Season's Greetings!

Thanks so much for choosing *With Love at Christmas* out of all the other seasonal books that are on offer out there. I think you've made a great choice – but then I'm very biased!

The story is about a busy, chaotic, loving family Christmas. I think so often in the run-up to Christmas we can get really caught up in all the commercialism that now surrounds it, that it becomes a really fraught and stressful time and we can so easily forget what it's really all about. Despite all the hype, it's a time for sharing with family and friends, and for love and laughter.

I'm sure this novel will put you in the right mood for Christmas and you'll be glad – I hope – that your own family Christmas isn't as mad as the Joyce's is! So, try to take a step back, and put your feet up for a breather. Five minutes dipping into *With Love at Christmas* will give you a real festive tonic. No one will mind if you don't turn out perfect, homemade mince pies – get Mr Kipling in to do them for you. Better that you approach Christmas chilled out and looking forward to it, rather than dreading all the work it entails.

Thank you once again for including me in your Christmas. I wish you a happy, stress-free holiday with your loved ones around you.

Wishing you a very merry Christmas and a fabulous new year.

Love Carole ☺ xx

# With Love at Christmas x

## Carole Matthews

sphere

SPHERE

First published in Great Britain in 2012 by Sphere
This paperback edition published in 2012 by Sphere

Copyright © Carole Matthews 2012

The moral right of the author has been asserted.

A CIP catalogue record for this book
is available from the British Library.

ISBN 978-0-7515-4548-7

Printed and bound in Great Britain by
Clays Ltd, St Ives plc

Papers used by Sphere are from well-managed forests
and other responsible sources.

MIX
Paper from
responsible sources
FSC
www.fsc.org    FSC® C104740

Sphere
An imprint of
Little, Brown Book Group
100 Victoria Embankment
London EC4Y 0DY

An Hachette UK Company
www.hachette.co.uk

www.littlebrown.co.uk

22/2/24

To the wonderful team at Little, Brown. You've all made me so welcome and I'm blown away by your energy and enthusiasm for my books. Long may it continue! Particular thanks to David, Cath, Manpreet, Hannah and Kate. You're all fab.

# Chapter 1

You can tell that Christmas is just around the corner. Slade's 'Merry Christmas Everybody' is belting out of the speakers, filling the busy supermarket aisles with festive cheer. That's a pension-fund song if ever there was one, and it never fails to get me humming along. I ask you: what would Christmas be without the dulcet tones of Noddy Holder?

I love this time of year. Even something as mundane as the weekly food shop is transformed into a magical experience. I'm at the bread counter in Tesco, squeezing the loaves to check their freshness. Cheery Santas hang above my head. Silver tinsel and colour-coordinated balls spiral down from the ceiling. I wish it could look as jolly all year round. Someone at head office has put a lot of effort into planning this. Perhaps I could borrow their theme and refresh my decorations this year. My husband, Rick, would have a fit. He's considerably more 'bah humbug' than I am when it comes to Christmas – the original Scrooge. Every year the expense of it all nearly gives him a heart attack. Every year I vow to cut back. And

1

every year, I don't. Maybe, for the sake of marital harmony, I'd better get out the 'old faithfuls' one more time.

I'm happy to say for the record that I'm the complete opposite of my husband. My name is Juliet Joyce. I'm a forty-five-year-old woman with one gorgeous grandchild, two troublesome, supposedly grown-up children, an annoying mother, a gay father, a very grumbly husband and a rather stinky dog. I am also a shameless Christmas addict. And I'm not the slightest bit interested in a twelve-step plan to cure me of it.

Slade slides seamlessly into Wizzard and 'I Wish It Could Be Christmas Every Day'. Heartily agree with that! We all need a bit of escapism from the daily grind of life, don't we? Jesus picked a lovely time of year to be born into the world, as it really cheers up the long winter months. It just wouldn't be the same if he'd been born, say, in July.

Skipping down the 'seasonal produce' aisle, I slip a Christmas pudding into my trolley, rapidly followed by some mince pies and a panettone, which has somehow become a must-have. None of the family is that keen on it really, but, like Brussels sprouts, Christmas just isn't Christmas without it. I put in an extra box of mince pies – just in case. You can never have too many mince pies, can you? I don't like to be caught out without some nibbles in case people drop in. I'd better get some Eat Me dates, too, and some assorted nuts.

I'd like to tell you that I make my own pudding, Christmas cake and all that – but I don't. I'm working full-time now in the office of a busy estate agent, and with that and the demands of the family, I hardly get time to breathe, let alone anything else. I aspire to producing a completely home-made Christmas, but every year it seems to slip further beyond my reach. I love the thought of creating a decadent Nigella-style celebration, with a bit of Kirstie Allsopp thrown in for good measure but, at this rate, that will have to wait – possibly until I retire. Even for a modest Tesco-based affair like my own, you have to start early. That's the key. I was very organised and bought my Christmas cards in the January sales. What's the point in paying full price when you don't have to? I picked up a couple of great presents at craft fairs in the summer. It's nice to find the perfect gift, isn't it? And, of course, you never do when you're looking too hard. Like middle age, perfect presents just sneak up on you. The special napkins were safely secured in August, as were the crackers for the table. The only thing I have to do now is find the 'safe place' where I can put them all. It will mean a trip into the loft for Rick, which he'll be cross about.

Since the first week of September I've been putting a few seasonal bits and bobs of food in the back of the cupboard but now, at the beginning of December, the Christmas food-shopping must start in earnest. I've got a few things in here for Dad and his partner, Samuel, too, just to help out, as I know how busy they are. Queuing at the checkout, I close my eyes and listen to the sounds of 'Do They Know It's Christmas?'. In front of me, a harassed-looking woman is berating her child, who's whining for sweets.

'I've no money for naffing sweets, Beyoncé,' she shrieks as she shakes her little girl by the arm more roughly than is right. 'If you don't start bloody behaving right now, Santa won't come to visit. He'll throw your Wii out of the sleigh and it will break into a million pieces. Then what will you do?'

The child screams. I think I would too. I should step in and remind them both about the true message of Christmas but, before I can, she's through the till and out, dragging the sweet-less and still screaming Beyoncé behind her.

Would they both think I was mad if I'd told them that at Beyoncé's age I was given one of my dad's old knitted socks – washed, I hope – filled with an orange and some nuts? That was it. Sum total of Christmas present exchange. I couldn't eat the nuts because Mum could never find the ancient pair of nut-crackers needed to open them, and the orange went straight back into the fruit bowl where it had come from. I couldn't ever buy presents myself because I was never given pocket money. But I was given some paper, glitter and some Gloy glue with which to make Christmas cards.

Times were different then. We had so little. Our family Christmases were always cheerless, meagre affairs. We never had any visitors calling. My mother put the moth-eaten tree up for as short a time as possible. Sometimes it didn't appear until Christmas Eve, late in the afternoon when I was almost beside myself with longing, and only then with much sighing. It was usually gone again shortly after Boxing Day. My dad used to do his best to liven things up. He'd laugh too heartily at the Christmas shows – *Morecambe and Wise* was his favourite. Tears would roll down his cheeks, and I used to find that funnier than the programme. But Mum was never a Christmas person. To her, it was absolute torture every year and, consequently, we all had to suffer. Perhaps that's why I like to make Christmas so special now. I like my home filled with laughter and love, overflowing with presents and food. If you can't go completely over the top at Christmas, when can you?

'One hundred and forty-seven pounds and thirty-two pence,' the checkout girl says when she's rung through my shopping. Even I wince as I hand over the money. It's going to be yet another bill that I'll hide from Rick.

Outside, the sky is white and heavy. A few flakes of snow are starting to fall, drifting, drifting down into the car park. The first this year. I smile inside. I love snow, too. Though I realise that I'm in the minority, as everyone else grumbles about how difficult it is to get around. And it's fair to say that the country does usually grind to a halt once there's anything more than a sprinkling on the ground. Me, I'd be happy to be trapped indoors and let it cascade down until it was three feet deep. Holding out my hands, I let the flakes settle. They're delicate, lacy and land on my upturned palms like filigree butterflies before instantly melting away. I shake snow from my short brown bob and remember that I need to wear my hat. It would be lovely if we had a white Christmas this year. A bit of snow makes everything look so much better, the icing on the cake.

Someone honks their horn in a bad-tempered manner. I glance up from the joy of snow on my hands. The car park is heaving now, and it looks like there's a dispute over a parking space. One driver winds down his window. A carol blares out: *Peace on earth, goodwill to all men.*

'Oi, arsehole,' he shouts at the other man, 'I was here first.'

The other driver, who has a sticker stating that 'Santa Does It With Reindeer' in his back window, clearly doesn't agree with his opinion and shouts back: 'Fuck off. This space is mine.'

I push my heavily laden trolley, which wants to go in the other direction, towards my trusty little Corsa. Heaving out the bags, I load them into the boot.

Both drivers jump out of their cars and shake their fists at each other. One has an aerial with a star and some tinsel on it. The other driver snaps it off and stamps it into the sprinkling of snow.

I sigh to myself. Not everyone, it seems, enjoys Christmas as much as me.

# Chapter 2

I pull into the drive of number ten, Chadwick Close and kill the engine. What I need now is a restorative cup of tea and perhaps my first mince pie of the season. They're possibly my most favourite festive food. I know that the shops start selling them in earnest in July now, but I like to put off the moment for as long as is humanly possible so that I can really savour it. This year I have excelled myself. I hope it also means that I won't have to spend as long on a diet after Christmas as I usually do.

My family and I live in a lovely part of Stony Stratford, a pretty market town in the heart of Buckinghamshire, a stone's throw away from the ever-encroaching city of Milton Keynes. We've been here for years, and have brought up our two children in this solid 1970s home. I suspect this is where we'll see out our days.

Rick is up the ladder, busy draping the front of the house with Christmas lights. That's good: I like to have them up nice and early to make the most of them. All my husband's abhorrence of Christmas disappears when – and only when – it comes to decorating the house with lights. It's a job he relishes. Every year Rick likes to adorn the place until it looks like Santa's grotto. It's the one trip of the year that he doesn't mind making up to the loft. He disappears in there for hours, searching out and sorting, and then he lifts down the lights gently, like treasured children.

We now have LED icicles with changing patterns dangling down from the rafters. We have a string of coloured bulbs across the garage that flash on and off at regular intervals. The front of the house has a sleigh and reindeer in white above the porch. The big cherry blossom in the front garden has its own string of lanterns. On the lawn, we have a wire reindeer covered in tiny lights. The rest of our neighbours don't bother much at all. Though number two do, on alternate years, throw a sparkling net of lights over their cotoneaster bush. We're the one and only house in the close that attempts to create a Christmassy spectacle. I don't quite know when or why this started, but I'm glad that Rick enters into the spirit at least in this one small area.

I climb out of the car. Rick comes down the ladder. My husband is one of those men who's grown more attractive as he's aged. At least he has to me and, I guess, that's all that matters. His long, lean frame is all knees and elbows – always has been. We seem to have so little quality time together now and, somehow, it seems even harder to find time for ourselves once the Christmas frenzy is upon us. Every year I vow that it will be different, and every year it isn't. I smile as he comes towards me, but he seems to be in a hurry and somewhat red in the face.

'Have you seen that?' he rages without preamble. A finger shoots out and points in an accusatory fashion at the house opposite.

Chadwick Close is a very staid neighbourhood, quiet. There's never any excitement to be had. That's why we like it here. Any scandal that there has been has in the past mostly emanated from the Joyce household anyway.

'Look,' he reiterates.

I look.

Across the close, directly opposite our house, is the sight that's offending him so much. Our good friend, Stacey Lovejoy, used to live at number five, but last summer she moved out. Now she's in Gran Canaria living the high life with Rick's old boss, Hal, and they're both having a lovely time according to the intermittent email updates she sends. The new people weren't here last Christmas, so Rick could hardly have expected to see this.

Our new neighbours, it seems, also like Christmas lights on their house. There's no one in sight, but it's clear that, like Rick, Neil Harrison has been very busy this morning. They have a display that far outshines ours.

'How nice,' I say. 'It's lovely.'

'*Lovely?*' Rick has gone quite purple in the face now.

'What's the matter?'

'*We're* the house that has lights up,' he points out.

I shrug. 'Now we're *one* of the houses that has lights up. I think it looks pretty.'

'Typical female response,' he snorts. Rick runs a hand through his hair, mussing it into his customary Stan Laurel do.

9

He's never been able to tame his hair, and now it's sticking out all over the place. I know that's the fashion for seventeen-year-old boys, but in a gentleman of a certain age it just looks like mad hair.

'You don't have to view it as a challenge to your supremacy.' Clearly Rick thinks that this is Neil banging his chest and roaring in his face. 'Maybe Neil just likes Christmas lights.'

Further snorting from Rick. 'I'll have to get some more,' he mutters. 'I want ours to be the *best* house.' He casts an envious glance at the giant-sized blow-up Santa, complete with his own chimney, that's fixed to Neil's roof.

'Ours look great, Rick. Especially with a little bit of snow on them. Very festive. Already I feel quite in the Christmas mood.'

My husband tuts. I'm disappointed that all this pointless willy-waving has soured his mood.

'Come on,' I say. 'Help me in with the shopping and I'll make you a cuppa and you can have a mince pie with it.'

With an exaggerated sigh, Rick puts down his screwdriver. I flick open the boot.

'Good God, woman!' He recoils in horror. 'What the hell have you got in here? It's not the feeding of the five thousand, you know.'

'It's Christmas,' I say. 'We have to have a little bit extra in. Just in case.'

'Just in case what?' Rick looks perplexed. 'You've got enough for the Joyce clan to survive a nuclear holocaust. The shops barely shut for ten minutes these days. We can always run out and get a loaf if we're stuck.'

'Oh, Rick,' I chide, 'you know you always enjoy it.'

'You know I always want to go away to the Bahamas, just the two of us, and ignore the whole bloody thing.' He heaves two carrier bags out of the boot, making a big show of how heavy they are. 'Instead we'll stay at home, suffer your mother, the Queen's speech and eat too much and drink nowhere near enough to ease the pain.'

'It's not that bad.'

Again he casts a dark glance at our neighbour's display. 'Putting up the lights was the only pleasure I had,' he complains. 'Now even that's been taken away from me.'

'You could go down to Homebase and buy a few more bits if you want to,' I suggest. 'They've got some very pretty things in.'

Rick rubs his chin. 'I need something with more impact,' he says under his breath. 'Much more impact.'

With that, he brightens considerably.

# Chapter 3

My mother, Rita Britten, is sitting in the kitchen when Rick and I struggle in with the shopping. She's wearing a cardigan that's buttoned up all wrong, and it doesn't look as if she's combed her hair since getting up.

'Get the kettle on, Rita, love,' Rick says.

She looks at him, perplexed. 'Why would I want to do that?'

'We'll all have a cup of tea, Mum.'

'Oh.'

'Here, you're done up all higgledy-piggledy.' I go to her and she tries to stare me down while I rebutton her cardigan.

'You do *fuss*, Juliet.'

'That's better.' I resist the urge to untangle her hair.

Rick rolls his eyes at me and I shrug back. My mum's not herself. I blame her trip to Australia. She's never been quite the same since. When she turned seventy, she dumped my true and faithful father, who had stood by her stoically despite her being a fairly miserably and demanding wife. She moved in with me and Rick, uninvited. My husband was not impressed, but what could I do? She had to live somewhere and, no matter how we tried to cajole her, she wouldn't go home to Dad. Then, to make matters worse, she took up with a pensioner toy boy, Arnold. We had to endure weeks of them 'doing it' in our back bedroom, which our daughter had been required to vacate to accommodate her. It was horrendous. The only way I could get any sleep was to clamp a pillow over my head. They'd only been together for five minutes when she and Arnold decided that they wanted to see the world. At the age of seventy, I ask you. Before you could say hip replacement they went out, booked two tickets to Australia, rented a camper van and set off touring in the outback.

I was beside myself. She'd never even been abroad before; now she was going to Australia for the foreseeable future with a man she barely knew. I thought it was children who were supposed to give their parents problems! Isn't that the way it happens? Rick was delighted, as he thought we'd seen the back of her for good. He was sure that in Australia, being the continent with the most venomous and lethal animals, she'd come to some great harm. No such luck. He hadn't reckoned on my mother's tenacity. After six months she was back, bronzed and broke, and poor Arnold had disappeared into the wilderness never to be seen again. I am distraught that Arnold, an elderly and rather pleasant gentleman, is missing in a strange land. My mother, however, doesn't seem too bothered by this turn of events. Rick thinks that the hapless Arnold most likely threw himself to a pack of wild dingos in an attempt to get away from my mother. He has a point. After spending six months in a glorified caravan with her, I'm sure anyone would feel the same.

Rick is rooting through the carrier bags. 'Panettone?' he says. 'What is it?'

'It's like a cake or bread. A bit of both. You've had it before.'

'Really? I don't remember.'

'We all like it,' I assure him.

'I don't,' my mum adds helpfully.

'Dad does.'

'Your father has gone all foreign,' she counters.

Which, I have to say, is partly true. Frank Britten was, until my mother abandoned him, the most unadventurous man on the planet. His comfort zone was never more than a foot away from his armchair. My dad, a man who, until he was seventy-two, thought that anything other than a half of bitter was for 'nancy boys', decided he'd been gay all along. Then he met Samuel, a charming bookseller who is younger than both myself and Rick, who has made his life infinitely more colour-ful. No one was more surprised than me when they moved in together. Well, except perhaps for my mother. I'm still not sure that she fully grasps the nature of their relationship. Anyway, now that Dad is a fully paid-up and enthusiastic member of the 'nancy boys' club, thanks to Samuel, his tastes have become distinctly more adventurous – and not just in 'that' department. He loves foreign food, foreign travel, enjoys good wine, speaks a smattering of several languages, plays chess, knocks up meals from Jamie Oliver and Nigel Slater cook-books and is generally very lovely to be around. It's taken him a long time to discover domestic bliss, but I'm so pleased that he has.

'Your dad phoned to say that he's coming round later with Samuel,' Rick says.

'Oh, that's nice. There are some bits for them in one of the other carrier bags. They can take them home with them.'

'I thought they were coming here for Christmas?'

'They are.'

'So why are you buying them Christmas food?'

'Christmas isn't just one day, Rick.'

'No,' he mutters. 'It's from bloody August onwards.' He stamps out to get the other bags.

'Are we having a cup of tea, or what?' Mum asks.

Now Mum is back for good, and is currently ensconced in Chloe's bedroom once again, much to the consternation of my daughter. Chloe had moved out when she accidentally fell pregnant with her first child and was renting a flat with her partner, Mitch – the father of baby Jaden and a man she barely knew. Not surprisingly, they've now split up and she's also back at home with Jaden in tow. But I can hardly wag my finger at her as, all those years ago, Rick and I tied the knot rather hastily when I fell pregnant with Tom.

Chloe won't ever really say what went wrong in their relationship. I guess it comes from having a baby with someone whose favourite drink, film and holiday destination are a total mystery to you. The pressure on them both was enormous. Right from the start she was coming home every two weeks over some row or other. Rick said we should have turned her round and sent her straight back to deal with it, but I couldn't.

That's what my mother would have done to me, and I couldn't watch Chloe suffer. I know she found it hard that Mitch was working long hours and, instead of being out partying, she was sitting at home every night with a baby. Then last month, with no justifiable explanation, she flounced home, supposedly for good. Mitch appeared on the doorstep every night for two weeks begging her to go back to him, but she wouldn't listen.

She's just had difficulty adjusting to being a responsible adult with a young child to care for. The fact that responsibility has been thrust on her rather than it being of her choosing must have something to do with it too, a case of too much too soon. Chloe has always been selfish, and still tends to think only of what she wants. Mitch, on the other hand, seems saintly. I know it's different when you live with someone – you see all their little foibles in sharp relief. But I don't know what else she could want in a man. Yet only Chloe can decide that. I can only be here for her, help her and hope that one day she'll realise what she might lose and she'll grow up, and sooner rather than later.

As if she's reading my thoughts, on cue Chloe waddles in. 'What's to eat?'

Oh, and the worst thing is that she's expecting again. Another little 'accident'. This time it is the same father, though, so I should be grateful for small mercies, I suppose. Maybe the imminent birth has triggered her flight home; I don't know. I have no idea how we'll all manage with another tot in the house. Jaden's a lovely boy, but he is a handful. I don't remember Tom being quite so boisterous at his age. I think it's something they put in the food now – all those 'E' numbers. The new baby is due in the middle of January and, already, Chloe is huge. She's certainly taking the whole 'eating for two' thing to heart.

'Who are you?' my mother asks.

'Don't be soft, Gran,' Chloe says. 'Put your specs on.' She flops down into the chair next to her grandmother. 'Hello, Buster, baby,' she coos at the dog. 'Didn't anyone give you your advent calendar choccy-woccy today?'

The dog barks that they didn't. Chloe, despite her concern, doesn't move to rectify the situation. So I get up and open the Simpsons advent calendar and pop the little chocolate Bart in Buster's mouth.

'What exactly do the Simpsons have to do with Christmas?' Rick asks as he heaves in two more bags. 'Aren't advent calendars supposed to be religious?'

'Get a life, Dad,' Chloe advises. 'Christmas is about fun and presents. What's God got to do with it?'

I do wonder sometimes if my Christmas excesses have given out the wrong message.

# Chapter 4

Rick mutters under his breath and stomps straight out again to get the remainder of the shopping. That should be about it. Even I'm concerned about the amount of bags. I'm sure it looks more than it really is. Everything is in such big boxes now.

I'm worried about Mum. Even for her she's acting a bit strangely, and it's not just the usual things. Since she's been living here we've had to get used to her penchant for wearing clothing more suited to a seventeen-year-old, dyeing her hair inappropriate colours, bringing strange men home from night-clubs and smoking marijuana on the sly when she thinks Rick and I aren't watching. All those things we are, unfortunately, well accustomed to. But now she seems to be developing a whole new range of troubling habits. When she goes into the bathroom, she often leaves the taps running – once with the plug still in, which flooded the place. She's prone to leaving the rings of the cooker on and wandering off into the garden. More often than not she puts her cardigan on inside out or, like today, buttons it up all skew-whiff. Last week she went out wearing odd shoes, and not in a Helena Bonham Carter way. Perhaps it's just an age thing. She's always been, at best, eccentric. Maybe, as she gets older, it's just ratcheting up a few notches. I'm concerned, though, that these little incidents are happening on a more regular basis.

'*I'll* put the kettle on, shall I?' Rick asks loudly as he dumps down the last two carrier bags. I think his blood pressure is getting the better of him.

'Let me,' I say soothingly. 'You sit down.'

'I'm going to the shed,' Rick says darkly. It's probably just as well, as he currently looks as if he'd like to break something.

'I'll bring your tea down there for you.' The shed is his retreat, his sanctuary, the only place where Rick manages to get any peace these days, as the house seems to be bursting at the seams.

Flicking on the kettle, I lift out the mince pies, which have been strategically placed at the top of one of the carriers.

My son Tom comes in. 'Did I hear the kettle go on?'

'Sit down, Frank, love,' my mother says. 'I'll put your tea on in a minute.' It's not yet three o'clock.

'This is Tom,' I gently remind Mum. 'Your grandson.'

'Oh.' She looks at him blankly.

'Wotcha, Gran,' Tom says. He gives her a hug and kisses her dry, wrinkled cheek. It sometimes surprises me that my own mother could have become so old. 'Got any good weed going spare?'

'Don't encourage her,' I implore.

'Break out the mince pies, Mum,' my son instructs. 'I'm starving.'

Tom has been perpetually hungry since he popped out of my womb.

'That boy's got hollow legs,' my mother notes.

He does.

'You wouldn't eat so much if you had to pay for it,' Rick grumbles as he goes out of the door.

'Chill, Dad,' Tom says. 'I'll get a job.' Then, when Rick is just out of earshot: 'Eventually.'

This is a frequent refrain from Tom. It's fair to say that he has had a lot more girlfriends – and boyfriends – than he has had jobs. We can't quite keep up with Tom's sexuality. Sometimes there's a trail of random young men through the house. Sometimes it's a string of unsuitable women. Sometimes both on one day. We try to ignore it as best we can. I don't want to think of my children having sex at all, frankly. And, at the end of the day, all we want is for him to be settled and happy. Well, actually all Rick wants is for him to be out of our house and earning his own living.

'Where have you been all day?'

'In bed,' he says, in a tone that queries why he would ever have been anywhere else.

'Lazy bastard,' Chloe notes.

'You've been in the bathroom all morning,' he complains. 'What was I supposed to do?'

My heart's desire is to have a house with two bathrooms. With six of us living here, and Chloe using the bath like her personal office, toilet visits have to be timed very carefully. We would live more harmoniously as a family if we had two bathrooms.

Tom has also just moved back home. Thankfully, he is less fond of washing than my daughter. My son is a twenty-six-year-old university graduate with a degree in nothing remotely useful, it seems. Since graduating, he's never held down a proper job, and his £30,000-worth of student loan shows no sign of ever being repaid. He's been away in China, supposedly teaching English as a foreign language. He lasted about a month doing that, then he split up with the girlfriend he went to China with – I can't even remember her name now, and I suspect Tom would struggle. When they parted company he moved on to Australia and someone new. The bar work he did there failed to keep pace with his bar *bill* and, eventually, he was forced by his financial circumstances to come home again. We had to book his flight online *and* pay for it, which Rick was *not* happy about. Understatement. I do sometimes wonder whether our son will ever willingly leave home. We make it too easy for him, Rick says. He may well have a point.

With all the bedrooms occupied, Tom's sleeping in the dining room on a futon that we bought from eBay. I don't like Tom sleeping in the dining room because I am never sure who – male or female – will wander through the kitchen in the morning wearing nothing but their underwear. We think he's bisexual, but you don't like to ask outright, do you? It's not really our business what his particular orientation is now that he's an adult. We try to be accepting of his many and varied relationships but, in all honesty, we just do our best to ignore it. It seems pointless to say that as a guest in someone's house

I would never have behaved like that, but they just don't care now. The fact that we rarely see the same face twice doesn't help. I'm sure that Rick's blood pressure will slide down a few notches when Tom does leave for good. It's not the girls in their undies he finds so distressing, obviously, but a few weeks ago there was a man in pink underpants, and I thought Rick was going to have heart failure. No one needs to see that at breakfast-time.

'Be a love and put the kettle on again,' I ask him.

'Aw, Mum! Why can't *she* do it?' He flicks a finger at Chloe, who sticks her tongue out at him.

'Because I asked you, love,' I say.

He hauls himself out of his chair as if he's preparing to scale the north face of the Eiger, not make a brew. He helps himself to a mince pie as he passes.

'Give one of those to your gran.'

''Scuse fingers,' he says as he hands her one.

I nearly remark that we do have plates in the house, but that's exactly the sort of thing that Rick would say, so I bite my lip.

I want to move Jaden from the little bedroom to share with Chloe so that Tom can have a proper bedroom, but Rick says it will only encourage him to stay. However, there is only a single bed in there, so it would be trickier for him to entertain overnight guests, which I can only view as a good thing. I am well aware that both of my children have sex, I just never envisaged I'd end up having it rubbed in my face morning, noon and night. To have sex when we were young, we had to avail ourselves of the back of Rick's car or get our own home.

There was never any question of having carnal knowledge under our parents' roof. It simply wasn't the done thing. I'm just sorry that those standards have gone.

To fit in the futon, the dining-room table was dismantled – I'd fallen out of love with it anyway – shortly after we found Tom bonking one of his numerous conquests on it some time ago. No mother needs to see her son's bare bottom bobbing up and down in that manner. The offending table is covered in plastic and resides in the garage, but it's going to have to be pressed into service again soon otherwise we'll have nowhere to eat our Christmas lunch en masse.

I worry about my children. We tried to do our best by them, but I wonder if we really did. Chloe is twenty-four, but seems so young. I'm sure I was more mature than she is when I was fifteen. Yet she's a single mum with a son of her own and another child on the way. When will she ever grow up and stand on her own two feet?

Tom, too, is the eternal teenager. He has no drive, no ambition and is quite content to spend his days playing computer games and hanging out with mates, who all seem similarly juvenile. Not one of them is married or has their own place. They all seem happy just to go out drinking or stay at home and play on the Wii. Is that normal behaviour for a man his age? Perhaps it is. None of them seems to have a desire to get on and provide for themselves.

I never set out to spoil them, but I think somehow we have.

Tom, distracted by the newspaper on top of one of my carrier bags, has failed to work his way towards the kettle. As no one else is likely to do it, I make the promised tea.

'Think I'll ask Santa for a Porsche this Christmas,' Tom says as he flicks through the newspaper.

'Well sick,' Chloe agrees. 'Could I get a baby seat in one of those?'

See what I mean? No wonder, some days, I feel so old. My family are ageing me in dog years. Soon Buster and I will be a hundred and ten years old, and who will care for us all then?

# Chapter 5

Rick breathed a sigh of relief once he was safely inside the shed. Listen to that. *Nothing*.

He felt his heart lift as he settled into his sunlounger. This was more like it! He glanced at his watch. Too early for a tot of whisky? Perhaps. No doubt he'd be on chauffeur duty for someone or other later on tonight. Tom always bleated about having no money, but that didn't seem to stop him going out drinking with his mates every night of the week. Chloe was still doing her fair share of partying, too – despite the fact that she was *with child*. Which meant that he and Juliet did more than their share of babysitting for Jaden.

Last summer their worn-out, rotting shed had been replaced by an all-singing, all-dancing fancy number. No expense had been spared. This was the finest shed Homebase could offer; a shed that dreams are made of. He had promised himself this treat since he and Juliet first moved here many moons ago. The new shed was long overdue. Now he was determined to make the most of it. This was his refuge, his island. He wished he could dig a moat round it and fill it with man-eating sharks, but Juliet would probably object. The older he got, the more he seemed to need some solitude.

At this time in his life, he'd thought that the kids would be off his hands. He'd hoped they'd be settled down with great jobs and families of their own. Well, part of that was true, he supposed. Chloe was certainly well on the way to a family of her own – it was just the great job that was sorely missing. Goodness only knows what the future held for Tom. His son seemed happy to be a perpetual adolescent. All very well if it wasn't always someone else picking up the bills. And that was the problem. What Rick hadn't envisaged was that they'd all keep bouncing back like bloody boomerangs – and particularly resilient ones at that. It looked as if their kids would never be off their hands. He'd hoped that, at their age, he and Juliet would be on their own again, able to do the things they'd missed out on when they were young and had two children and no money to splash about. Now they weren't getting any younger, still had two kids on their hands and no money to splash about. This hadn't been his life plan. Perhaps he and Juliet should move to the tiniest cottage they could find, preferably with just the one bedroom, so that none of them could so much as come and stay for the night.

There was a knock on the door and then it swung open. Juliet appeared bearing a tray. On it were two cups of tea and a plate of mince pies.

'It's getting chilly out there.' She shivered as she came inside. 'Room for a small one?'

'Let me put up another lounger.' Rick jumped up and set down the other chair next to his own.

'It's very tidy in here. I'm impressed.'

'I thought you'd been out to do it,' Rick said.

'No. Not me. Perhaps it's a self-tidying model.'

Rick shrugged. 'Must be.'

Juliet made herself comfortable and they sipped their tea in unison.

'It's still snowing,' she said. 'A sprinkling has settled on the grass. It looks very pretty.'

'I know.' The swirling flakes were hypnotic, and were slowly sending him into a pleasant trance. 'Just watching it and thinking.'

'Everything OK?'

He shrugged. 'Just one problem.' He rubbed his fingers together signifying money or, more accurately, a lack of it. 'Work's tough. Cash flow is pants.' Last year when his friend, Hal, had absconded to Gran Canaria to escape the complications of his love life, he'd left his flooring business to Rick. Walk All Over Me had been doing really well through the summer months – so much so that he'd taken on a young lad to help him out, Merak Kowalski. He was a great kid. Polish, enthusiastic, keen worker. Wanted to learn everything he could about the business. If only his own idle son had shown such an interest. He'd always fancied painting Joyce & Son on a van. Tom, it seemed, had other ideas, though goodness only knew what they were. Flooring was clearly beneath him – no pun intended.

Rick sighed inwardly. 'There's hardly anything in the book for January.'

'Money's tight for everyone.'

'It might pick up.' He sounded more optimistic than he felt. December was busy, but the Christmas holidays stretched for nearly two weeks this year. That was OK if you were on a nice fat salary and a generous holiday entitlement. Being self-employed, it simply meant two weeks that he wasn't earning. Plus, with the state of the economy, people were putting off home improvements if they didn't really need to do them. Everyone was making their carpet last that little bit longer. If the laminate was a bit chipped, a bit jaded, they'd scrape another year out of it. It was a worry.

'Last thing I want to do is lay off Merak. He's such a good kid.'

'I'm sure it won't come to that.'

Rick wasn't quite so certain.

'Do you want to give up on the idea of going away for a few days before Christmas?'

'No, no.'

'I don't mind.'

'It'll be fine. You've been talking about it for ages. I'll get the money together somehow.'

'I was going to ask Dad and Samuel for some ideas of where we could go. But we don't have to. I've not booked anything yet.'

'You go ahead and organise it,' Rick insisted. It was the last thing he wanted, really, but how could he let Juliet down when, in truth, she asked so little of him? He'd promised her a glamorous break for their twenty-fifth wedding anniversary which had been and gone over two years ago, and he still hadn't delivered on it. How could he say no now? 'We're going to have precious little time together once the second baby is on the scene.'

'Hmm.' Juliet took in the ambience of the shed. 'This is nice, just the two of us.'

'Doesn't happen enough.'

'I can't believe we're going to leave the lot of them to it for a whole *weekend*.'

'Sounds wonderful,' Rick agreed. 'Though knowing our lot, we'll be lucky if the place is still standing when we get back.'

'It won't have to cost much,' she insisted. 'I'm due to get a little Christmas bonus from work. We could put that towards it. It would do us good to get away. What with having Chloe and Jaden here – and my mother – we haven't managed a holiday this year. And you're right, with another baby due very soon, it could be some time before we can sneak off by ourselves again.'

That was true enough.

'If you can find something cheap and cheerful,' Rick said, 'then let's book it.'

Juliet kissed him. 'I do love Christmas,' she breathed.

He only wished that he could feel the same. To him it was all about stress, expense and unnecessary work.

# Chapter 6

Rick has brought the decorations down from the loft. There are boxes and boxes of them, and he always grumbles. Sometimes we splash out and have a real tree, but this year – in a vain attempt at saving money – we've gone for the artificial one we've had for donkey's years. I bought it just after Christmas many years ago in the sales, half price. In Woolworths, when they still existed. That's how old it is.

The tree in question is a six-foot blue spruce that has 'snow' sprayed on the leaves. Every time you touch it more of the snow falls off onto the carpet. Rick has already put it up and it's standing in the corner ready for my artistic additions. Despite its advancing years, it doesn't look too bad at all. Buster is lying beneath it, hiding at the back, clearly wondering how long it will be before he's turfed out from under it. We had to stop putting chocolate decorations on it years ago because the dog used to snaffle them all. Now that we've got Jaden, I've relented and bought a few. Though I've taken the precaution of putting them on the higher branches, out of the way of little fingers and doggy jaws. For me, the best job out of all of the Christmas preparations is putting up the tree. It really gets me in the mood. Which is just as well, as no one else in this household wants to do it.

I have my little time-honoured ritual that I like to stick to. On goes *The Christmas Album*. All my favourite festive songs are on there. I pour myself a glass of red wine, even though it's a bit early to be cracking open the booze, and line up another mince pie. Then I open all the boxes and spread out the decorations on the living-room floor, excited as always to rediscover what we've had tucked away for the last year.

The decorations have been collected over years and years. I like to buy one to mark special occasions, and I try to pick one up wherever we go on holiday. There's one for when Chloe was born. One for Tom. Another for my first grandson. A silver horseshoe highlighted with glitter marks my twenty-fifth wedding anniversary, which was over two years ago now. There were times when I thought that Rick and I wouldn't make it, but here we are and, thankfully, still going strong.

The fashion is for everything to be tasteful now, isn't it? All your baubles have to be coordinating. But I still yearn for the days when living rooms were draped with paper chains all over the ceiling and pinned with concertina Chinese lanterns. I was always envious of my schoolfriends whose parents went overboard at Christmas, as my mother could never be bothered. When we first moved into this house, I wasn't happy until every available surface was draped with clashing colours of gaudy tinsel. Now everything's very muted. I have twigs with tiny twinkling lights in a glass vase for the dining room, and a silver garland that wraps round the banister, but I don't go to town any more. I think that might have to change.

'Hey.' Chloe comes into the living room. She has Jaden in her arms. It looks like he's just woken up from his afternoon sleep. A bit late, I think. He'll be a devil to get down tonight. I can't quite impress on my daughter the joy of a routine when it comes to little ones, but she's going to have to get a lot more organised when she's got two on her hands, that's for sure. Jaden is blond with big blue eyes, just like his mother. I can only hope that he inherits his father's temperament. 'I'm popping out to meet Sarah for a coffee,' my daughter says.

She certainly looks all dolled up.

'Can you look after Jaden for an hour?'

'I thought I was babysitting tonight, so that you could see Mitch.' Now that Mitch and Chloe seem to be meeting up again, I'm doing everything I can to encourage it.

'Yeah,' she says. 'This is just while I nip out.'

'I was going to put up the tree, Chloe.'

'Jaden will help you.'

He's just turned two. He'll try to eat all the decorations, or stand on them. My pleasant little ritual will go out of the window and, instead of sifting through all my pretty baubles and running through the memories associated with each of them, picking the special place on the tree that they'll occupy, I'll be run ragged trying to keep Jaden entertained. This was one hour I was looking forward to having by myself.

'Can't you take him with you?' I want to add, *He's your son*, but I don't.

'Please,' she begs. 'Please, Mum. I'll do anything you ask.'

I know full well that she won't.

'It's really hard to kick back and chat when he's around. I've got to have eyes in my backside.' She tells me this as if I'm blissfully unaware of the joys of child-rearing. I'm clearly not looking convinced, as she says, 'Shall I get Gran to, instead?'

'No, leave her alone. I think she's tired. She's gone for a lie-down.' In truth, I packed her off for a nap so that she'd be out of the way too.

'Nan-nan,' Jaden says, and holds out his arms to me and, of course, my heart softens.

I stand up and lift him from Chloe. 'You're getting to be a big boy,' I say. His blond hair is sleep-flattened. He has a thumb in his mouth, a ragged teddy in the other hand.

'It'll be nice for him this Christmas,' Chloe says. 'It'll be the first one he understands.' I remember back to when my own children were that age, and how magical it was for them. Who knew then how life would turn out for them, for us all.

'Tree,' Jaden says.

'I'm outta here.' My daughter seizes her chance to escape. She kisses her son.

Would she be a more caring, more attentive mother if I wasn't always here to take up the slack? I can't fault Mitch, Jaden's dad, but sometimes I think that my own child takes her responsibilities far too lightly. I wonder what she'll be like when she has a baby on each hip?

'Be good for Nana.'

'Don't be out for long, Chloe.'

'Don't stress, Mum.' She kisses me too and bolts out of the room.

'Looks like we're going to do the tree together, Jaden.'

'Tree,' he says again.

The doorbell rings. 'Frank and Samuel are here, Mum,' Chloe shouts, and I hear her say, 'Love you, Grandad.' My father brings out the softer side of my daughter. She adores him, and they've always been close. Seconds later, the front door slams. Shortly after, my dad and his partner join me in the living room.

'We're not interrupting you, are we, love?' Dad asks. He has always been my favourite parent. Gentle where my mother is spiky; caring where my mother is self-obsessed. Normal where my mother is bonkers – I've added that one for Rick.

'Of course not. I was just going to put the tree up, but I find myself on babysitting duties. There's a bottle of wine and some mince pies there if you want to join me.'

'I know how much you like doing the tree,' Dad says. 'Remember when we used to do it together?'

I do. Sometimes I think it's why my mum refused to have it out until the last minute possible. My mother never had the patience for such things, so it was always Dad who was the teacher, the nurturer. In his own quiet, contained way he taught me how to read, ride a bike, climb a tree, fish for minnows. He did the same for his grandchildren, and now I hope that his great-grandchildren will get the benefit of his love and knowledge for years to come.

Looking as dapper as ever, he slips off his trilby and coat and lays it over the sofa. 'You crack on, love.' Dad takes Jaden from my arms.

'Poppee,' his great-grandson says with a beaming smile.

'We'll look after this little one, won't we, Samuel?' They both dote on Jaden, and love to look after him whenever they can. Which helps me out no end.

'Absolutely, Francis.' Samuel unbuttons his jacket slowly, methodically. There's a slight pallor to his cheeks and he coughs a little dry cough.

'Not well, Samuel?' I ask.

'A little under the weather,' he admits.

'I keep telling him to go to the doctor,' Dad says. 'But you know what these young people are like. Won't listen.'

They smile indulgently at each other. Dad and Samuel have been together now for over two years, and they are still incredibly happy together. I can easily say that I've never met a nicer couple. Samuel is the epitome of pleasant. Nothing is too much trouble for him, and he is so solicitous towards my father that it makes my heart glad to watch them together. Even my mother thinks that Samuel is wonderful, and she actually likes very few people.

'Can I get you anything for it, Samuel, or are you happy to rely on the medicinal properties of red wine?'

'A glass of wine would be excellent.'

Both men make themselves comfy on the sofa, Jaden wriggling between them, while I get two more glasses and some napkins so that they can have a mince pie.

'We're just planning our next trip,' Dad informs me as he sips his wine. 'Samuel and I are thinking of a cruise to Russia in the summer.'

'Wow,' I say. 'Russia!' I sift through my decorations as we talk.

35

'*Da!*' my dad says proudly. 'That's Russian for yes.'

'Da, da, da,' Jaden repeats.

'You two certainly like getting about.' In the last couple of years, having persuaded my dad to stop thinking of Bournemouth as exotic, Samuel has encouraged him to venture further afield. Together they've been to half of Europe, and certainly a lot more places than I ever have. Now I feel that Dad is trying to cram every moment of his days with wonderful experiences, and good luck to him.

'You *can* teach an old dog new tricks.' He winks at me. Buster looks doubtful. 'Life is for living, Juliet. Never forget that.'

My life, I muse, is for looking after everyone else. But I don't voice that opinion.

'I was going to pick your brains. Rick and I are thinking of going away for a quick weekend break before Christmas, just the two of us. We've actually been promising ourselves a romantic weekend away, somewhere like Paris or Rome, since our twenty-fifth wedding anniversary, and have never quite managed it. There's always something else to do, isn't there?'

'You need to spoil yourselves,' Dad says. 'That's what keeps love alive.'

God knows how we've managed to keep ours breathing, then. It could be on its last legs. 'Any ideas?'

'Why not go to one of the Christmas markets?' Samuel pipes up instantly. 'They have some nice ones in this country, or you could nip across to Europe. The market in Bruges is particularly nice. We loved it there in the spring, didn't we, Francis?'

36

'Oh, the chocolate!' Dad exclaims. 'You have to go for that alone.'

Nipping across to Europe sounds very nice. It's something I've never done before. Which is ridiculous, considering it's on our doorstep. I wonder, could I sell that to Rick?

'I can show you some of the sites that we use on the internet, if that would help,' Samuel offers.

'That'd be great. And I have another favour to ask, Dad.' I focus on the bauble in my hand and lower my voice. In this house, walls have ears. My mother, who is as deaf as a post when she wants to be, misses nothing. 'I'm worried about Mum.'

'Oh?'

I sigh. 'It's little things,' I tell him, trying to shrug it off. 'But I'm concerned about leaving her alone if we do go away.' It used to be the children I was frightened to leave at home on their own in case they burned the house down. Now it's my mum. Actually, I still wouldn't trust the kids entirely, and I certainly wouldn't leave them in charge of their tricky grandma. 'Could you and Samuel come and stay here to keep an eye on her?'

'Of course,' Dad says. 'Wouldn't like to see the old girl on her own.'

Concerned as I am about her frailty, the 'old girl' would still be capable of slicing off dad's balls with a blunt knife if she heard him call her that.

# Chapter 7

Samuel brings their wine glasses through to the kitchen, rinses them thoroughly and puts them in the dishwasher. He is the most domesticated person I know. Whenever you visit their house, there isn't so much as a hair out of place.

'Thank you,' I say.

'No worries. Nice mince pies.' He pats his tummy, which is cuddly like a teddy bear's.

'Sadly not home-made.'

'I can do some for you,' Samuel offers. 'Don't feel you have to do everything for Christmas, Juliet. You have so much on your plate.' As if subconsciously, he glances upstairs to where my mother is dozing. 'Francis and I are delighted to be invited, and we're more than willing to help out.'

'I know you are. And of course you're invited, you're family.'

'Thank you.' Samuel has big eyes in his round face, and he flutters his eyelashes at me proudly. 'I can do the Christmas cake for you, if you like.'

'Tesco has already done the honours.'

He laughs at that. I don't know if he thinks I'm joking. I'm not. 'I'll make some sausage rolls, then. They freeze easily. Francis does a mean cheese straw.'

I stand back and look at my dad's partner. 'I never thought I'd live to see the day someone said that of my dear dad.' We giggle together. Samuel is a consummate giggler. 'You have turned his life around, Samuel, and for that, I'm truly grateful. You've made him the man he always wanted to be. Thank you.'

Samuel flushes.

'I don't have to worry about him at all.'

'You don't,' he assures me. 'I'll always look after him. He's changed my life, too, Juliet. I was very lonely before I met Francis.'

'I can't imagine that at all.' Samuel is such easy company to be around, and he embraces every day with joy. In the two years that I've known him, I don't think I've ever seen Samuel in a bad mood.

'Beneath all this bluster, I'm actually very shy,' he adds. As a couple they now have a terrific circle of supportive friends, but they much prefer to be alone together.

'You hide it very well.' Before he becomes too self-conscious, I change the subject. 'What have you bought Dad for Christmas?'

'I've booked us afternoon tea together at the Ritz,' he confides. 'It's so charming, Francis will love it.'

'Oh, he will,' I agree. I wonder why I can't think of wonderful presents like that.

Rick comes in from the shed. 'Brrr,' he says. 'Getting cold out there. Hiya, Samuel.' He claps Samuel on the back.

Samuel always tries to be more gruff and manly when Rick is around, and fails miserably. 'Hi, Rick.'

'Do you want some more tea?' I ask him.

Rick rubs his hands together. 'Oh, yes.'

'Dad's in the living room, keeping an eye on Jaden. Can you see if he wants any, please?'

'Will do.' Rick disappears.

'It's not like Francis to turn down a cuppa,' Samuel says.

'No.'

'You sit down, Juliet. I can do this.'

'You are a love,' I tell him. Then Samuel coughs again, and it really catches his breath. He puts a hand to his chest.

'You really should go to the doctor about that,' I advise. 'You might need antibiotics.'

'I'll make an appointment,' he assures me. 'It has gone on for too long.'

'Can't you take a couple of days off work and stay in bed?'

'We're so busy at the bookshop in the run-up to Christmas, and I couldn't leave the others in the lurch.'

Samuel and I share a love of books, as does my dad. I currently have a job in one of the many estate agents' offices in the High Street in Stony Stratford but, before that, I was an assistant at the town library for years, a place that's now under constant threat of closure due to council cutbacks. 'It sounds like you should be the one having a rest. I'm glad you're busy at work, but take it easy. The last thing we want is for you to be poorly on the big day. I'm looking to you to lead the karaoke, Samuel.'

He titters again at that. Samuel specialises in the songs of Gloria Gaynor and is always the life and soul of the party, while my father sits and smiles adoringly at him.

'Chloe said she's got some new songs for the Singstar.'

'Oh, you know Chloe. She likes to make everything into a competition. It's *Back to the 80s*, or something. I'm surprised she's not been practising.'

'Sounds just up my street.' He coughs again. 'I'm hoping to have a few days off over the holidays so that Francis and I can sit with our feet up and catch up with some reading.'

'You go and sit down right now.' I usher him towards the door. 'Why don't you stay for dinner tonight? It will save you cooking.' I never want my dad and Samuel to go home. If we had room, I'd want them here all the time. 'I'm going to roast a chicken. Dad's favourite.'

'That's settles it, then,' Samuel says.

'Good.' We smile at each other. 'Perhaps we can have a look at the internet later, and you can help me decide on a destination for our trip.'

'I'd love to.'

Rick pops his head round the door. 'Tea all round,' he says.

'Fancy a bit of cake, Samuel?'

'I don't like to spoil my dinner.'

'Just a little slice? That won't hurt.'

'Oh, go on then. You've twisted my arm. I wouldn't say no to a tiny morsel.'

'I might open that Tesco Christmas cake now, and we could have a home-made one for Christmas proper.'

'I'm happy to oblige,' Samuel says. 'There's a nice recipe I'd like to try.'

'Then let's do that.' I make the tea, open the cake and, bracing myself, even take a cup up to Mum.

# Chapter 8

Dad and Samuel do stay for dinner, so we all crowd round the table in the kitchen. It's fair to say that there's not much elbow room. Any more and it will be standing-room only. But this is when I love my home the most. I'd have no idea what to do if it was just Rick and me again.

'We'll have to get that dining-room table back in, Rick,' I say to him while he's spooning carrots into a serving dish.

'I'll do it,' he says. 'I promise.'

I stir some hot milk and butter into the mashed potatoes. Rick drains the pan of peas. 'Dinner's ready, Mum,' I shout up the stairs for the second time. I start to carve the chicken. Thank goodness it's a big one. I think they must have been feeding it neat steroids, but I try not to dwell on that. Rick makes up some gravy granules. Delia would throw herself on her sword.

I cut up some of the scraps and put them in Buster's bowl. He trots over gratefully, always worried that he'll be lost in the crowd.

My mother wafts in. She's wearing a spangled evening dress in black and is carrying a clutch bag, though it's clear she hasn't combed her hair since she woke up from her nap. Rick and I roll our eyes at each other. She has lipstick on, but has almost entirely missed her mouth. As I'm just about to dish up, I don't have time to go and help her change. 'Sit down, Mum.'

Samuel moves up to create a space between him and Dad.

'Hello, young man,' she says to him. 'Have we been introduced?'

'Yes, Rita. We've met before.'

'Oh, lovely,' she continues. 'Was it in Cairo?'

'Mum, you've never been to Cairo.'

'Really?' She looks surprised at that. 'I'm sure I was there in eighty-two.'

She wasn't.

Mum sits down. 'Are you here with someone?'

'Yes,' Samuel says. 'I'm here with Francis.'

'My husband?'

'Er . . .' He looks at me, slightly panicked.

'Samuel is a . . . a friend . . . of Dad's.'

'How nice,' she says. 'From the Conservative Club?'

He nods uncertainly.

'Well, any friend of Frank's is a friend of mine.' She shakes his hand. Then she takes a compact from her handbag and powders her nose.

'Gran,' Chloe says with a laugh. 'You're losing the plot.'

'She thinks she's in the bloody cocktail lounge of the QE2,' Rick mutters to me.

'Shut up,' I mutter back. 'Just help me serve.'

We load up the table with food and everyone tucks in.

'Champagne, madam?' Rick says to Mum.

'I don't mind if I do.'

He pours her a glass of the Tesco own-brand orange juice that everyone else is having. 'Buck's Fizz.'

'My favourite.' She swigs it down and holds out her glass for more. Rick obliges.

Mum is definitely more malleable these days if she's drunk or thinks she's drunk. But I am concerned that her grip on reality seems to waver. Sometimes she's very lucid, just like the mum I've always known – cantankerous, opinionated, difficult. At other times she seems to slip into a world of her own, just out of reach. I must try to persuade her to go to the doctor's with me.

'I bet you're glad she pissed off, aren't you, Grandad?' Chloe says as she cuts up Jaden's chicken.

'Chloe!' I admonish. Mum, however, is intent on her food, and doesn't seem to notice that the conversation concerns her.

'Well,' Chloe counters. 'He's much happier with Samuel, aren't you?'

My dad nods. 'I am. But relationships are complicated, Chloe. They need work all the time.'

'You and Samuel get along OK.'

'You're right,' he says. 'We do, and I try never to take that for granted.'

I think that, discreetly, Dad and the object of his affections squeeze hands under the table.

'I'm going out with Mitch tonight.' Chloe wrinkles her nose. 'What do you reckon?'

'You should try to make it work with him,' Dad advises. 'He's Jaden's father, after all. Life would be a lot less complicated in the future if you could figure out how to get along.'

'I should take you on our date with us, Grandad. You'd sort us out.'

'I'm going up to the Living Room for a few bevvies,' Tom says, still shovelling food into his mouth. 'I'll give you a lift if you want, Chloe.'

I wish they were like this all the time, rather than constantly bickering as they normally are. But they've been like it since they could talk, so I don't think it's going to change now.

'Cheers, bro.'

'That'll be in your mother's car,' Rick notes.

'Well, it's not as if you two ever go anywhere,' Tom flings back.

That just about sums up our life.

'It's fine,' I say. 'We're not going out.' As if.

'We might go out,' Rick offers.

I raise my eyebrows at him. 'Really?'

'You can't,' Chloe says. 'You're babysitting. Remember?'

That just about sums up our life too.

'Can I please take your car, dear mother?' my son asks. 'If it's not too much trouble.'

'Dad will run you both up to the city centre,' I say. 'I don't want you drinking and driving. I'll give you the money for a taxi home.'

'Come on, fatso.' Tom to Chloe. 'Are you ready?'

'Tell him, Mum.'

'Don't call her fatso, Tom. It's not nice.'

46

'You look like you're about to drop, sis. Better not get too much of a swagger on tonight on the dance floor.'

'Mitch and I are going somewhere quiet where we can talk.'

'Good luck with that, love,' Dad says. 'You try to make up with him. He's a nice lad.'

'I don't want *you* eyeing him up, Grandad,' she teases. 'He's mine.' Then she puts her arms round his neck and kisses him, pressing her face against his. She adores her grandad, and they have a lovely bond. I sigh inside. Sometimes I wish that my daughter could be as soft and cuddly with me as she is with my dad. All we ever seem to do is bump up against each other. Dad knows how to sweet-talk Chloe in a way that no one else can. I think that if Chloe and Mitch do get together, then he should give that boy some lessons. 'Here,' she hands Jaden to me. 'Go to Nana. Be good for her. Kiss Mummy goodbye.'

Jaden, always an angel, does as he's told.

'I love you to the moon and back,' she tells him.

He wriggles to get comfortable on my lap, and then I reach for his plate and feed him the rest of his dinner.

'I want you back before midnight,' Rick says to Chloe.

'Get a life, Dad.'

'If I had a life of my own, I wouldn't be able to spend it running you two everywhere.'

'True.' Chloe picks at the last of her chicken and then stands up. 'I'm ready.'

I want to tell her to wear a cardigan, put on a warm coat, not to drink any alcohol, but I keep my lip buttoned.

'Laters,' Tom says. 'Might not be home tonight, Mum. If I'm lucky.' He gives me a hug and kiss.

'See you, Samuel. See you, Grandad. See you, Gran.' Chloe kisses me too.

'Are you off out somewhere?' my mum says.

'Fill her in,' Chloe throws over her shoulder. 'Byeee, darling!' She waves at Jaden.

'Laters!' Rick mimics as he picks up his keys with a reluctant air.

'Parteeeee!' Chloe says, and she and Tom dance out of the door, their father trailing unhappily in their wake.

'I want to go with Chloe.' Mum pulls a petulant face.

'You can't, Mum. She's seeing Mitch,' I remind her. 'You're to stay here with us. That'll be fun, too.'

Even Samuel and Dad look at me as if to say, *That's stretching it*.

'Oh,' Mum says. 'Is there something on in the ballroom tonight?'

'No,' I say. 'Thought we might just sit and watch *Emmerdale*.'

'Oh.' So no fun at all, really. I feel as disappointed as Mum looks. It would be nice to be drifting into a ballroom now for some cocktails and entertainment. Sadly, it's not to be.

'We'll clear up,' Samuel says. 'Won't we, Francis?'

'You'll do no such thing. Leave it to me. Take Mum through to the living room and give her some Baileys, or whatever she fancies.'

Her face brightens at that.

# Chapter 9

While Dad and Samuel keep my mother entertained, I take Jaden upstairs, give him a quick bath and put him to bed.

'Story, Nana,' he says.

'A quick one.'

'*The Snail and the Whale.*'

Current must-have. 'We did that last night.'

'Again.' Jaden pats the bed. 'Lie down, Nana.'

So I feed myself onto the bed alongside his little body and open the book. This is a dangerous time of the day, as I could so very easily fall into a deep sleep myself. Sometimes it's a toss-up who will be in the land of nod first. I read the story that I've trotted out so many times before, but neither Jaden nor I tire of it.

Tonight Jaden cracks first and is asleep after just a few pages. Slowly, I lever myself up and slither away. I kiss him and tuck him in, then leave him with just his little night light on. He hates waking up by himself in the dark.

Rick comes back from the city and I sneak upstairs with

Samuel to look at Christmas markets on the internet. With his advice, I print off a few details of a trip that looks great but won't break the Joyce budget. Then we all sit together and watch a repeat on ITV of Michael Bublé's *Home for Christmas*.

'Is that Dean Martin?' my mum says.

'Yes,' we all chorus.

We ply her with Baileys and Cointreau until she tires of Dean Martin/Michael Bublé and falls asleep in her chair. When they think no one's watching, my dad slips his arm through Samuel's. I nudge Rick, and we exchange a secret smile.

He runs Dad and Samuel home at ten o'clock as Samuel looks very tired, even though they insist that they can quite easily walk.

I wake Mum up and help her up the stairs. She grumbles as I peel off her spangly outfit and gently jiggle her into her nightie. Then I pull back her covers and ease her into bed. The strong, robust woman I have known for so long is becoming more frail all the time. Sometimes it pulls me up short. The flesh on her hands is thin, loose and mottled with brown spots. I reach out and stroke her mad, brightly coloured hair.

'Don't do that, Juliet,' she says. 'I don't like having my hair touched.'

I drop my hand. 'Do you want anything? Hot milk, camomile tea?'

'That dinner's sitting very heavily,' she says. 'I think I'll just read for a while.'

I pass her book over and help to plump up her pillows.

'Don't read for too long or you'll be tired tomorrow.'

'Don't fuss,' she says. 'I'm fine.'

'Night, Mum.' I kiss her powdery cheek.

'I'm not sure I like your father's friend,' she says. 'He seems very familiar with him.'

'You love Samuel,' I say. 'We all do.' She still looks unconvinced.

I hear a key in the front door and realise that it's Rick, back from running Dad and Samuel home.

'Sleep tight,' I say, and leave my mother to it. I know that she'll settle down right away; she just likes everyone to think that she's an insomniac when, in reality, she enjoys the sleep of the just.

In the kitchen, Rick is clipping on Buster's lead. 'I'll give him a quick constitutional,' Rick says. 'We could go together.'

'I'm worried about leaving Jaden alone with just mum.'

Now we can't even do our usual nightly walk together without regimental planning, so it's easier not to bother.

'I won't be long then.'

Quickly, I jump in the bath while the bathroom is free for once and I'm unlikely to be interrupted. I'm just climbing into bed when Rick comes back with Buster. I listen to him closing up the house, as he has done for the last twenty-seven years. I hear him grumbling away to Buster and smile to myself. I think this Christmas will be a good one.

Rick comes up and, with a minimum of fuss, climbs in beside me. 'What have you got here?'

'Trip to Bruges to visit the Christmas market.' I hand him the sheet I printed out. 'Samuel liked the look of it.'

'Our resident travel expert.'

'He's been there before, a couple of times.'

Rick turns to me. 'Is he all right? Thought he didn't look too well tonight.'

'He's a bit under the weather, a bug or something, and he's overworked. They're really busy at the bookshop. I'm sure he'll be fine once he gets to Christmas.'

'I hope he doesn't pass it on to your dad. You know what it's like when they get to his age. One bad bug over winter can finish them off.'

'Thanks for that, Rick.' Now I've got something else to worry about. 'I don't think it's anything serious, just something that's going round. I've told Samuel to go to the doctor, but you know what you men are like. I'll keep my eye on him.' Rick's probably more worried that he'll catch something himself. I try to turn his attention back to the matter in hand.

'What do you think of the trip? It's very good value. Everything's included. It goes by train from St Pancras, so it would be really easy to get to.'

'Hmm,' Rick says. He studies it intently. 'Looks good.'

'Do you think we can afford it?'

'No,' he says, honestly. 'But if it's what you really want, then we'll make it happen somehow.'

I kiss his cheek. 'Thank you.'

'I might need just an extra bit of persuasion,' he says.

'Oh, really? And what form would that take?'

'I'm sure we can think of something.'

I abandon the Christmas market itinerary and we snuggle down in the bed. Our bodies mould along the length of each other with the familiarity of a couple who've been married as long as we have. I know every dip and hollow of Rick's body, and there's a lovely comfort in that.

As he moves in to kiss me, there's an anguished cry from Jaden's bedroom. 'Nana,' he says. 'Where's Mummy? I want Mummy!'

Rick and I exchange a resigned glance. 'Put that cuddle in the bank,' I say as I haul myself out of bed and try to find my slippers.

'Along with all the others,' Rick mutters.

We both know that it will be a long night, with our fidgety grandson sandwiched between us.

# Chapter 10

The next morning, Rick felt like death warmed up. It was getting harder and harder to function on just a few hours' sleep, and Jaden had spent more time in their bed than he liked. Whenever Chloe was out on the lash, he ended up coming in with them. They'd never let their own children sleep in their bed – it was something he'd been particularly strict about – but he'd found that being a grandparent meant that he broke all the rules of good parenting. This was one that left him red-eyed and yawning all day.

Rick glanced at his watch. Minute-perfect. He was just finishing his toast when Merak arrived, ready and willing, as always, to start the day. Every morning his assistant walked from his own place to Chadwick Close in time for them to set off. You could set the clock by him. Buster greeted Rick's apprentice enthusiastically. That was mainly because Merak, more often than not, had some small treat tucked away in his pocket for the dog – a little biscuit or something.

'Morning, Merak,' Juliet said as she was gathering her

belongings ready to go off to work herself. 'Everything all right with you?'

Rick had hoped that his wife wouldn't have to be working full-time at this stage of her life, but there was no doubt that the extra money to help out Chloe came in handy. Plus Tom's being back at home was a drain on their finances. If nothing else, the shopping bill had doubled overnight. His son might be mostly immobile in front of the computer, but it seemed to take a lot of food to fuel his inertia.

'Oh, yes, Mrs Joyce,' Merak replied. 'I am very well indeed.'

The lad's English was improving all the time. His manners were impeccable, and all the customers loved his formal charm. He was tall and blond, which also seemed to go down particularly well with the ladies of a certain age whose flooring they laid. Rick's assistant had a pale, solemn face that looked as if it had rarely been troubled by the sun. He frequently appeared to have the weight of the world on his shoulders, and seldom smiled, but that didn't seem to put them off either.

At that moment, his own son appeared. Unusual for this time of day. Tom was scratching his head and his crown jewels at the same time. Rick's heart sank. Sometimes he couldn't believe this was a child of his loins. He might have inherited some of his genes, but the work ethic one clearly wasn't among them.

'Yo, Merak,' Tom said, and high-fived him.

'Good morning, Tom.'

'Don't suppose you're going to be doing anything useful today?' Rick snapped.

'No,' Tom said. 'Not really. It's pointless looking for a new job until after Christmas, if that's what you're banging on about. No one's hiring.'

This conclusion, Rick assumed, had been reached through hearsay as this week his son hadn't even gone as far as opening the local paper to see if there were any vacancies in it. He must think he could somehow absorb them by osmosis.

'A friend of mine is working in bar in the city centre as manager,' Merak offered. 'They are still looking for extra Christmas staff, I believe. It is good place to work. Is busy. I am doing three nights each week myself. I could give your name to him.'

'Nah,' Tom said. 'Had my fill of bar work. Thanks all the same.'

'No,' Rick said. 'Don't put yourself out when you can sit at home all day and have your mother running round after you.'

Unperturbed, Tom filled the kettle. 'I'll find something in the new year. Don't sweat.'

That was one thing his son was never in danger of doing – breaking a sweat. Rick and Juliet exchanged a glance. His wife sighed. She came to kiss him. 'I'll see you later. Have a good day.'

'Come on, Merak,' Rick said. 'Some of us have work to do.'

It didn't matter what he said, it was like water off a duck's back to Tom, who simply raised a hand in cheery farewell.

The two men drove out to Great Linford where their current job was, listening to Radio 2 on the way. It was only ten minutes away from home and, as usual, he let Merak drive the van. The lad whistled along to the songs as he went.

This was a big job, these days. One of the more successful building companies Rick knew had asked him to lay all the flooring in a brand new five-bed house. There weren't enough of those around at the moment. The building boom had ground to an abrupt halt with the recession, and half the small businesses he used to rely on for work had gone under. The good contracts to supply the flooring for whole estates – the ones that kept them employed for weeks on end – had all but dried up. Now Rick always seemed to be scratching around for jobs and, at the end of them, people were getting slower and slower at paying up. He was too soft, he knew. He was a sucker for every sob-story, and the cheques that were promised time and time again invariably never arrived. It was getting bad. He needed to get some money in soon, otherwise Walk All Over Me would also cease to be a going concern and he and Merak would be heading down to the job centre and boosting the unemployment statistics. It wouldn't just be Tom sitting at home on his bum all day. The last thing he needed was this trip to Bruges that Juliet had set her sights on, but how could he deny her when she was hardly demanding to start with? His wife always put herself at the bottom of a very long list. It would be nice for her to have a treat for once. He was just worried about how his credit card might take it.

He dropped Merak off at the big house, happy that he was quite capable of carrying on by himself for an hour while Rick went to do a quote. Some days Merak would get so into the job that Rick actually had to persuade the lad to stop for a bite to eat, or a drink, and now he'd found out that on top of his

57

day job he was doing extra evening work too. He might have been able to do that once, probably when he was Merak's age, but now Rick felt every day in his bones. His back ached from bending over, his knees had been giving him gyp for years with all the kneeling down the job involved, and he couldn't lift the heavy rolls of carpet or the stacks of wood planks like he used to. Now he definitely needed an extra pair of hands, and every day he was glad of Merak's help. He only wished Tom was similarly motivated. Despite a decent education and a university degree, he'd made nothing of his life. Merak had no family here to fall back on – they were all in Poland, he told him, and Merak regularly sent money back home to help them out. Rick laughed to himself: he could never see Tom doing that. What money that did find its way into Tom's hands was definitely on a one-way street.

Rick left Merak behind with a wave and drove to the other side of Milton Keynes to Cublington Parslow, a small village a good half an hour's drive away. Once upon a time, when Hal ran the business, all the jobs would be concentrated in the city, but now Rick was having to travel further and further afield to keep the work coming in. This particular job was a favour for a friend of a friend, and he'd made it obvious that the work would need to be more than keenly priced.

It was a bright day, and it was nice to get away from the rigid layout of the grid system employed in Milton Keynes and out into the rolling Buckinghamshire countryside. He wound his way through the undulating lanes and wide-open fields, enjoying the blue sky, the birdsong and the drive. In days gone by he and Juliet used to go out for a drive on a Sunday afternoon just for the sheer hell of it. Those days were long gone now. There was always so much else to do. Every time he crossed a chore off his DIY list, three more tasks were added to the bottom. It seemed to regenerate relentlessly, rather like the doctor in *Doctor Who*.

Eventually, Rick bowled up in Cublington Parslow. It was a nice enough village, a bit in the middle of nowhere, but Rick always thought it sounded like the name of someone who'd been in *Dallas* or *Dynasty*. He remembered a time when the duplicitous shenanigans of the Ewing brothers had been the sole source of Saturday-night entertainment for Juliet and him. At least that had a bit of excitement. Now, with Rita hogging the remote control, they had to sit through hour after hour of talentless wannabes on *X-Factor* or *Britain's Got Talent*, and then people he'd never heard of who were supposed to be celebrities on *Strictly Come Dancing*. It just wasn't the same.

Rick took in the village. There wasn't much to write home about. Cublington Parslow consisted of one main street and a single pub; no shop, no post office. There was a duck pond at the crossroads, but if you blinked you could miss it. A family of moorhens picked their way daintily around its periphery. He couldn't live out here; there wasn't enough going on. Not that Stony Stratford was the centre of the universe, but there was a heart to it. Here, everyone seemed to be hiding behind their net curtains.

The houses were an eclectic mix of pretty, ancient cottages and soulless seventies boxes. But on the main drag, it all looked quite well heeled. Rick checked the address he'd been given and then turned off into a side street.

He pulled the van up outside the customer's house. On time. Good. He was always striving to maintain a reputation for good, punctual service. He wanted Walk All Over Me to be a business people could rely on.

This was a row of what looked like 1960s ex-council houses. It wasn't quite so salubrious here, but most of the houses were well kept, with pebble-dashed fronts and tidy gardens. Yet the one he'd stopped at looked decidedly run-down compared to the rest in the quiet street. This was a rental place, and he was doing a quote to replace some flooring for the landlord who was best mates with a friend of Rick's. There'd been a burst pipe in the recent cold snap, and the whole of the downstairs had flooded. Bad news for the tenant and the landlord, but welcome business for Walk All Over Me.

Rick got out of the van. Most of the slats of the once-white picket fence were broken, and the wrought-iron gate hung off its hinges. The garden was overgrown with straggly pampas grass and untamed laurel bushes. It didn't look like the small, scrubby patch of grass had been troubled by a lawnmower in a long time. All the window frames needed a good coat of paint and, though there were two wicker hanging baskets on either side, they both carried long-dead blooms.

He knocked on the door and a young girl opened it. On her hip was a child, a little girl about the same age as Jaden, he'd guess – perhaps a bit older. But, unlike his own grandson, this child had untidy hair, a snotty nose and a dirty face.

'Hiya,' the girl said. 'Come on in.' She was thin, pale-faced, her hair lank. He thought of Chloe who was shiny, rosy-cheeked and plump with child.

Rick stepped inside. The house was damp and smelled fetid. He followed the girl down the hall and into the lounge. In each of the downstairs rooms, the sodden carpet had been rolled up, but it was still in situ and the floorboards were wet. There were a few meagre sticks of furniture. The sofa looked as if you could grow mushrooms on it.

'This is a bit of a mess, love,' Rick observed as he assessed the damage. 'How long has it been like this?'

The girl shrugged. 'Weeks,' she said. 'Every time I phone him the landlord keeps promising to fix it, but he never seems to get round to it.'

'I can't lay flooring on this,' Rick said. 'It's soaked through.'

'The boiler's been broken for over a month, so we've no heating or hot water.'

'Nothing?'

She shook her head. 'I boil a pan on the stove.'

'How do you get a decent wash or have a bath?'

'I boil a lot of pans.'

The child coughed and it rattled in her chest. 'She doesn't sound well.'

A tear sprang to the girl's eye. 'She's on antibiotics, her third lot. Her cough's not shifting at all. It's just so damp here. Water runs down the bedroom walls.'

It didn't take an expert to judge that this place wasn't fit for human habitation. 'Why don't you get out?'

'I'm trying to,' she said, her chin jutting in defiance. 'I've only been here a few months. My contract runs for a minimum of six. I've asked the council to rehome us, but it's not that easy. They just ignore me.'

What was she, nineteen? Twenty? Something like that. Younger than Chloe, he reckoned. No wonder both the landlord and the council thought they could fob her off.

It wasn't a bad house. Underneath the years of neglect, it was probably solidly built. It just needed a fortune spending on it to bring it back up to scratch. A quick glance up at the gutters had told him that they needed replacing. He couldn't imagine why she'd chosen to rent here in the first place. For now, all he was able to do was help her out as best he could.

'I'll get you some heaters,' Rick said. He knew he'd got a couple kicking around in the garage at home the girl could make good use of.

'I can't afford to run them,' she said.

'It's none of my business, but if you don't mind me saying so, miss, you seem to be in a bit of a pickle.'

At that, the girl burst into tears.

# Chapter 11

Some mornings, I'm so glad to get out of the house. In an effort to get fit, save money, avoid usage arguments with Chloe, I have abandoned my car and am now walking to work every day. It only takes me ten minutes if I stride out. I do, however, invariably arrive at the office breathless, hot and a little bit sweaty, but it does make me feel quite virtuous.

The High Street's pretty, old-fashioned and still harbours plenty of quirky, individual shops that attract visitors from all around the area. The downside of its popularity is that there is far too much traffic so that, instead of noticing all the pretty buildings, you tend to focus on all the cars. The offices of Westcroft & Co. are slap bang in the middle – housed in one of the not-so-pretty buildings that were renovated in the seventies by stripping all the character from them. It is, however, very handy for a quick trip to Budgens at lunchtime.

'Morning, Juliet.' One of the boys greets me as I swing in ready to face the day, phone already to his ear. I probably shouldn't call them boys – they are men. But each of them is young enough to be my son and, as is so often the way with estate agents, not one of them looks over fifteen. They're all highly strung. Sometimes it's like having five more kids and trying to keep them under control too. Now there's a thought. And they all treat me like their mum. Whatever problems they have – whether at home or with work – they always feel the urge to come and tell me. I always want to try to sort their difficulties out for them. The girls are just the same, too. There are two of them, and they're both long, willowy and unbelievably high-maintenance. The only good thing I draw from it is that it makes me realise that it's not just Tom and Chloe who are totally self-focused.

'Morning.' I unwind my scarf, peel off my coat and settle at my desk, which is tucked away in a corner at the back of the main office.

When I left the library I didn't do very much for about a year, and then I found this job advertised in the local paper. Amid stiff competition, and to my complete surprise, I got it.

I'm the office administrator, rather than being at the cutting edge of the selling part of being an estate agent. I deal with paperwork, appointments and look after some of the rental side of the business. Nothing too taxing. But it's a very busy office, and it suits me just fine. I'm efficient and organised and, as long as I keep on top of the paperwork, I take it more or less in my stride. Sometimes I miss the quiet calm of the library, the joy of the slightly musty books, but I try not to think about it too much. I work from nine to five here, and only the occasional weekend when pressure of work dictates.

Despite the recession, property in Stony Stratford always

goes well. There's generally more demand than there is supply. All of which goes to keeping my boss, Robin Westcroft, a happy bunny. His father ran the business before him, but it's Robin who's been at the helm for the last twenty years and who's turned it into the successful concern that it is. There are seven agents who work in the office, and there's another lady, Angela, who comes in just at weekends when the office is busiest. Then there are two other branches that Robin has added over the years. One in Olney, a very nice town near here, and one up in Towcester. We are the flagship branch, though. We don't usually see much of the other staff, but Robin has a barbecue for us all each summer and, of course, there's the Christmas party, which is coming up soon.

Robin Westcroft is a bit older than me, early fifties. He's a good-looking man. There's a touch of the Rufus Sewell about him – never a bad thing. He's very smart, always wears an expensive suit, well-polished shoes and a nice watch. Someone who looks after himself. He runs, works out, that kind of thing. Though when he gets time to do it I don't know, as he always seems to be at the office, morning, noon and night. When he's not at our branch, he's invariably at one of the others. He has an easy charm that makes him a pleasure to work for. All the staff love him.

'Morning, Juliet,' Robin says as he emerges from his office. Most days I believe he gets in at about seven o'clock, but I'm never here to witness it.

'Hello, Robin. How are you today?'

'Well enough,' he says. 'How are the plans for the Christmas party coming along?'

'All organised,' I tell him. 'I've booked the dinner and disco at The Cock Hotel again.' A nice place in the centre of the High Street, just a bit farther down from the office. 'It's still very reasonable, and we all enjoyed it last year.'

He shrugs his approval. 'Excellent idea.'

The truth is I was so busy that I didn't have time to shop around to find anywhere else that might have been more suitable. I kept meaning to, but I had to book this up in September to make sure we got in. Next year, I'll start earlier – about June! – and we might go somewhere more glamorous. I'm not sure where, though. The Cock Hotel is convenient for the other staff to get to as well. Robin puts on a minibus for them so they don't have to drive.

'I've put it in your diary.'

'Thanks.'

Then I hesitate. 'I've booked for Rosemary, too. Will she be coming along this year?'

I'm never sure what's the right thing to do. The appearance or not at office dos of Robin's wife is a constant source of gossip. Sometimes she turns up and is lovely; sometimes she turns up and is drunk. Sometimes she doesn't turn up at all. Even at the barbecue – which is held at their house. I know it embarrasses Robin terribly.

'I'm not certain,' he says, and there's a sadness behind his eyes. 'We'll have to see nearer the time.'

Usually about ten minutes beforehand, in my experience. 'Sure everything's OK?'

'Yes, yes.' He waves away my concern. Robin surveys the office. 'About time we put the Christmas decorations up?

It looks a bit miserable in here. Olney have got theirs up already.'

'I'm going to do it as soon as I can this week. If I can grab an hour to spare.'

'I knew you'd be on the case.' He smiles at me, but it doesn't quite reach his eyes. 'You're lovely, Juliet,' he says. 'I don't know how I'd manage without you now.'

I flush at that. 'Thanks.' I'm always flustered when Robin praises me. He does it quite often. Perhaps it's because I'm not used to the attention, as most of my family treat me with as much respect as they do the wallpaper. Even the dog gets more fuss than I do.

# Chapter 12

Rick looked at the kettle on the hob. 'A watched kettle never boils,' he said sagely.

The girl tried a laugh through her tears.

It had taken an age. In fact, his blood was boiling more than this kettle. What sort of landlord was happy to have someone living in a tip like this – and a youngster with a sickly kid at that?

He was seething.

Finally, the kettle sent out a meagre jet of steam and a whistle and Rick made tea in two chipped mugs. He gave one to the girl. 'Nature's cure for everything,' he said as he sat down at the kitchen table opposite her. 'A nice cup of tea.'

When he'd looked in the cupboards for tea bags, there was hardly anything in there either. You couldn't move for the Christmas stuff that Juliet had packed into their cupboards at home. The contrast was marked.

'I'm sorry,' she said, sniffling. 'I didn't mean to cry. It's just all got a bit on top of me.'

'That's understandable, love,' he said, sympathetically. 'I think I'd feel like weeping myself.' If Rick didn't need the work, he'd be straight on the phone and giving this landlord a piece of his mind. Might still do. The man was probably only fixing the floors at all because he could get the money back off his insurance company. The boiler was staying broken because he'd have to shell out for that himself. 'Don't worry, at least I can get your floors sorted out for you.'

'Thanks.' She sipped gratefully at the tea.

The little girl smiled warily at him and he tickled her under the chin, eliciting a full-blown grin. 'I'm Rick, by the way. Rick Joyce.'

He held out his hand to the girl and, hesitantly, she shook it. Her hand was insubstantial, as light as a feather in his.

'Lisa Hall,' she said. 'This is Izzy. Say hello to the nice man, Izzy.'

'Hello,' the little girl whispered, thumb in mouth.

'She's lovely. I have a grandson who's about the same age.'

'You don't look old enough to be a grandfather,' Lisa said.

He tried a laugh, feeling ridiculously flattered by that. 'Oh, believe me, I am.'

Rick looked round at the shabby kitchen. The front was off the broken boiler, the lino in here was ripped, half the cupboard doors were missing. *And my grandson has a very different life to this*, he thought. Rick took a swig of his tea to clear the lump that was suddenly in his throat. 'If you don't mind me saying, Lisa,' the name felt strange on his tongue, 'you seem to be a bit out on a limb here. If you're going to get the council to move you, wouldn't you be better trying to get into Milton Keynes?'

'I'll have to,' she sighed. 'That's where I lived before, but I wanted to get out of the city. I got in with a bad crowd, Rick,' Lisa admitted. 'I didn't want that for Izzy. The only way to break from them was to move right away. But it hasn't been as easy as I thought. I always dreamed of living in the country. I even had this picture in my head of what village life would be like.' The girl gave a bitter laugh. 'It hasn't quite worked out like that. To live here you need plenty of cash, a car and a posh accent. No one talks to me. They all look at me as if it's my fault the house is in this state. The landlord promised to do it up when I moved in.' She looked around her and said, needlessly, 'He never has.'

'I'll put in a good price for the floors,' Rick said. 'One that he can't refuse. At least we can make a start on those. I'll remind him gently about the boiler, too.'

'Why would you do that?' Lisa said. 'You don't know us from Adam.'

'It's coming up to Christmas, love. You can't stay in this freezing place over the winter. It's not fair on the youngster.'

'I've got nowhere else to go.'

'No family that can help you out?'

Lisa shook her head sadly. 'No. They live miles away, and I never see them.'

He wondered how that had happened. Sometimes he *wished* his kids would move miles away! He thought of Chloe and Tom, who had every comfort they could think of provided for them. Not that they were rich, but neither of his children had ever had to worry about where their next penny was coming from. Not like this young lass. Rick's heart went out to her. 'Then I'll see what I can do.'

'Thanks, Rick.' Her thin, grateful smile created a knot in his stomach.

He might be getting old and grey, but he still remembered how hard it was when he was young and had nothing. Rick drained his tea. 'I'll get these floors measured up, and I'll drop you some heaters back later today.' Producing his wallet he pulled out a twenty-pound note and handed it over to her. It was all he had on him. 'Use this to pay for running them.'

'I can't accept your money,' Lisa protested.

He folded the note into her palm. 'Take it for Izzy,' he instructed.

She looked at him, bewildered. 'I don't know what to say.'

'Say you'll get on to that council again and ask them to move you somewhere better.'

Lisa smiled, and it made her look younger than ever. 'I will,' she said.

# Chapter 13

Of course, I don't get a minute to myself all day. Now that Robin has mentioned the lack of Christmas decorations, I want to get cracking with them. It's not like me to be so late. I always want to enjoy them for as long as we possibly can, and would put them up in the office in September if I could – and at home, too. So I give Rick a call and tell him that I'm going to stay late and decorate the office, otherwise it could be February next year before I get round to it. He's got an extra call to make, he says, so dinner at Chadwick Close will be late tonight, and the rest of the clan will just have to put up with that.

When everyone else has departed for the day, I tidy away the paperwork on my desk and go to rummage in the darkest depths of the walk-in stationery cupboard at the back of the office. Eventually, under piles of paper and sundry stationery that's been dumped in there, I find the half-dozen big boxes that contain the Christmas decorations. There's a nice selection, although they do look a little too corporate for my own tastes. We have big snowflakes and fluffy snowballs that hang from the ceiling, and a range of glittering silver reindeer that gambol across the big front windows. There's a smiley polystyrene snowman that sits in the corner, and a big white sparkly Christmas tree with green and red baubles.

I lower the lights in the office and lock the door so that we won't get any late stragglers coming in trying to arrange to view a property. First, I'm going to put up the Christmas tree and then, when the High Street has emptied completely, and no one can see me climbing on the desks, I'll start on the window displays.

Unpacking the tree, I straighten out its branches and dust them off. Just as I'm about to put the three separate parts of it together, Robin's door opens and he comes out bearing his briefcase. He starts when he sees me.

'You made me jump, Juliet,' he says, hand on heart. 'I thought everyone had gone home.'

'Putting up the decorations,' I say. Although he's probably worked that out, due to the fact that I'm surrounded by boxes with tinsel spilling out of them and am standing next to a Christmas tree. 'I never got a chance today, and I thought I might as well stay for an hour and get it out of the way.'

'You didn't need to do that.'

I shrug. 'I don't mind. I love putting up decorations.' Sitting back on my desk, I say, 'I have a little ritual at home. I have my album of Christmas songs on the iPod, and I normally have a glass of wine and a mince pie or two.'

'That can also be arranged here.'

I laugh. 'If I'd thought about it in advance I could quite easily have brought something in.'

'No need,' Robin says with a grin. 'Wait five minutes.'

He puts down his briefcase and dashes out of the door. I look after him, bewildered, and then carry on assembling the Christmas tree. Goodness only knows what he's up to. I set up the tree in the corner and stand back to admire it. Our bare little office looks better already.

Minutes later, Robin reappears bearing a bottle of red wine, a box of Mr Kipling's finest mince pies and a CD of Christmas music. Like an excited child, he holds his stash aloft.

'All from Budgens.'

'Oh, Robin! That's fantastic. What a lovely idea.'

Stripping off his coat and jacket, he dashes to his office. 'I've got glasses, too.' Soon, he's pouring out wine for both of us. He clinks his glass against mine. 'Cheers.'

'Cheers,' I echo. 'Merry Christmas.'

'Merry Christmas, Juliet.' He takes a hearty swig. 'I'd like to stay and help. If that's OK.'

'You don't have to do that.'

'I'd like to,' Robin says as he loosens his tie. 'To be honest, this is the first bit of Christmas cheer I've had.' He holds up his glass again and his eyes avoid mine. 'I'm afraid there's not much festive spirit in the Westcroft household at the moment.'

'I'm sorry to hear that.'

'Things aren't good between Rosemary and me,' he confesses. 'I'm sure you know that from the office gossip.' I try a non-commital mumble. Of course Robin and his troubled relationship are regularly the hot topic. The opinion of most of the staff is that Robin should have left his wife years ago.

'Haven't been for a while.' My boss picks up a few of the

Christmas-tree baubles and goes to hang them. I do the same. We stand at opposite sides of the tree and fiddle with the baubles and the branches. 'I think the phrase is "we've grown apart",' he continues.

'All marriages go through their rough patches,' I offer. 'Goodness only knows, Rick and I have had our moments.'

'Really?' Robin seems surprised by this. 'I always thought of you as the perfect couple.'

I laugh at that. 'Far from it!' I shake my head, still smiling. 'We're fine now,' I add hastily. 'Absolutely fine. But it hasn't always been the case. We've weathered some storms in our time.' A couple of years ago, I even considered leaving Rick for another man, something I never thought would happen, not in a million years. With any relationship, no matter how long it has endured, you can't just rest on your laurels. I wonder why Rosemary Westcroft is unhappy with her husband. If you asked for my opinion, I'd say that she'd have to go a long way to find a nicer man. But then you never know what goes on behind closed doors, do you? Who knows, he could have a whole range of despicable habits once he takes off his smart suit jacket for the night. I pick up another bauble to hang. 'If you want my advice, Robin, just stick with it. I'm sure, given time, that you'll come out the other side.'

'You think so?'

'I'm sure so.'

'What got you through it all?'

'I just came to realise that I was happier as a married woman at the heart of my family. That's where I wanted to be.'

'I wish Rosemary could appreciate that. Perhaps the fact that we've never had kids hasn't given us that cement. As it's just the two of us, maybe it's too easy to see the faults. I love her, Juliet, but I'm not sure that she feels the same any more. There's a terrible gulf between us, and I don't know how to bridge it.' He looks at the gaudy bauble in his hand. 'Look at me. I'd rather be here with you, having a glass of wine and a laugh and putting up the Christmas decorations than at home with my wife. I'm always frightened of what's waiting for me. I can never tell if we'll be OK or if she'll be hurling plates at me.'

'Oh, Robin.' My heart goes out to him. 'You can't go on like that.'

'I know. I'm envious of your family life, Juliet. You always seem so tight-knit. You talk of them all with such pride.'

Do I? My thoughts go to my cantankerous mother, my late-onset gay dad, my troublesome daughter, my idle son, my grumpy husband and I realise that, despite everything, I do love them all. They are my world.

'I hope you work it out,' I say to Robin.

'Me too.' He nods his head towards the windows and paints a smile on his face. 'Shall I make a start on the reindeer?'

'That sounds like an excellent idea.' I'd rather Robin risk life and limb to do the window display than me.

I carry on decorating the tree but, out of the corner of my eye, I watch him clamber over the desks and fuss with putting the reindeer in an arc across the large expanse of glass.

He turns back to me, red-faced with exertion. 'Look good, Juliet?'

'Looks great.'

He gives me the thumbs-up and titivates the reindeer some more. His jollity is forced, and I wonder if he thinks he's said too much. I get a lump in my throat when I realise that, for all his wealth, his good looks and his charm, Robin Westcroft is lonely.

# Chapter 14

'Come on, Chloe,' I shout up the stairs. 'Hurry up or we'll miss the switching on of the lights.'

'What lights?' Mum asks.

'The Christmas lights in the High Street,' I explain for the third time.

We're all going to see the turning on of the Christmas lights in Stony Stratford High Street. It's something we've done as a family for years now and signals, for me, the start of the festive season in earnest.

'Is that why I've got my coat on?'

'Yes, Mum. We've done it for years.'

'Have we?' She looks round, baffled. 'I'd rather be watching *Emmerdale*.'

'*Emmerdale* isn't on today. This'll be fun. You'll enjoy it.'

'If that girl's not down here in two minutes,' Rick grumbles, 'we're going without her.'

The rest of us are ready. Even Tom's coming along with us today, which is lovely as his attendance at family events is somewhat sporadic these days. Dad and Samuel are going to be there too, and they're meeting us in the Market Place by the library. Merak will also be joining us. This is his first year in England, his first British Christmas, and I thought he might find it fun. I don't know what they do in Poland, but I don't want him feeling left out. As usual, he's arrived spot on time. Only Buster is staying behind and, because he senses his impending abandonment, the dog's distressed and is whining pathetically. Feeling guilty, I give him tomorrow's chocolate from the advent calendar to placate him. And to anyone who says that dogs aren't supposed to have chocolate, Buster has been happily gorging himself on it since he was a puppy and at thirteen years old, I don't think he'd be happy to stop now. Much like myself.

Eventually, Chloe comes down the stairs with Jaden, who's all wrapped up as if he's going on an Arctic expedition, bless him. His big blue eyes look out from between a bobble hat and a scarf that looks like it might be strangling him. He's in more danger of overheating in that lot than he is of freezing. 'Let's go then,' she says.

Surreptitiously, I loosen Jaden's scarf as I organise him into his buggy and we all set off for the short walk to the centre of town. I take the pram and Chloe links her arm through her grandma's.

The switching-on ceremony is always preceded by a day of fun. The High Street is closed off to traffic and is lined with a mishmash of craft stalls, fairground rides and street performers. For weeks before, local people have been making festive paper lanterns to take part in a twilight parade. The sun is sinking as we hit the town and Market Square is bustling with activity. Street performers go through their various acts to entertain the people. In one corner is an enormous inflated bouncy snowman. If I was considerably younger, that's exactly where I'd be heading as it looks like great fun. As it is, there are a few big boys on there bouncing into each other, and I think it might be too boisterous for Jaden. Next year, when he can hold his own, he'll be able to go on that. The centre ground of the Market Square holds the towering Christmas tree, strung with pretty white lights. Around the periphery there's a huge variety of food stalls.

The medley of smells is so very tempting. Surely we've got time to stop for a little something to keep us going? I've got a chilli on the timer in the oven for when we get home, but that's ages away and it doesn't stop me from saying, 'Shall we have a coffee and a hot doughnut?'

'Hmm.' Rick rubs his hands together. 'Sounds good.'

'What do we all want?' I ask, then I try to remember who's requested what as they simultaneously shout out their orders.

Rick and I queue up. There are only a couple of people ahead of us, and the staff move quickly and efficiently. Soon we have a tray bearing our stash of various flavoured coffees and a big bag of hot, sugary doughnuts fresh out of the fryer. That should keep the cold at bay for a while, at least.

I hand them out to Jaden, Chloe, Tom and Merak. Then I give one to Rick.

'Thanks, love.'

'Where's Mum?'

Everyone looks about them, but she's nowhere to be seen. My heart goes cold. 'She was with you, Chloe.'

My daughter looks guilty. 'I don't know where she is. I was watching Jaden. She must be here somewhere.'

'Mum!' I shout out. 'Mum!' But I can't see her anywhere in the crowd.

Rick takes up the call. 'Rita! Rita!'

Heads spin round, but not one of them is Mum's. In a panic, I give Rick the remaining coffee and bag of doughnuts and fish for my mobile. When I find it, I punch in her number. The phone rings, unanswered.

'It's probably on the kitchen table where it usually is,' Rick tuts.

I'm frantic now. 'Do you think she'll have gone on into the High Street without us?'

'I don't know,' Rick says. 'She may be heading back towards home.'

We'll have to find her before she goes too far. 'Tom, you take Chloe and Jaden to watch the parade. Merak, go with them. There's no point in all of us missing it.' I chew at my fingernail. 'Keep your eye out for Gran, though. Dad and I will look for her and we'll catch you up.'

'She can't have gone far,' Tom offers.

'I hope not.'

'I will stay with Rick,' Merak says.

So Tom, our portable dustbin, is given the coffee and doughnuts to finish off and the children head into the High Street while we three go in search of my errant mother.

'Let's split up,' Rick says to me. 'You walk back towards the house. I'll go this way with Merak.' He points down the nearby shopping alley. It's so crowded with people that I can hardly see a space between them and I wonder how we'll ever find her here. 'What's she wearing?'

'A blue coat and a white woolly hat.'

'OK. I'll give you a ring in five minutes and we can see where we are.'

'Right.' I set off briskly, retracing our steps back towards Chadwick Close.

The wind nips at my cheeks as the temperature is now dropping. I stride out, going as fast as my legs will carry me.

I'm just turning off Calverton Road when Rick rings me. 'It's packed here, love,' he says. 'We can't see Rita anywhere.'

That makes my heart sink further but then, as I look ahead of me, I catch sight of Mum's coat. 'I can see her, Rick. Looks like she's on her way home.'

'Thank goodness. Are you going to bring her back?'

'If she'll come.'

'OK. Do you want me to come over to you?'

'No, no. I can handle it.'

'We'll go and meet up with the kids then. Text me to let me know what you're doing,' Rick says, and hangs up.

I put on another spurt and, within seconds, have caught up with her. 'Mum,' I say. 'What are you doing here? Why are you going home?'

'I want to watch *Emmerdale*,' she says without breaking her step.

'But it isn't on.'

That stops her. 'Isn't it?'

I shake my head. 'We were all going to watch the Christmas lights being turned on in the High Street.'

'How lovely,' she says. 'Every year I enjoy that.'

'I know. You love it. We all do. Why did you go wandering off like that?'

She looks at me blankly.

'You had us all worried.'

'Did I?'

'Come on, Mum,' I cajole. 'We have to go back now, or we'll miss it.'

Without arguing, for once, she lets me take her arm and guide her back towards the town.

'Don't rush me,' she says as she trots along beside me. 'My legs aren't as young as they used to be, Frank.'

I don't correct her slip. I'm just grateful to have found her so quickly. I know that she's been getting more and more forgetful, but this is the first time that Mum's wandered off like this and it's worrying. The alarm bells that should have been sounding have just gone unheard amid all the other noise. What with Chloe being back and Tom, and looking after Jaden and the run-up to Christmas and everything else that's going on, perhaps I hadn't really noticed that she isn't just getting old and mad, that perhaps she is actually unwell. There's a word that's whirling round my brain and I don't want it to. I can't even bring myself to say it out loud. *Alzheimer's*. Is that what Mum has? At what point does forgetfulness tip over into becoming an illness? I don't know. But I think it's something that I'm going to have to address.

'Is *Emmerdale* on tonight?' she asks as we head back to join the festivities. 'I like *Emmerdale*.'

And I realise that this isn't good. It isn't good at all.

# Chapter 15

The parade is in full flow by the time we both get here, and the street is full of revellers carrying paper lanterns lit with candles. Hundreds of people, some in elaborate fancy-dress costumes, some simply wrapped up against the cold, carry them aloft. There are lanterns shaped like polar bears, Christmas trees, angels, stars, all jiggling through the watching crowds to the sound of drums and trumpets.

'Look how pretty it is, Mum.'

'Oh, yes. Lovely, dear.' For the moment, she seems completely normal again. 'You're holding my arm too tight, Juliet.'

'Sorry.' She's probably right. I'm clinging on to her for dear life now, and I wish that they did those harness-with-reins contraptions for pensioners like they do for toddlers.

I text Tom and find out whereabouts they all are, and then Mum and I join the rest of the family. They've found a good spot to watch from, and Tom has hoisted Jaden onto his shoulders for a better view. In front of us is the stage where shortly Santa will arrive and count down to the switching on of the lights. The Town Crier in his red and gold livery is already in place. The Salvation Army band are also ready to play a selection of carols after the lights come on, as they always do.

'Is she all right?' Rick asks.

'I'm worried about her,' I say, close to Rick's ear. 'I think it's something more than just her getting very forgetful.' I might well have been in denial about how erratic her behaviour has become over the last few years, but I can't ignore it any longer. 'I hope she doesn't make a habit of wandering off.'

I can tell by Rick's face that he's about to make a poor-taste joke about that. 'Don't even say what you're thinking,' I warn him. 'You'd be just as worried as anyone else if anything happened to her.'

'Devastated,' he dead-pans. 'Do you know that if you rearrange the letters in "mother-in-law" you can make Woman Hitler?'

'Yes, I do,' I say, digging him in the ribs. 'You tell me often enough. Now watch the parade.'

A stream of brightly coloured Christmas puddings, teddies and snowmen dance down the road. Across the street in the crowd I see Robin with his wife. Hopefully, if they've come out together, it means that things are a little better between them. I wave frantically and, after a moment's peering at me, recognition kicks in and he waves back. Maybe it was my hat that fooled him.

Rick leans over towards me. 'I thought your dad and Samuel were supposed to be up here too.'

'They are.'

'I haven't seen them anywhere.'

'I'll text Dad. Let him know where we are.' I do just that.

'This is very good,' Merak says. His eyes are shining bright, just like a child's. There is a rare glimmer of a smile on his face.

I put my arm round him and give him a squeeze. 'Glad you could come. Stay with us for some chilli afterwards?'

'I am afraid I cannot. I have to work in bar tonight.'

'Shame.' He's a nice kid, and works hard for Rick. It must be difficult to be living over here alone, without his family. We try to do as much as we can to support him, but he seems quite self-sufficient. 'Are you going home at Christmas?'

'Yes. I hope so.'

'That's nice. I'm sure your mum's missing you.'

'Yes,' he says, eyes downcast. 'Very much.'

As the musicians head up the High Street and the last of the lanterns pass by in front of us, Santa arrives and takes to the platform erected outside the church. The Town Crier steps up too. Ringing his bell, he shouts out, 'Let the countdown to Christmas begin!'

'Ten! Nine! Eight!' We all join in. 'Seven! Six! Five!' Jaden is getting very confused as he's only done counting forwards. So I try to help him by holding up the appropriate number of fingers. Chloe is busy texting. 'Four! Three! Two! One!'

Santa hits the switch and the lights come on. There's an appreciative gasp from the crowd. Strings of twinkling lights grace the street with angels and stars hanging from them. All of the shops have small trees fixed above their doors, and they glow with coloured bulbs.

'It's Christmas!' the Town Crier booms out. Everyone cheers. The Salvation Army band starts up with 'Joy To The World.' Now the festive season has well and truly started.

I hug Rick and say, 'Let's hope it's a good one.'

He kisses me even though we are in the High Street and there are people we know out here. Before I can hug the rest of the family, my phone rings. It's Dad. 'Where are you, Dad?'

'I'm still at home,' he says, but I can hardly hear him above the noise.

'Everything all right?'

'Can you come over, love?' His voice is trembling. 'Samuel's fallen asleep and I can't seem to wake him up.'

# Chapter 16

'There's something wrong with Samuel,' I tell Rick as soon as I hang up. 'We need to get round to Dad's right away.'

'Want to go back and get the car in case we need to take him to the hospital?'

'No. Let's just go straight there.' Dad's house is a stone's throw from the town centre. Even with all the crowds it should take us less than ten minutes to walk there.

'What's wrong?'

'He says he can't wake Samuel up.'

Rick's face blanches. 'Has he phoned for an ambulance?'

'I don't know.'

'I'll call one just in case.'

'Perhaps we should see what's wrong first. It might be nothing.'

'Better safe than sorry,' Rick counters and punches 999 into his phone. 'It's Saturday night. It could take them a bloody hour to get there.'

I call the family into a huddle. 'We're going to see

Grandad,' I explain. 'Samuel's not well. Tom and Chloe, why don't you take Jaden to see the children's fairground rides?'

'I want to come and see if Grandad's all right,' Chloe says.

'Stay here with Jaden,' I insist. 'Don't spoil it for him. I'll text you to let you know what's happening as soon as I get there.'

'Can I help?' Merak asks.

'No, lad,' Rick says. 'You need to get off to your bar job. We can manage.'

'I can phone in and tell them I will be late. It is an emergency.'

'Everything's fine, I'm certain,' I tell him. 'We'll keep you posted.'

'If you are sure,' he says.

'I am, but thank you. You're very thoughtful.' Somewhat reluctantly, Merak heads off to the city centre to his bar job while I make a plan. 'Tom, can I put you in charge of looking after my mum?'

'Sure.'

'If you let her wander off it will be on pain of death.'

'You're not going anywhere, are you, Gran?'

'I don't think so,' Mum says.

'We won't be long,' I promise. 'We'll be back as soon as we can. If we don't see you here, we'll catch up with you at home. The chilli will be ready in about an hour.'

Rick and I leave the children and dash round to Dad's. Ten minutes later, we're outside, puffing heavily with exertion.

This was my childhood home, the one that my dad shared with my mum for so many years, and now Dad and Samuel live here together. Despite being separated for well over two years now, my parents have never officially divorced or even taken that terrible step of carving up their assets between them. With Mum moving straight in with us, there's never really been the need to. But now the house is looking tired and needs some money spending on it, and I wonder whether the time has come for us to do something about it. What we should do is anyone's guess.

My hands are shaking as I reach for the knocker, and I wonder why. As soon as we knock, Dad opens the door and we hurry inside.

'I've tried and tried to wake him up, but I can't,' he says, wringing his hands.

In the small living room Samuel is sitting in the armchair. He looks for all the world as if he's fast asleep. But something tells me that he isn't. His face is too pale, too waxen. He looks just too peaceful. I feel the colour drain from my own face.

'How long's he been like this?'

'For a couple of hours, I think,' Dad tells me. He shakes his head, confused. He looks every one of his seventy-odd years and more. For the first time in his life he seems old and bent. 'He said he was tired and was going to have a nap before we went up to see the lights. You know Samuel, he's always up for some fun.' Tears fill Dad's eyes and he struggles to speak. 'He was so looking forward to it.'

I hand him a crumpled tissue that's in my pocket and he dabs his eyes.

'When it was time for us to get going, I couldn't wake him up. I shook him and shook him. But nothing.'

I kneel down beside Samuel and shake his hand gently. 'Samuel,' I whisper. 'Wake up.' But I can tell instantly that Samuel is no longer with us. Any hope that I might have had seeps out of me. A lump stops in my throat. He's gone. The vibrant, funny Samuel has gone. I hold his cold hand to my cheek. My tears wet his skin and I know that he won't ever feel it. Oh, Lord. What are we all going to do without him?

I look up. Rick and I exchange a worried glance. I force out, 'Have you phoned an ambulance, Dad?'

'No.' He looks bewildered. 'Do you think we need one?'

'I think perhaps we do. Rick has already called one. Just in case.' Thank God he did. 'I hope it will be here soon.'

'It's not looking good, is it?' Dad says.

'No, Dad. I'm afraid it isn't.'

'Has he gone?'

My eyes fill with tears and I nod. 'I think so.'

With that, he sinks down into my arms. Cradled on the floor, I hold him until his body is no longer wracked with sobs. We hold each other tightly, rocking back and forth. For the moment, I am the parent, my dad the child. His keening breaks my heart. I can hear Rick crying, too. We all love Samuel. We love him so much.

'Come on, Frank,' Rick says. He helps to lift my father from the floor and together we ease him into the nearest chair. Dad looks small and crumpled.

'I used to worry what would happen to him when I was gone,' Dad says, tears still rolling down his cheeks. I cry with him. 'I wanted him to find someone else, someone his own age. He used to laugh it off and say, "You're only as old as you feel, Francis. There's plenty of life in you yet." There was, with Samuel. He made me feel like a young man again. With Samuel I could be anyone I wanted to be.'

'You're still that person, Dad. You won't go back to how you used to be.' Until he met Samuel, my dad hardly used to put a foot out of the door. He had a lonely existence, just him and his beloved books. And my nagging mother. When he first got together with Samuel, I did wonder how we'd feel about their partnership. We've learned to accept Tom's wide and varied choice of partners over the years, but with your own dad, it's different. He was my dad. I'd only ever known him as part of my mum. I can't say I wanted that to change. As it turned out, we needn't have worried. Dad and Samuel were so happy together, who could possibly deny them that pleasure? They were always fun to be with, and I know that Dad will be utterly bereft without him. As will I. Putting my arms round him, I hold him tightly. 'You've got us. We'll look after you.'

'At least he won't have to nurse me as a doddery old man, will he? I never wanted to be a burden to him.' He cries again.

'You're not a burden to anyone, Dad. We all love you.'

We hear the ambulance outside and, a moment later, two paramedics knock at the door. Rick lets them in.

'Perhaps he *is* just asleep.' Dad glances back over his shoulder at Samuel, forlorn hope in his eyes.

'I don't think so.'

'No.' He sighs, and his whole body shudders.

The paramedics confirm that Samuel, still in his prime and

against the order of nature, has left us. They tell us to call Samuel's GP and a funeral director. We offer them tea, which they politely refuse and then they leave. That's it. They leave us alone to our grief and utter disbelief. It feels as if a bomb has exploded in our midst, and I look at my father and don't know how he'll pull himself back from this.

I look at Samuel sitting, still and unmoving in the armchair, and I want to grab him by his cardigan and shake him back into life. It's all I can do to stop myself. How can he have done this? How can he have left my dad behind? Who will love him as Samuel did?

The paramedics might not need tea, but I do before I can make the other calls. Samuel's family will have to know, our kids too. 'I'll phone the kids.'

'We'll tell them when we get home,' Rick says. 'Let them enjoy their time at the fair.'

I nod my agreement. Of course; there's plenty of time for tears. My dad sits on the pouffe at his lover's knee and tenderly holds Samuel's lifeless hand in his, stroking it softly.

I gesture to Rick to come into the kitchen with me and we leave them alone together. Then, in Rick's arms, I break down and shed more tears for the loss of this lovely man.

'Hush, hush,' Rick says, patting my back. 'We'll sort it out. Everything will be fine.'

But I know that it won't. 'We'll have to take Dad home with us,' I say when the tears start to abate.

'I know. He can't stay here. We'll find room.'

I'm not sure where we're going to put him, but I can't possibly leave him here by himself.

My heart is breaking for Samuel, and for my father who's left behind. These things are terrible no matter when they happen, but why does it always seem so much worse when they happen at Christmas?

# Chapter 17

The doctor comes, and is followed quickly by the funeral director. With an alacrity that's quite startling, they take Samuel's body away. On Monday we have to go into their office to complete the paperwork. We are all stunned at how quickly he is gone from our lives, gone from the house.

'I'll go and get the car,' Rick says. 'We'll take your dad home.'

I nod. In the kitchen, I find the bottle of brandy and pour one for Dad and one for me. We knock it back without speaking.

'Get a bag of things together, Dad.'

'I'll be all right here, love,' Dad insists. 'You've got a house full already.'

'I'm not having you here by yourself. You'll be as close to Samuel at our house as you are here.'

He clings to my arm unable to move, paralysed by grief. 'You sit,' I say and lead him to the chair again. 'I'll find you a few bits and bobs.'

I go upstairs to their bedroom and pull out some necessities for Dad. As I get his pyjamas from under the pillow, I try not to look at the bed, so neatly made, and imagine my dad there, alone again. In the bathroom, I gather up his shaving things and well up again at the two toothbrushes standing side by side.

Rick returns with the car, and I help my compliant father into his overcoat and lead him to the car. It's late when we let ourselves into Chadwick Close – gone midnight. I help Dad as he stumbles over the step. When she hears us, Chloe flies out of the living room and nearly knocks Dad over with a bear hug.

He and Chloe cry together, and she makes soothing noises. I do what I always do and put the kettle on. Chloe takes Dad through to the living room and settles him on the sofa, still gripping him as if she'll never let go.

Thankfully, Mum has gone to bed. There will be time enough to tell her tomorrow.

Rick, looking drained, takes Buster for his walk. I don't know what I would have done without him tonight. He's been a rock, and I expect he's glad of a bit of fresh air. It's been a terrible night. Tom appears from the dining room and lounges on the door frame.

'Is Grandad OK?'

'No,' I say. 'Naturally, he's very upset.' Distraught, devastated are closer to the mark. I fear that he may never be 'OK' again. He is grey with pain. 'Can I ask you to sleep on the sofa tonight? I thought we'd put Grandad in the dining room for now, and then sort out bedrooms tomorrow.'

'Sure. Is there anything else I can do?'

'Be kind,' I say.

'I loved Samuel too,' Tom says, and then he surprises me by breaking down. He comes to cuddle me like he did when he was a child. He sobs in my arms, and I don't think I've ever seen him cry like this and I'm touched at the softness of his heart. It's easy to forget that he has feelings at all when most of his life is spent whizzing in and out of the family like a whirlwind. He sniffs up his tears and wipes his eyes on his sleeve. 'Don't tell Dad.'

'Tears are nothing to be ashamed of,' I tell him. 'There'll be plenty more where those came from.' I rub my thumb over his cheek. 'We'll all miss Samuel.'

'It makes me worry about you two,' he says, choked. 'You're not getting any younger either.'

'Thanks, Tom.' That's more like my son.

We both let out a teary laugh. 'You know what I mean.'

Unfortunately, I do. 'Let me make some tea for Grandad. You can take it through to him.' I make tea and a cheese sandwich for him and Tom delivers it while I go to sort out our sleeping arrangements, which are becoming more complicated by the minute.

I change the sheets on the futon and, when Rick comes back with Buster, I persuade him to go into the loft to find the sleeping bag for Tom. It could do with an airing, but I'm sure he's slept in worse places. I've seen some of his photographs from Thailand.

In the living room, Dad is sitting looking dazed. At least Chloe has released her death-grip on him – poor choice of words – and is now just holding his hand and leaning against his shoulder. He's drunk his tea, but his sandwich is untouched.

'Eat that, Tom,' I say, and my son does. 'Fancy a nice hot bath, Dad? It will help you sleep.'

He nods at me, and I lead him upstairs as if he's Jaden's age, carrying his overnight bag. In the bathroom, he sits on the loo seat and waits patiently while I run his bath and find him a clean towel.

'Here are your wash things and your pyjamas.' I put them out for him. 'Are you all right undressing yourself?'

He nods again that he is.

'I'm going to wait right outside, Dad. Don't lock the door, and just call out if you need anything.'

His fingers fumble with the buttons of his shirt as his hands are trembling and it's all I can do to stop myself from jumping in and helping, but I want to leave him with his dignity intact. I want to make him manage.

'Take your time. I'll be just here.' I close the door on the bathroom and then take up my place outside. Sitting with my back against the wall on the landing, I listen to my father cry. The tears roll down my own cheeks. Rick comes up to see where I am and brings me some more tea. I am awash with tea and would really rather have more brandy, but I take it grate-fully nevertheless. Rick sits down next to me. 'All right?'

'Yes.' I wipe my face with my hands.

'You're doing a great job, Juliet.'

'I feel so helpless.'

'We'll look after Frank. He'll be fine.'

I lean against Rick. 'Promise me you'll never die,' I whisper. 'I don't think I could bear it without you.'

'Can I have that in writing?'

'Don't tease,' I say. 'I mean it.'

'Then I promise I won't die,' he says solemnly. 'Not ever.'

# Chapter 18

'Those heaters that I dropped by did the job OK,' Rick noted.

'Yes.' Lisa was making tea for him. 'Thanks for that. It made all the difference in the world. For the first time this winter, Izzy and I have been warm.' She rubbed absently at her thin arms.

'The floorboards have dried out nicely, so I can get on and lay that living-room carpet today.'

'It'd be nice to be a bit more tidy for Christmas.'

He'd come to the job alone today. Merak was more than happy cracking on by himself in Great Linford, and he didn't want to leave Lisa any longer than he had to without anything on the floor. He'd dropped his assistant off at the big house this morning and would collect him again at the end of the day. Someday soon, he hoped they might bring in enough business so that they could get another van and Merak could build up his own customers. It was a risk. There was always the chance that someone you had spent long hours training up would then leave and set up in competition with you. But he didn't think Merak was that kind. He seemed like a loyal sort of bloke, so Rick thought it was worth it. But first, business would have to pick up considerably.

The landlord here had gone for the cheapest laminate and carpet, of course, plus the room was so tiny that it wasn't going to be loads of heavy lifting for him. A couple of days should see the job done.

Lisa handed him a cup of sweet tea. Was it Rick's imagination, or had she made a bit more effort with her appearance today? He thought she looked a bit tidier, and there was more make-up in evidence. Mind you, Juliet always nagged him that he never noticed these things when it was her, so he could be entirely mistaken.

'Has the landlord sent anyone out to fix your boiler yet?' The day after he'd first come to the house, Rick had called the man to remind him gently that there was a young kid and a baby in one of his properties with no heating or hot water in the depths of winter.

'No, but he said he's coming in the next few days when the part he needs arrives.'

Rick tried not to let out a cynical snort. Maybe the landlord was fobbing her off. Maybe he wasn't.

'Keep me posted,' Rick said. 'I'll give him another little nudge if he doesn't turn up soon.' What he'd really like to see is the bloke here today. How would he feel if it was *his* daughter left abandoned in this cold, damp hole? And charged royally for the privilege? He could fix up this place in no time with a bit of effort and some well-aimed cash.

\*

At home, they'd had a terrible week after Samuel's death. Naturally, Frank was devastated and barely functioning. Rick's father-in-law had moved back in with them for the time being, so Tom had been ousted from the futon in the dining room and was currently sleeping on the sofa. Juliet had said that Jaden would have to share Chloe's room which – judging by the amount of vociferous moaning she was doing – his daughter wasn't exactly keen on. Rick hadn't pointed out that she actually had her *own* home to go to if only she wasn't so stubborn and would give her relationship with Mitch another go.

Due to a last-minute rush before Christmas – what was it about this time of year that made everyone feel they needed new carpet? – Merak and he were working flat out, so the lion's share of organising the funeral and all the paperwork that needed to be completed had been left to Juliet.

He couldn't complain about the extra money that this rush of work was bringing in – goodness knows, they needed it. Against his better judgement, he'd agreed that he and Juliet should take the quick break together before Christmas, and Juliet had booked up the trip to Bruges that she fancied. Now – more than ever – she really needed the break. Bruges was somewhere neither of them had ever been to before. It sounded nice enough, but even a couple of days was going to take some paying for. Finances were also tougher now that they helped out Chloe with stuff for herself and the little one. He loved his grandkiddy more than life itself. Jaden was a great little fella, but they were such an expense these days. He seemed to need new shoes, new clothes every ten minutes. Of course, Chloe wanted everything in the house to be organic for him. *Her* child wasn't going to be sullied by pesticides. Not that it stopped her sticking a decidedly non-organic sausage roll, or a Gregg's dummy as Rick called it, in his mouth when it suited her.

It sounded as if he begrudged them the money. But he didn't, not a penny. Yet there was no denying that it all added up. Even when the work was coming in, people were more reluctant to pay up. It was getting harder and harder for him to collect the cash at the end of a job. There was always some excuse, some reason to delay, more bounced cheques, more homes repossessed the minute they'd finished laying new flooring. The customers who paid promptly without any quibble were becoming few and far between.

Samuel's funeral was scheduled for tomorrow, and he was taking a day off to be able to attend. It was only right. Merak would have to work on his own on a small job they'd picked up, and maybe Rick could go and help him out later when the funeral was over.

At lunchtime, he stopped work for half an hour. He couldn't carry on right the way through the day like he used to. Now he needed to take a breather, even if it was a snatched one. Rick sat at Lisa's kitchen table with a cup of tea and the girl sat opposite him. He'd made a sandwich to bring with him, and felt self-conscious eating while Lisa seemed to have nothing more than a Cup-a-Soup for sustenance. No wonder she was so skinny. She definitely looked a bit brighter today, though. Perhaps it was just the fact that she was finally getting her carpet replaced and wouldn't be living with bare, wet floorboards.

Izzy was on the kitchen floor at her feet on a colourful blanket playing with a moth-eaten doll. He wondered whether Jaden had some spare toys that he could bring for her. At home he was always falling over something or other that had been left lying around. The place was like a flipping branch of Toys R Us.

'How do you get around living out here,' he asked, 'if you've got no car?'

'I bought a second-hand bike and one of those kiddy trailers out of the paper,' Lisa said. 'It's bloody hard work. I like to think that it keeps me fit. But I have to cycle up to Wing or down to Stewkley if I want even a loaf or some milk.'

'That's a long way on a bike.'

'If I go to Wing there are fewer hills.' She shrugged. 'It's not ideal. I have to catch a bus to Leighton Buzzard or Aylesbury if I want to do a big shop, and that's a fortune. The nearest doctor's surgery is miles away. I didn't really think this through properly. All I wanted was for Izzy to have a nice life somewhere that didn't have car alarms going off all night or druggies on every corner.'

'You've tried,' Rick said. 'There's no harm in having a rethink. Perhaps you could move out to the country again if your circumstances change in the future.'

'Yes,' Lisa said. 'I could do that, couldn't I?'

'I don't see why not.' And it hurt his chest to see the faint hope shining in her eyes.

# Chapter 19

The funeral cars pull up outside the house. It's only three o'clock, but the sky is heavy with black clouds and night is already threatening to close in around us. There's the bite of ice in the air, and the weathermen are predicting more snow later in the week.

As I'm pulling on my coat, Mum comes downstairs in a brightly coloured, flouncy dress that I can't even recall seeing in her wardrobe. It's topped with a straw hat complete with blousy flower and worn at a jaunty angle, and white cotton gloves.

'Mum.' I'm aghast. 'What are you wearing?'

My troublesome parent gives me an indignant glare. 'My best dress.'

It was probably her best dress in 1975. 'We're going to a funeral,' I remind her.

'Are we?' She looks genuinely surprised. 'I thought you said it was a garden party.'

'It's Samuel's *funeral* today.'

'Who's Samuel?' She stares round at everyone, who have congregated in the kitchen – Rick, Chloe, Tom, Dad, Samuel's parents. 'I don't know a Samuel.'

I look over at Joshua and Kate Scott and mouth, 'She's not well.'

'There's nothing the matter with me,' my mother snaps.

Bat ears – as Rick likes to call her.

Samuel's mother and father are a gentle, retired couple. We've met them a couple of times before – mainly at Christmas – but not in terrible circumstances such as these. Joshua, like his son, is a gentle giant. Kate is petite and, today, looks even smaller than ever. It's as if the life has been sucked out of her too at the untimely departure of their only son. I can barely imagine how awful she must feel. Some days I think I could gladly strangle Chloe or Tom, but the reality of it is that if anything happened to either of them I have no idea how life would continue. It's the worst possible thing for a parent to go through. You never imagine that you will outlive your own children, do you? There's just nothing right about it.

Mr and Mrs Scott live on the east coast now, in Sheringham, which is a good three-hour drive away from here. They've travelled over for today and are staying at the Jury's Inn in the city centre overnight with some other members of Samuel's family from various corners of the UK, none of whom we know. I would have loved to have offered for them to stay here but we're all out of beds. Dad, in his black coat, which suddenly looks ten sizes too big for him, is standing with them and it's clear to see that Samuel's parents are both several years younger than him.

Samuel is to be cremated at Crownhill, and the thought of it makes me want to weep. He died of a pulmonary embolism – an errant piece of thickened blood meandering into his lung – at the grand old age of forty-four, and I don't think anyone would argue if I said that's far too young an age to be departing this planet. The worst thing is that there was no indication this might happen: no symptoms, no alarm bells. Apart from the cough that had dogged him for weeks, apparently unconnected to his death, Samuel was, by all accounts, in robust health for his age. He was on statins for his cholesterol and there was no doubt that he enjoyed his food and a glass or two of wine, but is that reason enough to cause his premature death? Idiopathic, the doctor called it. Just a random chance that his own body would turn on him without warning.

'Thank you for having us,' Kate says. 'We do appreciate it.'

'Oh, goodness me, don't mention it,' I say. All of the family are coming back here afterwards for something to eat. To coax Dad out of his despondency, I cajoled him into baking some of Samuel's favourites from one of Jamie Oliver's books, and we spent a pleasant couple of hours cooking together. 'It's the least we could do. We all loved Samuel.'

'I still have no idea who this Samuel is!' my mum announces at the top of her voice. 'Why are we all talking about him as if he's dead?'

Kate flinches. I want the ground to open up and swallow me. No, what I actually want is for the ground to open up and swallow my mother.

'Mum,' I hiss. 'You do know Samuel. He was Dad's ...' and then words fail me. Friend hardly encompasses it. What was he? He was more than Dad's boyfriend or partner or whatever you want to call him. He was his life. In the few years that they'd been together, he had become Dad's life. They were inseparable, like an old married couple but without the arguing. Samuel had shown my dad, late in life, what it was to be loved and to live for the moment. I look at Dad's drawn features and my heart breaks. In death Samuel will be missed beyond belief.

'If we don't get a move on,' my mother says in theatrical tones, 'all the best cake will be gone.'

'We are not going to a bloody garden party, Rita!' Rick snaps.

'I'll stay at home with you, Gran,' Tom suggests. 'We can watch some rubbish telly.'

'I want to go to the party,' Mum shouts. 'I don't want to stay at home.' She flails her arms, having a tantrum, the likes of which Jaden is just trying out for size.

'Let's lock her in the basement,' my husband suggests under his breath.

'We haven't got a basement.'

'More's the pity,' Rick mutters darkly. 'Remind me to dig one.'

'I. Want. To. Go. To. The. Party!' Now Mum is going purple in the face.

'For heaven's sake, get her in the car,' Rick says.

I take my mother by the arm and hustle her towards one of the waiting funeral cars, grabbing a coat for her from the rack in the hall as I leave. At least it will cover the worst of the flouncy dress.

'Do you think we could get a two-for-one deal while we're there?' my husband mutters as he stomps down the path after me.

'Rick!'

'Just a thought. I'll stay with Genghis Khan, you get your dad.'

I usher Mum into the back of the car, glad to leave her in the tender loving care of my husband.

'Budge up, Rita,' I hear him say. 'We've all got to get in here. You're not the bloody Queen.'

I return to the house and help Dad. As we walk along the path, I glance back at the house. Rick's multiplicity of Christmas lights twinkle, flash and strobe on the front of the house. Damn it, I should have got him to turn them all off.

'I'll get Rick to take those down, Dad,' I say. 'I should have thought of it before now.'

'You've had a lot going on, love. Thanks for doing everything. Don't think I could have faced it.' Now Dad turns round and a glimmer of a smile moves his mouth. 'They look lovely. Samuel always liked your lights. He loved Christmas. It was his favourite time of the year too.' Now he tries a weak laugh. 'All that food!'

'Perhaps we'll get a new light in his honour.'

'That would be nice. Something very sparkly. Perhaps a star.'

'I'll get Rick to take you to Homebase and you can choose one together.'

'I will miss him.' Dad's lip trembles.

I tuck my arm through his. 'We all will.'

109

'Come on, Frank,' my mum shouts from the funeral car. As well as everything else, I sometimes think she forgets that she's not actually married to my dad any more. 'Don't dilly-dally. It's starting soon, and we'll not get a good seat.'

Dad rolls his eyes at me. 'Is it wrong on the way to a funeral to be considering murdering someone?'

'No,' I say. 'And don't think you're the only one.'

# Chapter 20

I sit at the front of the chapel of rest with Dad. Chloe is like a limpet against him on the other side. She's been very solicitous towards him this last week. Rick keeps my mother at the back, though quite why we think that will be any better is anyone's guess.

The service is a really lovely affair. Dad manages to read out one of Samuel's favourite poems, and one of his cousins tells some stories of Samuel's life, and, deep down, I wish that we had known him longer.

The final song that Dad has chosen comes on. Andrea Bocelli's 'Time To Say Goodnight', and there isn't a dry eye among us.

Just as I think all is about to pass off without incident, my mother shouts out from the back, 'Can't you put on something more cheerful? This is very dreary!'

I turn to my husband and Rick gives me an exasperated look. To be honest, I'm glad he's managed to keep her quiet for so long. She has always been 'straight-talking' throughout her life – a euphemism for downright rude, if you ask me. Now she seems to have lost her edit button entirely. Whatever she's thinking seems to come straight out of her mouth without any concern for others.

'How can we dance to this?' she adds at full volume. But she's totally oblivious when everyone turns to stare at her.

She only disgraces herself once more when we all file out of the chapel at the crematorium and she snatches one of the beautiful red roses left by Samuel's aunt from the top of the coffin, puts it between her teeth and dances out. This time, everyone pretends they haven't seen her do it.

In muted mood, we all come straight back to Chadwick Close after the funeral. As soon as I get the chance, I grab Samuel's rose off my mother and now it's in a bud vase in pride of place in the middle of the buffet table. My mother is, quite honestly, proving to be more trouble than Jaden.

I settle Dad in an armchair next to Samuel's parents and get them all tea. Rick is looking after the rest of the relatives who, thankfully, seem to be just as affable as Samuel was. Then my breath catches in my chest. I can't believe that I'm referring to him so readily in the past tense.

I'm biting back the tears when Tom comes over. 'Nice spread, Mum,' he says, slinging his arm round my shoulders. 'You've done Samuel proud.'

'Thanks. Keep an eye on Grandad for me.'

'He's doing fine.' Tom helps himself from the sausage-roll mountain and wanders off.

When I've seen that everyone else has had plenty to eat, I sit down with some sandwiches myself. My fear is always that food will run out so, as usual, I have catered for twice as many people as have turned up. We're going to be eating sausage rolls from now until New Year. I was up and making quiche at six o'clock this morning. Needless to say, Rick pointed out that I was mad.

I've managed to persuade Mum to go and have a lie-down so that she's out of harm's way at least for the moment. I'm not entirely sure, but I think Rick might have slipped a sleeping tablet into her tea. I saw him looking very furtive over the PG Tips. If he has, it was a jolly fine idea and I wish I'd thought of it. Hopefully, Samuel's family will all have left by the time she graces us with her presence again. Jaden is playing on the floor with his Timbertown train set which we've set up in the corner. Mitch is kneeling next to him.

I go over. 'Everything OK?'

'Thanks for asking me to stay, Juliet,' he says.

Mitch looked after his son while we were all at the funeral, and I persuaded him to come in for something to eat when he dropped Jaden back. 'You're family,' I tell him. 'I just wish it was a nicer occasion. I'll look after Jaden for a few minutes while you have a chat with Chloe.'

'Thanks.'

I beckon to Jaden. 'Come and have something to eat with Nana.'

Filling a plate from the buffet table, we find a spare chair. He climbs onto my lap and tucks into a ham sandwich and a couple of little sausages. I glance over to where Chloe and Mitch are sitting together, deep in conversation. Every now and then, my daughter throws back her head and lets out a raucous laugh. Not the best thing to do at a wake – do people still call them that? – but I'll take the laughter if it means that things are going well between them.

Oh, I do so hope that they can get their relationship back on track. They had a 'date' the other night which, by all accounts, was 'OK'. It must have been wonderful as it's like trying to get blood out of a stone, eliciting praise from my daughter.

If one good thing could come out of today it would be that those two realise how silly they're being. But then, I have to confess, I think it's Chloe who's being the silly one. From the outside, it looked to me that Mitch was trying his hardest to be a good father in difficult circumstances. Chloe was the one who was feeling 'stifled'. Suddenly becoming a mother was, it seems, too much of a culture shock for her. Once she realised that the partying and the free-and-easy lifestyle couldn't continue, I think she panicked. Now, with another baby on the way, I'm going to have to sit her down and make her reassess her priorities. Perhaps if we weren't always here picking up the pieces for her then she'd have to face up to her responsibilities. But we can't just turf her out on the street, can we?

Rick sidles over to me. He's looking uncomfortable in his one good dark suit. His tie has been loosened already. In his hand is a paper plate filled with mini-Scotch eggs, cheese twirls and crisps.

'When I've finished this,' he nods at his plate, 'mind if I slip away to go and see what Merak's up to? He should be finishing about now.'

'That's fine.'

'Sure you can manage?'

'They'll all be heading off soon.'

'Leave the tidying up. I'll give you a hand when I get back.'

'Don't be too late.'

'No.'

Rick turns to go.

'Take Merak some food,' I suggest. 'There's going to be heaps of it left, and he can probably make use of it. There's plenty still in the kitchen. Take what you want. I'll keep some of the sandwiches to pack up for you both tomorrow for your lunch.'

'Good idea.' Rick kisses me on the forehead. 'You've done your dad and Samuel proud, love.'

'You think so?'

'No one could have asked for more.'

I'm pleased to hear it.

'I'll say goodbye to Samuel's folks and then make myself scarce.'

A moment later, I see Rick slip quietly from the room. Soon life will be back to normal. But then I remember: we are the Joyces of Chadwick Close, and life in this house can very rarely be classed as normal.

# Chapter 21

Merak was just finishing up when Rick arrived at the job in Great Linford. As always, he'd done exemplary work, and was now running the vacuum cleaner round to clear up after himself. He could relax when Merak was around, as Rick knew his back was covered.

'Nice job,' he said.

'Thank you.' Merak smiled shyly with pride. 'How did funeral go?'

'As well as these things can.' Rick punctuated the sentence with a sigh. 'Come on. Let's get this van loaded up and I'll take you home.'

They both threw the tools in the back of the van and set off towards Stony Stratford. He always dropped Merak in the centre of the town where he said he rented a room in a house within walking distance.

The lad climbed out of the van. 'There's a carrier bag here for you,' Rick said. 'A doggy bag.'

'I am begging your pardon?'

'Food from the buffet. Juliet thought you might want some for your tea.'

'Thank you,' Merak said and peered into the bag. 'That was very thoughtful of her. Please say thank you.'

'It's OK, lad. Don't bring any sandwiches tomorrow, either. I'll sort us out.'

'I will see you in morning.'

'Usual time,' Rick said. Not that he ever had to remind him.

Merak closed the van door and then, with a backward wave, walked off down the High Street. Rick looked after him. He couldn't help feeling that sometimes Merak was lonely. He hoped that he had a good bunch of mates around him to have some laughs with. Whereas his own dear son was too much play and not enough work, he wondered whether Merak was the opposite.

Rick tutted to himself. What was wrong with him at the moment? He seemed to want to take on the woes of the world. As if he hadn't got enough to worry about of his own!

He glanced at his watch. A two-minute drive would see him safely back at home. Yet, in the back of the van, there was another carrier bag stacked with surplus food that he'd a mind to deliver. When he'd seen quite how much was likely to be left over from the buffet, he'd not only filled a bag for Merak, but he'd filled one for Lisa and Izzy too.

It was getting late now, and he'd promised Juliet that he wouldn't hang about. Still, it was hard to think of that girl and her little one and not want to help her out with a bit of dinner. There was nothing in her cupboards. This would be a nice treat for them. Surely?

The sensible thing would be to head straight home. Rick sat in the van, unmoving. That would be the sensible thing to do.

He put the van in gear and headed towards Cublington Parslow.

Lisa looked surprised when she opened the door to him. But no more surprised than Rick was to find himself here again so soon, he'd guess.

'Rick,' she said, a smile lighting up her thin face.

'I'm not intruding, am I?'

'Well, Johnny Depp and I were about to get down to it on my new flooring,' she said cheekily. 'But I'm sure he won't mind waiting a minute.' She stood aside. 'Come in.'

He stepped over the threshold. It was still colder than the inside of a fridge in here. 'Still no boiler?'

'No,' she said. 'I called the landlord again today. I'm sure he never picks up when he sees it's my number. All I could do was leave a message. Another one.'

'I'll ring him again too.' He needed to get his payment from the guy as well. This money was going to pay for the Bruges extravaganza.

'That can't be all you came out here for.'

'No.' Now he was embarrassed. He'd no good reason for being there, really. 'I brought this.' Rick held up his carrier bag. 'My father-in-law recently lost his partner.' He didn't want to explain the complexities of Frank's love life. Not when he felt himself choking up whenever he thought of Samuel. 'It was his funeral today. Juliet, my wife, made far too much food. I just thought that you and Izzy might like some. Have a little party, the two of you.'

'A party? Izzy, did you hear that?'

'Par-tee,' the little girl echoed.

Lisa peered into the depths of the carrier bag. 'Wow,' she said. 'It looks lovely. Your wife made all of this?'

'Mostly.'

'She's a clever lady.'

'Yes,' he said. 'I ought to get straight back and help her tidy up, or she'll be a very cross one.'

'Stay,' Lisa said. 'I was just thinking what to have for our dinner. Now you've saved me a job. I'll put the kettle on.'

'Better not. I really have to go.'

'Oh.' She looked genuinely disappointed.

Rick shuffled from foot to foot. 'I'll see you then,' he said. 'Take care.'

Lisa stood up on tiptoe and kissed him on the cheek. 'You're a lovely bloke, Rick Joyce,' she said. 'Do you know that?'

But sometimes, in trying to be a nice bloke, he often seemed to do completely the wrong thing.

# Chapter 22

'Oh, you go off and enjoy yourself,' Mum says, tight-lipped. 'Don't think about us here at home. You two have *fun*.'

She spits it out like a swear word.

'It's for two nights, Mum.' I try not to sound cross. I try not to sound like a whiny five-year-old. I try to sound like a calm and in-control grown-up who simply harbours a desire to spend some time alone with her husband. 'When did Rick and I last have a couple of days away together?'

My mother turns her head away from me.

'Dad's still here. He'll look after you.'

'Since when has your father been any use for anything?' she says out of the back of her head.

Dad rolls his eyes. 'We'll be fine,' he says quietly. 'I'm cooking her favourite tonight.'

'I can hear you,' Mum snaps. 'What did he say?'

'I said, I'm cooking your favourite tonight, Rita. I've got a chicken pie ready to go in the oven.'

'There's no need to shout,' Mum says.

'I think that's Mum-speak for "that sounds lovely",' I whisper to Dad.

'She'll be fine,' he reassures me. 'You go off and enjoy yourselves.'

This said in a totally different tone to my mother's. I can't believe that we are actually going. We really are going away and leaving our family to fend for themselves. That Rick and I will be alone together for longer than the ten minutes when we fall into bed exhausted before sleep claims us. I want this trip, am desperate for this trip and we're going, come hell or high water. I'm so excited, I feel like a teenager again. Rick had better watch himself.

'It'll be like old times, with just me and your mum,' Dad adds. 'God help me.'

I smile at that. 'If you're sure.'

'You young things should have some time to yourself. All you do is run around after everyone else. Samuel always said—' and then his words dry up.

Putting my arms round him, I pat his back. 'I know. I know.'

'Go on then.' Dad gathers himself together. It's the small things that catch him out. 'Or you'll miss that train.'

'We've both got our mobiles,' I remind him. 'Don't hesitate to call us if you need anything. If there's a problem.'

'Don't fuss, Juliet.' He gives a wobbly laugh. 'What could possibly go wrong?'

It's snowing, quite heavily. Our train to Bruges is at eight o'clock tonight, and Tom is taking us to Milton Keynes

Central station to catch our connection. I'm worried about the weather. Does snow affect the Eurostar? It seems to bring everything else to a grinding halt.

I kiss Chloe and then Jaden. My grandson clings to my neck. 'Want Nana,' he says.

'It's just for a few days, sweetheart,' I tell him. 'We'll be back very soon.'

'Have a blast,' Chloe says. 'Have you put all the food in the freezer?'

'Yes,' I say. 'There's plenty to keep you going. Grandad's cooking tonight. Don't forget to give him a hand. If there's anything you need, you know where we are.'

'I can't believe that you're actually going.' She pouts slightly.

'Me neither, but Dad and I really need this break, and we're not going to get the time once your new little one comes along.'

Chloe huffs and looks down at her bump. 'I don't think it's ever going to come.'

'Trust me, it'll be here before you know it.'

'We'd better get going,' Rick says. Already there's an inch or two on the road outside and, of course, it hasn't been gritted. 'This weather will make Bruges look very pretty,' Rick says, peering anxiously out of the window, 'if it's snowing over there too.'

Tom lifts our bags into the car and we kiss Mum, Dad, Chloe and Jaden. I feel quite teary going off without them. Our son is driving, and everyone waves from the front door – even Mum – as we slither off down Chadwick Close.

Apparently, the Christmas fair is on during the whole of

December, so I'm really looking forward to that. I'm thinking lovely food, nice drinks to sample. There's a Snow and Ice Sculpture festival on at the same time too. I'm going to find a few moments on the train to swot up on the guidebook, as I haven't had a chance to do that yet. Thanks to Samuel's excellent recommendations, our hotel is centrally located right by the Belfry Tower, close to all the attractions. There's an ice rink right in the main square, and I'm wondering if I could persuade my husband to don ice skates for the first time in umpteen years. We used to take the children when they were small, and Rick cut quite a fine figure on the ice way back when – he liked to show off by skating backwards. Maybe it's like riding a bike, something you don't forget. It would be fun to do something like that again, glide around on skates, feel the chill breeze lifting my hair. Maybe have a cup of warming glühwein afterwards.

'What are you grinning at?' Rick asks.

'Nothing. Just happy.'

'Watch the road,' he says to Tom. 'I don't want a crash on the way to the station.'

'It's cool,' Tom replies, as the wheels spin beneath us. 'Chill out, Dad.'

Rick tuts.

We slither and slide our way along the dual carriageways towards the city.

It takes us three times longer to get there than it normally does, and there's an enormous queue of taxis outside the station that's blocking the entrance road but, thankfully, we've allowed plenty of time.

When we finally crawl forward and reach the front of the station, Tom helps us to unload our wheelie cases from the boot.

'Have a great time, Mum,' he says, and kisses me.

'Look after your gran and grandad. Look after the house. Don't argue with your sister. Don't bring strange women home.' Or men. And certainly don't entertain them in our bed, I want to add.

'You worry too much.'

I actually think that I don't worry enough.

'Watch how you drive,' Rick adds. 'I don't want a dent on that car when I get back.'

'Relax.' Tom holds his hands up. 'Everything will be cool. The house will still be standing when you get home. The car will still be here. It will be dent-free.'

Rick harrumphs. Perhaps we *do* worry too much. It's no wonder we never manage to get away by ourselves.

Tom claps his father on the back. 'Make sure Mum has a great time, she deserves it.'

I take a deep breath. He's right: I do deserve some time, some *romantic* time, with just me and my lovely husband.

Rick takes my hand and grins at me as we head towards the station. 'Come on, then,' he says. 'Let's go and show Bruges what we're made of.'

# Chapter 23

We get down to St Pancras and the Eurostar terminal without incident, but when we arrive we learn that the snow on the Continent is far worse than it is here. France has had four inches in the last hour and the Eurostar, though still running, has developed lengthy delays.

'I knew it,' Rick mutters. 'I knew it was too bloody good to be true.'

'We'll be fine,' I say. There are fantastic shops here, lovely restaurants and posh-looking bars. 'This terminal is so fabulous you could spend your entire holiday here.'

'Don't be in too much of a rush to say that out loud.' Rick studies the departure board. It's saying that our eight o'clock train will now depart at ten o'clock. 'We might well be doing it yet.'

'We could go and have something to eat, or a drink at the Champagne Bar.' How decadent would that be!

'We'll be able to do both at this rate.'

Tearing ourselves away from the departure board, we head

upstairs to the Champagne Bar by the platforms. Although everywhere is crowded, we manage to get seats and, at great expense, Rick orders two glasses for us. He even does so without flinching.

'Shall I ring home?' I pull out my phone. 'See how they all are?'

'We've been gone for less than two hours, Juliet. They're all fine.'

'Just a quick call.'

'They can manage without us,' he insists.

Reluctantly, I put my phone away again.

'Besides, you don't want to worry them. They'll all think we're happily on our way to Bruges, not stuck here at St Pancras for the foreseeable future.'

That's true enough.

The champagne arrives, and Rick clinks his glass against mine. 'To us,' he says. 'To a romantic weekend away together.'

'To us,' I echo, and my husband kisses me tenderly on the lips. 'Are you sure I shouldn't just call?'

'Do I have to confiscate your phone, Juliet?'

'No,' I say. 'I just worry about them all.'

'Let's focus on us for once,' Rick suggests. 'Just the two of us.'

I am trying to do that, but it's not easy simply to step out of your normal role in the family, is it? I'm the matriarch, the one who holds it all together. It's hard to remember that, first and foremost, I am a wife and lover before I'm a mother, a daughter, a grandmother and an all-round dogsbody.

'When did we last do this?' Rick says.

'We never have.' That's why I'm determined to enjoy it.

In an attempt to recapture my inner sex goddess, I went out and bought myself some deliciously sexy underwear and a sheer nightie that doesn't involve fleece, anywhere. It's probably more suitable for someone half my age but, at the risk of being ridiculed, I thought I'd give it a go. I also went to that rather tacky sex shop that's everywhere on the high street now and, hoping that no one recognised me, bought a red, very festive feather boa and even a set of matching furry handcuffs. Very cheeky, for me. I'm not usually one to go for that sort of thing. I might like to think that inside I'm a smouldering sex siren, but I'm probably the most staid person I know. I'm sure Rick will like it. He'll certainly be surprised. Rick and I have been married for twenty-seven years now, and it's hard to keep the sex sparkling after all that time. To be honest, it's hard to fit it into the schedule at all. Who would have thought that at our age, our bedroom would be bordered on one side by my mother and on the other by our daughter and grandson? It's nigh on impossible to be spontaneous and sexy when there's a risk everyone else might be able to hear – particularly your mother. That aside, how do you continue to find a thrill in skin that's as familiar to you as your own? Rick works so hard that the last thing on his mind, I'm sure, is swinging from the chandeliers – not that we have any. I'm hoping we might rectify that, at least a little bit, this weekend.

Although our sex life might not be the stuff of the glossy magazines, I think we're lucky still to be in love after all this time. So few of our friends who married at the same time as we did have made it this far. Yet somehow Rick and I have weathered our storms. We even survived the threat of an affair with my old flame, Stephen Aubrey, a couple of years ago. With hindsight, I think it was something of a midlife crisis for me, but at the time it felt very real and I was almost ready to turn my back on Rick, my family, all that was familiar. I can't believe it now. It was a close-run thing, and it shook us both to the core. But we came out of it stronger as a couple, more determined to make it.

'A penny for them?' Rick says.

'I'm just thinking that I'm very lucky to have you,' I tell him. 'Let's make this weekend extra special.'

'A toast to that,' Rick says, and we entwine our arms and sip champagne again.

Three hours later, and we've had more champagne, enjoyed a very nice meal at a cramped and busy restaurant where we could hardly hear ourselves speak, and still our train isn't ready to leave.

But I'm fine about it. That's got to be a bad sign, hasn't it? I shouldn't really consider sitting in a heaving railway terminal as a chance to grab a bit of peace – if not necessarily quiet – with my husband. At home, I just don't have time to stop and think about anything. It's all rushing around, fighting fires. When was I last able to kick back and drift? Or, apart from writing Christmas shopping lists, when did I have time to sit and plan for the future? It's all about the here and now, and I'm not sure the frantic pace that we live at is good for any of us. I get up early, go at full tilt all day until I fall into bed with every bone in my body aching, exhausted. When did that become the norm? Perhaps Tom is the one who's got it right, after all.

I take Rick's hand in mine.

'What?' he says.

'Nothing. It's just nice to be together.'

It's now past eleven o'clock at night, and all the bars and restaurants are closing up and my eyes are growing heavy. There's not a seat to be had, so we're sitting on our wheelie cases, staring at the board, willing it to change. It's disappointing that there's been a delay, as we have so little time away to eat into – but that's life, isn't it? We should have been in Bruges by now, maybe even checked into our hotel, perhaps enjoying a little late-night stroll, taking a nightcap in one of the bars. On the plus side, I have had time to read about all the wonderful things that we could be doing in our as-yet-unused guidebook.

'Our train's up on the board,' Rick announces, standing up in surprise. 'Good God. We could still be in Bruges before dawn. Get your case, Juliet. Get your case.'

I jump up too and, hurrying along together, we join the surge of people now heading towards the check-in desks. 'I can't believe we're finally going!'

Just wait until I hit that Christmas market tomorrow. I'm hoping that I can find something unusual to bring back for Jaden – maybe a nice handmade toy. They're sure to have some great chocolate, too. My mouth's watering just thinking about it. I'd also like to get a couple of new decorations for the tree, just to remind myself of our trip.

We're in the queue, shuffling forward now, dragging our wheelie cases behind us. The sense of relief is palpable.

'I just hope we don't have any trouble on our way back,' Rick says. 'I can't afford to be late for work on Monday.'

'We'll be fine,' I assure him. 'It's usually only the first few days of snowfall that's a problem. After that, everything soon gets back to normal.'

Two couples are in front of us now, then it's us. We check in and go straight through to the departure area. The train is already boarding. Clearly, now that it's moving, they're not hanging about. We hurry along the platform and climb on board. My excitement is rising now. We're going. We're on our way!

We're jostled through the carriage until Rick finds our pre-booked seats. The train is spacious and rather sophisticated, in a sparse way. 'This is nice,' he says, clearly impressed. 'Here, give me your case. There's no room overhead. I'll put it at the end of the carriage near the door.'

As I'm handing him my case, my phone rings. 'It's Chloe's number,' I say to Rick.

He rolls his eyes. 'She's probably ringing to find out how to make a cup of tea for herself.'

'Rick,' I chide, as I click to answer.

'Hello, love. Everything all right?' It's hard to hear her as the signal is cutting in and out, but she sounds like she's crying. My insides turn to water. What if something's happened to Jaden? 'You'll have to speak up, Chloe. I can hardly hear you.'

'It's coming,' she shouts. 'The baby. It's coming. My labour's started. Mum, what am I going to do?'

# Chapter 24

We bundle ourselves off the train and are still striding down the platform – the wrong way – as it pulls out. Everyone else is heading to Bruges. Everyone but us.

Rick does not look amused.

'I'm her birthing partner.'

'Humph,' he says.

As they're technically apart now, Chloe doesn't want Mitch to be present at the birth. On the one hand, I can understand it. But, on the other, it seems so terribly sad. 'What else can I do?' I ask him.

'Nothing,' he mutters, but it doesn't look like he sees the imminent birth of our second grandchild as being on the same level of emergency that I do.

Secretly, I think he feels that we should leave Chloe to get on with it and see the new arrival when we get back from our trip. But I've promised her that I'll be there with her. I wasn't to know that the baby would decide to pop out just as we were about to go on our first romantic break together since time began, was I?

'This new baby clearly isn't going to take after Chloe,' Rick grumbles on. 'If it was its mother's child, it'd be a month late rather than early. Why couldn't she have waited until Monday?'

'Don't go on, Rick.' I might as well join in the complaining. 'What's done is done.'

Anyway, it's too late now for what ifs. We're off the train and heading home.

How could I possibly go to Bruges for a romantic getaway, drink hot chocolate, ice-skate, prance round a hotel room in nothing but lacy lingerie when our only daughter is giving birth? I just couldn't do that. I couldn't. How could I let her struggle to bring a new life into the world all by herself? Rick will see that it's the right thing to do when we get back and hold that little baby in our arms.

'We'll have to hurry if we want to catch the midnight train back home,' I say.

Rick puffs but, nevertheless, we both pick up speed as we dash out of St Pancras and race down the slush of Euston Road.

'It might be quicker to take a taxi home,' I pant.

'No taxi,' Rick huffs. 'That'd cost nearly the same as our weekend away.'

'It can't be helped,' I counter. 'It's an emergency.'

'I wonder, will the holiday insurance cover it?' He continues to complain as we run.

We hit the midnight train with seconds to spare and throw ourselves into two of the few spare seats among the late-night drunks and revellers. Not quite the calm oasis of the Eurostar.

We chug slowly back to Milton Keynes, stopping at all stations known to man and a few places that I've never even heard of. At a snail's pace, we crawl through the deserted night-time stations of Apsley, Berkhamsted, Tring and Cheddington. No one gets off. No one gets on. This is pure torture.

It's past one in the morning now, and I've been trying to ring Chloe all the way home from London but there's no reply from her phone. I'm assuming she's in the delivery room already. I try Tom too, but no luck there either. Her brother is the one who will have taken her into the maternity unit, and that thought doesn't fill me with the greatest comfort.

Eventually, when I'm just about ready to weep, we pull into the bright lights of Milton Keynes station and everyone disgorges. A short and expensive taxi ride from the station and, not a moment too soon, we swing through the hospital doors, a couple of hundred pounds lighter and a couple of years older. Still, it's been worth it. At least I am able to be here. Supposing we had already been in Bruges? Then what would I have done? I would have spent our romantic weekend chewing my fingernails to the quick and wishing I was at home. As it is, we're cutting it fine. I hate to think of Chloe going through this on her own, and can only hope that she's managed to hang on until I get here.

Ragged and exhausted, we bowl into the maternity unit to find Mitch pacing up and down in the corridor.

'Is she OK?' I ask, grabbing him in a bear hug. He might be estranged from our daughter but, to my mind, he's still the father of her children and a very nice young man to boot.

'I don't know,' Mitch says, hugging me in return. 'She won't let me go in to see her. I've been waiting out here for hours.'

'Where's Tom?'

'He left as soon as I got here.'

Typical. 'And Jaden?'

'Frank's looking after him.' At least my grandson is in safe hands.

'Have you had anything to drink, to eat?'

'I'm not hungry,' he says.

'Rick could get you some tea from the machine,' I offer.

He shakes his head. 'I just want to know if she's all right.'

'Let me see if I can find someone to tell us what's going on.'

Nurses seem in short supply at this time of the morning but, eventually, I find someone tucked away in a side room, eating a Mars bar and filling out paperwork.

'She's right in here,' the nurse says, and leads me through to a small room where my daughter is just being helped off a trolley bed by another nurse.

My child's face is pale, washed out.

'Chloe!'

'Mum!' She throws herself into my arms. 'False alarm,' she sobs. 'I can go home. I thought the baby was coming, but it's not.'

'Oh.' I think of the Eurostar speeding to Bruges without us, of the fancy nightie tucked in the depths of my case, of the baby still comfortable in Chloe's tummy, of how miserable Rick is going to be when we tell him the news.

I put my arm round my daughter and steer her towards the door. 'Let's go home and put the kettle on, then.'

# Chapter 25

Another taxi. This time back to Chadwick Close. At least Rick's display of Christmas lights blink welcomingly to us in the cold, dark night.

'The house looks pretty,' I offer. The snow has started again and fat flakes drift lazily from the sky to decorate the street. I sigh happily to myself. I do like living here.

Rick grunts. He looks as if he is ready to commit murder. Chloe has alternately cried and grumbled all the way home.

'I wish this baby would just hurry up,' she mutters. 'Then I can get on with my life.'

It must be her hormones. She seems to think that the baby should arrive at a convenient time between the hours of nine and five. But perhaps the harsh reality of her situation was just starting to set in when she thought that the delivery of baby number two was actually happening. There'll be no 'getting on with her life' for some time to come.

'I should have been going out with my mates tonight,' she continues glumly. 'I bet they're having a brilliant time.'

I don't want to risk the waterworks again by pointing out to her that we should be on our way to our romantic weekend in Bruges, and would have been arriving there at this very moment instead of being back at home.

'Stop complaining,' Rick snaps. 'Your mother and I should be on a romantic two-day break in Bruges now.'

Chloe promptly starts crying again.

'Rick,' I admonish. 'Now look what you've done.'

'It's not all about her,' he complains. 'We've probably lost a small fortune on that trip.'

'She wasn't to know it was a false alarm,' I remind him.

More wailing from the back seat as the cab pulls up outside the house. Rick grumbles as he pays the fare.

'Put the lights on full beam would you, mate?' Rick asks the taxi driver. The man obliges.

Sure enough, his headlights pick out my mother in her night-dress and slippers, walking purposefully away from our house and down Chadwick Close.

'Oh , Lord,' Rick says. Simultaneously, Rick and I jump out of the car and race down the road after her.

'Mum,' I shout. 'Mum!'

She turns round to face us.

It takes only seconds for us to catch up with her. 'What are you doing out here?'

My mum looks down at herself and seems not to know why she's out here.

'You should be tucked up in bed. It's freezing.' I rub her arms. 'You've only got your nightie on. Where's your coat?'

Rick strips off his own coat and wraps it round Mum's shoulders. I turn her back towards home.

'Where are you taking me?' she asks. 'It's cold out here.'

'I'm taking you home, Mum. I don't know what you're doing out here in the first place.'

'I'm looking for Frank,' she says. 'I'm sure he lives round here somewhere.'

'Dad's at home in bed.'

'Oh,' she says.

While I'm ushering Mum back inside, Rick helps a still snivelling Chloe to the front door across the slippy pavement.

Inside, and Rick heads straight to the kitchen to flick on the kettle. His tea levels are probably dangerously low by now. Murderously low.

I take Mum straight upstairs to her bedroom. 'Come on, Mum. Climb into bed.'

'I'm cold,' she says, and meekly lets me help her under the covers.

'This'll make you nice and warm again. I'll bring you up a hot-water bottle in a minute.' I sit down on the bed beside her. 'You shouldn't go outside, Mum. Not on your own.'

She starts to cry. 'I don't remember doing it.'

I rock her in my arms like a baby. 'Don't worry,' I murmur. 'Don't worry. Everything will be all right.'

'Sometimes I'm frightened,' she says.

'No need to be. We'll look after you.' I smooth her hair. 'How about we go and see the doctor on Monday?'

'No.' She sounds pitiful. 'I don't want to see the doctor.'

'It might be for the best,' I suggest.

But she's adamant. 'No.'

I don't want to upset her further by pushing it so, instead, I say, 'Want a nice cup of tea?'

Mum shakes her head. 'I'm tired.'

All my life my mother has been strong and irascible. I hate to see her like this now. When I take her hand in mine, the skin is dry, wafer-thin, mottled with age. It feels like the hand of someone I don't know.

'Settle down then. I'll come and slip that hot-water bottle in for you in a minute. You go to sleep now.'

'You're a very nice lady,' Mum says. 'Your mother must be very proud of you.'

My throat constricts. 'I think she probably is.'

Mum turns over, her back to me, and pulls the covers over herself so that just a shock of dyed red hair is sticking out.

With a heavy heart, I make my way downstairs. I'm just about to go back into the kitchen when I hear a strange noise coming from the living room. Hesitantly, I open the door and, dreading what I'm about to find, see that Dad isn't in bed as I'd thought. Instead, my poor father is flat out asleep on the floor with Jaden curled up at his side, surrounded by a mountain of toys. The noise is a combination of Dad's snores and with the chugging of Jaden's train set, which is still happily pootling round the track all by itself.

I realise in a startling moment of clarity that my parents are getting too old to be left alone. They, like my grandson, are going to need constant attention.

'Dad.' I kneel down beside him and shake his arm. 'Wake up. It's late.'

He snorts himself awake, then rouses, blinking his eyes sleepily. 'What time is it?'

'It's gone three in the morning, Dad.'

'I must have dropped off.'

I'm well aware that looking after Jaden for just a few hours is exhausting, and have to acknowledge that it's probably too much for Dad to do on his own now.

'My old bones are stiff,' Dad says as he eases himself up. I give him a hand.

'Off you go to bed. Do you want any tea or cocoa?'

'No thanks, love,' he says. 'I'll only have to get up in the night if I do.'

'There's not much of the night left.'

'I suppose so. How's Chloe? Has she had the baby yet?'

'False alarm,' I tell him. 'She's back home with us.'

'Oh,' he says. 'She must be very disappointed.'

'She is.' I pick Jaden up in my arms. He's almost getting too heavy to lift now. His eyes roll back in his head as if he's drunk. Looking after this little bundle of trouble will soon take my daughter's mind off her woes.

Dad shuffles back towards the dining room where he's camped out on the futon, and I carry Jaden through to the kitchen.

Chloe is sitting drinking tea at the kitchen table, while Rick is filling a hot-water bottle for Mum.

'One tired little boy,' I say.

'Can you take him up, Mum?' Chloe says. 'I'm exhausted. I'm just going to finish my tea. Though I am hungry. I'd love some toast.' She looks round to see if there are any takers.

'You're pregnant, Chloe,' Rick grumbles. 'Not paralysed.'

Nevertheless, Rick slams two slices of bread into the toaster.

Tucking Mum's hot-water bottle under one arm, I carry Jaden upstairs. Someone has already changed him into his favourite Bob the Builder pyjamas – Dad, I assume – so all I have to do is put him down in his little bed. We've moved him in with Chloe, so that Tom can have a proper bed. Now that Dad's going to be here full-time, we might need to have yet another rethink of the sleeping arrangements. My poor old father can't sleep on a futon for ever. Chloe's room is cramped now, with two beds squashed in here, and it can't be easy to be so short on space. It's far from ideal, and it saddens me to think that Chloe does have her own nice little place to go to if only she could patch things up with Mitch.

Jaden stirs as I cover him over. He slips his thumb into his mouth and sucks it. Soon, before any of us know it, he'll be all grown up with trials and tribulations of his own. For now, I just want him to have the best childhood that we can possibly give him and, if that means having him and Chloe living here with us, then so be it.

I kiss Jaden goodnight and turn off the light. Through in Mum's room, she's already fast asleep. I tuck the covers round her again and slide the hot-water bottle in by her feet, where she likes it best. In the darkness she looks so small and frail, like another child. She seems to have gone downhill very quickly and, if it continues, I wonder how much longer we'll be able to look after Mum at home. The last thing on earth she'd want would be to go into a nursing home, but what will

I do if she starts to need full-time care, or if she wanders off on a regular basis?

There comes a time in your life when you realise that you have become the mother of your own mother, and I think that I have just reached it.

# Chapter 26

Back in the kitchen and Chloe, shoes kicked off and feet up on a chair, is polishing off her toast.

'Feel better now?' I ask.

'Yeah,' she says. 'I might have a lie-in tomorrow. This is all very draining.'

'Tell me about it,' Rick complains.

'You'll look after Jaden in the morning, won't you?'

'Of course,' I say. 'You've got to rest.'

'Night, Mum.' She hauls herself from the chair and kisses my cheek. 'Night, Dad. Top toast.'

'Don't wake Jaden up,' I say as she heads out of the kitchen.

'You're too soft with her,' Rick says when Chloe has climbed the stairs and is out of earshot. 'She takes advantage of you.'

'She's got one heck of a shock coming to her,' I remind him. 'I don't mind doing all that I can for her now.' I can still remember exactly what it was like when we added Chloe to her brother. Having one child was a life-changing experience;

having two took it to a whole new level. Flopping down into a chair, I let out a heartfelt sigh.

'Exactly how I feel,' Rick says.

'It's been a long day.' And a long night.

'Tea and toast?'

'That would be wonderful.'

My husband puts the kettle on again and slots two more slices of bread into the toaster.

'We're what they call the sandwich generation,' Rick says. 'We're stuck between still looking after our own kids and caring for our parents. It sounds nicer than it is, don't you think?'

'Hmm.' The toaster jettisons the bread and, when he's liberally buttered it, Rick brings it over to me. My tea follows.

'We have to help them,' I remind him. 'That's what families do.'

'When does it end? When do they start helping us? At this rate, I'll still be working until I'm ninety to pay for this lot.'

Is there a point when your offspring turn into adults, or do they for ever stay children in your mind? Is there a time when it's kinder to cut off your support and let them fend for themselves, whatever the consequences? Or is it your job as a parent always to be there to pick up the pieces?

'Perhaps we do too much for them, Rick, but my mum was never there for me.' She never once offered me guidance, or even showed me affection. With Mum, it was all about criticism and being made to feel that whatever you did wasn't good enough. When the kids were young, she never once offered to babysit or cook a meal. When we could have done

143

with an extra pair of hands, she was never there. If anyone, it was always Dad who stepped into the breach, and then she used to complain about that. It was as if she liked to see us struggle. I can't do that to Chloe or Tom. I want them always to know that, no matter what, I'll drop everything to help them. 'I vowed that I'd never be like that with my kids.'

'I know that. Rita's lucky that you're so good with her now.'

'She's my mother.' And, really, that says it all. Blood, when it comes down to it, *is* thicker than water. The ties that bind you aren't easily broken. If it means that I have to look after her, then I'll do it to the best of my ability. Whether I get thanks for it or not.

However, I do admit that I thought Rick and I would have the house to ourselves at this time in our lives, and not be thinking that we'd have to extend just to accommodate everyone.

Rick comes to join me, and I steal a piece of his toast. He lets it go without protest.

'I'm sorry about the weekend being ruined,' I say.

'We'll book up another one. I promise.'

But when, I think? It's taken long enough to organise this one. What chance will we have when we've another grandchild to care for?

Rick's phone bleeps to tell him he's got a text. 'Who on earth is that? Do they know what time it is?'

We both glance at the clock. It's a quarter past four. And it feels like it. My eyes are heavy and gritty. I can't wait to get into my bed.

'It's probably $O_2$ telling you that your bill's due or something.'

The only people who text me at four in the morning are people I owe money to.

Rick picks up his phone. He takes a look at the screen and then hurriedly sticks his phone in his pocket.

'Who is it?'

'Work,' he says.

'At this hour?'

'It can wait.'

I shrug. 'It's time we climbed the stairs to Bedfordshire.' The only member of the family who is happy about all this untoward nocturnal activity is Buster. I pick up a leftover crust from Chloe's toast and feed it to him. He gulps it down happily. 'Want to go outside for a minute, Buster?'

He wags his tail in agreement. So I open the back door and let him run out into the garden. The dog heads straight for his favourite bush and waters it. I lean on the door frame and stare out into the garden. Buster snuffles through the snow to his next favourite spot. Then my head snaps up. Did I just see someone hurrying across the bottom of the garden in the darkness?

'Rick,' I whisper. 'I just thought I saw someone in the garden.'

My husband comes to join me at the door. 'Where?'

'Down there. At the bottom. By the tree.'

'I can't see anything.'

'Near your shed.'

'My shed?' Now he sounds worried. 'It might have been a fox.'

'It was about six foot tall. Bloody big fox.'

'I'll get my shoes on,' Rick says, and disappears into the hall.

Moments later, he returns all kitted up in his shoes and coat. 'Where's the torch?'

'Here.' I lift it from the drawer and switch it on, but it's as dead as a doornail. 'No battery.'

'Typical.'

'Be careful,' I say. 'Shall I come with you?'

'No. Stay here. I'll take this in case I need to hit someone on the head with it.'

Rick goes out into the garden with his dead torch, muttering away to himself. Any burglar will have been long gone by now.

I can just make him out as he plods along the path, Buster scampering in his wake. The light of the shed snaps on and, seconds later, off again. Rick comes marching back.

'I can see some footprints,' he pants. His breath is visible in the cold air. 'It's possible that someone was sniffing around out there, but the shed is still locked up and there's nothing gone from inside. Maybe you disturbed them.'

'We should get some security lights put up. Number six was burgled last year.'

'I'll get a couple from B&Q. I said I'd take Frank anyway, so that he can choose a Christmas light for Samuel.'

'That'd be nice.' I touch Rick's arm. 'Do you think our work for the day is finally done?'

'I bloody hope so.' He locks the back door, checking it twice. 'I'm not sure George Clooney has to put up with all this crap in his life.'

'I expect not.'

'Lucky bastard,' Rick says.

Hand in hand, we climb the stairs. 'I put something very saucy in my weekend case,' I tell him in a whisper.

'Oh really?'

'It will have to wait now. I can hardly keep my eyes open. Perhaps we can sneak a night alone over Christmas.'

'Hmm. I must admit, I can't wait till my head hits the pillow.' He squeezes my fingers. 'I will hold you to that, though.'

Bone-weary, I open the bedroom door and switch on the light.

There's a cry and a voice says, 'What the fuck?'

Rick and I freeze in the doorway.

In our bed, our son sits up and shades his eyes.

'Oh, hi,' Tom says. 'You nearly gave me a heart attack. Thought you two would be out for the night.'

'No,' Rick says tightly, as if he's the one about to suffer a cardiac arrest. 'We're back. And, if possible, your mother and I would like our bed vacated.'

'There was nowhere else to go,' Tom complains. 'Grandad's on the futon.'

'What's wrong with your bed?'

Next to him, a girl sits up and hugs the duvet to her. 'Hello.'

Now it's Rick's turn to say, 'What the fuck?'

Tom tries to flatten down his hair. 'This is ... er ... er ...'

'Kelly,' the girl supplies. She tries to straighten her hair too. 'Nice to meet you.'

'We thought we'd be more ... comfortable ... in here,' our son reasons. 'Didn't we ... er ... er ...'

'Kelly,' the girl supplies again.

'I want you out,' Rick splutters. 'You and *Kelly*. In five minutes.'

'Where are we supposed to go?' Tom complains.

'To a hotel.'

'Aw, man! Now? There's only a couple of hours of the night left.'

I don't point out to Tom that he rarely rises before midday.

'The single bed in the spare room is free, and one of you can kip down on the sofa,' Tom suggests. 'It won't kill you.'

Unlike our son, I recognise that look on Rick's face and take a firm grip of his arm before he launches himself into our bedroom and *kills* Tom.

'You take the bed. I'll take the sofa, Rick,' I say. 'It'll be fine for one night.' What little there is of it left. Plus, I don't think I'll ever want to sleep in my own bed again, now that I know what Tom's been doing in it.

# Chapter 27

As always, Monday morning comes round too quickly. I don't know why the weekends always seem to go so fast and, as Christmas approaches, they whizz by even quicker. I've been so busy at home that I wonder how I would have coped if we *had* made it to Bruges.

Plus all this hot-bedding is exhausting. With all that's been going on, I don't feel as if I've had a decent night's sleep for a week. Dad is going home today – he assures me that he's feeling happy enough to do that. If he's vacating the futon, then Tom could go back into the dining room – alone – and Jaden could have the spare room again. From tonight, assuming that we have no more unexpected visitors, Rick and I can stake permanent claim to our double divan once more. Bliss!

I hand Dad his toast. 'All right, Dad?'

'Yes, love. Champion.' My dad is one of those old-school gentlemen who never complains about anything. To me, he looks smaller and less robust since Samuel has gone, but he seems to be coping well, considering. I kiss his forehead and, in return, Dad smiles up at me. For some reason, it makes me want to cry.

Quickly, I turn away and say, 'What would you like for breakfast today, Merak?'

'May I please have some toast, Juliet?'

'Of course.' I slip some more bread into the toaster.

Merak has taken to coming in a bit earlier each morning, in time to have something to eat before he and Rick set out to work. I'm so pleased, as I was a bit worried that he wasn't eating properly. He's as thin as a rake, even though he's over six foot tall. You know what lads are like when they live on their own. If Tom was in Merak's situation, I'd like to think someone's mum would look after him. But, of course, Tom isn't in Merak's situation. Our dear son is still fast asleep in bed. Thankfully not *our* bed. I hand over Merak's toast. 'Jam's out on the table. Help yourself.'

'Thank you.'

I move my beautiful, red poinsettia from the table, so that it's not waving in Merak's face. Chloe brought it home for me yesterday in a rare moment of thoughtfulness, along with an apology for making us miss our longed-for trip to Bruges. It's just lovely, and not simply because it shows that Chloe can think of someone other than herself when she has a mind to.

I take Mum her breakfast in bed as a treat. All she likes is a small glass of orange juice, a slice of brown bread and a banana. 'How are you feeling this morning?'

'Fine,' she says.

'Sleep well?'

'On and off.'

My mother sleeps like the dead; she just doesn't like to admit it. I help her to sit up and plump the pillows behind her. Then I slip on her bed jacket so she's nice and cosy. She's looking perkier this morning. Thank goodness. 'I'm off to work now,' I tell her. 'You know where I am if you need me.'

'I think I might pop into the library today,' she says. 'I haven't got any books.'

There are half a dozen on her bedside cabinet.

'I don't work at the library any more, Mum. I'm in the estate agents' office now. Westcroft's. In the High Street.'

'Oh.'

'You've lots of books here. Have you read them all?'

'I don't know,' she says. Mum frowns at them as if she's never seen them before.

'We'll go through them together when I get home. It might jog your memory.'

'All right, dear.'

So I leave her sitting like the Queen in her bed jacket with a tray on her lap.

Back in the kitchen and Rick comes in from the garden. Wiping his feet on the mat, he rubs his hands together. 'Brrr. It's parky outside there today. Glad we're working inside, Merak.'

'Yes,' he agrees. 'It is very cold.'

'Couldn't see anything clearly,' Rick nods towards his shed. 'There might have been a track up to the shed, but Buster could be responsible for that. It's been snowing heavily for the last half-hour, so any footprints that were made overnight would have gone now, anyway.'

'That's a shame.' I'm pretty sure that I saw someone coming

out of Rick's shed again last night, but when he went to check, as before, everything was in order. Perhaps all the stress of the last few days is making me hallucinate.

'Weird thing is,' Rick says, 'the inside of my shed looks even tidier.' He shrugs at life's strange mysteries.

'Has someone broken into your shed?' Dad asks.

'I don't think so, but it looks like someone's been mooching about in the garden. Juliet thought she saw someone out there on Friday night, and again last night.'

'There's a lot of it about,' Dad says. 'You need to get a bigger padlock. Maybe that CCTV.'

'There's nothing in there worth pinching, unless someone wants a ten-year-old Flymo.' Then, 'Bloody hell, Juliet. Do we have to listen to Christmas songs morning, noon and night? It's two weeks away yet.'

'Yes, we do.' I smile at him and turn the radio up a notch. 'Frosty The Snowman' fills the kitchen. My husband sighs in resignation. One day I'm determined I'll make him a fan of Christmas. 'More toast, Merak?'

'Thank you very much, Juliet.'

I slip him another slice.

'Get that down you, lad. We've got a lot on today. I'll go and load up the van.'

'I will be very quick.' Merak bolts down his tea and starts to get up.

'You take your time.' I lay a hand on Merak's shoulder and ease him back into his seat. 'You know what Rick's like. He'll be faffing about for ten minutes yet. Do you want anything else to eat?'

'No, thank you. This is very good.'

'I've made you both sandwiches today. Cheese OK?'

Merak nods. 'You are very kind to me.'

'It's what anyone would do.'

'I do not think so,' Merak says. 'I think that many people would not do it at all.'

'Well, it sets you up for the day. I can't have you going out there hungry.' I take up my bag and throw my phone in. 'I'll see you all later. Dad, do you want a lift home?'

'No thanks, love. I'll take your mum a cup of tea in a minute, then I'll sort her out when she's finished her breakfast.'

'To be honest, I'd be happier if you'd stay all day.' Otherwise my mum will be at the mercy of Chloe and Tom. 'Have you got anything to get home for?'

'Not really, love.'

'Stay another day.'

'I could help Rita to write her Christmas cards. But I'll go home tonight. You've got enough on.'

'Don't worry about me. I'm fine.' I just can't face Dad going home to an empty house by himself. 'The bed's small, but you could have the spare room. Or we could bump Tom off the futon again.'

'I don't want to put you to any trouble.'

I slip my arm round him. 'It's no trouble having my lovely dad here. Just stay. We'll sort out who goes where later.'

'If you're sure,' he says.

Of course I'm sure. He'll rattle around in that house without Samuel, and it physically hurts me to think of it. Is it selfish of me to want to keep him here for good? I wonder what Rick would think of that? Maybe I'll broach it with him later.

Still, it's time to get to work, or our tortured sleeping arrangements will be the least of my worries. 'Bye, Merak,' I say. 'See you later. You can always join us for dinner.'

'I am working in bar again tonight.'

'Another time, then.'

With that, I swing out of the door. Still in the driveway, Rick is fiddling about in the back of his van.

'I'm off now,' I tell him.

'Right.' He doesn't look up.

'I think I'm going to walk in again rather than take the car.' There's a lot of snow about, and now that I'm not having to run Dad home, it would be safer to go on foot and it would be nice to get some exercise. Buster's walks have been severely truncated due to the weather, which means that I'm going to struggle to keep my weight down over Christmas.

'Good idea.'

'Busy day ahead?'

'Yes.' He seems distracted.

'Everything OK?'

'Yeah. Yeah.'

'I love you.'

'Love you too,' Rick says.

But I can tell that he's just repeated what I said.

'I can't wait for Christmas,' I add. 'What about you?'

'Yeah,' Rick says. 'Can't wait.'

And now I know without a shadow of a doubt that he hasn't listened to a word I've said.

# Chapter 28

They'd finished the job in Great Linford. Unfortunately for Rick, the customer hadn't yet paid up, even though the customer had said that they were really pleased with the job. Often, these days, it was the folks in the poshest houses who seemed to be most strapped for cash, and with Christmas coming everyone had a million different demands on the same amount of money. Rick was no exception to that.

Merak drove the van and sang along, tunelessly, with Shakin' Stevens and 'Merry Christmas Everyone'. Juliet was clearly indoctrinating the lad, and Rick realised that he was fighting a losing battle.

He thought he'd like to give Merak a bit of a bonus this year. A small token of thanks for all his hard work, but he didn't know if it was going to be possible. Cash flow was still tight. But then he thought of Lisa and little Izzy – they were the ones who knew what it was like to have nothing.

He'd thought about the girl a lot over the weekend. Perhaps that wasn't right. She'd texted him a couple of times too and, each time, her messages seemed to highlight her loneliness. Stupidly, he'd lied to Juliet when she'd asked who the text was from. In his defence, it *was* about four in the morning, and he hadn't been able to think quickly enough to explain why a teenager would be texting him at that hour. Evading the answer had seemed a lot easier when Juliet had so much else on her plate. Would his wife really understand why he felt so drawn to this vulnerable and lonely slip of a girl? He wasn't sure he entirely understood it himself. The truth was, he felt so sorry for Lisa, stuck out there in that damp house, all alone with only a small child for company.

The job they had on this morning was only a small one. Some tiling in a utility room over in Tattenhoe. Merak could do it with his eyes closed. He didn't really need Rick around. In fact, he'd probably be in the way. And Tattenhoe wasn't that far from where Lisa lived. Fifteen, twenty minutes. No more.

Before he could think what he was saying, Rick said, 'I might just drop you off this morning. I've got a few things to do. Can you manage?'

'Of course,' Merak said.

'I'll come back before lunch.'

His apprentice shrugged his acceptance.

Half an hour later, and he'd settled Merak in to the job. Rick had shown the lad what to do and Merak, as always, had wasted no time getting stuck in.

Five minutes later, when he pulled up outside the big Morrisons supermarket at Westcroft, it was as if Rick was on autopilot. He went inside and, without really thinking about it, filled a basket with some shopping basics. What would Juliet buy for the week? She was the one who always did the shopping, usually going on a Thursday after work. It was a thankless task. Rick hated it, and out of choice hadn't been near a supermarket for years. It made him think how much Juliet did for them all without complaint.

He threw some fruit into the basket. Nothing fancy – just apples, a bag of satsumas. Everyone liked those at Christmas, didn't they? Some veg, too. But what? Carrots. Even he would suffer carrots, and veg wasn't high on his list of favourite things to eat. Rick put in some cheese, crackers, some chicken breasts, a big carton of milk and a wholemeal loaf. He had no idea what he was buying and why, but it was something he felt compelled to do.

When he'd finished filling the basket with practical things, he threw in one of those fancy tins of extra-chocolatey biscuits that they only did at this time of year. Wouldn't hurt to have a few treats.

He queued up behind women with trolleys piled high with seasonal goodies. Rick looked down at his basket, and thought that it made his offering look measly. Too late now: he needed to get away from those bloody Christmas songs, and fast. There was no way he could face doing all that again with a trolley. Rick had no idea how Juliet did it every week. Perhaps he should man up and offer to do it for her every now and again.

Back in the van, he headed out of Milton Keynes. In the city, the main roads were pretty clear now, but farther out into the country and there was snow everywhere, and just narrow tracks of tarmac were visible in the undulating roads. The snow was banked high on the verges, and swept like sand dunes over the hedges. The sun sat low and brooding in the sky, barely visible through the milky veil of cloud. Against the whiteness, the spidery trees looked like they were tipped with crystal.

Soon enough he was dropping down the big hill into Cublington Parslow and pulling up outside Lisa's shabby-looking house. Maybe he should have called her before he just turned up here. But one of the texts she'd sent him at the weekend had invited him to drop in at any time. It wasn't like him to roll up unannounced, though, and he wondered for the umpteenth time what was propelling him to act like this. Perhaps he should just text her now, even though he was sitting outside her place. He patted himself down, but he couldn't find his phone. Bugger. He must have left it back at the job with Merak. She'd just have to turn him away if it was inconvenient.

Lifting the two carrier bags of shopping from the passenger seat, he lugged them to Lisa's door and rang the bell. Sure enough, moments later the girl answered, child on hip in her customary pose.

'Rick,' her eyes lit up again. This time her free arm went round his neck and she hugged him to her and Izzy. 'I hoped you'd call by.'

'I didn't know if you'd be in.'

'We're always in. We never go anywhere.'

'I can't stop,' he said, suddenly conscious of being there.

Her face fell with disappointment. 'Not even for a quick cuppa?'

158

'Well ...' He softened. 'Maybe I've time for a quickie.' Then he flushed. 'A quick cuppa. A cuppa. That's all.'

'We love having visitors, don't we, Izzy? No one ever comes to see us.'

He followed her into the kitchen. The house was still cold and damp. 'No luck with the boiler?'

'Not yet.' She shrugged. 'I keep ringing the landlord. He said he might do it next week.'

*Might.* Rick gritted his teeth. Next week was Christmas week, and he couldn't bear the thought of the pair of them being here, alone and cold.

'I brought this.' Rick held out his offering.

'There's no need for that,' Lisa said. 'You're too good to us.'

'It's just a few bits to keep you going. I thought you might not be able to get out to the shops with the snow and that.'

'We are down to slightly weird meals,' she admitted. 'Last night we had Cornish pasties from the freezer and boiled rice.'

They both pulled a rueful face at that.

'It was a low point,' she offered. 'I was going to try to get more organised today.'

'Well, I hope this helps.'

'Thanks.' Bashfully, Lisa took the bags and peeped inside. She rooted through the groceries, her face rapt. 'It's like *Ready Steady Cook*,' she laughed, and put the carriers to one side. 'I'll have to see what I can rustle up.' Then, 'You don't need to bring me presents, you know. I just like seeing you.' She tucked her hair behind her ear, and it struck Rick how young she really was. 'I'll put that kettle on.'

'There's milk in there, too,' Rick said.

'You're a lifesaver.'

Lisa made them tea, and he sat and drank it, feeling elated and guilty and relaxed and edgy and a hundred different emotions that he couldn't identify. He kept his eye on the clock on the ancient cooker while he told her about Chloe's false alarm and the abandoned trip to Bruges. She made sympathetic noises in all the right places. Half an hour later, he said, 'I have to go now.'

'It's been nice seeing you.' Lisa stood on tiptoe to kiss his cheek. 'Say goodbye to Rick,' she told Izzy.

'Bye-bye,' the little girl said.

'Come back soon,' Lisa said as she showed him to the door.

'I'll try to,' Rick replied. 'If I'm passing.'

'Thanks again for the shopping.'

'No worries.' He held up a hand in farewell, went across to his van and climbed in.

Minutes later, he was heading back through the lanes to Milton Keynes. He should call Merak and tell him he was on his way. But then he remembered he hadn't got his phone.

# Chapter 29

The morning goes by in such a blur that I don't have time to think about my family once, or the fact that Christmas is looming large and I've still got masses to do. The office has been frantic this morning, and I can't imagine why anyone would be thinking about buying, selling or renting a home at this time of year. They should be writing Christmas cards, wrapping presents and buying turkeys.

I'm eating my sandwich at lunchtime and making yet another Christmas list when Robin comes out of his office. 'What have you got planned after work tonight, Juliet?' he asks. 'Anything arranged?'

'No.' I shake my head. 'I need to feed my family, but there's nothing new there.'

'If you and I finished work an hour early, could you do a little favour for me?'

'Of course.' If the boss asks you to knock off early, you're hardly going to say no, are you? 'What can I help you with?'

'Christmas present for Rosemary.' He perches on my desk.

'I thought jewellery. Something nice. But I'm clueless. I thought I'd try that new place that's opened in the High Street. Will you come with me?'

'I'd love to.'

'We'll leave at four,' Robin says. 'Then I can take my time.' He smiles at me. 'Till then.'

Sandwich finished, I work like a mad thing all afternoon to get through the admin that's piling up. I'm making good headway and am just sorting out a tenancy agreement for a new rental client when a mobile bleeps in my handbag, though it's not my tone. When I rummage inside, I realise that – stupidly – I must have picked Rick's phone up as well as my own. I bet he's going crazy without it. That may even be him texting me from Merak's phone to find out where it is.

But when I check the message, it isn't from Merak's phone. I sit back in my chair. It's from a woman named Lisa. *Hi*, it says. *Great to see you today. Thanks for everything. Luv Lisa.* And there are kisses – a whole row of them.

Scrolling back through the messages, I find that over the last few days this *Lisa* has messaged my husband quite a lot. Including at four in the morning, when Rick told me that it was to do with work. I knew that sounded fishy even then.

Staring at the phone, heart pounding, a taste of bile in my throat, I feel as if the stuffing has been knocked out of me. Does he think I'm totally stupid? I read the text again. What does this mean, then? Is Rick seeing someone else? If he is, then when exactly does he find the time? I have to say that there's nothing too overtly sexy in the messages, but they do have quite a cosy tone to them. It's clear that he's seen this lady

162

more than once. I check to see if I can find texts that he's sent to her, but they've all been deleted. I'm not sure I like that, either. Now what do I do? I could simply ask Rick to explain himself when I get home. That, surely, would be the best thing to do. Get everything out into the open. But it's the run-up to Christmas. Do I really want to rock the boat now? What if the answer is something that I don't want to hear? I thought I could trust my husband with my life, but then I know how easy it is to be tempted. When things aren't great at home, it seems the solution can be another pair of waiting arms. I feel sick to think of it. Would Rick really do this to me? We've had no time for each other recently. But what's new? The demands of family life are relentless, and he knows the pressure we've both been under, what with Mum, Dad back at home, Samuel's death, Chloe's break-up and the impending baby. We could both easily have cracked under the strain of holding everything together. Would he really start an affair, in the circumstances? But the truth is, I have no idea. People, even reliable husbands, do strange things when the heat is on. Does this woman offer him some peace and quiet from the madness? Does she offer him the passionate sex that's sadly missing at home? My brain creates an image that I just don't want to see. What I do know is that sitting here staring at the phone in an accusatory manner isn't going to bring about any kind of resolution. I have to do something.

But, failing to come up with a plan of any kind, I do nothing more than slip Rick's phone back into my bag with trembling fingers and stew on it for the rest of the afternoon.

Just before four, I ring Chloe. 'Hello, love. Everything OK?'

'Other than I'm still as fat as a house, fine.'

'I'm going to do a bit of Christmas shopping with Robin Westcroft tonight. Help him out with a pressie for his wife.'

'All right for some,' Chloe tuts.

'I've left a shepherd's pie in the fridge for dinner. Can you put it in and sort out some veg to go with it?'

There's a huff. 'Why didn't you phone Dad?'

'Because I have your father's mobile in my handbag,' I explain. 'Besides, your dad's got a full day. You're not working at the moment, Chloe. It won't hurt you to peel a few carrots for when he gets home.'

'I'm looking after Jaden.'

I can hear my dad singing away to my grandson in the background. Chloe's probably had her feet up watching television all afternoon. It's clear that my daughter needs a few lessons in home management. 'Just do it, please. It won't kill you.'

Another huff. 'OK.'

'I won't be that late,' I promise. 'Tell Dad where I am. Oh, and can you save me some dinner please? Just a bit.'

'Yep. Anything else?'

'No.' A sigh escapes my lips. 'That's all.'

I hang up and wonder, really, why I bother.

# Chapter 30

At four o'clock on the dot, Robin appears in front of my desk. 'Ready?'

'Two minutes.' I shuffle the pile of papers on my desk into a semblance of order and then shrug on my coat.

'See you tomorrow, everyone,' Robin says to the rest of the staff, and he and I leave the office to its own devices.

Outside on the pavement, I have a fit of the giggles.

'What's wrong?' Robin says.

'This feels slightly naughty,' I tell him. 'As if we're sneaking off to play hookey.'

'Let's make the most of it, then.'

The air is sharp, tinged with frost. The snow that's on the ground is crisp and sparkles in the streetlight. It's treacherous underfoot. I slither towards the kerb.

'Whoa,' Robin says, and he hooks his arm through mine to steady me. We set off in step on Mission Buy Rosemary's Christmas Present.

'The High Street looks very pretty,' I say as we progress side by side. All the coloured lights are twinkling and it looks homely, welcoming.

'So it does,' Robin agrees.

'Did you enjoy the switch-on event for the lights?'

'Yes,' he says. 'Very much so.'

'And Rosemary?'

He sighs. 'If I'm perfectly honest, I never know what Rosemary's thinking these days.'

'Oh.'

'That's why I want to get her something special this year. I thought this new jeweller's might be the right place.'

A well-respected local jeweller from Woburn has just opened a second branch of his shop, Ornato, here in Stony Stratford, and everyone is raving about it. Everyone who has money to buy jewellery, that is.

'I haven't been in here yet.' I haven't dared. It looks prohibitively expensive for someone of my limited budget, so I'm best staying away. This is the perfect opportunity for me to have a nosey inside.

We make our way along the High Street to the far end where the jeweller's is located and Robin holds the door open as I slip inside, grateful to be out of the biting cold. The bell rings to herald our arrival.

The shop is truly beautiful. I feel more calm already. This is a lovely distraction from the distress of this afternoon – although those texts are still nagging at the back of my mind. Inside the shop it's all white, with a dark wood floor and several crystal-clear glass display cases to show off the wares. Silver snowflakes adorn the walls to give it a tasteful, festive feel and soothing music wafts into the room.

'I should think Rosemary would be happy with absolutely anything from here,' I whisper. 'It's gorgeous.'

We browse the cases, filled with bracelets and necklaces glittering with diamonds. It's all exquisite, but I'm not sure what's making me gasp more, the stunning jewellery or the matching price tags.

'Which of these pendants do you like?' Robin points at a row of necklaces draped over white stones.

'They're all fabulous.'

'But if you had to choose one, which would you pick?'

There's a delicate silver necklace with a charm shaped like a teardrop. 'I like that one.'

'Me too,' Robin says. 'It's simple. Understated.'

'Can I help you? Sir? Madam?' A sleek, glossy sales assistant appears behind the counter.

Robin wheels round. 'I'm looking for a Christmas present for my wife,' he says. 'My friend here is going to help me choose.'

'What can I show you?'

'A bracelet? What do you think, Juliet?'

'These are lovely,' I offer, pointing out a particular range. I have no idea what Robin's thinking of paying, but I know that Rick would have heart failure just looking at the tags in here.

My husband isn't the best present-buyer in the world. I had a wheelbarrow for my fortieth birthday and last Christmas I had a bread-maker, which is still in its box under the stairs. A nice thought, I suppose, but when do I have time to make bread? We have never been the romantic kind of couple – primarily because all our money has been spent on the family, over the years. There's never been anything spare for lavish presents. Not like this. And it's never really bothered me. I'm not a flashy-jewellery type of person. Though Rick did surpass himself and bought me a beautiful diamond bracelet for our twenty-fifth wedding anniversary. It's my only good piece and I treasure it, which is a good thing as it may be my husband's only ever foray into the mysterious world of jewellery-buying. The thought of the illicit texts on his phone push forward again. What *is* going on there?

After finding out that Rick has a secret from me, I have no idea what to expect this Christmas. There's nothing I need, no trinket that I desire. All that I'd dearly love is for my husband to stay true and faithful to me. I hope that's not too much to ask. I thought we were always open with each other. It seems that I was wrong.

The tray of bracelets is put out on the counter for us to peruse, and it pulls me away from my dark thoughts.

'Do you have a budget in mind?' the assistant asks.

Robin ponders for a moment. 'About two thousand pounds.'

I try not to splutter. Two grand? Phew. Lucky Rosemary!

'Which do you like, Juliet?'

'They're all just beautiful.'

'Slip on a few.'

'Oh, I couldn't.'

'Do,' he urges. 'It would be a tremendous help.'

So, with the assistant's help, I slip a bracelet onto my wrist and model it for Robin, turning it this way and that.

He shrugs, unimpressed by its magnificence. 'Maybe this one?'

I try on a couple more, but they don't meet with Robin's approval. They all look utterly wonderful to me, so perhaps he hasn't brought the most objective of people with him. We move along the row.

'This is eighteen-carat gold set with rubies,' the assistant says.

It's a Tiffany-style bangle in brushed gold. 'It's very festive,' I say to Robin. The dark rubies glow like a fine wine.

'Try it on,' he says. 'Let me see what it looks like.'

I model the bangle. It feels weighty, substantial on my wrist. Everything about it screams quality. 'This really is gorgeous.'

'It suits you.' Robin looks at the bracelet. 'Do you think Rosemary would like it?'

'I think she'd love it.' Any woman would.

'The style is classic,' the assistant chips in. 'It will never date.'

'You don't think that a man should always buy diamonds?'

I try not to laugh. I can't ever imagine Rick coming out with *that* statement.

'This is an excellent alternative,' she assures him.

'It's different,' I add, for what it's worth. 'I think I like this one the best for a Christmas present.'

'Then let's take it,' Robin says.

The assistant goes to gift-wrap the bracelet, and I gaze longingly at some of the other displays. We thought Rick had won the lottery a few years ago but, of course, it was just a hideous mistake. I wonder if I'd be shopping in here now, if we really had. Would we be happier if our bank account was overflowing? Would he be seeking comfort with another woman if we were sickeningly wealthy?

Robin pays and takes his purchase. Moments later, we're back on the High Street. 'That was easily done.'

'It was a great choice. I don't think you needed my help at all.'

Robin smiles. 'But I appreciate it, all the same.' Then, 'It's not yet five o'clock. What shall we do now?'

'We could go back to the office for half an hour. I've a few things to tidy up.'

'I don't think so. If we're going to play hookey, then we'll do it in style.' Robin puts his hand under my elbow and steers me across the road. There's a lovely wine emporium in Odell's Yard, a little alley just off the High Street, and it looks like that's where we're headed. It's very cosy, and has just a few tables inside where you can enjoy a drink. 'The night is young, and so are we!'

I laugh, pushing down my anguish. 'I'm not so sure about that.'

'Let's have a drink to celebrate,' he suggests. 'A nice glass of red would work wonders now.'

That's a sentiment I couldn't agree with more.

# Chapter 31

We manage to bag the last table in the corner of the little wine bar. Robin orders a bottle of Shiraz Cabernet and a Greek platter to share between us.

'I'm supposed to be having the remains of a shepherd's pie with my family,' I tell him as the platter arrives. 'This is a *much* better idea.'

Robin pours us a glass of wine and waves away my objections, as I help myself to olives and hummus and deliciously warm pitta bread. The red wine is full-bodied, fruity and hits the spot perfectly. Relief washes over me and, briefly, my anxiety abates. I sigh with pleasure. The restorative properties of red wine are working their magic.

'Good?' Robin asks.

I nod in agreement. 'Excellent.'

We eat and drink in companionable silence for a few minutes. I didn't know that I was hungry, but it seems that I am. Mellow jazz music washes over us. I can push my troubles to the back of my mind for now.

'This seems like a very grown-up thing to do,' I say, sipping my wine. Rick and I should come here sometime. Perhaps it would help our situation if he could see me again as his loving wife and not just a domestic drudge at everyone's beck and call. 'Thanks for persuading me.'

'I don't seem to recall you needing much persuasion.'

'No,' I laugh. 'I guess not.'

'Don't you and Rick get out much together?'

'Hardly ever. There's always someone in the family who needs us. We get very little time to ourselves. Our trip to Bruges was supposed to be the big romantic weekend we've promised ourselves for years, and you know what a disaster that turned out to be.' If we had gone, I wonder, would things be different now? If that sexy nightie had come out of the suitcase, would our love have been rekindled? Would he have blocked those texts from reaching his phone?

Now it's Robin's turn to laugh. 'It was a shame you had to come home! Terrible timing.'

'The joys of being a mother. And a grandmother!'

'You don't look old enough,' he says, flirtatiously.

'I frequently feel it.'

'Even though we've not got children, Rosemary and I never come out like this any more, either. I don't know why. We've just got out of the habit.' He helps himself to more pitta bread, toys with the hummus and avoids my eyes. 'She's out most nights of the week – book group, choral society, Pilates, Women's Institute. You name it, Rosemary does it. I can't even remember what else is on the list.' He looks at me sadly. 'We lead separate lives now, and I don't know how to get back to where we were.'

'It takes a lot of hard work,' I say. 'And you both have to want to do it. Maybe you need to sit down with Rosemary and explain to her how you feel.' Who am I to be giving advice when I can't even keep my own husband interested in me?

'We men are so rubbish at that, aren't we? Instead of facing up to our problems, I spend longer and longer at work. Which, on the bright side, is great for business –' he tries to make light of his words '– but not so good for us as a couple. I sometimes wonder if we're going to get through this at all, or whether this is how it's always going to be.'

'You have to do something if you're not happy, Robin.' Here I am, dishing it out again. 'I'm sure Rosemary doesn't like the situation, either.'

'I don't know. People stay together for years when they're not particularly happy with each other, don't they?'

I think of my parents as a prime example. I think of Rick and me. I thought we were happy together. Perhaps I'm wrong about that.

'We all deserve the love we desire,' I offer. 'But you can create that, if you really want to.'

'Think a beautiful ruby bracelet will help?'

I smile at Robin. 'I'm sure it will be an excellent start. See if you can get her to come to the office party, too.'

'I don't know if she'd view that as a great night out.'

'It's usually fun, and the business is an important part of your life.'

'I'll try.' He pours us more wine.

That's one bottle polished off, and I really should go home

soon. I'm feeling quite squiffy, and I'm sure there are things I should be doing – apart from finding out what's going on underneath the surface of my marriage. Christmas isn't going to sort itself out, and my To Do list doesn't seem to be going down much. My head is whirring. It's a good job I walked to work this morning, otherwise I'd have to leave the car here overnight.

'You and Rick seem so solid.'

'It hasn't always been like that,' I confess. 'We've had our moments. A few years ago I thought about leaving him.'

'You surprise me.'

'An old flame came back to town, and I was sorely tempted to rekindle the fire.' I don't know why I'm telling Robin this. We've grown close over the years as we're the only ones of a certain age in our office, and he's confided a lot in me about his wife. The lines between boss and employee have been blurred, and I'd consider him a friend. He probably knows more than he should about my family. Perhaps the two and a half glasses of good wine are loosening my lips, too. I feel that I need someone to talk to and Robin's here, and he's sad about his relationship too. 'Luckily for me, I didn't.'

Robin sounds shocked when he says, 'That doesn't seem like you at all, Juliet.'

'It wasn't like me. I was acting like someone I didn't know. I was at a low point, I felt vulnerable, taken for granted and, frankly, unloved. Stephen swept in and made me feel like a desirable woman again. It's a heady feeling.' I offer a weak laugh to try to hide my embarrassment. 'I thought I could turn my back on everything that was dear to me and start a new life with this man.' Is this what Rick's affair is about? Has he held this against me for the last two years? Does he think that he deserves a fling, some passion in his life? I thought he had forgiven me. More than I'd forgiven myself. 'It would have been a disaster. Fortunately, I came to my senses and realised that my family was more important to me than anything else.' How true that is. I thought Rick knew that. But perhaps he's feeling unloved and taken for granted. I place my hand over Robin's. 'Don't give up on your relationship just yet. It sounds like there's hope. Keep going.'

'I will,' he says. 'You're a wonderful woman, Juliet. Rick's very lucky.'

'I'll remind him,' I joke.

I wish I could tell him of my own anxieties. But I can't. I have to keep it all in. Rick has a secret and, in turn, I now have one too. In reality, there are some things that Robin doesn't need to know about. There are things I wish I didn't know myself. Beneath my wine-induced bonhomie, my stomach is churning and I try not to think of the string of now familiar text messages on Rick's phone from an unknown woman, or whether my husband is as happy with me as I am with him.

# Chapter 32

The dancing display of Christmas lights on the house welcomes me when I get home. Which is just as well, as no one else does.

Mum and Dad are ensconced on the sofa watching *Mary, Queen of Shops*. Dad looks up and says, 'Hello, love,' and then goes back to his telly. Mum fails to register my appearance at all. Chloe is sitting in the armchair with her iPod on while Jaden plays with his train at her feet, both absorbed in their own worlds. Looks like Tom is out, as usual. There's no sign of Rick or Buster either, so I'm assuming they're on their evening walk. It's a shame I didn't pass them on the way or I could have walked with them. The snow is still lovely and crisp on the ground and the moon is full in the sky.

In the kitchen, I peel off my coat and kick off my shoes. With very little persuasion I'd crack open another bottle of wine and keep drinking. Resisting temptation, instead I settle for flicking on the kettle.

Moments later, Rick comes through the door and throws

his keys on the counter. Buster jumps all over me. Sometimes I wish it could be the other way round.

'Where did you get to?' Rick says. 'I was out of my mind with worry.'

'Didn't Chloe tell you?'

'You *are* kidding?' He tuts as he pulls off his walking boots. 'That bloody girl.' More tutting. 'Whatever you told her probably disappeared from her head less than two seconds later.'

I should have known.

'I tried your mobile a dozen times.'

I check my phone. The ring tone must have got turned off in my handbag. There are, indeed, a dozen missed calls. 'Sorry. I didn't realise. I went with Robin to choose his wife's Christmas present,' I explain. 'Then we stopped at the Stony Wine Emporium for a drink. We should go there together sometime. It's lovely.'

'When do we ever get the time to go out?'

'That's what I said to Robin. But we should make time.'

'Pah,' he says. 'We should also predict the lottery numbers and invent a cure for cancer, but we can't seem to do that either.'

'I'd asked Chloe to make dinner, too.'

'That was a waste of breath. We'd have been eating at midnight.' Rick towels down Buster as he speaks. 'I found a shepherd's pie in the fridge and stuck that in the oven. Merak stayed for dinner too.'

'That's nice.'

'He's a good lad. He peeled the carrots.'

'Is there any food left?'

'No,' Rick says. 'Why? Did you want some?'

'It doesn't matter. I had something to eat at the wine place.'

I make the tea and put one on the table in front of Rick. Then I watch him as he fusses the dog. I can see nothing different about him. He just looks like Rick always does. He looks like the man that I have known and loved for the vast majority of my life. He doesn't look like a man with a secret.

'What?' He catches me staring at him.

'Nothing.' I turn away.

When Buster is back in his basket, Rick sits down. 'Mmm.' He swigs his tea. 'Thanks for that, love. You always make a good brew.'

'Plenty of practice.' I sit opposite him. 'Rick. Things are OK between us, aren't they?'

'Of course they are,' he says.

'You'd tell me if they weren't?'

He seems bemused. 'There's nothing wrong.'

'I took your phone today. By mistake.'

A look of relief washes over him. 'Thank Christ for that,' he says. 'All my contact numbers are on there. I wondered what the hell I'd done with it. I had to borrow Chloe's to call you.'

He doesn't look like a guilty man at all. This would be the moment to tell him that I know someone called Lisa is texting him rather regularly. I could ask who she is. I could ask my husband what she means to him, if I have cause to worry. I could tell him that I'm frightened that he doesn't love me any more. But I don't.

My voice is stoppered in my throat. My brain won't make the right words. My heart doesn't think it could stand the pain. So, instead, I push the phone across the table to him and I keep quiet.

# Chapter 33

'Rick,' Merak said. 'You have been in very quiet mood today.'

They were loading up the van after finishing off a job – living-room carpet in Castlethorpe – before heading home for the day.

'Lot on my mind, Merak,' Rick replied as he stacked his tools.

'Is it something I may help with?'

Rick smiled. 'If you can find a way of making our customers pay up, that would do it.'

Take the job they'd just finished, for example. The woman was full of praise for the way they'd worked. She *loved* the carpet. She *loved* how polite Merak was. She *loved* how they'd tidied up after themselves. Blah, blah, blah. But when it came down to coughing up with the cash or a cheque, she suddenly didn't *love* that idea so much. She didn't have the money on her. She'd have to get it out of the bank next week, she'd said. Why hadn't she bothered to get the money for them today, so that she could pay her debts there and then? It meant another trip back to Castlethorpe now – something he could well do without. It meant an extra hour on his day that he wouldn't be paid for. It also meant that the feeling of pride that resulted in a job well done was replaced by a sour taste in his mouth.

'Why do they not like to pay?'

'Money's tight, Merak. For everyone.'

'I know. For us too, though.'

'For us too.'

'There is enough work?'

'The book for January's not as busy as I'd like.' Not by half.

The weeks were racing by, and he needed to go and do some quotes that were outstanding that might bring in some work for the start of next year. Maybe he and Merak could pop some flyers through doors whenever they had a quiet day after the holiday to drum up some business, too.

'I do not wish to lose my job.'

'It shouldn't come to that, lad. You know I'll do everything I can to keep us working.'

With the time between now and Christmas being eaten away at an alarming rate, Juliet had given him a long list of DIY jobs that she wanted doing. Some of them – like putting the loo-roll holder back up after Tom had knocked it off the wall one night when he'd come home drunk – had needed doing for ages. So why did it matter now whether it was rectified in time for Christmas Day? Did anyone really object on that particular day to just picking up the loo roll off the shelf next to the loo like they had done for the last six months or more? Why couldn't Tom himself fix it? Well, that was clearly a stupid question. Perhaps if there wasn't enough flooring work in January, Merak could do some stuff around the house to fill his time. It would keep Juliet happy, and the last thing Rick wanted to do was lay Merak off, as he'd never find such a good worker again. The lad was pure gold dust.

'We need to make a call on the way home. That OK?'

'Sure.'

'Remember the job we did in Woodman Rise? Can you head there?'

They jumped into the van, and Merak swung out and drove back towards the other side of Milton Keynes. At the house where they'd laid twelve square metres of black slate tiles in the kitchen, and more than twice that in oak laminate in the dining room and hall, Merak pulled up. They'd done it for a knock-down price. Needless to say, their bill was still outstanding.

'I won't be a minute, lad.' Rick jumped out of the van and, taking a deep breath, he knocked at the door.

The man answered. The man who had been all sweetness and light while they were working for him. Now he only cracked the door ajar and, in his hand, he held the lead of what looked like a pit bull terrier. Rick hadn't remembered a dog when they laid the flooring there.

'I've come about the outstanding invoice,' Rick said.

'You'll get your money.' Both man and dog snarled. 'I've just got some cash-flow issues.'

'So will I, if you don't settle up with me.'

'I told you,' the man snapped. 'You'll get it.'

'This is the third time of asking,' Rick pointed out. 'It's overdue by three months.'

'Come back in another few weeks. I have to go, I can't hold this dog much longer.'

Rick sighed inwardly. 'I *will* be back.'

The door slammed in his face.

Merak watched him carefully as he climbed back in the van and stared out of the window.

'That did not go well,' Merak said.

'No,' Rick conceded. 'I hate doing this. People should pay what they owe without me having to beg.'

'They should,' Merak agreed.

'Let's go home. There's not much else we can do.' He felt like breaking the bloody door down and ripping up the flooring that they'd effectively stolen from him. But where would that get him?

Though the radio was on, his apprentice didn't indulge in his usual sing-along – even though they were playing a Kylie Minogue tune, which were normally his favourites. Instead, Merak frowned all the way and they both sat in silence until they hit Stony Stratford. It seemed as if Rick's dark mood was catching.

'Rick,' Merak said. 'May I borrow the van this evening?'

'Yeah.' Rick shrugged. 'For a particular reason?'

He also shrugged. 'I have some errands to do.'

'OK. No drinking and driving.'

'No. Of course not.' Merak pulled the van up outside Chadwick Close. 'I will bring it back later.'

'Take it home with you, lad. Pick me up in the morning.'

'I prefer to bring it back.'

'Suit yourself.' Rick jumped down. 'Stop in and we'll have

a beer when you do. If you're not doing anything else. Juliet's at her office party tonight. We could have our own one.'

'Thank you.'

Rick stood on the pavement and watched the van drive off. Across the road, his neighbour's Christmas lights pulsed, throbbed, flickered and twinkled. Neil Harrison had an arc of reindeers travelling across his roof. His eaves were decorated with multi-function LED icicles. The front of the house sported an angel with moving wings. Every tree was adorned with a string of coloured lights. On the garage was a waterfall curtain. In the centre of the garden a big, brightly lit, cone-shaped Christmas tree shone out. Over the drive were three enormous hoops of lights. Where were those from? Neil must get these from abroad somewhere. Rick had never seen anything like them in B&Q.

He studied his own house. They were better than his, Rick thought miserably. Much better. As if he didn't have enough to worry about.

# Chapter 34

I always look forward to the office Christmas party. This will be my third one at Westcroft's. At the library it was a much more sedate affair – a couple of drinks at the end of the day and some mince pies. All very low-key. Robin, on the other hand, pays for all of the staff from the three Westcroft branches to go to a hotel for dinner and a disco. We've been to the Holiday Inn before now, and some years before I joined they all went to Wilton Hall – which is very nice. But this year it's The Cock again. It's a lovely place, but not exactly The Ritz. Even so, it means that Robin still has to dig deep in his pocket to entertain us all. The people I work with are all much younger than me – apart from Robin – and certainly know how to party.

This year, I've even splashed out and bought myself a new dress for the occasion. It's odd when you get to my age, though; I feel I've become invisible to clothes manufacturers. What do you wear for a Christmas party? I don't do bling all that well, so I don't like anything too sparkly. I don't like my cleavage on show. I'm not that keen on my arms. I like something that hides my expanding waistline and flatters my bottom. I want to look fashionable, yet not like mutton dressed as lamb – always a fine line. The term 'glamorous' worries me these days. It is the close cousin of 'overdone'. The dress I've chosen is from one of the posher shops in Milton Keynes – still high street, but at the top end of it. Rick would die if he knew how much I'd paid, particularly with money being tight. But then I get so little opportunity to dress up now that I wanted to push the boat out. I thought about getting something radical done with the safe bob that I've sported for years, but bottled out as usual.

I look at myself in the mirror. I've not scrubbed up too badly, even though I say it myself. The dress is scarlet, a wrap-over number that clings in all the right places. On go the high heels – which I know are going to cripple me within an hour. I'm a flatties sort of woman these days, and don't do tottering well. But needs must. I slip on my diamond bracelet, too. That doesn't get much of an airing either, but it's nice to have something special to wear. I've even painted my nails – toes *and* fingers – scarlet to match. Then my confidence crumbles as I wonder how I compare with unknown female Lisa. Is she younger than me? Glamorous in the real sense of the word? Stylish? Beautiful? I only wish that I knew.

Rick's going to drop me off at the hotel, and then I'll get a taxi home in case it's a late finish. As far as I remember, the party goes on until one o'clock – though I'm not sure that I'll be one of the stalwarts who stays so long.

As I'm finishing off with a squirt of Chanel No. 5, Chloe comes into the bedroom and leans against the wall. 'Mum, I think Jaden's got a temperature. Can you come and look at him?'

I follow her through to my grandson's bedroom. In his bed, Jaden's cheeks are flushed and I feel his forehead. 'He is hot,' I say. 'Have you taken his temperature?'

'No.'

'The thermometer's in the bathroom cabinet.'

Chloe lingers for a second or two. Then, when it becomes clear that she's the one who should go and get it, she pads away. A moment later, she's back and I slip the thermometer under Jaden's tongue. 'It's a little high, but not too bad. Give him a bit of Calpol. You could get a cool flannel and just wipe him down.'

'Can't you do it?' Chloe says. 'You're better at these things.'

'That's because I've had a lot of practice,' I remind her. 'When you've had a lot of practice, you'll be good at it too.'

'Mum ...'

'I'm on my way out to the office party, Chloe. You'll be fine. If there are any problems, you've got my phone number.'

'I was thinking of popping out tonight.' My daughter does big eyes.

'Then you'll have to think again,' I tell her.

'Tom has asked me to go for a drink with him and his mates.'

'Much as it's nice to hear that you and Tom aren't bickering as you normally do, it won't hurt you to stay in for one night. It wouldn't hurt Tom, either.'

The dark looks say that she's not too keen on my assessment of her social plans. So be it.

'It's Christmas.'

'And Jaden's your son. You need to be here for him.' I hand her the thermometer. 'Besides, it's *my* big night out tonight. I'm sure you wouldn't want me to miss that.'

My dear child very much looks as if she would actually like me to miss my party for her. Well, it's not going to happen. Not this time. For once, I'm putting myself first. Chloe will just have to learn to take her responsibilities more seriously.

'Have a nice time,' she says reluctantly. 'I'm sure I'll manage.'

'I'm sure you will.' I give her a twirl. 'Do I look OK?'

'Fine.'

Feigning such extreme disinterest is surely an art form. I probably shouldn't have expected more. One last look in the mirror and *I* think I'll do. Then doubts swamp me again. Am I still an attractive woman? Or do I now look every one of my forty-five years? What does Rick think when he sees me? Is the spark for him still there, or has it died? Is that why he is exchanging texts with another woman? I don't want to think about that. Tonight, I just want to leave everyone behind and go out and have fun.

Downstairs, and Mum and Dad are watching television. No change there. Despite their differences, they seem to be rubbing along quite nicely, and Dad is certainly helping me to keep an eye on Mum.

'I'll be back later,' I say. 'Be good.' Rick has taken to marking the bottles of alcohol after we caught Mum necking the Croft Original straight from the bottle last week.

'Where are you going?' Mum asks, tearing herself away from *The One Show*.

'To my office Christmas party.'

'Aren't you going to dress up?'

'I am dressed up, Mum.' This is as dressed up as I get.

'Oh.'

'You look very nice, dear,' Dad offers.

'Thanks.'

'Very Christmassy.'

Good. Because that's what I was aiming for.

In the kitchen, Rick's reading the paper. He doesn't actually like reading the paper, it gets his blood pressure soaring sky high. I think he's just trying to grab a moment of peace. If he didn't have to run me into the town centre, he'd probably already be in his shed.

'Da-da!' I say.

'You look lovely,' Rick tells me. 'Very lovely.'

The expression on his face says that he still likes what he sees.

'Really?'

'You'll be the belle of the ball,' he assures me. 'I almost wish I was coming with you.'

'You did have your chance,' I remind him. When I booked this I asked Rick if he wanted to be included, and he chose not to. Most of the staff aren't married and don't take partners, so if you do take your other half along they are a bit of a spare part.

'I know.'

'Besides, I'm glad you're staying here to keep an eye on this lot. Jaden's running a temperature and I've put Chloe in charge.'

189

'God help us.'

'She needs to do it, Rick. It's time she realised that her son needs her and she can't just palm him off on us all the time.'

'We've been too soft with her.'

'I know. I don't want to stop helping her completely, but I am trying to wean her off being totally dependent on us.'

'Not before time.'

I check my watch. 'I'd better get going or the turkey will be on the table without me.' As I've booked it all, I feel responsible for making sure it all runs smoothly.

Rick grabs his keys and drives me into the High Street. The Cock Hotel is situated right in the centre, and it only takes a few minutes by car from our house. When Rick pulls up I can see Robin Westcroft just ahead of us walking towards the venue. He looks very handsome and smart in his dark cashmere coat and silk scarf, but his head is down and his shoulders are hunched against the cold. His wife, it seems, is not accompanying him after all. As he turns into the hotel, he cuts a lonely figure.

'Thanks for the lift.' I kiss Rick. 'See you later.'

'No coming home in the early hours drunk and unnecessary and trying to ravish my body like you did last year.'

'Really?'

'Only if you insist.'

I kiss him again. 'You'll have to see what Santa brings.'

My husband smiles at me. 'Can't wait.'

'Me neither.'

But, in the meantime, I want to forget all our troubles and have some fun. I have several glasses of wine to consume and a four-course Christmas dinner to eat. Bring it on!

# Chapter 35

It was about eight o'clock when Merak returned with the van. Rick had waited in the kitchen for him. When his apprentice walked in he was dressed all in black and was wearing a leather jacket and sunglasses, even though it was dark.

'That's a new look for you,' Rick noted. 'Very smart.' If slightly menacing.

'Thank you,' he replied proudly. Merak took off the sunglasses, carefully folded them and put them in his top pocket.

'Where have you been all poshed up like that?'

'I have been busy,' Merak said.

'Had anything to eat, lad?'

'No. I have not.'

'Could rustle you up a bacon sarnie, if that would tickle your fancy?'

Merak nodded solemnly. 'I think my fancy would be tickled.'

'Deal done then.' Rick clapped his hands together and set about cooking. 'Help yourself to a beer.'

'Thank you. May I pour one for you too?'

'That would be champion.'

'Champion,' Merak echoed.

Rick slid the bacon under the grill and Merak cracked open two bottles of Stella. He clinked his bottle against Merak's. 'It's not much of a Christmas party for the staff of Walk All Over Me, but hopefully next year we might do better. Thanks for all your help, Merak. I don't know how I'd manage without you now. I'd hoped to give you a bit of a bonus. Show my appreciation, but, well . . . ' Rick's sentence tailed off.

'Money is tight.'

Rick shrugged. 'Got it in one.'

Merak frowned. 'I have something to tell you.'

Rick turned back to the bacon and flipped it over. 'This will be ready in five.'

'Something important,' Merak insisted.

'Do I need to sit down?'

'Perhaps it would be a good thing.'

Rick wasn't sure he wanted to hear this. Maybe all this talk about money being tight had made Merak look for a new job. Could be that he was going to give him his notice, and next year Rick would be back to doing all the humping and dumping on his own. He'd hate it if that happened. He'd got used to having Merak around, and he'd struggle to find anyone half as good to replace him. Still, if the lad wanted to move on, he wouldn't be the one to stop him. Whatever he wanted to tell him, he'd take it on the chin. So he made a bacon butty for himself too, even though he wasn't all that hungry. Comfort food.

'We'll wander down to my shed with this,' Rick said. 'My sanctuary. You'll like it in there. Not many people get invited into the inner circle. We can have a good chat. Do you want your bacon on bread or toast?'

'Bread, please.'

Minutes later, they were heading down the garden, a pile of bacon sandwiches on a tray. Rick unlocked the shed. They settled themselves on the sunloungers.

'Look,' Rick said. He opened his man-fridge, his pride and joy. It was round, stainless steel with a glass top and had wheels on the bottom so that he could use it in the garden when they had a barbecue. There were more beers in the fridge. In fact, more than he remembered being in there. Perhaps Juliet had treated him to a few and had forgotten to mention it.

'Right,' Rick said as he bit appreciatively into his sarnie. 'Spill the beans.'

'I do not have beans,' Merak said.

'It means tell me the story.'

'Oh. I see.' With a sigh, the lad reached into his inside jacket pocket and pulled out a thick wedge of money. He held it out to Rick.

Carefully wiping his greasy fingers on the bit of kitchen roll he'd wisely taken with him, Rick put down his bacon sarnie before he took the cash in his open hands.

'That's a lot of money.' Rick could feel his eyes widening.

'It is eight thousand, four hundred and ninety-two pounds.' Merak reached into his pocket again. 'And fifteen pence.' He put the coins in Rick's hands too.

193

'Eight thousand, four hundred and ninety-two pounds,' Rick repeated, open-mouthed.

'And fifteen pence,' Merak stressed.

'What did you do, lad? Rob a bank?' Rick laughed nervously. He hoped that this wasn't the moment when he discovered that his apprentice wasn't quite the straightforward and polite kid he'd grown so fond of.

'I went round to customers who owed us money,' he said flatly. 'I collected this money. Tomorrow night I will visit some more.'

'Bloody hell,' Rick said. He put the money on the little coffee table in front of them both. Staring at the pile of cash, he rubbed his hands through his hair. 'Who paid up?'

Merak delved into another pocket. He produced a small notebook. Inside, neatly written, was a list of names. 'Mr Taylor, one, Woodman Rise: two thousand, three hundred and fifty-one pounds.'

'You went back there?'

'I did. He was not happy to see me.'

'I'll bet!' Rick was dumbfounded. 'But he paid up?'

'Yes. He did.'

'And the dog?'

Merak's expression didn't change. 'The dog, he tasted my shoe.'

Rick let out a giggle that, even to himself, sounded crazed.

Merak cleared his throat and continued. 'Mr Bateman-Smith, The Elms: three thousand, nine hundred and eighty-four pounds. Mr and Mrs Davis, seventy-three, The Spinney: nine hundred and eighteen pounds. Mr Ackersley, ten, Grandley Gardens: one thousand, two hundred and thirty-nine pounds and . . . '

'Fifteen pence,' they finished together.

Merak closed the notebook, but not before Rick had registered that there were still several names on his list. The rest of his customers who hadn't paid up didn't all owe such large sums of money, but it was cash he'd rather have in his own bank account, where it rightly belonged, than in theirs.

'I've been trying for months to get this money out of them. What did you do? Threaten to take a sledgehammer to their cars?'

Merak shifted uncomfortably on his sunlounger.

'Tell me you didn't!'

'I told them that I was Russian mafia, and simply reminded them that swimming with fishes is very cold at this time of year. I told them that it was advisable for them to pay their debts to avoid this experience.'

'*Are* you Russian mafia?'

'No. Of course not.' Merak shrugged. 'But you English people think that we all sound the same. Polish, Lithuanian, Albanian, Russian. It is the same to you.'

'That's probably true enough,' Rick admitted. 'But you can't go round threatening our customers, Merak.'

'I only threatened them little bit.'

'If you do that, we'll have none left.'

'Might I say that we do not want to have customers who do not pay their bills.'

Rick risked a smile. 'That's true enough.'

'I watch you. Many times, you have asked them politely

and still they do not pay. It is your money. I think they now understand that.'

Rick laughed out loud. 'Bloody hell, Merak, I can't believe you've done this.' He clinked his bottle against Merak's again. 'Eight bloody grand! That solves a lot of our problems.'

'Then you are not angry with me?'

'No,' Rick laughed. 'Not angry at all.' In fact, he felt as if a huge weight had been lifted from his shoulders. He had enough cash now to see them through the Christmas lay-off and well into January. If Merak could get all of the outstanding money in, then he'd be for ever indebted to him. 'I thought you'd got yourself another job,' he confessed. 'I thought that's what you were going to tell me.'

'No. Never,' Merak said fiercely. 'I would not do that.'

'I'm glad to hear it.' Rick laughed again. 'I want to give you a bonus. A little something to say thanks.'

'It is not necessary.'

'Here,' Rick peeled off a roll of notes. 'That's about five per cent. You can have that on whatever else you manage to collect in.'

'That is very generous, Rick. Thank you.'

He settled back onto his sunlounger and swigged his beer. There would be turkey on the table after all this Christmas. He could afford to buy Juliet a nice present, something special. And maybe, and the thought pricked at his conscience, a little something for Lisa and Izzy, too. Perhaps he'd pop in to see them again in the next couple of days, if he could find a moment.

Rick threw his head back and chuckled loudly. 'Bloody Russian mafia!'

Merak laughed too – a rare sound – and relaxed back on his lounger. 'If you let me help, Rick, I will find new customers for us.'

'We'll do it together. Grow the business. I'm going to put you in charge of credit control from now on.'

They laughed together.

'Now, let's kick back and chill for an hour. Make yourself at home.' He got Merak another beer from the fridge. 'How do you like my shed, lad?'

The kid looked around appreciatively. 'I like it very much indeed,' he said.

# Chapter 36

The room for our party is beautiful, decked out like a winter wonderland, and The Cock Hotel have made an excellent effort. There's a huge tree in the corner hung with decorations themed in pink, lime and burgundy, which makes mine at home look very old-fashioned. Perhaps I'll have a total revamp next year. The tables are set to match. And, as the party is so large, we've taken over the entire place. At least we don't have to worry about upsetting any other diners if the antics of the youngsters get a bit out of hand. Office parties are a lot more raucous now than when I was at the library.

Even the youngest of the boys are in dinner jackets, and they all look so smart. The girls are in their party best, all spangly and barely there. I'm so glad I splashed out and bought a new dress. No one wants to be the old frump on the dance floor.

We all snap our crackers, put on our hats and swap jokes. Robin sits at the head of the table, and I'm next to him.

'Excellent work, Juliet,' he says. 'This looks great.'

'Thanks.' I have to say that I'm pleased with it myself. It's always nerve-wracking booking a party for other people. Now I can relax and enjoy it too.

Robin raises his glass. 'Merry Christmas, everyone!'

The staff cheer, and then everyone throws the streamers that I've bought for the table and we're instantly covered with multicoloured strings. Spirits are high, and it's nice to see my colleagues outside of our usual surroundings and everyone letting their hair down.

The dinner is superb. Succulent turkey and all the trimmings. Which, like a full English breakfast, somehow always tastes better when you don't have to cook it yourself. Even the sprouts are cooked to perfection, which is always tricky with large-scale catering. It's just a shame that nearly everyone has left them. We had little smoked-salmon canapés and cocktails to start with when we got here, too. Even though I've squeezed a hearty portion of Christmas pudding within the confines of my dress, after the main course, I've still managed to top it with two mince pies. Now that we are all far too full to move, the tables are being pushed back against the walls to clear a space for the dance floor.

Already my colleagues have drunk deeply at the well of Westcroft's free booze account. I'm not doing too badly myself. Four glasses of wine – twice my usual quota – and a Baileys coffee and, it's fair to say, I'm feeling mellow.

While there's a hiatus in the proceedings before the disco starts, I take a moment to walk out of the hotel and onto the High Street for a breath of fresh air. This would be a good time to check in at home to see that Jaden's slight fever hasn't got any worse in my absence.

Out on the street, the temperature has dropped again and I'm glad that I thought to collect my coat on the way. Pulling it round me tightly, I fish my phone from my handbag. The weathermen have forecast yet more snow for later this week, and it looks as if my wish for a white Christmas might well come true. This winter has seen the most sustained period of snow that I can remember in years. Because the temperatures have stayed low, the snow that has already fallen is still lying on the ground on top of a good coating of ice, making the pavements treacherous. Not the best thing to negotiate in high heels.

On his hands and knees, farther down the street, someone is being sick into the gutter.

'Are you all right?' I ask.

He nods at me and pulls himself to his feet, swaying alarmingly. 'Merry Christmas, love,' he says, and weaves off down the road.

'Merry Christmas,' I reply. There is such a thing as *too* much Christmas spirit, I guess.

I punch in the number for home. The landline gives me nothing but the busy tone, so I try Rick's mobile phone. That goes straight to voicemail. I leave a message to say that I'm trying to contact him – anyone – to see how things are going. Then I try Chloe's mobile, which is also engaged. I hope she's not on to NHS Direct. Moving on, I try Mum's phone. After two rings, she answers.

'Mrs Rita Britten speaking.'

'Hello, Mum,' I say. 'Just phoning to check that everything's OK at home.'

'Who is this?'

'It's Juliet.'

'Juliet who?'

'Juliet, your daughter.' Freezing her butt off outside in the snow.

'Oh,' she says. 'That Juliet.' My mother knows no other Juliets – and, particularly, none that is her daughter. 'How are you, dear?'

'I'm fine, Mum. I'm just phoning to check that everything's OK there.'

'It's lovely, thank you very much. Nice talking to you again. You must drop by for tea sometime.'

'Mum!' But she's hung up already. Christ on a bike!

I ring Dad. His mobile goes straight to voicemail. Sometimes it's worth ringing Dad's phone just to listen to his message. Today, it breaks my heart as Dad hasn't changed his message and it's Samuel's voice that you hear first.

Samuel: 'Press that button, Francis, and then speak.'

Dad: 'What, this one?'

Samuel: 'Yes.'

In the background I can hear Noel Edmonds and *Deal or No Deal* at full tilt.

Dad: 'I still can't hear anything.'

Samuel: 'Have you pressed the button?'

Dad: 'Which one?'

Samuel: 'That one there.'

Dad: 'Is that the banker on the phone?'

Samuel: 'Yes. He's offered ten thousand pounds.'

Dad: 'Hmm. I think he should take it. I've pressed the button. What shall I say now?'

201

Samuel: 'Ask them to leave a message and say you'll call back.'

Dad: 'Whoever this is phoning me, can you ...'

Then the tone cuts Dad off and I leave a message. 'Dad, can you ring me, please? I've tried everyone else.' I realise that I sound shrill. 'I just want to know that everything's OK.'

I stand in the cold for five minutes more, admiring the Christmas lights that are strung across the street, swinging in the icy breeze. Then, just as I'm about to abandon my quest to contact my family, my mobile rings. It's Dad.

'Hello, love,' Dad says. 'Where's the fire?'

'What's everyone up to?' I ask. 'I just want to know that you're all fine. How's Jaden? What's Chloe doing? Is Mum OK? Where's Rick?'

'Jaden's fine,' Dad says soothingly. 'His temperature is down a little bit. Chloe's still upstairs, lying on the bed next to him.'

That's nice. Even if she is on the phone to someone while she does it. Maybe it's Mitch. That would also be nice.

'Mum just went off for a bit of a wander,' Dad continues, 'but I've brought her back now.'

God. This does seem to be an increasingly regular occurrence. How are we going to stop her from going walkabout? I wonder if we can get one of those electronic tags that they put on criminals for her? 'Where did she go?'

'She was going across the road to look at the Harrisons' lights.'

'Oh, Dad.'

'She's fine now,' he assures me.

'Someone called Juliet's been ringing me,' I hear my mum shout.

'This is Juliet,' Dad explains. 'She says hello.'

'I don't know who she is,' Mum says. 'Tell her to fuck off.'

'Mum says hello too.' Dad is good at subtext.

'And where's Rick, for heaven's sake?'

'He's in the shed with Merak,' Dad says. 'I'm sure they're fine, too.' There's a sigh in my father's voice. 'Why don't you just go and enjoy your party? The house won't burn down while you're out. Even if it does, I'm still quite capable of dialling 999.'

'I know.'

'Then go and have some fun.'

'I will.' I hang up. Right. As I am currently superfluous to my family's requirements, fun, here I come.

# Chapter 37

Uncertain as to whether I'm reassured or not, I swing back into the hotel. As I'm hanging up my coat, Robin appears behind me.

'Oh,' I say. 'Hi there.'

'I was just wondering where you'd got to,' Robin says.

'Trying to make contact with my family,' I explain. 'Despite the multiplicity of technology available to me, it would be a damn sight quicker to send out smoke signals.'

'You're missing the party.'

'I know. My father has instructed me to have fun,' I tell Robin. 'I think that might involve me drinking more alcohol.'

'Then I'm happy to oblige. There's plenty of champagne on offer.'

I follow Robin back into the party room. The disco is in full flow. Coloured lights sweep the room, glittering off the Christmas tree, and the walls vibrate. Our colleagues gyrate alarmingly. Robin and I exchange a worried glance.

'Someone's going to put their back out. Or lose an eye,' he notes.

I laugh as Robin pours me a glass of champagne.

'To a very happy Christmas, Juliet,' he says.

'Happy Christmas, Robin.'

We clink glasses and drink together.

'Come on,' he says when we've finished our drink – in double-quick time. 'They're playing our tune.'

'I didn't know we had a tune.'

They are, in fact, playing Kings of Leon and 'Sex On Fire'. While the rest of the room are bouncing to the song, punching fists in the air, Robin takes me in his arms and pulls me close. In the corner of the dance floor we circle slowly to the pulsing beat. My boss holds me tight and I feel his cheek against my hair, his breath on my neck. His hand is hot in the small of my back. My heart is beating faster than it should.

The music changes to the Black-Eyed Peas and 'I Gotta Feeling' and, not surprisingly, still we are the only smoochers. It feels strange to have Robin's lean body pressed up against mine. Did he do this at last year's party? If he did, I don't remember. I start to relax and enjoy it, entirely aided by the champagne. Robin dances nicely, moving smoothly with the rhythm, holding me close. On the rare occasion that I can drag Rick onto a dance floor, he moves to a rhythm utterly of his own making, and not necessarily connected to the music, but I've got used to it after all these years.

When that song finishes, Robin leans in close and whispers, 'My ears are bleeding now. Shall we move to somewhere quieter for a coffee?'

'That sounds nice.'

Grabbing a bottle of champagne and our glasses on the

way, he steers me along a corridor and into a quiet bar where there are squashy leather sofas. There are just a handful of other lightweights in here. We both flop down into the welcoming cushions.

'I like to think that I'm still young and trendy,' Robin admits. 'But it's at times like this that I realise I'm not.'

I giggle. 'Me too. When I'm at home every night with my cocoa, I long for a party like this. Then when I'm out, I realise that I like being at home with my cocoa.'

'We are very sad people,' Robin agrees.

'I'm sure our colleagues will be the first to tell us that tomorrow.'

'They're all having a great time,' he notes.

'That's because they're young and foolish and don't mind having a monstrous headache that wipes out the following day.'

'We can have our own more civilised party here.' He pours us more champagne.

What I actually need is the coffee that he promised, but then I remember my father's instruction to have fun, so I knock back the proffered fizz. It goes straight to my head. Why do bubbles make you feel squiffy more quickly?

'Was everything all right at home?'

'Oh, yes.' I give an airy wave of my hand. 'I don't know why I worry myself sick about them. They all manage quite perfectly without me.'

'I'm sure that's not true.'

'No, you're right. It isn't.'

'You seem to be at the very centre of your universe.' He

turns to me. 'I envy you that. I seem to be on the periphery of my own.'

'You couldn't persuade Rosemary to come along tonight?'

Robin shakes his head. 'Pressing matters at the book group.'

'Ah.'

'The sad thing is,' he continues, 'that I haven't actually missed her.' He tops up our champagne again. 'Without her here, I can relax.' Robin turns to me on the sofa. 'What I like about you, Juliet ... what I *love* about you ... is that I can be myself with you.'

I'm not sure what to say to that. Perhaps it's the drink talking. Both of us have probably had more than enough.

'That's why I wanted you to have this.' From his pocket he pulls a small white box.

It's one from Ornato. Now I'm an aficionado of their wares, I'd recognise it anywhere.

'I can't accept this.'

'You don't know what it is yet.' Robin smiles. 'I just wanted to buy you a little token of my affection,' he says. 'A thank you for all the support you give me.'

'Robin, I've done nothing.'

'I would disagree with you,' he counters. 'Just seeing you in the office every morning gives me a lift. You're always smiling, always cheerful.'

I'm bloody sure I'm not.

'You're always willing to listen,' he continues. 'And there's no one else I feel that I can talk to. I wanted to let you know how much I appreciate it.'

He hands the box to me and, as if I'm sleepwalking, I open it. Inside is the delicate silver teardrop necklace that I admired so much.

'Oh, Robin.'

'You like it?'

'You know I do. It's very, very lovely.'

He smiles shyly. 'Can I put it on for you?'

As luck, or fate, or something would have it, I don't have a necklace to wear with this dress. I sit forward on the sofa while Robin gently lifts my hair and fastens the delicate chain.

Then he sits back to admire me. 'It looks beautiful,' he says.

I don't even need to look at it to tell that it sits perfectly on my skin. It feels fantastic. 'I really can't accept this.'

'You can,' he insists.

'It's too much, Robin.'

'Let me be the judge of that.'

This is more than Rick will buy me. It's stunning. I run my fingers over the smooth teardrop. How can I possibly say no without offending him? This is so thoughtful – perhaps a little *too* thoughtful. And, I admit, the shallow part of me really, really wants this gorgeous necklace. 'Well. Thank you so much. It's too kind of you.'

He bats away my protest. 'Just a small Christmas present from me. Nothing more.'

But I think it possibly is much more, and my thoughts are confirmed when he leans towards me and kisses me tenderly on the lips.

'Robin . . .'

He puts his finger to the place where he's just kissed. 'I know. You love your husband.'

'I do.'

'Bizarrely, your devotion, your loyalty, it only serves to make you more attractive to me. You are a truly wonderful woman.'

'Really, I'm not. I have a small, ordinary life. I'm nothing special, Robin.'

'That's where you are so very wrong.' He leans in to kiss me again and I place my hand on his chest gently to block it. I don't want Robin to cross the line and make it difficult for me to work with him. I love my job. I love my boss. But not like that.

'You need to make things right with Rosemary,' I remind him.

'Oh, I am trying,' he assures me. 'Really, I am. I'm blaming this kiss on the madness of the moment.' He looks at me regretfully and sighs. 'But Rome wasn't built in a day, Juliet. I'm not content to settle for what Rosemary and I have any more. It has to be better than just existing together. I want the sort of relationship that you have with Rick. I'm very jealous of him.'

'We're hardly the perfect couple.' I think again of the secret texts that Robin knows nothing about. Perhaps it's just as well, or maybe he'd have tried to press that kiss home.

'I'd be a very happy man if I could have what you two have with my own wife.' His eyes fill with tears.

'Oh, Robin.'

'I've said too much.' He holds up a hand. 'Just consider

yourself a friend, a colleague who I'm very, very fond of.' Robin picks up the bottle of champagne again and drains it into our glasses. 'Now. I think we should go and join the party again, and get absolutely rat-arsed.'

I laugh. 'That sounds like a splendid idea.'

# Chapter 38

It's gone midnight, and I'm ridiculously drunk. More drunk than I've been in aeons. And now the office Christmas party is over for another year.

My colleagues, too, are more than a little worse for wear. The staff from Olney and Towcester totter off to their respective minibuses. At least, I hope they all get on the right ones. The state that they're in, they could end up anywhere. We wave them goodbye with much whooping and hollering.

Then the staff from our own branch, in turn, all kiss me goodbye and say that they'll see me in the morning. Robin has, very graciously and very sensibly, decided to open all of the offices at ten o'clock in the morning to give us a little lie-in. Frankly, I'm not sure that some of them will make it in at all. We stand together and watch the youngsters dance off down the High Street, still singing 'I Gotta Feeling' at the tops of their voices. If there was a nightclub in Stony Stratford, I'm sure they'd be heading straight there. As it is, they seem content to career off into the cold, cold night

211

without a care in the world. Most of them don't even have coats on.

Robin has offered to escort me home. He's already called a cab for us, and we're just waiting for it to arrive. As everyone else departs, my boss and I are left alone.

'It's been a lovely evening,' I say. 'Thank you so much. And thank you again for my present, too.'

'You're welcome.' Robin glances at his watch. 'The cab should be here any minute now. I'll go and find our coats.'

I'm desperately in need of mine. Already, hypothermia is setting in. I give an involuntary shiver and rub my arms as we go back inside the hotel reception area.

Robin heads towards the cloakroom and leaves me to my own devices.

*If* there was a nightclub in Stony Stratford and my colleagues were going to it, I might well be tempted to go too. I feel light and energised. Given half a chance I'd waltz along the High Street, take my shoes off and twirl in the snow, swinging round the lamp posts in the style of Gene Kelly.

I feel frisky, too. Perhaps too much fizz is the key to unlocking our sedate sex life. I could go home and ravish Rick. If we didn't have a house full of family, I could ravish him on the rug in front of the fire. As it is, we'll have to stick to our bedroom. But I want to be a sexy, saucy seductress. My husband gave me a strong enough hint that he'd like it, too. I wonder, does he rue the waning of our love life more than I do? I should make the effort more. Especially now that I'm competing with someone else.

Then I notice that there's a table set out advertising the

hotel's Christmas lunch package. The table is set with shiny silverware, sparkling crystal and festive flowers. The whole ensemble is decorated with Christmas confetti in red, green and gold. It looks beautiful.

What if I pinched some of the confetti to give Rick a Christmas treat? I'm thinking a little striptease routine followed by a confetti shower reveal. Without any further planning, and buoyed by too much alcohol, I take generous handfuls of the confetti from the table and scoop it into my bra. I shake it down – bit scratchy – and pile in some more. Admittedly, the enticing table looks a little bare now, but my bra is a secret holder of seasonal delights. Just wait until Rick gets an eyeful of this.

Robin returns with our coats and, as I'm shrugging mine on, our cab pulls up at the entrance. My boss holds the door open for me and I totter across the glassy pavement to flop inside. As we travel the ten minutes to Chadwick Close, I let my head rest back on the seat.

I know only too well how easy it is to start an affair. I'm feeling drunk and incredibly sexy. What if Rick and I were going through a really bad rough patch? What if I thought, *What's good for the goose is good for the gander* and decided to have a fling of my own? One moment of weakness is all it takes. What would my boss think if he knew my bra was bursting with Christmas confetti? Would he find that too much of a temptation? What if he and Rosemary haven't slept together for months, just as Rick and I haven't? A surfeit of drink and a rising of sexual desire is a dangerous situation. If Robin leaned in now to kiss me again, would I be able to

213

resist? Or would I let him snog me senseless in the back of a taxi? Then I realise that if I am old enough to use the word 'snog' then I am also old enough to know better.

Not a moment too soon, we pull up outside number ten. 'We're here,' I say pointlessly.

'So we are. Then I'll wish you goodnight.' This time Robin's kiss chastely finds my cheek, but his lips linger longer than they should.

'Goodnight, Robin. I'll see you tomorrow.' I step out of the cab – only slightly unsteadily.

I stand and watch as the car turns round and whisks him away.

# Chapter 39

'Sssh,' I say to Buster as I creep into the kitchen. He wags his tail enthusiastically, thumping it against the table leg. He's clearly thinking that it's time for walkies. He is about to be cruelly disappointed.

'Go to sleep,' I whisper to the dog. 'It's the middle of the night.'

He slinks back to his basket.

A second later, as I'm about to head for bed, I hear another key in the lock. Another second and the kitchen door bangs open.

'Ssh,' I say to Tom.

'Wotcha, Mum.' He does not *ssh*. 'What are you doing up so late?'

'Been to my office party. What are *you* doing up so late?'

'Just out with mates in the city. Stick some toast in, Mum. I could eat a horse.'

'Make your own toast,' I say. 'I'm going to bed. Dad's got to get up to go to work in the morning.'

'Aw, but you do it so much better, Mummy.'

I sigh. 'You treat this house like a hotel.'

'Now you sound just like Dad,' my son offers.

I give in. Resistance is futile. Sliding two slices of bread in the toaster, I realise that I'm actually peckish too, and put in another two pieces. What is it about drinking too much that gives you the munchies?

'Might as well put the kettle on,' Tom suggests.

Indeed, I might as well.

When it's ready, I sit opposite Tom at the kitchen table and we eat our hot buttered toast and drink tea together in companionable silence. I wave half a slice at Buster and he comes to sit at my feet while he wolfs it down.

'I hardly ever see you now,' I say to Tom. 'We're like ships that pass in the night.'

My son shrugs. 'You know what Dad's like. It works better if I stay out of the way.'

'He only wants what's best for you,' I tell him. 'He worries that you're not settled.'

'It's different now. Being married, having a career, a pension, it's not seen as the be-all and end-all.'

'Still being at home can't be ideal.'

'I get my toast made for me in the middle of the night. What more could I want?' Tom laughs.

My son doesn't laugh often. He may like to think he has a free and easy lifestyle, but he doesn't seem to have much fun that isn't drink-induced. I look at him closely and his skin is pale and there are dark shadows round his eyes.

'Don't worry about me, Mum,' he says in answer to my scrutiny. 'I'm fine.'

But will he still be telling me the same thing when he is thirty, forty, fifty? God forbid. When will he grow up, see responsibility as a good thing, enjoy the love of a good woman – or man? I don't mind which way his sexual proclivities lie.

'Look at Chloe,' he says. 'I wouldn't want to be in her shoes. One kid already and another on the way.' Tom snorts. 'That's not for me.'

'I just want you to be happy.' I take his hands. I miss the days when he would readily twine his fingers in mine. 'I hope that you find someone special to share your life with.'

'Mum, I don't even know if I want to settle down with a man or a woman. I'm not going to rush into anything.'

'I can see that.' Sometimes I wonder, is this the same quiet boy who I used to curl up on the sofa with and watch Disney films for hours on end on rainy Sundays? Where did that mild-mannered, shy child go?

'I'm having a good time looking,' he says, grin widening. 'If that's any consolation.'

'Tom,' I admonish.

He just laughs at me. Old-fashioned fuddy-duddy that I clearly am. I'm well aware that my son has what might be called an 'adventurous' sex life. I only wish his mother could say the same. Is it the lack of passion in our love life that's causing Rick to stray? I'd assumed that, like me, he'd got used to the fact that sex was at the very bottom of the To Do list and had just learned to accept it. Perhaps I'm wrong. I should be up there now, tripping the light fandango for him, but I have so little time with Tom that I don't want to tear myself away. All my flirty thoughts have been packed away again.

217

I turn my attention back to Tom. 'It would be nice if you brought someone home to meet us.'

'I do,' he protests.

'I mean *really* meet us, not just find them naked in our bed.' Or on our dining-room table.

My son shrugs. 'If that's what you want.'

I sigh and stroke his hair. 'All I want is for you to be happy.' I drink up my tea. 'Now I really must go to bed. Your dad will be wondering where I am.' Most likely Rick will be fast asleep and snoring.

I plant a kiss on top of Tom's head before he can resist. It used to smell of shampoo and sweets. Now it smells of stale cigarettes and beer, but I still relish the closeness. 'I love you.'

'I love you too, Mum.'

Those are words that I don't hear enough. I let my hand linger on his hair. 'Goodnight, Tom.'

# Chapter 40

Eventually, I climb the stairs and tiptoe into our bedroom. My feet are really hurting now, and I carry my heels in my hand. The bedside light is off and, as predicted, I can hear Rick snoring softly.

It's late. Gone two o'clock now. All ideas of being a frisky, fruity femme fatale have gone out of my head. Toast, it seems, is a counter-aphrodisiac. Rick has to get up in the morning, and I'm sure he wouldn't appreciate being woken up for a quick late-night tumble. See, this is what happens to all my good intentions.

I'll just slide quietly in beside him and cuddle up. I look down at my husband sleeping soundly and my heart is filled with love. Perhaps we didn't come together in the best of circumstances, but I could have done a lot worse than marry Rick. We have made a good life and have two wonderful children. Well, mostly they're wonderful.

Dropping my shoes on the floor, I reach up to undo the necklace from Robin and put it back in its posh box.

'Juliet?' It's Rick's voice coming sleepily from the bed. 'Is that you?'

It's a good question because frankly, these days, it could be anyone in our bedroom.

'Yes,' I whisper. 'Sorry I woke you.'

'It's OK. Did you have a good time?'

'Yes,' I say. 'I did.'

'You sound a little slurry.'

'Do I?' Perhaps I am.

Rick switches on the bedside lamp and sits up in bed. He rubs his eyes. 'Last year when you came home squiffy you wanted bouncy cuddles.'

'Hmm,' I say. 'So I did.'

'How much have you had to drink?'

'Enough,' I say, and though I try to sound seductive, Rick may indeed be right when he says I'm slurring. 'You're not tired?'

'It's the middle of the night, Juliet. Of course I'm tired.' He hesitates. 'But I'm not *too* tired.'

'Oh.' Rick is clearly giving out buying signals. Then I remember all the festive confetti in my bra and how I was going to do a sexy striptease. 'I'm not that tired either.' I stifle a yawn.

Rick laughs. 'Come here and give me a cuddle. We can do this another time.'

But when? I can't even remember the last time my husband and I made love. There are always other things, other people to consider. Our needs are right down at the bottom of the pile.

'I don't think so.' I start to sway and lift my arms to pile my

220

hair on the top of my head. I pout at Rick. His face says that five minutes of the missionary position will be quite enough, thank you very much, but I want to make this a night to remember. I want him to know that I'm still his lover as well as his wife.

I dance a little around the floor, singing 'Santa Baby' in a Marilyn Monroe-style breathy voice and tripping slightly on the rug.

Rick, I have to say, looks more bemused than aroused.

Turning to shake my booty at him, I see Rick yawn. Better get on with this before the mood goes off. So I slip the shoulders of my dress down as I'd imagine Dita Von Teese would. I can see why burlesque is becoming popular again; it's very empowering. A shimmy or two, then step out of the dress. Just undies. Decent ones. Ta-da!

My husband is looking a little more impressed now.

I climb up onto the bed. A bit of a wobble there.

'Be careful, Juliet,' Rick says. 'You're a bit unsteady on your feet.'

'I'm fine,' I assure him.

'You'll wake the whole house,' he says.

'Ssshhh.'

Standing on the bed, I gyrate a bit more, even though I'm now feeling very tired. Rick looks quite concerned. A sudden longing for the comfort of my bed washes over me.

I lean forward, ready for my big finale. Undoing the hook of my bra, I plan a theatrical fling, showering Rick with the Christmas confetti. Vigorous lovemaking will ensue and we can still both be asleep by three.

But as flinging commences, I somehow trip on the duvet and slip forwards. My bra comes off in more of a fumble than a fling, but the Christmas confetti is still jettisoned over Rick's head. Lots of it. How did quite so much fit into my bra? Some of it goes into his mouth, which has dropped open in surprise. Rick starts to splutter and I start to fall. He lunges to catch me but misses and I scramble to get purchase on the duvet. But it's no good; I'm slipping, sliding sideways off the bed, taking the duvet with me.

I land with an unhealthy thump on the floor, ankle twisted beneath me. The pain is excruciating – even the alcohol is failing to block it.

'What's going on in there?' I hear my mother shout from the next room. 'Keep the noise down. Some of us are trying to sleep.'

'Ouch,' I complain. 'Very ouch.'

Rick's face appears at the edge of the bed. He has Christmas confetti in his hair and stuck to his skin. He looks down at me and smiles. There's confetti between his teeth when he asks, 'I suppose a shag's out of the question now?'

# Chapter 41

'I am *not* going to A&E.' I hold up my hand so that Rick knows I mean business. How stupid would I feel explaining to them what has happened? 'All I need is to put my foot up with an ice pack.'

My ankle is swelling nicely and is already turning a disturbing shade of lilac. Rick helps me into bed, props up my ankle on a pillow and trots off to find me some ice.

When he comes back, he's got a bag of frozen peas, a cup of tea and a packet of tablets.

'I found these,' he says, and hands over the pills.

They're anti-inflammatories that have been lurking in the back of the medicine cabinet. As they're only six months out of date, I take two.

'Feeling OK?'

'Stupid. That's how I'm feeling.' Though my ankle is throbbing, if I'm truthful it's my pride that's hurt more than anything.

'It was very funny,' Rick says.

'I'm not sure that "funny" was the emotion I was aiming for.'

Then we laugh together.

'The bedroom's covered in that Christmas confetti,' he notes. 'We'll be hoovering it up for weeks. What were you thinking?'

'I was thinking it would be sexy and seductive.' Seems I was mistaken.

Rick lies down next to me and wraps his arms round me. 'I find you sexy, confetti or not, Mrs Joyce.'

I snuggle into him. 'Do you really?'

'Of course I do.'

Again, this would be the perfect moment to tell him that I've seen his texts to another woman, and that I'm worried about them. How can I go through Christmas with this doubt drumming away inside of me? In my head, I start to formulate the words I need into a sentence.

Then Rick says, 'Are you going to go to work tomorrow?' and the moment has gone.

'Yes. I'll have to go and face the ribbing.'

'You can tell them you fell over Buster.'

That sounds plausible enough. It's possibly only Robin who will realise just how drunk I was. I curl into Rick's arms. 'This isn't quite how I envisaged the evening ending.'

'It's the thought that counts,' Rick says, and within seconds we're both asleep.


A couple of hours later and it's time to get up again. I hop through the confetti on the floor and look out of the window.

Already I can tell that there's been a heavy snowfall overnight, as there's that thick silence that comes with it. Outside, everything is covered by a blanket of white and looks stunning.

Rick texts Merak to tell him not to come in until later. Then, with Rick's assistance, I get showered and dressed. When eventually, with a judicious application of thick slap, I don't look like I've been up all night, I hop downstairs. In the kitchen, unusually, the family are up in full force. Rick is well into his toast marathon. Chloe is giving Jaden his breakfast. My grandson looks bright-eyed and bushy-tailed – more than can be said for his nana.

'How is he?' I ask.

'He's very well.' Her look says, *No thanks to you*.

'What was all that row last night?' Mum asks. Her red hair is standing on end and her dressing gown is buttoned up all wrong. She has put on bright pink lipstick, but again has missed her mouth completely. I'll have to organise dressing her properly before I go to work.

'What row?' Chloe wants to know.

'I fell over the dog.' The lie trips from my tongue. Only Tom looks up and raises an eyebrow, but he doesn't dob me in. 'I've sprained my ankle. Only slightly. I'm fine. Really. Fine.'

'Come and sit down, love,' Dad says. 'Let me get you some tea.'

'I've got it, Frank,' Rick says. 'Anyone for more toast?' Tom is the sole taker.

Merak arrives, and is instantly given tea and toast.

'Come on, Mum, let me get you dressed before I go.'

'I want Frank to do it,' she says petulantly, arms folded in front of her. 'I want Frank.'

I glance across at Dad. 'I'll do it, love,' he says with a nod. 'You go off to work. I don't mind.'

'If you're sure.'

'Of course he's sure,' Mum snaps. 'We've been married for twenty years.'

They were married for the best part of fifty years, and separated for nearly three – something else my mother seems to have forgotten. 'He's seen me in my knickers before.'

'I do apologise, Merak,' I say to our guest. No one needs to know about my mother's knickers at this time in the morning.

'Let's go to work,' Rick says. 'Before the whole bloody day is gone.'

I limp to get my coat, which Merak helps me into. I can't quite put my weight on my foot, but it seems to be better than I expected. The three of us pile into the van.

'This snow's sticking,' Rick notes.

'More is forecast in the next few days.'

He tuts. 'Fabulous.'

The van slithers its way into the High Street, and then Rick helps me across the pavement and into my office.

'See you later,' he says. He turns away and then, as an afterthought, turns back. 'It was fun last night.'

I laugh. 'No it wasn't.'

'Well, it *nearly* was.' Rick grins back at me. 'We could have an early night tonight,' he suggests.

'In our house? What do you think the chances of that are?'

'Slim,' he agrees. 'But it shouldn't stop us from trying.'

My heart surges to think that he still wants to. 'It's a date,' I say.

Then I kiss him goodbye before I head into the office to face the teasing from my colleagues.

# Chapter 42

Rick worked for the rest of the morning with Merak, laying a laminate floor for the back room and kitchen of a run-down solicitor's office.

The snow was getting heavier, and his thoughts turned again to Lisa and Izzy. What if they hadn't been able to get out for a few days? What if they had no shopping in? What if their bastard landlord still hadn't fixed the boiler?

At lunchtime he cracked and phoned her. It was the first time he'd done that. He'd texted her a couple of times just to see if she was OK, but it was the first time he'd called to speak to her. Merak was out getting them both some hot soup and bacon rolls from the bakery just along the street. Before he came back, Rick punched in Lisa's number. Why did he feel that he had to do it in secret? Why couldn't he have called her in front of his assistant? And, for that matter, why had he still not mentioned her to Juliet?

Lisa answered instantly.

'Hi,' he said. 'I was just worried about you and Izzy with all this snow. Is it bad out there?'

'Terrible,' she said. 'I don't think I'm going to be able to get out today at this rate.'

'Have you got plenty in the cupboards?'

A hesitation. 'Enough to keep us going.' He knew that she hadn't.

'And the boiler?'

'Still not working.'

How could the landlord be so bloody uncaring with a kiddie in the house? It made Rick's blood boil.

'Look,' he said. 'I'll try to pop out and see you later. Bring some groceries. Is there anything in particular you need?'

'Just some basic stuff,' Lisa said. 'If you can't make it, there's no need to worry about us.'

But he was worried.

Merak returned, and they had their soup and rolls together.

'The snow is bad,' Merak said. 'I am glad that we are working near to home.'

'Can you walk to your place from here? I've got to pop out at the end of the day. You'll be OK?'

Merak nodded. 'Yes.'

'Not thinking of going round roughing up our customers?' he teased.

'Not today,' Merak dead-panned.

'Thanks again for that, lad.'

He shrugged. 'It is not problem.'

They returned to work and, after getting their heads down and cracking on, finished the floor at about three o'clock.

'Want to go home now?' Rick said as they loaded the van. The snow was still coming down thick and fast. It was freezing out here, too. Rick rubbed his hands together. Only a madman would consider driving in this. 'There's nothing else to be done today. Can I drop you off somewhere?'

'No,' Merak said. 'I will walk.'

'Take my coat, lad. It's warmer than yours.' It was the first time he'd noticed that Merak was wearing nothing more than a fleece hoodie. 'Haven't you got a warm coat?'

'No,' Merak admitted. 'I have not.'

'I'll have a look at what I've got in my cupboards. There are enough coats in there to stock a branch of Millets. In the meantime—' Rick slipped off his thick jacket and handed it over. 'I don't want you freezing to death.'

'Now you will be cold,' Merak noted.

'I've got the van heater.'

'We will swap. Take this.' Merak handed over his fleece. Rick reluctantly agreed. It was so thin it barely made a difference. He couldn't believe that he hadn't noticed the lad was walking round in nothing but this in the freezing weather. The boy was lucky he hadn't got hypothermia. They must make them from tough stuff in Poland.

Merak shrugged on the warm jacket gratefully. He patted it down, admiring the fit.

'Suits you.' Rick thought that he might as well keep it. He was sure he had another one just like it somewhere. Juliet would be able to root it out.

'I will see you in morning,' Merak said.

'We might have a slow start again, if this keeps up. I'll text you.'

Then he watched Merak as he walked away down the High

230

Street. The snow was up to his ankles, and it nearly covered his work boots. After a few hundred yards he had disappeared, and Rick couldn't see him in the white-out at all.

Time was getting tight now. If he was going to buy some shopping for Lisa and run it over there, and be back in time to collect Juliet from work at half past five, then he was going to have to get a serious move on. He texted Lisa to say that he was on his way.

Then he slotted the van into gear and eased it out into the road. It slipped and slithered where the roads hadn't been gritted – always a bone of contention. The first sign of bad weather in the UK, and all the gritters seemed to go into hibernation.

Following the path he'd trodden before, he headed to the supermarket. He braved the relentless battering of Christmas songs and filled a basket full of essentials and headed out to Cublington Parslow and to Lisa's house.

The going was tough. The country lanes were treacherous. It was a hard job just to keep the van in a straight line, and not end up buried in a hedge or one of the rapidly growing snowdrifts. He crawled along at a pace that even a snail would be embarrassed by. The windscreen wipers were working overtime, just trying to keep the snow from piling up and blocking his view completely. It took him nearly two hours to complete a journey that would normally take him a shade under half an hour. A dozen times he nearly turned back, but it was the thought of Lisa and Izzy being cut off in that cold house with no food that kept him going. Some people would say that it wasn't his problem, but somehow he had made it so, and he couldn't just leave them to the mercy of the elements now.

There were cars abandoned everywhere on the rapidly disappearing road. One was upside down in a ditch. Rick narrowed his eyes, which were scratchy with tiredness, and peered through the rhythmic clack-clack-clack of the wipers and into the driving snow. Darkness was falling, and his fingers were cramped with tension on the steering wheel. This was hell. It was sheer lunacy even to attempt to drive in this weather.

When he finally reached Cublington Parslow, he could have wept with relief. He turned into Lisa's road and slithered the last few metres to her house. The light was on in the front room, and he thought he'd never seen anything more welcoming in his life.

Parking the van, Rick noted that all the cars in view were fast being buried by the steady onslaught. Already he was too late to pick up Juliet. He punched her number into his mobile.

'Hello, love,' he said when she answered. 'How's the ankle?'

'Better. Just painful rather than excruciating. How are you? Job finished? I was beginning to wonder where you'd got to.'

'I'm just calling to say that I'm still tied up with work.' He glanced guiltily at Lisa's house. 'I'm out in Cublington Parslow. I had a devil of a job getting here. It took me the best part of two hours.'

'Oh, Rick. What are you doing there?'

'Just a few loose ends to tie up before Christmas,' he said, feeling bad that he was avoiding the question. 'Can you ask Tom to pick you up after work, or jump in a taxi? It could take me another couple of hours to get back. I'm not going to be there in time to collect you.'

'OK. I'll try to find Tom.'

'It's bad on the roads,' Rick said. 'Tell him to take it easy. You might be better getting a taxi.'

'I don't think there'll be many taxis out in this.'

Rick hadn't thought of that.

'I could walk if it wasn't for this wretched ankle.'

He thought about his wife weaving about above him on the bed in nothing but her underwear and smiled at the memory. 'Not a good idea. The pavements are like glass. I don't want you injuring your one good ankle.'

'Don't worry, I'll take it easy. I'll see you when I see you, then,' Juliet said. 'Be careful yourself.'

'I will.' He hung up and put his phone in his pocket. Rick wished that he'd said *I love you*, but it seemed silly to call her back just to say that now.

Instead, he jumped out of the van and, crossing the treacherous pavement, carried the shopping to Lisa's door. It was already open when he got there.

'We've been watching at the window for you for over an hour,' she said. 'I was worried you wouldn't make it.'

'Me too.'

'I'm so grateful for this,' Lisa said as she took the shopping from him and went into the kitchen. 'The kettle's on. I've already boiled it a dozen times.'

'I can't stay,' Rick said. 'I'm going to have to turn straight round and go back.'

'But it's taken you hours. You need to have a hot drink and at least a sandwich. You can't go out in this without anything inside you. It could take you hours to get home again.'

'A quick cuppa,' he said. 'Then I have to go.'

'Take a sandwich with you.' She made the tea and handed it to him. Pulling the sliced loaf and packet of cheese out of the carrier bag, Lisa set about making him a sandwich. 'Thanks again for all this.'

She looked at it as if he'd given her a bag filled with the Crown Jewels, not just a few bits and bobs of shopping. How she lived from hand to mouth was humbling. Perhaps it was the sheer glut and greed that this season encouraged in people that brought her circumstances into sharp contrast. If he had come across her at any other time of the year, would he be so concerned about their plight? It was a hard question to answer.

While he drank from his mug, Izzy handed him her battered dolly and slid cautiously to perch on his knee. The child's face was always so solemn and unsmiling that it tightened the cords around his heart.

There was still no heating, and even the kitchen was freezing. 'No word from your landlord?'

'No.' She shook her head. 'I can't see him coming out in this either. Can you?'

'Let me try.' He indicated that she should give him her phone.

Lisa pulled up the number. 'You can try, but he just doesn't answer.'

Sure enough, the call went straight to voicemail and Rick left him a message asking him to ring. Perhaps he'd return his call if he didn't realise it was on Lisa's behalf.

'Izzy and I have been sleeping on the sofa under the duvet,

so we've been able to keep the fire on all night. It's not been too bad. I'm dreading the bill, though.'

'There's no need to worry about that,' Rick said. 'I'll see you right.'

'You're too good to us,' Lisa sighed. 'We really do appreciate it.'

'Are you going to be OK for a few days?'

'We'll be fine,' she assured him. 'Now that we've got this.' Lisa glanced for the hundredth time at the shopping as if she still couldn't quite believe her luck. 'I can't thank you enough. We'd have been stuffed without it.'

Tea finished, he stood up. 'I'd better go.'

She scooped Izzy into her arms. 'Say goodbye to Rick.'

'Bye-bye,' Izzy said. 'Come again soon.'

He laughed. 'I will.'

At the front door, Lisa kissed him gently on the cheek. 'Drive carefully.'

But, as the snow showed no sign of letting up, he realised it could be some time before he reached home again.

# Chapter 43

'How did you hurt your ankle again?' Robin asks.

'I tripped over the dog.' I wipe the condensation from his car window and peer outside.

'Taking strong drink is a very bad idea,' he laughs.

My boss doesn't need to know how I actually did sprain my ankle. That can stay a lifelong secret between me and my husband. 'It was a nice evening. A lot of fun.'

'Yes,' Robin agrees. 'It was. Everyone seemed to enjoy it.'

Judging by the monumental hangovers that most of Robin's staff had today, I think he's probably right. I doubt that very much work was actually done at the various branches of Westcroft & Co. at all. Most of my colleagues spent the day slumped over their desks in a state of extreme inertia. I'm sure I wouldn't have been missed if I'd stayed in bed for the day.

'Thank you for offering to take me home.'

'I wouldn't hear of anything else.'

When Robin overheard that Rick wasn't able to pick me up at the end of the day, he jumped in at once to rescue me. I'd phoned half a dozen taxi firms but with no luck and, of course, Tom was nowhere to be found. Robin had insisted he drive me home. Now, we're sitting in a queue of traffic that snakes down the High Street and have been for some time. The traffic reporter on the radio is working overtime, and it looks as if everything in Buckinghamshire has come to a grinding halt. Had I been able, it would have been infinitely quicker to walk.

'We could go for a drink and wait until this dies down,' Robin suggests. 'There's a parking space right outside the pub. You wouldn't have to hop too far.'

'I'd better not drink for a few days,' I say. 'I'm taking tablets.' Only out-of-date anti-inflammatories, but Robin doesn't need to know that either. I think it's better if my boss and I aren't involved in any more cosy, solo drinking sessions. I don't want Robin to get the wrong idea. 'But thanks for the offer.'

We inch forward, following the stream of red tail lights, mesmerised by the windscreen wipers. Robin turns off the radio.

'Rosemary didn't come home last night,' Robin says into the silence. He looks straight ahead. 'Not at all.'

'From book group?'

'I don't think she was there after all.' He tries a smile, but it doesn't reach his eyes. 'Unless it was a particularly riveting book.'

'Is she all right?'

A weary sigh. 'Oh, I think she's just fine.'

I was having visions of her lying in a ditch somewhere, but obviously Robin is imaging her lying in someone else's bed.

'You must have been out of your mind with worry.'

'There wasn't much sleep had in the Westcroft household.' Robin tries another smile, but the result is as far off the mark as the previous one. 'I could have phoned round her friends, but there didn't seem much point in dragging them from their beds. I managed to get hold of my wife just before lunchtime. She told me it was none of my business where she'd been. That couldn't really be considered a good thing in a marriage, could it?' Now he looks at me.

'No,' I say. 'I don't think it could.'

'Any advice?'

'You have a right to know where she's been and if there's someone else involved.'

'Yes,' he says. 'I think I do.'

I'm not the best person to dole out advice when I can't confront the present situation in my own relationship. Perhaps I should take a little of my own medicine.

We carry on in silence and, eventually, arrive at Chadwick Close.

'That was a bit of a marathon,' I apologise. A ten-minute journey has taken over half an hour, and I wonder just how long it will take Rick to make his way back from Cublington Parslow. 'I'm sorry to take you out of your way.'

'It's not a problem, Juliet. It's always a pleasure. I'll see you safely to the door.'

'Come in and have some tea, or something. I have mince pies.'

'Tempting as that is, I think I need to go home and talk to my wife.'

238

'That's probably a good idea.'

Robin comes round and opens the door for me and helps me out. My foot can take most of my weight now, though it still feels weak. He escorts me along my icy path to the front door. We stand facing each other in the snow.

'I do love her, you know,' he says.

'Then I hope that you manage to work things out.'

He kisses me on the cheek. 'Thanks, Juliet.'

I watch as Robin goes back to his car and swings out of the close. Then I let myself inside the house and try not to trip over the dog.

# Chapter 44

Rick had tried every way out of the village possible. In the brief time he'd been here, the road he'd come in on from Milton Keynes was now so covered with deep snowdrifts that it was impossible even to see where the edge of the tarmac finished and the fields began. There was no going back in that direction. The next lane he'd travelled down had such a steep hill that he simply couldn't get up it no matter how hard he tried. Every time he took a run at it, even in a low gear, the wheels just skidded beneath him. Cars and vans that had similarly failed before him littered the verges.

When he turned round and attempted the other route – which would take him on to the main road – there was a lorry jackknifed on a sharp bend, which had completely blocked the road. Three other cars had crashed in its wake. With the snow still coming down at the rate it was, Rick was sure that little lot wasn't going to be cleared in a hurry.

There was no choice. He wouldn't be able to get back up the other hill into the village either. He was stuck here in this dip for the foreseeable future, and was just going to have to stay in the van and sit it out until the road cleared, even if that took until morning – which was looking the most likely scenario.

He pulled over into the adjacent lay-by so that he was out of the way of the carnage – only the bright yellow waste bin by the side of it giving him a steer on where the lay-by stopped and the ditch began. It was cold – already below freezing he'd guess, even though it was still not yet six o'clock in the evening. The van would only hold its heat for a few minutes, and there was no point wishing now that he had his thick jacket to wear instead of Merak's thin hoodie, which was about as much use as a piece of tissue paper.

Rick called Juliet to tell her not to worry.

'You're going to stay in the van?' she said, in response to his plan. 'But it's freezing.'

'I'll be fine.'

'You won't,' Juliet insisted. 'You'll die of hypothermia. If you really are stuck, can't you walk back into the village and see if there's a pub? They might have a room.'

That was a better idea. He'd seen a pub by the crossroads, The Bird in the Hand, or the Bush, or something like that. Even if they didn't have a room available, he could stay in there until closing, which would minimise the time he'd have to spend in the van. Perhaps they would have a roaring log fire. He could almost see it.

'I will,' he promised. 'Perhaps I can get a hot meal too.' As nice as the cheese sandwiches were that Lisa had made for him, they might well keep him from starving but they wouldn't warm him up any and already he was starting to shiver.

'Phone me again,' Juliet said. 'Let me know that you're all right.'

And so, moments after he'd rung off, Rick found himself zipping Merak's hoodie right up and reluctantly venturing out into the snowy landscape.

As he climbed out of the van, the snow was coming down thick and fast. Crunching it underfoot, Rick headed back towards the village as he'd promised Juliet he would. Within seconds, he put up his hood and jammed his hands deep into his pockets. Gloves would have been a useful addition. And a woolly hat. Maybe a sled and a pack of huskies. The walk back to civilisation felt like a million miles, though it could have been no more than two. The bottom of his work jeans were soaked through, and he was glad of his heavy boots as his feet were sinking deep in the fresh snow.

It was over half an hour before he was back at the village. His face was raw and wet from the pelting snow. The light grey hoodie was now soaked to dark grey. When he was sat in front of that roaring log fire, he'd start to steam. The thought of it spurred him on, and Rick crossed to the pub with hope in his heart. It was only when he was inches away from the front door that he then noticed the small scrap of paper stuck to it with a ripped piece of parcel tape. In black marker pen, it read: *Closed due to power cut.*

His heart sank. He felt like collapsing to his knees in the snow. Banging on the door. Pleading for sanctuary. Surely they would take pity on him. He peered in at the window.

Deserted. He rapped at the knocker and waited, but no one came. If there was anyone at home, it was clear that they didn't intend to offer comfort to stranded strangers. So much for all the tales in the newspapers of saintly publicans taking in distraught trapped motorists and housing them for days on end filled with jolly japes and drinking the place dry. Clearly the Christmas spirit hadn't troubled the landlord of The Bird in the Whatever, Cublington Parslow. Now what? Only the thought of a good pub curry or some egg and chips had kept him going. Not only was a hot meal and a warm by the fire not on the cards, but it definitely looked like there was no chance of a bed either. He'd have to face that long walk back to the van for a night with nothing but a cheese sandwich for sustenance.

Then his phone rang. He assumed it would be Juliet for an update on his progress but, instead, he saw that it was Lisa.

'Hey,' she said. 'Just checking to see if you got back safely.'

That made Rick laugh, when a minute ago he'd felt like kicking the pub door in. 'Not exactly. I'm still at the end of your street.'

'What?'

'I can't get out of the village. All the roads are blocked.'

'I saw that it was bad on the news. Where exactly are you?'

'I'm outside the pub.' He looked up at the sign for the first time. 'The Bird in the Hand. I was hoping to get a room for the night, but it's all locked up. They've had a power cut.'

'So have we,' Lisa said. 'Look, why don't you come straight back here? I can make you something proper to eat. Luckily someone brought me a load of shopping earlier.'

Rick laughed again. 'I don't want to impose.'

'Don't be a pillock,' Lisa said. 'Get yourself round here now. I'm not having you out on the roads in this. You can kip down with us.'

'I can't do that.' How would he begin to explain this to Juliet? Surely it was much safer to risk freezing to death in the van. If Juliet found out that he was spending the night at another woman's house, he'd have a near-death experience when he got home anyway.

'You'll stay here and I'll have no arguments.' Lisa's voice cut into his thoughts. 'Say you'll come.'

What else was he to do? With heavy heart, Rick said, 'I'll come.'

He could hear the smile in her voice at his acquiescence.

'Good. That's what mates are for.'

He hung up and trudged towards her house, wondering on the way if that's what they really were – just mates.

# Chapter 45

This Christmas, I will be channelling Delia. Nigella is too smug, Gordon too sweary, Jamie too much bish, bash, bosh. You know where you are with Delia. She is the one person I would like to emulate in the cooking department. If Delia says you need to make a tent with extra-wide foil within which to roast your turkey so that it comes out buttery and moist, then that's exactly what you must do to ensure success. She'll never let you down. And the one day of the year you don't want dinner to be a trauma is Christmas Day.

I have knocked out more Christmas dinners than I care to remember, but they still always seem fraught with danger. So much has to come together at once. One slight slip and it can all go to rack and ruin. I remember the time that, amid all the mayhem, I actually forgot to order the turkey, and had the devil's own job to get one big enough in time. After a little too much festive cheer one year, I dropped all the roast potatoes and parsnips on the floor as I was about to serve. Everything had to go back in the oven for another hour while I peeled and cooked some more. Now I take the precaution of having an 'emergency' back-up Christmas dinner in the freezer – frozen roasties, frozen veggies and a Bernard Matthews turkey roll – just in case of tragedy.

This year I want it all to be perfect. As the years pass, you never know when it could be the last one with your parents. Samuel's untimely passing has only served to underline it. He will be sorely missed around the table this Christmas, and I can hardly bear to think of Mum or Dad not being here too.

Speaking of which, I've come out into the kitchen to write my Christmas food-shopping list, version Twenty-two – in peace. All of my Delia cookery books are stacked on the table, so that I can flick through the recipes and make sure I've got everything I need.

*Coronation Street* is blasting out in the living room at a decibel level suitable only for the stone deaf. It's a good job we don't live in a semi-detached house, otherwise there would be complaints. As it is, there are cracks appearing in the ceiling due to sound vibration.

I have Delia's *Christmas* open in front of me. The family like her Parmesan-baked parsnips and braised red cabbage with apples. None of us likes Brussels sprouts, but we have to have them because it's Christmas, so I use Delia's white-wine and bacon recipe, as that makes them taste a bit less sprouty. Normally the dog ends up finishing them off, and then no one will speak to him for three days. We make him stay well behind us when he goes for his walks. Every year I plan to make Delia's classic Christmas pudding, and every year I fail. Shop-bought again. This year, though, I'm eschewing Mr

Kipling and will definitely – come hell or high water – be baking Delia's lattice mince pies for Christmas Day.

Dad comes in. 'No Rick yet, love?'

'He's stuck in the snow, Dad. Out in Cublington Parslow.'

'Oh, dear. That's not good.' He's opening and closing cupboard doors. 'Have we got any biscuits, love? The tin seems to be empty again.'

I have to stash my biscuits secretly now, as the family would get through ten packets a day if I let them.

'What do you want, Dad? Bourbons or custard creams?'

'Oh, both would be nice. They're for your mother.'

They're not. Dad is the biggest biscuit-snaffler in the house. But if that's his only vice, then I'm happy to indulge him. The kids like all the new-fangled ones, but Dad's a traditionalist when it comes to his biscuits. Custard creams. Bourbons. He'll go mad for a Tunnock's caramel wafer or teacake.

'Everything OK?'

Dad shrugs. 'Fine, love.'

'I'll bring you some biscuits through. Want a cup of tea?'

'That'd be lovely. Though your mother's on the wine again.'

'She's not good, is she, Dad?'

'She's just a little bit confused, I think. There's no fun in getting old, love.'

'No.' Even at my age, I've worked that out. My body, that would once bounce back from anything, now takes days to get over the most insignificant setback. A pulled muscle that would ease overnight now needs nine months of physio and a truckload of Nurofen before it will even think about going. I have to get new glasses every couple of years, and

I've long since given in to the hair dye. The title on every tub in the bathroom cabinet starts with the words 'age-defying'. But none of them – not a single one – does anything to defy age.

Dad shuffles out again and I notice that, despite saying he's fine, his shoulders are in a permanently sagged position since Samuel's been gone. I think it's only the fact that he's keeping an eye on Mum that's helping him get through this.

I put on the kettle and ring Rick. 'Did you get sorted out at the pub?'

'Yes,' he says. 'The snow's even worse now. I'll be back as soon as I can in the morning. I'm hoping they'll manage to get at least one of the roads open by then.'

'OK. Keep warm. I love you.'

'Yes,' Rick says. 'Me too.'

Gosh, it didn't exactly sound like the pub is a jumping joint. There wasn't a sound in the background. Mind you, I bet few people are risking going out in this. At least Rick is safe and warm.

I take a pot of tea and a plate piled high with biscuits into the living room for Mum and Dad.

'Thanks, love,' Dad says. His eyes light up at the biscuits, and it makes my heart clench at how little it takes to keep him happy.

'You're welcome.'

'I hope it's not weak,' is Mum's contribution.

'Leave it to brew for a minute, if you want it stronger.'

Then, as my ears threaten to bleed from the volume of the television, I turn to leave. Out of the corner of my eye, from the living-room window, I catch sight of a shadow moving in the garden.

'There's someone out there,' I say.

'What?' Mum wants to know.

'There's someone in my garden again!'

Despite my limp, I put on a spurt and shoot out of the back door and into the garden in my slippers. Buster follows, barking happily and wagging his tail.

Some guard dog he's proving to be. I would have hoped that at the sight of an intruder on his patch, he'd have turned into an uncontrollable, snarling beast. No such luck. Buster looks as if he might want to lick our burglar to death.

Heart pounding, I hobble down the garden as fast as I can shouting, 'Hey, you! Stop! Stop!'

Quite what I plan to do if he stops, I don't know. I wish I'd have thought to grab my rolling pin or something to look threatening with. But, instead of stopping, the dark figure sprints across the snow and expertly scales the back fence. Looks like he's done that a time or two before.

I slow my pace, as I'm never going to catch him now, and stand puffing in the middle of the lawn. Buster takes the opportunity to sniff out a few plants and water them. Footprints come from Rick's shed but, when I check the lock, it hasn't been tampered with. Perhaps I caught him just in time. I peer through the windows, but nothing seems to be disturbed there. In fact, it's looking tidier than ever.

Why does this keep happening? What are they after in Rick's shed? Has he got something valuable in there that he's not telling me about? Or are they just chancers, looking for a bit of something to sell at a car boot sale in these straitened times?

It worries me that there's someone lurking in our garden while Rick is away. Maybe I should call the police, but it seems pointless as there's no damage and nothing stolen, and they're reluctant to come out at the best of times.

I call Buster and turn back towards the house, shivering. I'll make sure the doors and windows are double-locked tonight. I'm concerned, and I'd really love to call Rick but that would only worry him more. And he's got enough to think about at the moment.

# Chapter 46

'I'm not much of a cook,' Lisa said. 'Not like your wife. Will a couple of eggs and some oven chips do?'

'That'd be fantastic,' Rick answered. It was exactly what his tastebuds had geared up for. 'I'm just grateful for anything. It was looking like a night in the van for me.'

'I can't believe you didn't ring me straight away,' she tutted over her shoulder.

'I didn't think.' The truth was, he wouldn't have liked to impose himself on Lisa and Izzy anyway. Never mind what Juliet might have to say on the subject.

'I don't much like this gas cooker,' Lisa said. 'It's a bit temperamental. But I'm glad I've got it now. I don't know how we would have managed otherwise.'

Due to the absence of electricity for the foreseeable future, the kitchen was lit by a dozen stubs of candles that were stuck in saucers round the room. Lisa, he'd noticed, had switched on one of the portable bottled gas heaters he'd lent her as soon as he'd arrived, but it was making little impression on the biting cold.

'The heat from the oven will warm it up in here,' she said as if reading his mind. 'We'll be toasty in minutes, won't we, Izzy?'

The little girl nodded. She was wearing pyjamas but had a jumper on top, thick socks and a knitted hat. Rick thought how talkative Jaden was compared to Izzy. Most of his chatter might be non-stop babble, but he was never quiet for a second. Izzy chewed thoughtfully on a piece of toast.

'Is that nice?' he asked, and received a solemn nod in return.

'We tend to stay in here after our tea until it starts to get colder,' Lisa continued. 'Then we go through to the living room when it's time for Izzy to go to bed.'

This was terrible. Terrible. *More* than terrible.

There was an old battery-operated radio on the windowsill above the sink, and Rick listened to the local weather forecast. It wasn't heartening. There was chaos and carnage on every road. He would definitely be here until morning.

Lisa put down the plate of egg and chips in front of him. 'You're not eating?'

She shook her head. 'Had something with Izzy earlier.'

Rick wondered if she really had. There was nothing of her but skin and bones. He ate the meal she'd prepared, but felt as if every mouthful was taking food from her and Izzy. Was there something, *anything*, he could do for her to make her situation more comfortable? Her landlord had better ring him back and fast.

When he'd eaten and the welcome heat from the oven had started to dissipate, Lisa said, 'Shall we go into the other room now? I like to try and get it warmed up for the night.'

She scooped up Izzy and carried her into the living room. Rick followed, bringing the candles on a plate. He went to the window and flicked the curtain aside. Outside, everywhere was still in pitch darkness. It didn't look likely that the power was going to come on again any time soon. The snow was still falling, the cars in the road had a fresh couple of inches on the roofs. So would his van. If it continued at this rate, he'd have to dig himself out in the morning. He wondered if Lisa would have a spade – it seemed unlikely – or whether he could borrow one from a neighbour. Rick let the curtain drop and dotted the candles round the place: on a little side table, on the fireplace. Then he went back to the kitchen and wheeled in the heater. It was as much use as lighting a match in a freezer.

He thought how different it was to his own living room at home. There were no Christmas decorations at all here, nothing to make it feel festive in the slightest. It was cold, bare, and it made him shiver just looking at the place. Juliet always went all out for it at Chadwick Close. Even though she'd got out their old tree again this year, it still seemed to take up half the room and it was hung with a million different baubles that she'd carefully collected over the years, and was draped with half a mile of tinsel. She was a great card-sender, too, so they always got dozens and dozens in return, which graced every free surface. He wasn't a big fan of Christmas himself, but he was suddenly very glad that Juliet was.

'Time for bed, young lady.' Izzy climbed onto the sofa and snuggled down at one end. Lisa pulled a neatly folded duvet from behind the sofa and shook it out.

'You sleep in here?'

'It's too cold to go upstairs,' she told him. 'Even if you want to go to the loo, you have to run up and down as quick as you can. There's no way we could sleep up there. There's ice on the inside of the windows.'

Tenderly, she tucked the duvet round her daughter's tiny frame. Rick felt choked. He hadn't really thought that people might live so frugally in this day and age. There was no doubt that he saw some sights when he went into other people's homes. Some folks clearly didn't know what bleach was for, while others lived in mansions. But he didn't know anyone who had to sleep in their living room because the rest of the house was too cold.

'Won't we keep her awake?'

'Nah,' Lisa said. 'Izzy's a good girl. She'll be off in minutes. Would you like to read her story to her?'

'It's one of the things I like doing for my grandson, Jaden.'

'Want Rick to read your story?'

The little girl, thumb already in mouth, nodded and her wide, unsmiling eyes fixed on him.

'Just tell me which one.'

Lisa handed him a book called *Giraffes Can't Dance* and Rick sat at one end of the sofa while Izzy curled into the other. He picked up a candle and held it to the page and read as he often did to Jaden. As Lisa had predicted, the child was asleep minutes later.

When he was sure she'd gone off soundly, he closed the book.

Lisa was in one of the armchairs in the room and Rick took the other one. She tucked her knees into her and huddled into the chair.

'So, where do you sleep?' It sounded like a loaded, cheesy question, but it wasn't.

'More often than not on the sofa, too. Izzy doesn't take up much room.' She glanced across at him. 'Will you be OK on an armchair? That one reclines. It's not too bad.'

It sounded like she'd spent more than one night on that, too.

Rick felt despair wash over him. 'Is there no one who can help you to get out of this place? No family, no friends?'

Lisa shook her head. 'No.' She tried a laugh, but it came out thick. 'If I'm honest, Rick, you're the only friend we've got. I can't think of anyone else who's done so much for us.'

'Izzy's dad isn't around?'

'Nah. I should never have got involved with him. He was a bad boy, Rick. Stupid girls like a bad boy. We'd only been together for a few months when I found out I was pregnant with Izzy.' She tucked her hair behind her ear and looked down at the floor. 'I tried to stick it out with him. But he turned out to be handier with his fists than he was at pushing a pram.'

'Do you see him now?'

'That was one of my reasons for moving out of the city. He knew where to find me and often did when he'd had a few bevvies too many.'

'Couldn't you have gone back home then?'

'My mum's into her vodka more than she is having a teenage kid with a daughter of her own. She's not exactly ideal grandmother material.'

Rick thought about how nurturing his own wife was with Jaden.

'When she was drunk and out of it, my stepdad often got a bit too touchy-feely. If you know what I mean,' Lisa went on. 'It might be hard, but Izzy and me, we're better off on our own.'

He looked round him. If the girl really thought like that, then things must have been pretty rough before.

Lisa yawned. 'I guess we should get some sleep. I'm usually well in the land of nod by now.'

He guessed that sleep was a blessed escape from such a bleak existence.

'I've got blankets for us both,' she said, and padded across the floor to retrieve them from behind the sofa where the duvet had been stashed. 'This is a nice one.'

Lisa handed him a loosely knitted throw. It was nice. But it also felt cold and damp. Christ, this wasn't good for either of them.

'Going to risk the bathroom?'

'Yeah,' Rick said.

'It's at the top of the stairs. I put a clean towel out for you. Good luck. I'll boil a pan of water for us all in the morning.'

Rick took a candle and made his way up the stairs. Lisa was right. It was bitterly cold. In the bathroom, he did what he had to, but his resolve to have a good wash evaporated in the chilly air. He quickly rinsed his face in the icy water and rubbed it over with the threadbare towel. Tomorrow would be fine for him too.

Back in the living room, Lisa was already curled under a blanket on her chair. He did the same.

'It's a good job it's bedtime. I think the candles are just

about to give up the ghost.' She blew the remains of hers out. 'Night, Rick.'

'Goodnight, Lisa.'

'Sleep tight,' she said. 'Don't let the bed bugs bite.'

He felt like crying. Of course, he'd known that their situation was bad, he just hadn't realised quite how bad. He thought of his wife, and how much he'd like to be curled up next to her in his nice warm bed in his nice warm house. What he needed to do was talk to Juliet about Lisa and the child. See if there was something they could do to help. He should have done it long before. As soon as he got home tomorrow, he'd sit Juliet down and tell her all about it.

# Chapter 47

It's the weekend before Christmas, and I've still got so much left to do that you wouldn't believe it.

Normally, I won't go near the shopping centre this close to 25 December, but needs must. Chloe and I are going together, which undoubtedly means that my darling daughter is more than likely to swan off shopping by herself and leave me to wrestle Jaden's pushchair in and out of the shops. Believe me, there's going to be a serious regime-change round here when the second baby arrives. We're taking my mother too, which I think is a bad idea, but I've left her alone enough with Dad this week, and he needs a break too.

From the radio, it sounds as if the main roads are cleared now and the snowploughs and gritters have, finally, been out and about. Rick called first thing to say that he was making his way home, but that progress was slow on the country lanes. I'd hoped that he'd be here by now. As usual, there's no sign of Tom, and I didn't want to leave Dad by himself.

'Chloe,' I shout up the stairs. 'Aren't you ready yet?'

'Keep your hair on, Mum,' comes the reply.

My mother appears at the top of the stairs and gingerly makes her way down. It breaks my heart to see how frail she's becoming and how quickly. This is not the same woman who just a short time ago was taking on the outback of Australia with a toy-boy lover.

She stands in front of me now dressed in pink ballet flats that I think must be Chloe's. Beneath a floral skirt, she's wearing grey trousers and her jumper is on backwards, the pretty embroidered design gracing her shoulder blades rather than her bosom.

'I don't think that's quite right, Mum,' I say. 'You look as if you got dressed in the dark.'

'Do I?' She stares down at the trousers and skirt, seemingly perplexed at how they got there.

'Let me turn your jumper round.'

She strokes the front. 'This is new. The purple sweater I had before was embroidered with flowers.'

'You've got it on the wrong way round. Here, let me help.'

Without protest, she lifts her arms and I tug it off and then swizzle the jumper round until the embroidery is in its rightful place.

'You could take the skirt off too, Mum. It looks better with just the trousers.' Again, she doesn't move while I unbutton the skirt and then I help her step out of it. 'That's better.' But when I look up, I see that my mother is crying. Silent tears roll down her face.

'Oh, Mum. Don't cry. It doesn't matter. You look lovely now.'

She starts to sob. Her small shoulders shake and I take her in my arms. 'I think your father has another woman,' she blurts out.

'What?' Hadn't seen that one coming.

'He talks about someone called Juliet all the time. I think he's in love with her.'

'Mum, I'm Juliet,' I say.

'You're Juliet?' She stares at me, aghast. 'He's in love with *you*? But you're young enough to be his daughter.'

'That's because I *am* his daughter!'

Mum looks at me blankly. It frightens me that there's no recognition whatsoever in her eyes.

'He's my dad,' I explain patiently. 'I'm your daughter, Juliet.'

'I wanted to look nice for him,' she continues, sniffing sadly. 'He doesn't look at me the way he used to.'

Wearing all of your wardrobe at once is never going to attract the kind of looks that she wants, but how can I begin to explain that? Instead, I simply hold Mum tightly. It's no good: I need to take her to see the doctor. Perhaps there's something he can do for her. If this is Alzheimer's, then there are tablets you can get to help, aren't there? Or are they something else that has disappeared with the cutbacks? It's a nightmare to get an appointment to see our doctor at the best of times, and now I wonder if I'll even be able to get a slot at the surgery before Christmas.

'We're going shopping, Mum,' I remind her. I fish in my pocket and find a slightly crumpled but not much used tissue, and I wipe her eyes and face with it. It takes me back to when she'd do this for me as a child, except my mother would spit

260

on the tissue first and rub much harder. 'It'll do you good to go out. I'll treat us both to a nice cup of tea.'

Her face brightens. 'And cake?'

'Yes. Of course we can have cake.'

Chloe bounces down the stairs, Jaden in her wake. 'Bloody hell, Gran. Have you been nicking my shoes again?'

Mum looks down at her feet and, again, seems surprised at how her shoes have got there.

'Chloe,' I admonish. 'Leave your gran alone.'

'Yeah? See what you say when she starts pinching stuff out of *your* wardrobe.'

'She doesn't know what she's doing,' I whisper to her. 'Be kind.'

Chloe softens. 'If you're going to wear my shoes, Gran, let me pick them with you. I've got nicer ones than that.'

My mother looks pleased by the thought, while I realise that I never imagined there would be a time in my life when shoes would become such an emotive issue.

'Let's get going,' I say. 'Otherwise we'll never find a parking space.' We're just about to bundle out of the front door when I hear the sound of a key in the lock.

It's Rick. Home at last.

'Hello, love,' he says. 'Made it.'

He looks exhausted, drawn. I give him a hug and feel my body tremble as we touch. I knew that I'd missed him overnight, but I hadn't realised how worried I was about him. 'I'm glad you're home.'

'The journey was terrible, and I had to borrow a spade to dig the van out of the snow. Nightmare.'

'It looks like you've hardly slept a wink, too,' I note.

'Gan-Gan,' Jaden says, holding out his hands.

Rick lifts him up and hugs him tightly to him. 'How's my little man?' Rick asks, and I'm surprised to see his eyes filling up with tears. 'I missed you.'

'Dad's getting soft in his old age,' Chloe quips.

'Play trains, Gan-Gan?'

'Later, Jaden,' I intervene. 'Grandad will play later.' Now he looks like he needs a good rest. Then to Rick, 'We were just on our way out. You can have a bit of peace for a couple of hours.'

'Do you really need to? The roads are still pretty bad.'

'We're only going as far as the shopping centre. It's my last chance before Christmas.' We're not closing the office until the day before Christmas Eve, and I'll be too busy cooking on the 24th to contemplate doing anything else. 'I won't stay long. Dad's still here. Can you keep an eye on him for me? I've given him his breakfast and he's watching *Saturday Kitchen*.'

Rick nods. 'Perhaps I'll take him out and get a Christmas light for the front of the house for Samuel. If he's feeling up to it.'

'That'd be nice. But don't overdo it.'

'Let's get going,' Chloe says. 'We're missing valuable retail-therapy time hanging about here.'

I kiss Rick. 'See you later, love.'

Then, as Chloe takes Jaden outside, Rick pulls me to one side. 'Juliet, can we grab five minutes to have a chat later?'

'Of course we can. Is everything all right?'

'It's fine. Just something on my mind.'

'You look so tired,' I say, stroking his cheek. 'Why don't you go and have a nice hot bath and a lie-down? Did you not sleep well at the pub?'

Rick shrugs. 'So-so.'

I touch his arm. 'Take it easy today. You've had a busy week, and next week's not looking much better.'

'I might do that.'

He looks teary and emotional. Not like Rick at all. 'Are you sure everything's OK?'

'Yeah. Nothing to worry about.' But, despite his reassurance, I still feel unsettled. 'Was everything OK here?' he says.

'Yes, yes. Fine.' I decide that now's not the best time to tell him that we had another night-time intruder around his beloved shed.

Then Rick's phone beeps that he has a text message and we both stand and look at each other, but he makes no move to answer it. That's the point when my stomach goes cold and I wonder whether he was really snowed in at Cublington Parslow, and if he spent the night at the pub at all.

# Chapter 48

Rick did as instructed and had a long hot bath. As he lay in there, among the bubbles, he thought about Lisa and Izzy, who didn't have this luxury. When he got out, he rang Lisa's landlord again. This time the man made the mistake of answering his phone and Rick gave him both barrels on her behalf. Despite his being a customer too, Rick threatened the guy with Environmental Health, Trading Standards and *Watchdog*. He felt a lot better for doing so. Hopefully, that should motivate him to go and fix Lisa's boiler. He promised that he would. If not, he might well send Merak round there in his leather jacket and mean sunglasses. See if the threat of the 'Russian mafia' could motivate him to some compassion. He might take pleasure in going round to see the bloke himself.

Rick grabbed a quick half-hour kip while Frank was engrossed in his television programme. Again, spending a night in an armchair was all right every now and then – particularly when the alternative was sleeping in a cold van – but it made him fuming mad to think that Lisa and her child were forced to do that when they were paying bloody good rent for somewhere to live and they were just being abused.

When he finally went downstairs again, Frank was still sitting watching television with a cup of tea and a plate of biscuits by his side.

'Fancy going out to look for a Christmas light for Samuel, Frank?'

Juliet's dad looked up. 'In this weather?'

'We'll not go far. Just to B&Q. It'll give you a breath of fresh air.'

'I'll put my coat on then.' Frank ambled into the hall and Rick waited while he slowly shrugged on his smart black coat and placed his trilby at just the right angle. Even when Frank mowed the lawn, he always wore a shirt and tie.

In the van, they headed into the city centre and to the retail park, where a number of the big outlets were situated. The snow had stopped for the time being and the roads, while not great, were more readily passable.

Frank had to be the easiest company in the world. He just sat quietly in the passenger seat and watched the world go by. Rick had always got on well with Juliet's dad. He was no trouble at all. Her mother – well, she was a different kettle of fish altogether.

The two men toddled round B&Q together and looked at Christmas lights. Now that there was less than a week to go before the big day, the store looked like a plague of locusts had been through it. All the shelves had been picked clean of Christmas products but, thankfully, there was still a reasonable choice of lights left and – even better – they were now half price. There was nothing to compare with the audacious display that Neil Harrison had assembled, but Rick wasn't going to go down without a fight.

'See anything you think Samuel would have liked, Frank?'

Together they pored over the boxes. Rick favoured a rope light to thread through the hedge. The multicoloured one with variable programmes was especially nice. Frank was leaning more towards the illuminated silhouettes, and kept coming back to a flashing HO-HO-HO in shocking pink.

'That, I feel,' Frank said, stroking his chin, 'would be very Samuel.'

'Why don't we do up the shed in Samuel's honour?' Rick suggested. Why hadn't he thought of it before? 'We could really go to town then.'

He realised that Neil Harrison wouldn't be able to see it from his house, but that was hardly the point.

Frank smiled and his eyes filled with tears. 'That'd be lovely.'

So they did indeed go to town, buying silhouettes, rope lights, a white sparkling star and even a stylised Christmas tree with a star to fix on the top. When they'd filled a trolley with their purchases, Rick pushed it towards the small café in the centre of the store.

'Fancy a coffee here, Frank, while I just run off for five minutes and do a few chores?'

'Oh, yes,' Frank said. 'Have they got any biscuits?'

Rick bought him a cappuccino and chocolate-chip cookie and left his father-in-law looking after the trolley and flicking through a home furnishings catalogue that someone had left behind on the chair. Now that Frank was gay, Rick assumed that he'd be more interested in cushions than he'd previously been. He could also be completely wrong. Still, he needed a few minutes to himself, and Frank was always more than happy to entertain himself.

Across the road from B&Q there was a big Matalan store. Rick bolted over there, weaving in and out of the queues of traffic waiting to go into the car park. There was a lot of honking of horns. The store was hot and crowded, and he felt panic sweep over him. Present-buying had never been his strong suit. He had no idea what Lisa and Izzy might like for Christmas, but he felt that he should get them both a little something. A token. He suspected there wouldn't be much Christmas cheer in their household this year.

Not really knowing what he was buying, he picked up what looked like a good thick jumper for Lisa. He was sure it was the sort of thing that Chloe would wear, so he hoped that meant it was trendy. For Izzy, he picked out a little outfit with matching trousers, sweater and hat. He avoided the obvious pink and went for something a little more serviceable in navy with yellow trim.

There was a monster queue snaking halfway round the store, but it moved quickly and minutes later he was heading back to find Frank and pay for the Christmas lights. Merak collecting that money from his customers had helped to take a weight off his shoulders, and there was certainly less pressure on his finances than there had been. It gave him a lightness in his heart that he hadn't previously realised was missing. He was only glad that he'd been able to give the lad a bit of a

Christmas bonus too. Help him out. It was only right. He certainly deserved it.

Frank was still sitting there waiting patiently when Rick returned. They paid for the lights – another queue – and were just heading for the car when Rick's phone rang. It was Juliet.

'Rick,' she said, sounding totally stressed. 'I need you to come quickly.'

Cold dread gripped him. 'What's wrong?'

'I'm in the shopping centre. John Lewis's. Just get down here as fast as you can. You won't believe what's happened.'

# Chapter 49

I'm still frantically searching John Lewis's when Rick arrives. I grab hold of him. 'I've looked everywhere,' I say. 'Not a trace of her.'

Mum has gone missing again.

'They're putting out announcements for her, but nothing yet.'

'How long has she been gone?' Rick wants to know.

'Nearly half an hour now.' It's packed up at the shopping centre. Everyone is shuffling along cheek by jowl. Chloe had stopped to look at one of the make-up counters, and I was so worried about losing Jaden that I took my eye off Mum for one second and she'd gone.

'I've tried her mobile, but that was a dead loss. It's not switched on.' I've told her a thousand times about that, but she doesn't listen. If I'm honest, I don't even know if she's got her phone with her.

'We'll find her, love,' Dad says. 'Don't you worry. Her legs aren't that fast. She can't have gone far.'

'Chloe's looking in Middleton Hall.' There's a busy Christmas market there with lots of little stalls selling festive trinkets and food. We walked through there earlier and, despite the crush, Mum loved it all. It's not beyond the realms of possibility that she's wandered back to it. I have Jaden held tightly on his reins.

'We should be used to this now,' Rick says. 'I'll go with Frank and take the left-hand side of the shopping centre first. You just keep looking here in case she comes back.'

Then, just as we're about to split up, my mobile rings. It's my mother's number, but on the other end is a policeman. He has called the number that we registered under ICE – In Case of Emergency – on Mum's phone, and I'm so glad we took the time to do that now.

'We're with your mother in Campbell Park, down by the Grand Union Canal,' the officer says. 'She's a little confused.'

I heave a relieved sigh. 'We've been searching high and low for her.'

'Well, she's safe now. Can you come and collect her?'

'We're just in John Lewis's. I can be with you in five minutes.'

He hangs up.

'She's in Campbell Park, down by the canal,' I tell Rick and Dad. That's quite a walk, considering. I can't believe she's got that far.

'Let's get going then,' Rick says.

'I haven't finished my shopping,' Chloe complains when I phone her with the good news.

'Then you'll have to get a taxi back when you're ready,' I say.

'Can't you take Jaden?'

'No. We have to go right now.' I hang up before I hear the inevitable tut. For once, Chloe will have to look after her own son. I can't deal with my daughter's selfishness now. I just want to know that Mum is all right.

Rick, Dad and I pile out of the shopping centre and, in our separate vehicles, set off down to the park.

It's a pretty place. There's a hill at one end where there are always kite-flyers. At the other end, a string of brightly painted narrowboats is moored on the canal. That's where we're headed now.

Minutes later, I see the police car and pull into the car park. As the police are there, I try not to spin the wheels. Rick and Dad are right behind me in the van.

Mum is sitting in the back of the police car with a woman officer. She has a blanket round her and she's drinking tea from a plastic cup. I rush over to her.

'Mum,' I say. 'Are you all right? How did you get down here?'

She looks at me blankly.

'It's Juliet. Your daughter.'

'Juliet said she was taking me shopping.'

'I did, Mum.' I'm close to tears. 'You wandered off when I wasn't looking.'

She turns to the police officer for confirmation and the woman nods.

'Did I?'

'We've been worried, but we've come to take you home now. We'll have a nice cup of tea.'

'I've got a cup of tea,' she answers. 'But it's not very nice.'

'I'm sorry,' I offer to the policewoman.

She smiles. 'It's OK. My colleague got her one from the burger van just up there.' The policewoman nods in the general direction of the man I must have spoken to on the phone. 'As long as she's safe and sound.'

I help Mum out of the car. 'Thank you. Thanks so much for looking after her.'

'Glad to help. You'll be all right now, Mrs Britten,' she says to Mum in a voice you would use for a child. Then the police officer lowers her voice as she speaks to me. 'You can get a personal locator alarm, you know. Very helpful if your mum's taken to wandering off on her own.'

'Thank you. I didn't know. This has only started recently, but it sounds like a good idea.' I give her the blanket back. Mum's coat is missing. 'Where's your coat, Mum?'

She shrugs. 'I haven't got a coat.'

'You were wearing your blue one.'

'I don't think so,' she insists.

'Here, love,' Dad strips off his coat. 'Put this round your shoulders. You'll catch your death.'

His choice of words make me wince, but he wraps his coat tenderly around Mum and guides her to my car.

'Thank you, young man,' she says to Dad, and we both exchange a worried glance.

'Jump in,' I instruct. Then to Rick, 'I'll take them both back with me. My heater's more efficient than yours. Do you think I should take her to the hospital for a check-up?'

'No,' Rick says. 'That would be even more traumatic. Let's just get her home. Don't look so worried. She's fine now. No harm done.'

But I am worried. Very worried indeed.

# Chapter 50

Dad's safely ensconced in front of *Deal or No Deal* with tea and biscuits. My mum's tucked up in bed with hot chocolate, her knitting and *Neighbours Omnibus* on the little telly.

Now Rick and I are sitting at the kitchen table drinking tea. What I want is brandy, a double. My nerves feel shredded by this morning's drama.

'We need to get something sorted,' I say to Rick. 'Mum's becoming a bit of a liability. The police officer suggested we get her a personal locator alarm so we could always find her.'

'A straitjacket would work too.'

'Rick.' I tut at him. 'Don't make fun. What if she'd got completely disorientated and fallen in the canal?'

'Really, Juliet,' he says, 'we couldn't be that lucky.'

'This is serious,' I admonish. 'And you know that, beneath it all, you love her. You'd be horrified if anything happened to her.'

'I know,' Rick sighs. 'We *will* do something. As soon as Christmas is over. Until then, we'll just have to keep a closer watch on her.'

'I'll phone the doctor later, and book her in to see him whether she likes it or not.' I can no longer bury my head in the sand and just hope that everything will be OK. It will be better if she can get professional help, I'm sure. 'I turned my back for two seconds.' I feel so guilty. 'While I was sorting Jaden out. I don't have enough pairs of hands.'

'Or eyes in your backside,' Rick agrees. 'Now that your mum needs you to look after her more, Chloe's just going to have to take on her own responsibilities.'

'I don't know how she'll manage when she's got two to look after,' I admit. 'That worries me too.'

'You can't worry about everyone.'

'But I do. Where's Tom, for instance? I haven't seen him for days. Who knows what he's up to.'

'I can hazard a good guess at that,' Rick suggests. 'It's *who* he's up to it with that's a more difficult question. That changes on an hourly basis.'

I sigh audibly. 'I'm just looking forward to Christmas so that I can have a rest and some relaxation.'

'We can keep your mother filled up with advocaat so she spends most of the holiday comatose on the sofa.'

It's true that she does rather like a snowball cocktail with a bit of extra brandy in it and a squeeze of lime juice. We try to keep her off the gin, as that makes her fighty. In some ways I prefer her when she's being obnoxious to when she's bewildered. It's horrible to see her like that. Alzheimer's is a cruel disease, and I still don't want to believe that this is what's wrong with Mum. It's like watching a photo of your loved one slowly fade in front of your eyes.

I put my head in my hands and bite my lip to keep the tears away. 'She will be all right, won't she?'

Rick comes to sit next to me and slips his arm round my shoulders. 'She'll be fine. She's just getting old, love. It happens to the best of us.'

'It's more than that, Rick. Getting old means aching bones when it's cold, or walking around looking for your specs while they're on your head, or running upstairs for something and forgetting what, or getting up in the night to wee. That's getting old. This is something worse.'

He lets out a weary breath. 'You're probably right.'

'I know I am.' I fill up again. 'I'd hate to think that this might be her last Christmas with us. I couldn't bear that.'

'There's plenty of life in her yet. And your dad. But we are going to have to look after them a bit more. It suddenly creeps up on you that they're not managing quite as well as they did.'

'Dad's OK, though?'

'When is your dad ever any trouble? We had a nice run out to B&Q, chose some lights for Samuel. Pink.' Rick shrugs at me. 'Your dad's choice. I'm going to do up the shed a bit. Thought Frank might like to help.'

'Don't let him get cold, though.'

'No. I'll get started out there when I've had this cup of tea, before it gets dark. I might see if Merak wants to come round and give me a hand. I don't know that the lad does much at the weekend.'

'I'm only making some curry for tonight. He's more than welcome to stay if he wants to.'

'I'll text him.'

As Rick reaches for his phone something clicks in my brain. 'This morning you said that you needed to talk to me.'

'Did I?' Rick avoids my gaze. 'Can't remember now.'

'It wasn't important?'

My husband shrugs. 'Can't have been.'

I kiss him on the cheek.

'What was that for?' he asks.

'I know you're not a big fan of Christmas,' I say to Rick, 'but it could be the last time the family are all together. Mum or Dad might not be here next year. Tom could leave home. Again. When Chloe's had her new baby she might want to move out into her own place – either with or without Mitch.'

'Chance would be a fine thing.'

'I don't know. Anything could happen between now and next Christmas.' I can't even voice the thought that I'm worried that my husband will still be here, or whether he'll be somewhere else enjoying Christmas with a new family. Tears spring to my eyes.

'Don't get upset,' Rick says as he thumbs my tears away. 'We'll never get rid of this lot, love. We just keep adding to the numbers.'

Sniffing attractively, I lean into him. 'Let's make it a really good one.'

'Of course we will.' He wraps his arms around me, and I can't believe that this man would ever do anything to hurt me. But, yet again, I let the opportunity to voice my fears pass by. I just enjoy being held, and try not to fret about a future that may not happen.

I want us all to have fun together, the way families should. I want to forget our troubles, and for Rick and I to be close once more. If nothing else, I want this Christmas to be truly memorable.

# Chapter 51

While Rick is out in the garden with Dad – putting what looks like a huge selection of lights on the shed – I decide to do some housework. I want everywhere looking lovely for Christmas.

Our bedroom is the worst mess. That needs a serious mucking out. Ever since I came home drunk and disorderly from the office party, I've been finding Christmas confetti all over the flipping place in there. It's stuck in the rug, under the bedside tables and everywhere else you can think of.

Dragging the hoover upstairs, I check that Mum's not fallen asleep, then I set to. I give the bathroom a good scrub, and then carry on into Chloe's room while she's still out. I check my watch. I thought she would have been back by now. I'll give her another half an hour and then I'll text her. Jaden will be exhausted, and I hope that he's managed to catch his afternoon nap in the buggy.

There's a little pile of clothes on the side, tiny Babygros, bootees and socks. We stored them all in the loft when Jaden grew out of them, and last week I got Rick to bring them all down again. Now they're washed and ready for Chloe's new arrival. I press a little jacket against my face. They smell of nothing but Lenor Pure Care fabric conditioner, but soon they'll smell of milky baby. How lovely! I hold up a white sleepsuit and marvel at how tiny it is. Was Jaden ever that small? Then I think of my own daughter. It hardly seems like five minutes since Chloe was this size. Now look at her: one child of her own already and soon to be a mother of two herself. A tear comes to my eye and I blink it away. It will be lovely to have another little grandchild to mollycoddle. I hope this time it's a girl. We'll know soon enough. Still, I can't sit here all afternoon, daydreaming. Must get on. I pile the clothes together again.

Back in my own room, I start to vacuum. Every time some of the confetti goes up the spout, the hoover rattles. What was I thinking, for heaven's sake!

As I'm pushing the hoover around, deep in thought, I hear the front door bang and it's my daughter finally arriving home. I hear her thump up the stairs with Jaden and a second later, the door flies open.

'Nan-nan!' Jaden shouts, and flings himself into my arms. I lift him up and cuddle him.

'Get all your shopping done?' I ask Chloe.

'Yeah. Sort of.' She flops down on my bed and Jaden wriggles until I put him down next to her. He cuddles into her side and yawns. Looks like he missed his nap. 'I bumped into Mitch.'

'Oh?'

'He wants to take me out tonight. Is it OK if you look after Jaden?'

'I'm exhausted after losing your gran, Chloe.'

'It's not as if you have to do much,' she protests. 'He'll be asleep.'

'Can you make sure he's bathed and in his pyjamas, then?'

'I've got to get ready.'

'Oh, Chloe.'

'When am I going to get the chance to go out after this?' She stares down at her bump. 'I'm going to spend the rest of my life staying in.'

I don't point out that, because of Chloe, her father and I spend most of our lives staying in!

'This is what you've signed up for, Chloe.'

'I know. I'm just trying to put off the inevitable,' she confesses.

That makes me laugh. 'You don't look like you've got long to wait.'

'I'm a waddling monster,' she says. 'I can't even believe that Mitch still wants to see me.' Then she looks up at me, and I see fear in her face and soften. 'I haven't been very nice to him, have I?'

'No,' I say.

'I do love him.'

I stroke her hair, the hair that has always been her pride and joy, the hair that I used to spend hours happily brushing and plaiting. 'Then it's time to show him.'

'Good,' she says. 'Then you will babysit?'

Inwardly I sigh to myself. 'Of course I will.' It may curtail my own plans, but a date with the ex sounds like a good idea to me. Mitch is a good man and is a steadying influence on my darling daughter – when she lets him be. I'd like to see them back together again, and if babysitting my adorable grandson will facilitate it, then I guess I shouldn't mind doing it.

She bounces up and gives me a kiss. 'Thanks, Mum. Love you loads.'

The term cupboard love has never been applied to anyone more fittingly than to Chloe.

'Aren't you going to ask how Gran is?'

'Oh, yeah. Is she all right? Where did she get to?'

'She'd wandered off to Campbell Park. But she's fine now.'

'You're going to have to put her on a lead like Buster,' she notes. 'You'll be going bonkers like that, soon.' She waddles out, Jaden in tow.

'Thanks, Chloe,' I mutter under my breath. 'And it's you who'll be driving me mad.'

I hoover ferociously. What am I going to do with her? What on *earth* am I going to do with her? I never brought her up to be like this. At some point I'll just have to stand back and let her get on with it, do things her own way. I can't make Chloe share my standards, and I do try to appreciate that it has all changed since my day. But I can't help but have Jaden's welfare as my top priority.

Bending down, I shove the nozzle under the bed. There's a load more confetti there. Grumbling, I get down on my hands and knees to make sure that I get it all.

Then, under the bed, tucked at the back on Rick's side, I spy a Matalan carrier bag. It's clearly something he's hidden there. Oh, that is so tempting! I know I shouldn't, but I'm dying to have a look. I've given no hints at all this year, so I've no idea what Rick might buy me. I only want something small, and I've told him that. With all the other expense we've got on, it's silly for the two of us to exchange presents. Neither of us really needs anything, and I'd rather make sure that everyone else has something they want than spend money unnecessarily on each other. I've got Rick some new jeans and a smart shirt. Not exactly exciting. But it could easily have been aftershave and socks.

Checking the door, I pull the carrier bag from under the bed. I hold it in my hands, knowing that I shouldn't peek, yet unable to resist. This is a bad thing to do. I'd be cross if Rick opened a secret present that I'd bought for him. I try to look into the carrier bag without opening it completely, but can't see very much. Finally, the temptation is too much to bear and I open it.

Inside there's a lovely sweater, the sort of thing that Chloe would wear and in a very small size. I don't think this can be for me. Does Rick really think I'm that tiny? Holding up the jumper, I know it won't go anywhere near me. But it's very pretty, so maybe I can exchange it for a bigger size. Underneath it, there's a child's outfit. Has he bought this for Jaden? I can't think why Rick would do that. Normally, I buy all our grandson's clothes – he has nothing to do with it, other than pay up. Plus this looks a bit girly with its lemon trim and, again, way too small. Jaden is quite a bruiser of a boy. I don't think this will do for him at all. Perhaps the jumper isn't for me, after all. It could be for Chloe. Perhaps he thought she'd need something nice once she's shed her baby weight. But I'm usually the one responsible for family present-buying. Why would he get something and not tell me?

Shall I ask him? Then maybe we could change them for the right size, before Christmas. But then that would spoil the surprise. Or should I just pretend I haven't seen it?

Eventually, I decide on the latter. Putting the clothes back in the bag, I secrete it away again under the bed. At least Rick's tried. That's nice. I'll just have to look suitably surprised on Christmas Day.

# Chapter 52

It's the day before Christmas Eve, my last day in the office for two weeks, and I don't know where the time has gone. At Westcroft's, we're finishing at three o'clock and then having a glass of wine and some mince pies in the office. I meant to make the mince pies with my own fair hands, but I ran out of time and had to shoot to Budgens instead. But when I get home tonight, I'm definitely going to set to in the kitchen.

Robin is doing the rounds of the staff, topping up glasses. I hand round the mince pies. Someone's hooked up an iPod and Coldplay's 'Christmas Lights' wafts into the office. It's been a good year for Westcroft's, and everyone can leave for the Christmas break safe in the knowledge that they have jobs to come back to next year. There's a good atmosphere, and all the team laugh and joke together. I realise that I'm lucky to work in a place where everyone gets on so well. Spirits are high, and I suspect that the Christmas bonus, modest though it is, will still be burning a hole in most of the staff's pockets. Wine drunk and mince pies eaten, gradually everyone drifts away and, by five o'clock, I'm left doing the washing-up in the little kitchen at the back of the office.

Robin comes in and picks up a tea towel and rubs pensively at the glasses I've already put on the draining board.

'I can manage,' I tell him.

'I quite like drying up,' he says. 'Very therapeutic.'

'Come round to my house any time. You can have all the therapy you need.'

He laughs at that. 'Of course, I'm speaking as a person who doesn't have to do it very often.'

'I'd gathered that.'

'All ready for Christmas, Juliet?'

'Nowhere near.'

'We've run out of time though, now.'

'I'm going to have a frantic dash round tonight and tomorrow,' I say. 'Get all the little outstanding bits done.' I stop washing up and glance at my boss. 'What about you?'

He shrugs, but doesn't offer a reply.

'Things at home any better?'

Robin shakes his head. 'Not a lot.' He studies the glass he's wiping, avoiding my eyes. 'It's just the two of us on Christmas Day. We normally go out for lunch with friends. I didn't think I could stand the tension this year, so I volunteered to cook. I hope it works out all right.'

'I'm sure it will.'

He takes the dish mop from me and puts it on the draining board. His hand goes to my face and he strokes it wistfully. Then, just as unexpectedly, he drops it to his side again. 'Go home, Juliet. You have more than enough to do. I'll finish off here.'

286

'Are you sure?'

'Go home to your family.'

I strip off the rubber gloves and smooth down my skirt. 'Have a lovely Christmas, Robin.'

'Next time I see you, it will all be over.'

'I guess so.'

John Lennon sings 'Happy Xmas (War is Over)' as I shrug on my coat. I don't really want to leave Robin here alone – he seems so melancholy, and no one should be feeling sad at Christmas. But I have things to do, family to organise, presents to wrap, mince pies to rustle up, and I must go.

'You will be all right, Robin? Won't you?'

'I'll be just dandy.'

'Call me,' I say. 'If you're not, call me.'

'Merry Christmas, Juliet.'

'Merry Christmas, Robin.'

Looking sadder than I've ever seen him, Robin raises a hand as I open the door and step out into the cold.

At home, Mum and Dad are watching *Midsomer Murders*. It looks as if they may have been on the sofa since I left the house this morning, and it pains me to see that Dad's world has grown so small again since Samuel has gone. I hope, in time, that he'll find his zest for life again, that he'll want to travel and eat at good restaurants and won't while away the rest of his years watching terrible daytime television. I, on the other hand, am quite happy for my mother never to venture farther than the living room, so that I know exactly where she is at all times.

'Hello, love,' Dad says. 'Busy day?'

'So-so.'

'Shall I come and make you a cup of tea?'

'I'll do it,' I say. 'You stay where you are.'

'Some exercise wouldn't go amiss. Haven't moved all day.'

Thought as much.

'Go easy with the milk,' Mum instructs. 'You're too heavy-handed. You make tea that tastes like rice pudding.'

Dad and I roll our eyes, and then he follows me through to the kitchen.

'Seen anything of Chloe and Jaden today, Dad?'

'She's gone out with a friend of hers,' Dad says. 'Said she wouldn't be long.'

I shouldn't be anxious when she takes Jaden out by herself, but I am. I can't help it. That girl has lost six mobile phones in the last year, and I do worry that she has the same casual attitude towards her child.

Glancing at the clock, I wonder what we might have for dinner. 'What do you fancy to eat?'

'Oh, you know me, love. I'll eat anything.'

'I've got some ham, and we could have a jacket potato.' It's not very exciting, but I think of all the rich food we'll eat over the coming days and decide that something simple would fit the bill.

'Sounds good to me. I'll set the table. Are we a full house?'

'Your guess is as good as mine, Dad.'

Rick should be home soon, and Chloe. Goodness knows where Tom is. I don't even ask any more.

'I'm going to make some mince pies later. Want to give me a hand?'

'Lovely,' Dad says. 'My pastry's as light as a feather.'

'I'm thinking of doing Delia's lattice-top ones.'

'Haven't tried those,' Dad admits, 'I'm a Michel Roux man myself. But I'm up for it if you are.'

Suddenly tears spring to my eyes. 'You are all right, Dad, aren't you?' I go and hold him tightly.

'Me?' Now his voice is choked too. 'I'm champion, love. Don't you worry about me.'

'But I do.'

'Rick and I are going to do up his shed tomorrow,' Dad says. 'All fancy. In Samuel's memory. That'll be nice.'

'He'll be with us this Christmas, you know that. We won't forget Samuel.'

'He'll be livid if he doesn't get Christmas pudding, wherever he is.'

My mum's shrill tones come from the living room. 'There are people dying of thirst in here!'

'If only,' Dad quips.

'Better get that kettle on,' I say as I give him a last little squeeze.

Rick arrives as it boils. He looks tired. I think the fact that it's taking so long to get to and from his job due to the heavy snow is making it a long day.

'No Merak?'

'The lad's working in the bar again tonight.'

'Are you sure he's going home for Christmas?'

Rick shrugs. 'That's what he said. But I can't say he's

mentioned it again. He hasn't told me if he's booked a flight or anything. I'd give him a run to the airport if he needs it.'

'Oh, Rick. Why didn't you ask him?'

Another shrug from my husband.

'I don't want him to be alone over the holiday if he's not.'

'We've only got a couple of hours' work to finish off in the morning. I'll check with him then.'

'You spend all day, every day together. Don't you two ever talk to each other?'

'Not really. We're blokes.'

'You never talk to me, either,' I complain.

'Hang on, Juliet,' he says, wearily. 'I'm hardly through the door. I've not even taken my coat off yet.' Then he pauses, and a serious expression clouds his features. 'Actually, there was something I wanted to discuss with you ...'

But before he can continue, the front door bangs open, sounding like it's coming off its hinges.

'Mum! Mum!' Chloe shouts.

I hear the pushchair hit the frame. Rick is already complaining how many chunks are missing out of the paintwork. That'll be another one gone. I dash out into the hall.

'What's wrong?'

My daughter is standing there pale-faced, shell-shocked. 'It's coming,' she says. 'The baby. This time it's *definitely* coming.'

# Chapter 53

'Good job I haven't taken my coat off,' Rick says, and we both help Chloe out to the car.

I go back and retrieve her overnight bag from her bedroom. After the last false alarm, I made sure that she'd got everything ready to take with her. This time I think she's right. Judging by the time between her contractions, the baby is already on its way.

By some miracle, Tom answered his mobile phone the first time I tried him, and he's come straight home in order to take Jaden to stay overnight with Mitch. The logistics of moving everyone around in this family gets more complicated every day. Why is it that no two people ever need to go in the same direction at the same time?

'Are you sure you'll be all right while we're out?' I ask Dad.

'Off you go, love. I'll take care of everything here. You just concentrate on Chloe.'

'I'll ring you as soon as we know anything,' I promise.

'Good luck, love.' He kisses Chloe.

'Thanks, Grandad.' She clutches at her belly. 'Let's get going. I'm not going to be able to hold this kid in for much longer.'

If only labour were so easy.

Dad waves us off. When I help Chloe to walk down the drive to the car, Rick is already in the driving seat, revving the engine. Chloe climbs into the back, moaning softly. I jump in too and off we go. My husband drives like the wind across the city. All the main roads have been cleared of snow, thank goodness. Though now night is falling and, along with it, the temperature, it is starting to ice up again. Despite that, less than half an hour later we're turning into the car park at Milton Keynes General Hospital.

Patiently, I help Chloe inside while Rick feeds the pay-and-display meter. Grabbing a wheelchair in Reception, I escort her up to the maternity ward, pushing her as briskly as I can.

But when we get there, a shock awaits us. 'Sorry,' the harassed-looking nurse says. 'We're full.'

'Full?' I query. 'You can't be.'

'It seems that a lot of our babies have decided to come in time for Christmas.' She glances at us sympathetically and then looks at the clipboard she's holding. 'There's room at Stoke Mandeville.'

'That's miles away.'

'It's the nearest hospital with free beds on the maternity ward,' she assures me.

'Mum!' Chloe is looking panic-stricken.

'Calm down, darling,' I say. 'Everything will be fine.' But inside I'm pumping adrenalin.

'I want to stay here.'

'Will you take her there by ambulance?' I ask.

'No ambulances either,' the nurse admits. 'They're mostly out at traffic accidents because of the weather. It'd be quicker to drive over there. You could do it in forty minutes, easily.' She tries to give us a comforting smile. 'These babies never rush themselves. It'll be plenty of time.'

I think back to Chloe's last labour, when she was pushing and shoving for the best part of twenty-four hours. My daughter might think she's in a desperate hurry, but these things *do* take time. There's probably hours and hours to wait yet.

By this time, Rick has joined us from the car park. 'What's the problem?'

'No beds,' I explain. 'We're to take her to Stoke Mandeville.'

'I don't want to go to Stoke Mandeville,' Chloe complains.

'It's a lovely hospital,' the nurse interjects. 'I'll phone to tell them you're on your way.'

'Bloody government cuts,' Rick rages. 'I pay my taxes!'

'Not now,' I sigh. 'They can't just magic beds out of thin air. Let's just get going.'

He tuts. A lot.

We wheel Chloe back into the car park and load her into the car. It's a bitter night, and the snow is developing a nice crust of ice.

'I'm not taking the wheelchair back,' Rick grumbles and, just to make a point, he dumps it in the car park.

Slowly, we make our way through Milton Keynes and out towards the village of Stewkley and then on to Wing. The roads are becoming much more treacherous. Once we leave the edge of the city and the main roads, the snow-clearing has obviously been much more sporadic. Rick has his satnav on, and it's speaking to us in measured tones. It must be the only thing in the car that's not panicking. For the first time in my life, I'm hating snow.

'How far?' I want to know.

'It's not that far. About twenty-five miles in total,' Rick says. His face bears a grim expression. 'But it's going to take a while tonight.'

'Mum!' Chloe wails.

'Hang on, darling,' I tell her. Reaching into the back seat, I grab her hand. She squeezes mine tightly. 'We're going as fast as we can.'

'Fucking hospitals! They're useless.'

I have to agree with her. This is the kind of stress that no one needs when they're about to have a baby.

We're heading out towards Aylesbury and then on to Stoke Mandeville. Due to the atrocious weather conditions, it's nearly an hour later and we're not yet halfway there. The car wheels slip and slide alarmingly. The snow has started again and splats against the glass, fat and wet. The windscreen wipers set up a steady battle to swish it away.

Rick and I exchange a worried glance. This is much worse than I thought. In the back seat, Chloe has stopped complaining and is crying softly.

'Nearly there,' I say to her, even though I might be lying. I glance at Rick, and the returning shake of his head tells me that I am. 'Not long now.'

Chloe cries out in pain. 'It's coming,' she pants. 'I know it is.'

'Just try to keep calm.'

'I DON'T WANT TO KEEP CALM,' she yells. 'I WANT THIS FUCKING THING OUT!'

'That's not going to help, Chloe. Try to breathe deeply and relax.'

'*Fucking relax*,' she mutters to herself. '*Fucking relax*.'

There's not much traffic out in this weather, but that's not what's holding us up. It seems that most people have, quite sensibly, stayed off the roads. Only those – like us – with emergency journeys would venture out in this. We head out to Wing along the bypass, settling into two clear grooves in the snow. My stomach is tense with anxiety for Chloe. Childbirth should be a pleasant, uplifting experience. But, let's face it, it never is. Doing it like this adds a whole other layer of stress and danger.

'I thought this way would be quicker,' Rick says anxiously. 'It's a shorter distance, but maybe I should have stuck to the main roads.'

'We'll be fine,' I say determinedly. 'Just fine.' Perhaps we should have had one of those paddling-pool births at home. But Chloe was never keen to go down the natural route. She likes to be knocked out at the start of it all and, I think, preferably be revived shortly after the child's twenty-first birthday.

Chloe cries out again. If these *are* contractions, then there's not much time between them at all. 'It's coming. Really it is.' She's whimpering now. 'Do something, Mum. I don't want my baby to be born in the car.'

Reaching back, I hold her hand. 'Just hold on a bit longer,

295

love. You're doing really well. Not too far now.' I still have no idea if that's true. We don't seem to be making very good headway at all. 'Rick?' I glance across at my husband.

'A little while yet,' he says somewhat crisply.

'It's coming,' Chloe insists and shouts out again. 'It is. The head's popping out.'

'Are you sure?'

She nods.

'Take deep breaths,' I say. 'Relax. Relax.' I make whooshing noises with my breath.

'How can I *fucking* relax,' she shouts. 'I'm about to have my baby in the back of the *fucking* car!'

Fair point. I'm trying to stay calm and think what to do. If only we had one of those 'Beam me up, Scotty' machines to speed us to Stoke Mandeville. If only Milton Keynes hospital could have had a bloody bed free.

'I'll turn down here,' Rick says. 'It's a short cut through the back roads.'

We turn off the main Aylesbury road and into the country lane that takes us through the tiny hamlet of Broughton. There's not much here but a smattering of cottages.

Soon the street lights disappear, the cottages thin out to a trickle and the black night envelops us. Thick, wet snow smacks persistently against the windscreen. There's nothing around us but open fields. We go over a small humpback bridge that spans the Grand Union Canal, and Chloe cries out.

'I can't wait,' she says. 'This is it.'

'Pull over, Rick,' I instruct. 'I'll get in the back with Chloe.'

'Don't stop,' Chloe says. 'Put your foot down!'

I fear it might be too late for that.

'There's a car park just up here beyond the bridge,' Rick says. 'We went for a walk along the canal from here last summer. I'll swing in there.'

He pulls in. The car park is dark, secluded and – Rick is right – borders the canal. At this time of night and in these conditions, there's not another living soul around. Rick parks up over by the deserted picnic tables. I jump out of the car and nip into the back seat. Chloe is pale and sweating.

'Slip off those leggings,' I instruct, 'and we'll have a little look at what's going on.'

Chloe, for once, does as she's told without protest. She's breathing heavily now.

She struggles out of her clothes and lies back on the seat so that I can have a look. Rick switches on the interior light.

'Oh, my goodness,' I say when I look at Chloe. My mouth goes dry. 'The head's crowning.'

'I knew it,' she wails. 'I knew!'

'I don't think we can go any farther, Rick,' I tell him. 'We'll have to do it here.'

'No!' Chloe cries out. 'I don't want my baby born in the car.'

'Can't we look for a farm, or something?' I ask. 'Perhaps there's a barn nearby.'

'She's not the bloody Virgin Mary, Juliet,' my husband snaps. 'Even I can tell there's no time. We'll have to cope. I'll phone the emergency services.'

Without waiting for further argument, he punches 999 into his phone.

'Breathe,' I say to Chloe. 'Remember what you did last time.'

'Last time I had every drug known to man,' she reminds me, 'and it still hurt like fuck!'

'You can do it,' I assure her, gripping her hand tightly. 'You can do it.'

Chloe cries out. It looks as if she'll have to cope. This baby isn't hanging about.

'It's coming,' I say. 'I'll put my coat on the seat.'

'Use my fleece,' my daughter says. 'Your coat will get ruined!'

'That doesn't matter. Needs must,' I tell her. 'We'll need the fleece to wrap the baby in.'

I strip off my coat and lay it down. 'Settle back.'

'Don't let it happen here, Mum,' she pleads.

'There's nothing else we can do.' I grip both of her hands and make eye contact with her. 'Listen, Chloe. I want you to focus. We can do this. You're my brave girl. Right?'

She nods, despite the fear in her eyes. Chloe leans back against the door, legs out on the back seat of the car. Never before have I wished that we had one of those great big hatch-back cars that we could spread out in.

Rick, on the phone, talks to the operator at the other end.

'My daughter's just about to have a baby in the car,' I hear him say as I try to make Chloe as comfortable as possible. She's not panicking so much now, and seems a lot calmer. I, on the other hand, can feel perspiration running down my arms despite being in just a thin blouse. My palms are damp and I wipe them on my skirt. 'Can you please send an ambulance as soon as you can?' He reels off our location. 'I'm to stay on the line,' Rick tells me. 'I've got a lovely lady to talk to and she'll give us all the instructions we need.' I see a gulp go down his throat and know that he's as worried as I am. He pats Chloe on the shoulder. 'We'll just do as the operator says, and there'll be nothing at all to worry about. It will be a piece of cake.'

'Pass my handbag,' I tell him. In there I have some gel wash that I keep for cleaning Jaden's sticky fingers. Rick finds it and I squirt it onto my hands. I ignore my banging heart and my trembling fingers, and instead, smiling at Chloe, I ask, 'Ready for this, sweetheart?'

Tearfully, she nods back.

I choke back a tear too. 'Then let's deliver this baby.'

# Chapter 54

'Have we got any blankets or towels?' Rick relays from the operator at the other end of the phone.

'In the boot. There's a picnic rug and a plastic bag with a couple of clean towels in it.' I keep some old, scruffy ones for rubbing Buster down if he's got too muddy to be allowed into the car when we've taken him for a walk in the woods. They may not look their best, but at least they've just been washed. Who knew that they would come in so handy?

'I'm scared, Mum,' Chloe says.

'No need to be.' I sound so assured that I could almost believe myself. 'You've done it before. This may not be as comfortable, but you can cope.'

Rick comes back with the rug and towels. I wish he could get into the back with us as I feel as if I need all the hands I can get, but there's simply no room. 'Thanks,' I take them from him. 'Put the Christmas songs on the CD player. That'll keep us all calm.'

For once, Rick doesn't object and the sounds of Johnny

Mathis singing 'When A Child Is Born' fill the car. How appropriate!

'The operator says not to rush,' Rick offers. 'Take your time. Nice and slow. The baby will come in its own time.'

Chloe cries out again. Rick grabs her hand while mine are busy. 'Hush, love,' he says softly. 'Nearly there. Nearly there. Easy goes.'

Rick and I exchange a glance and I nod at him. The baby isn't that far away now, if you ask me, and we need a bit more of Rick's soothing voice.

'I'm frightened, Dad,' she says.

'No, you're not. You've got me and Mum here. We'll make sure it's all OK.'

'Thanks,' she sobs.

'Pant,' I say to Chloe. 'Short breaths. Only push down when you can't help but do anything else.'

My darling daughter does exactly as she's told. The sweary, belligerent version of her disappears and a focused, mature adult slips into her place.

'Come on, Baby Joyce,' I cajole. 'You can do it.'

Chloe bears down again, clutching at Rick.

'The head's coming,' I tell her. 'One more little push.' Both Chloe and I are sweating profusely.

Rick takes one of the smallest towels and mops Chloe's brow and then mine in turn. 'You're both doing really well,' he says. 'You're fantastic.'

Wiping the tears from my eyes with the back of my arm, I support the head with both hands. I can see tears rolling down Rick's face too. 'Not long now.'

Chloe, teeth gritted, pushes again.

'Good girl,' I say. 'It's here. Baby's here. The head's fully out.'

She gives a relieved sob while I glance up at Rick, anxiously. I don't want to worry Chloe, but this isn't as it should be. My heart races. Rick looks down and he too, instantly, sees what's wrong.

'The cord's round the baby's neck,' he tells the operator in measured tones. He waits for a reply and then says to me, 'See if you can slip a finger underneath it and then gently ease it over the baby's head. There should be enough slack.'

My fingers shake as I find the umbilical cord and try to release it. As Rick says, it isn't tight and I do it without fuss. Relief washes over me. The baby is out of danger and is now free to be born.

'One more push,' I say to Chloe. 'Good girl.'

Crying out, my daughter bears down and, a moment later, a slithering bundle of bloody, slimy life slides into my hands. 'That's it! You've done it.'

Chloe collapses in tears.

'The operator wants to know is the baby pink and breathing?' Rick asks softly.

The baby lets out a disgruntled squall that fills the car. It's a beautiful, beautiful sound.

'Oh yes!' My new grandchild kicks out and, fists balled, arms flailing, makes its presence in the world known. Bright pink and yelling.

'Wipe the mucus from the nose and mouth,' Rick relays.

I take one of the towels and gently wipe the baby's face,

which wrinkles up in disdain. I laugh out loud. Oh, this is going to be its mother's child!

'She says to put the baby on Chloe's chest and keep it warm. Don't touch the umbilical cord or the placenta, the paramedics will deal with that. They'll be here soon. Any minute. Just wrap the baby up and keep it warm.' Rick grins. 'The operator says, "Welcome to the world, Baby Joyce."'

'Tell her thanks for all her help.' I can hardly speak for crying.

'Thanks,' Rick says into the phone. 'Thanks so much.' Then he hangs up and, dropping the phone into his lap, sags back against the seat, eyes closed. That's one worn out grandad.

Swaddled in one of Buster's dog-walking towels, I place the baby on Chloe's breast. 'Well done, Chloe. I'm so proud of you.'

Chloe, still crying, cuddles her baby to her. 'What have I got, Mum?'

'You've got a little girl,' I tell her. 'A beautiful little girl.'

# Chapter 55

An hour later, and Chloe is in the back of an ambulance cuddling her new daughter in her arms. The baby has been cleaned and is wrapped up tightly in Chloe's fleece, which has, thankfully, replaced the dog's towel.

'It's a shame she wasn't born in a Porsche,' Chloe says, smiling down at her child. 'You can't really call a kid Corsa, can you?'

'No,' I agree. 'You can't.' *Definitely* not. I'll make sure of that. She hands my new granddaughter to me. 'She's beautiful. Look, Rick.'

My husband comes to coo over her too. The baby's little red face is screwed up against the light and cold and she looks like she's thinking of trying her lungs out again. Now that it's all over, Rick's looking tired and emotional too. All in all, it's been a very long day. If I didn't have my arms full, I'd give him the hug he deserves, but that will have to wait. Instead, I give him a peck on the cheek. 'Well done, love.'

'I think you had the starring role.'

'Couldn't have managed without you.'

'Chloe did well,' he says. 'I didn't think she had it in her.'

'Perhaps we need to give our daughter more credit than we do. She'll come good.'

While I have the baby, Chloe phones Mitch and tearfully tells him that he's a daddy for the second time.

The ambulance arrived minutes after the baby was delivered – by my own fair hands! – which was a huge relief. I've never been happier to see those flashing blue lights coming out of the darkness. The two-man crew came and dealt with the aftermath of the birth swiftly and professionally. Now they've checked that the baby is all right and that Chloe is too. They both said that they were impressed with my handiwork. By all accounts, I've done a good job. The baby is alive and well and has all her fingers and toes. That's all that matters to me. They're taking Chloe on to Stoke Mandeville hospital where a bed – somewhat belatedly – is ready and waiting for her.

The crew have given me a blanket to wrap around myself as my coat is beyond salvage.

When Chloe hangs up, she's smiling.

'Is Mitch pleased?'

'Yeah.' She shrugs self-consciously, but I can tell that she's proud of herself. 'He was worried about us.' She kisses my cheek. 'Thanks, Mum. Couldn't have done it without you and Dad. That was a bit hairy.'

'I'd rather you'd have done it the conventional way,' I admit. 'But it will be an experience you'll always remember. We didn't do too bad between us.'

'Thanks, Dad,' Chloe says.

'I just wish I could have got you to the hospital on time.'

'It all turned out OK in the end,' Chloe says in a rare moment of magnanimity. 'You're top parents.'

We all hug each other tightly. This is one night that I certainly won't forget in a while.

I go with Chloe in the ambulance, and Rick follows in the car. On the way, I phone Dad and Tom and let them know the news. Dad is all teary and Tom, typically, can't really hear over the noise from the bar that he's in. We settle Chloe into the maternity ward, where they're going to keep mother and baby in just for observation.

Baby Joyce – as yet unnamed – after her unscheduled rush into the world, is now fast asleep, quite possibly exhausted by the ordeal. It looks like Chloe's eyes are rolling too.

'We'll go home now,' I tell her, 'but we'll come back tomorrow as soon as we can.' My daughter looks so young in her hospital-issue gown that I can't believe she's now the mother of two children of her own.

'OK,' she yawns. 'Mitch said he'll come in too, and bring Jaden.'

That has to be good.

'Can I borrow your fleece to wear home?' It's a small price to pay, but my coat has not come out of this unscathed.

'Sure,' she murmurs.

I slip on the fleece and kiss Chloe goodnight, but she's already sinking into sleep.

I link my arm through Rick's as we walk back to the car and give him a squeeze.

'All's well that ends well,' I say.

'Could have done with a bit less excitement,' Rick confesses. 'I think that's just shaved a few years off my life.'

'It's given me a few more white hairs too.' I sigh and make a cloud in the cold air. 'Makes me feel old,' I admit. 'Being a grandmother to two children now.'

'You still look good to me,' he says.

I stop in the car park in the still falling snow. 'Do I?'

'Of course you do.'

This is not the time to ask him about the woman who's texting him. We've been through too much together tonight. Though it's eating away at me inside, it could be perfectly innocent and it would spoil the mood of tired elation. I give Rick a sideways glance. Could he really be having an affair? Surely, after all we've been through together, we are too tightly bound to let anyone come between us now. At our age, it isn't just splitting up, it's ripping your shared history apart. Family is so important to both of us: would Rick really want to do that? I can hardly believe it. There must be another explanation, and soon I must find the time to hear it.

'I do love you,' I say. 'Despite the fact that we're old and going grey and our knees ache and we can never find time to have sex.'

'You say the nicest things.' Rick puts his arm round my shoulders and pulls me in close. 'I love you too.'

And, this time, to my absolute relief, he sounds like he really means it.

# Chapter 56

Rick and Frank carried the Christmas lights they'd bought in B&Q from the garage out to the shed. The snow was thick on the ground and Juliet had insisted they both wear wellies. Rick was also under instructions not to keep Frank out in the cold for too long, or 'there would be trouble'.

In truth, he was still exhausted after last night's shenanigans with his new granddaughter making a dramatic entrance into the world. He was definitely getting too old for this sort of thing. But, the fact of the matter was, it was Christmas Eve and if the lights didn't go up today then they might as well go up in the loft for next year. As he'd bought these in honour of Samuel, it only seemed right to make the effort.

He'd called Merak first thing that morning to tell him that he wasn't going to be at work today. Instead, he'd spent an hour cleaning out the back of Juliet's car. This childbirth was a messy business. It was a good job the seats in there were wipe-clean rather than cloth. Juliet's coat was beyond salvation, of course, and he threw that straight in the bin. Perhaps he'd buy her a new one in the sales after Christmas. She'd like that.

Later that afternoon, they were planning a trip over to Stoke Mandeville to see Chloe and the baby at visiting-time. Merak had told him that he'd finish off the job they were on by himself and he'd picked up the van first thing while Rick was still in his pyjamas. He wondered again how he'd manage without the marvellous Merak in his life.

Together he and Frank piled the boxes of lights on the ground. Rick opened up the shed. He'd put power and light in here, and they were going to have to run the Christmas lights from an extension cable. Inside, he stopped in his tracks. On his sunlounger there was a folded newspaper. A copy of the *Sun*. Who had been in here reading a paper? No one in his house read the *Sun*. Had Tom been sneaking out here and invading his personal space? Except that it couldn't possibly be Tom, as his errant son didn't ever stay at home long enough to sit down to read a paper. Looking closer, behind the sunlounger, there was something that he didn't recognise on the floor too. A folded black jumper. A man's one. It must be Tom. Who else could it possibly be? But what was he doing out here? Nothing remotely useful, that was for sure.

'Want me to make a start, Rick?' Frank asked.

'Sorry, Frank,' he said. 'Went into a trance for a minute, there. Let's get a move on.'

So he went outside again and draped some of the lights around the edge of the shed, fixing them with hooks that he'd bought for the purpose. The star went above the door, and the pink HO-HO-HO across the window. The hedge that bordered the shed and the pond was threaded with more rope lights. The stylish Christmas tree was set adjacent to the door, which was framed with a pulsing rope. The Santa and reindeer silhouettes were fixed to the side of the shed.

When they'd finished, Rick plugged them in and the two men stood back and admired their handiwork.

They flashed, sparkled and glowed.

'Nice,' Frank said.

'Bloody marvellous,' Rick agreed, rubbing his hands together at a job well done. Stick that in your pipe and smoke it, Neil Harrison. It was only a shame that his neighbour couldn't see this splendid display from his house.

Juliet came down the garden with a tray bearing mugs of hot chocolate and mince pies for them. 'Looks lovely. Very colourful.' She hugged her dad. 'Samuel would be pleased.'

'I think so,' Frank answered and, surreptitiously, wiped a tear from his eye.

'Have you seen Tom come down here?' Rick asked her as he tucked into his mince pie.

'No. He's hardly been at home for weeks.'

Rick frowned. 'That's what I thought.' He brushed the crumbs from the front of his jacket. 'There's a jumper in there that I don't recognise, and a newspaper.'

'How odd. Perhaps we've got a ghost.'

'Perhaps we've got a tramp.'

'It's a very tidy tramp,' Juliet noted. 'There's never a thing out of place in there.'

'That's true.'

'Come on in,' she said. 'I don't want Dad getting cold out here. It's freezing today.'

'I've a few things to do,' Rick said. 'Can I take the car, as Merak's got the van?'

'You're not going to be long, are you?'

'No, no. I'll be back in plenty of time to take you to see Chloe.'

'I can't wait to see her, but I've got so much to do today.'

'I'll help you with it all just as soon as I'm back.'

He felt bad leaving Juliet but, right now, he just needed an hour to himself.

# Chapter 57

Dad made some mince pies while I was out last night. I have one with a cup of coffee – just for quality control purposes. While I do, I call the hospital and check that Chloe is OK. Mother and baby, I'm told, are both sleeping. That has to be a good sign.

I open this morning's pile of Christmas cards as I pick the last of the crumbs off my plate with a licked fingertip. Dad makes excellent pastry. He said that he'd made two dozen, but I can only find twelve – perhaps he was a bit muddled. I'll need to do some more myself later, but this is a good start.

Every day in the run-up to Christmas, the waterfall of post cascading through the letter box has grown. Final delivery today, so this is the last of our Christmas communications. There are cards from people we see nearly every day; ones from people we don't see from one year to the next. There are cards from people overseas we might never see again, and from those who live close by and wish we didn't have to. I am in charge of card-sending in the Joyce household. If it was left to Rick, we'd never send another one. And not just at Christmas. Birthdays, Valentine's Day, Mother's Day, Easter, you name it – would all go unmarked by my husband. But I think it's a nice way to keep in touch, to say to someone that at this time of year we always think of you. Rick says I'm just buying into the commercial pressure of a cynical greetings-card industry, but I like sending cards. I take time to write out a round-robin letter, updating our friends on the comings and goings of our family. Actually, I don't. I usually miss out most of what has been going on so that we sound better on paper. I'm not completely on board with this new fad of sending email cards where you make dancing elves of the entire family, or which open when a cute puppy bounces across the screen with a Christmas cracker in its mouth. That somehow seems like cheating. Give me an old-fashioned, sent-through-the-post Christmas card any day of the week.

Still, I can't sit here all day. I have a list as long as my arm of things that I must do before we go off to visit Chloe and the new baby. Christmas is one deadline that can't be moved. Where to start? I consult my list. I've forgotten even what version this is as there have been so many. There are a few, last-minute presents to wrap, and I want to change all the bed-linen.

Then I hear Mum shouting, and a second later she cries out. As I'm about to fly to the living room where the noise is coming from, Dad pops his head round the door.

'Can you come quickly, love?' he says. 'It's your mother.'

In the living room, Mum is huddled into a corner of the sofa, knees drawn up to her chest.

'Go away,' she shouts. 'Don't touch me.'

There's a wild, disconnected look in her eye that frightens me.

'Mum? What's the matter?'

'I don't know what started her off,' Dad says, perplexed. 'One minute she was fine, the next she was like this.'

I go towards the sofa and she kicks out at me. Jumping back, the heel that's aimed at me just misses.

'Rita, love,' Dad says, distressed. 'Don't upset yourself. It's Juliet.'

'I don't know who she is, Frank. Don't let her hurt me.'

'I'm not going to hurt you, Mum. I only want to know what's wrong.'

'She's put me in a home, Frank. This isn't my house. Where's my house? I want to go home.'

Mum starts to cry now.

'You've been living here with us, Mum. Your family. With me, Rick, Chloe and Jaden.'

She looks over at Dad, her face a total blank. I might as well be speaking a foreign language.

'Take me home, Frank,' she says, flinging her arms out for Dad. 'Don't leave me here.'

'I'm not leaving you. I'm here with you.'

'I want to go home,' Mum reiterates. 'I want to go home to my house.'

I risk sitting on the sofa. 'You're safe here, Mum. We can look after you.'

She swings a punch at me, which I duck, but she manages to grab a handful of my hair and pulls it with a strength that she doesn't look like she possesses.

'Ouch!' Then she lets go and bursts into tears anew. Now what to do? I rub at the tender patch on my scalp. Dad looks at me for inspiration, but I have none.

'I don't know what to do,' I tell him.

'Take me home,' Mum sobs. 'Take me home. I'm frightened here, Frank.'

Now Dad sits next to her. 'No need to be, Rita love. You're all right with me. I'll look after you. I've always looked after you, haven't I?'

Mum nods pitifully, and it breaks my heart to see her like this.

Dad turns to me and drops his voice to a whisper. 'Perhaps I should take her back to the house for a couple of hours,' he suggests. 'See if she'll calm down. We could have a little walk up there.'

'The pavements are like glass, Dad.'

'We'll take it slowly.'

'I can't let you take her when she's like this. What if she turns on you?'

'She won't,' Dad says, more certain than I am. 'I'll take her back home for a little lie-down. Perhaps it'll reassure her.'

'She hasn't lived there for nearly three years, Dad. What if she doesn't recognise that house either?'

'Don't talk about me like I'm not here,' Mum snaps. 'I want to go home.'

'Just for an hour or two,' I say. 'I'd rather drive you, Dad.' I'm worried that once she's outside, Mum will try to make a break for it and Dad won't be able to give chase. I can't contend with her doing a runner today, on top of everything else. 'Are you sure you'll be all right with her?'

'Fine,' Dad assures me. 'Let me do this, Juliet. It'll give you a little break too. You've got enough to worry about.'

'I've got to pop to Budgens for some fresh stuff, cream and the like. I could drop you off at the house then. Shall we do that?'

'I think it's for the best,' Dad says. 'We can get out of your way for a couple of hours and come back later.'

'I'm going to see Chloe this afternoon,' I remind him.

'You give her our love,' he says. 'I can't wait to see our new great-grandchild. Did you hear that, Rita? We're great-grand-parents again.'

'We are?' She looks terrified by this prospect too.

But I wonder how we'll manage when Chloe comes home and there are two babies in the house and my mother, who is rapidly losing the plot, and my grieving father to care for. And I think that, perhaps, it's me who's the one who should be the most terrified of all.

# Chapter 58

The shed was looking very nice. Flashy even, but Rick had already realised that there was one major problem with having such an elaborate display in your back garden. Your neighbours couldn't see it.

As much as he hated to admit it, and as much as he'd tried to convince himself that it didn't matter, the truth was that it was troubling him that all that flashing, strobing and sparkling was going on and Neil Harrison couldn't even see it. Would it look too obvious if he invited the bloke round for a festive beer in his shed just so he could get an eyeful? Perhaps it would.

Rick was driving out to see Lisa and Izzy to deliver their Christmas presents. He'd taken the liberty of lifting some of Frank's mince pies in the hope that Juliet wouldn't notice, and he'd also picked up the now customary bag of groceries from Morrisons on the way.

The roads were clearer now as there had been no fresh snow overnight, and the temperature had risen fractionally.

He was making good time. Soon he pulled up outside Lisa's house and, as always, she flung open the door the minute she saw him.

'I can't stay,' Rick said.

'That's always the first thing you say,' Lisa admonished.

'I know,' he apologised, 'but I'm always in a rush and I've got a million things to do today.'

'You shouldn't have bothered about us.' Her sharp chin jutted out defiantly. 'We're fine. We can manage.'

'I didn't mean that,' he said, following her into the kitchen in what had become their usual way. She put on the kettle without asking, and he plonked the groceries on the counter. 'I wanted to see you both. Wish you a Merry Christmas and give you these.'

Rick held out his gift-wrapped presents. As he hadn't even told Juliet about Lisa and Izzy, he could hardly ask her to wrap their presents for him. So he'd sneaked some paper and had taken it down to the shed and done it himself. They looked like they'd been wrapped in the dark by a cack-handed octopus.

Lisa smiled at him. 'You shouldn't have, Rick.'

'It's just a little something. Nothing much at all.'

'It's a lovely thought.'

'Look, Izzy, Rick brought us presents.' The little girl was wide-eyed. 'What do we say?'

'Thank you, Uncle Rick.'

'You're welcome, sweetheart.' Tea was handed to him. 'Keep them for the morning.'

'I will. I'd put them under the tree if I had one.' Lisa

laughed hollowly. 'One year I'm going to give Izzy the best Christmas *ever*.'

'I'm sure you will.'

'Thanks again for the groceries, Rick. It'll be a lot better now than it would have been.'

He shrugged. 'I hope they'll keep you going.' Rick didn't have to look to be able to tell that the cupboards wouldn't be groaning with festive fayre like the cupboards at Chadwick Close. 'What are you doing tomorrow?'

'Nothing much,' Lisa said. 'Watch rubbish telly. Izzy hasn't seen *Bedknobs and Broomsticks*, so I hope that's on.'

'It's always on,' Rick assured her. 'It's one of Jaden's favourites.' He sat down – just for five minutes. It was rude to dash in and straight out again. 'Have you got a turkey?'

Lisa shrugged. 'I haven't bothered this year.'

'Look in the bag,' he said.

'Oh, Rick!'

'It's only a small one.' It was a crown or something, ready stuffed, with rashers of bacon on the top and enough for four, it said. 'I didn't want you to be eating it for days.'

If he'd thought ahead, he could have asked them both round for Christmas Day – goodness only knows, there was always enough food on their table for a few extra mouths. But how would he explain Lisa and Izzy's existence when, in all the time that he'd known the girls, he hadn't once mentioned them? The less he'd said about them, the worse it had become, and he'd never found the right moment to explain it all to Juliet. Now he felt terrible that he'd left it so long and that the two of them were to be alone in this *still* bloody freezing house.

319

'I'm gonna move out after Christmas,' Lisa said as if reading his mind. 'I've had enough. Izzy can't stay here any longer.'

'No,' he agreed. 'I think it's the right thing to do.'

'I shouldn't have stayed here all this time,' she admitted, 'but you think the best of people, don't you?'

'I guess so.'

'Well, come January, I'm outta here.'

'I'll help you all I can.'

'I know you will, Rick,' she said solemnly. 'I don't know what we would have done without you lately. I hoped you'd drop by, as we've got you a little present too.'

'You shouldn't have.' She handed him a tiny package.

'It's nothing much. This is from Izzy, really. She wanted to give you something. You're lucky because you nearly got her favourite toy, her Dora the Explorer phone.'

'No home should be without one.' They laughed at that.

'Shall I open it now?'

'No,' she said. 'When you're alone.'

He drained his tea. 'Now I really do have to go. I've a new granddaughter to visit.'

'Really?'

'An unexpected arrival, last night. We didn't make the hospital in time, and Juliet and I delivered the baby in the back of the car.'

'No way!'

'She's a lovely little thing. Six pounds something.' He couldn't really remember as last night had all been a blur, but he knew that these things matter to women. As dramas went, he could have done well without it and, no doubt, he'd have a few more grey hairs to show for it. Still, he was proud at how they'd handled the situation in the end and, thankfully, no harm had come to mother or baby. It had been much easier when his own kids were born, though he couldn't now, for the life of him, remember what weights they'd been either. 'No name as yet. I'm taking Juliet to the hospital this afternoon.'

'Then you'd better get a wiggle on.'

Rick ruffled Izzy's hair. 'Be a good girl for Santa.'

She nodded, but Rick suspected that there wouldn't be much Christmas cheer here tomorrow, no matter how hard Lisa tried. He headed to the door, and Lisa stood on tiptoe to kiss his cheek.

She sighed. 'I wish I'd had parents like you. My life could have turned out very different. Your kids are very lucky.'

'We just do our best for them. Nothing more.'

'Well it seems like you do a pretty good job to me.'

'Merry Christmas,' he said.

'Thanks, Rick. Merry Christmas to you.'

In the van, he read the label. *To Uncle Rick with love from Izzy*. Lisa had obviously written it, and she'd signed it for them both too. She'd put two kisses next to her own name. Rick opened the tiny present. Inside the cheap wrapping paper was a much-loved, grey Tatty Teddy that needed a wash. Across its tummy was a red sash that said I LOVE YOU WITH ALL OF MY HEART.

It brought tears to Rick's eyes and a lump to his throat. They had nothing, and yet still they wanted him to have this. The bear had clearly been one of Izzy's prized possessions, and now it would be one of his.

# Chapter 59

While I'm waiting for Rick to come home, I clean the oven. You don't want to be putting a turkey in a grubby oven now, do you? Cranking up the Christmas carols on the CD player, I get cracking with the Mr Muscle.

Reluctantly, I dropped Mum and Dad off at their house. When I went inside to settle them, it felt cold and unloved as Dad hasn't really been home since Samuel died. Now I'm worried sick about them both.

I cranked up the central heating for them and Dad was going to light a fire in the living room to warm that up. I also gave Dad some of the mince pies he baked in a cake tin so that they can have some with a cup of tea later. As soon as we're back from the hospital, I'll drop by and collect them.

Mum seemed to calm down pretty quickly once she knew they were going home for a while, but I'm anxious about what the future holds. I don't want them to go back to that house on their own, and Mum seems to have completely forgotten that she left Dad years ago. Sighing to myself, I think, 'Parents. Who'd have them?'

At home in the kitchen, I sit at the table alone nursing a much-needed cup of tea. The rare experience of being totally alone allows my feelings to flood in and swamp me. I sense that my family is unravelling. Everything is slowly fragmenting. I don't know what's going to happen to us – to Chloe, to Tom, Mum, Dad, Rick. The pressure of it is building up like steam in a pressure cooker, and I don't know how long I'll be able to hold it all in. They all come to me to solve their problems but, increasingly, the questions seem to be harder and I don't know the solutions. The older I get, the more complicated life becomes and the fewer answers I seem to have. Where is the wisdom that is supposed to come with age? Perhaps it's like Santa – a big fat lie that we all buy into.

Still, I can't sit here feeling sorry for myself. I've things to do, and I must get on. So I slip on my rubber gloves, thinking that I'll tackle the washing-up in the sink first. I switch on my Christmas songs in the search for some succour.

From the work surface, Judy Garland sings 'Have Yourself A Merry Little Christmas', and her urging to let my heart be light has me undone. My heart is not light. It's as heavy as a stone. I want this to be a fabulous Christmas. I want all of our hearts to be light. Mine, Rick's, Chloe's, Tom's, Mum's and Dad's. But I suspect that they're not. I want Chloe to be happily married, have a proper family with husband and children. I want Tom to find a fulfilling career and someone to love. I want to see Dad smile again and travel the world. And I want Mum to be well once more. But more than all that, I want

Rick to be my husband for the rest of my life and for him not to run off with someone who may be younger than some of the knickers I have in my underwear drawer. I sink to the floor, marigolds and all. Then I cry. I sob my heart out on the tiles amid the dusting of icing sugar on the floor that my father has failed to clean up after his mince-pie baking spree. I want my family to be happy and healthy. I want everything to be wonderful. Is that too much to ask?

# Chapter 60

By the time Rick comes home, I've pulled myself together again. The oven is clean, but the window of opportunity for baking mince pies has passed. Good job I picked up a few extras in the supermarket. Mr Kipling, you are my knight in shining armour!

'All right?' Rick asks. He regards me suspiciously.

'Yes, fine.'

'You haven't been crying?'

'No, no, no. My eyes are stinging from the oven cleaner.'

'Where's Frank and Rita?'

'Mum had a bit of a meltdown,' I tell him. 'They've gone back to Dad's house for a couple of hours to see if he can settle her.'

'That doesn't sound good.'

'No,' I agree. 'She didn't know who I was, or even where she was. Incidents like this are getting more regular. I phoned the doctor, and she has an appointment after Christmas. I hope there's something they can do.'

'Let's not worry about that now,' Rick says. 'We'll just make sure that we give her a good Christmas.'

'Thanks.' Rick has always had a tetchy relationship with my mum because she can be so damned difficult, and he doesn't think that she appreciates all that I do for her. Even after twenty-seven years of marriage, she never hesitates to tell me that I could have done better than Rick. I look at him now and don't think that I could. He has been the rock of this family through thick and thin. 'I know that you love her really.'

'She's your mother. *You* love her, and that's enough for me.'

She *is* my mother. And she may well be a tricky customer, but I hate to see her like this.

He rubs his hands together. 'Now, are you ready to go and see the baby?'

'I can't wait.' That's true enough. I'm dying to get over to the hospital as soon as possible. I wonder, will this baby hold a special place in my heart, as I had a helping hand in bringing her into the world?

'Me neither,' Rick confesses. A grin breaks out on his face. 'Our new granddaughter is a little smasher.'

'We did a good job.'

'So we did.' Rick puts his arms round me and we hold each other tightly.

'Chloe did well too.'

'Perhaps she's made of sterner stuff than we give her credit for,' Rick acknowledges. 'She's got you to thank for that. You've been a great mother to our children. I hope they appreciate that.'

'I'm sure they don't at all,' I say.

'Well, I do.' Rick gazes into my face, and he's not a natural gazer. 'I want you to know that.'

'Thank you.' I look at my husband tenderly. This is not a man who's thinking about walking out on us, surely? We have so much binding us together. Where else would he find the depth, the layers of love that his family offer? I don't like to think about that.

'We'd better get a move on then.'

As always, our family commitments, those that knit us together so closely, are the same ones that so often keep us apart. Reluctantly, we let go of each other.

'I'll get my boots on.'

Minutes later, we jump in the car – the car which has seen so much action in the last twenty-four hours – and, once again, head off to Stoke Mandeville hospital. The journey is certainly less fraught than the last one, and we arrive with the same number of passengers we started out with. Always a bonus.

In the maternity ward, Chloe is sitting up in bed. She's now wearing her own nightie rather than a hospital issue and Pooh Bear is gracing the front. I think she would look only marginally less out of place in the children's ward, and my heart squeezes with love for the mother who is still little more than a child herself. It's nice to see that Mitch and Jaden are here to meet the new arrival, and Mitch is cuddling the new addition to their . . .

I stop and sigh to myself. I was going to say their family, but that's hardly right. They're not a family any more. Jaden has Chloe's surname, and I wonder what this baby will be called. Surely Mitch won't insist on her having his surname – he didn't with Jaden – so she'll also be a Joyce. But it can't be easy for him, having a different name to his children.

'Hello, love.' Both Rick and I kiss Chloe, and then I peer into the bundle of hospital blankets that my granddaughter is swaddled in.

'Here you go, Juliet.' The ever affable Mitch hands her over.

'She's so beautiful.' Not to be left out, Jaden slides onto Rick's knee.

'We were just talking about names,' Chloe says. 'I was thinking Pepper, or Meadow.'

Out of the corner of my eye I see Rick recoil in horror. There's a flinch from Mitch too.

'What about Laken?' she continues pensively. 'That's nice. Or Rihanna?'

'What about something seasonal,' I suggest, 'to mark the fact that she's a Christmas baby? There's Ivy, or Joy. Or what about Carol?'

'Are you mad, Mum?' It's fair to say that Chloe looks unconvinced.

'You could call her Cracker,' Rick suggests, and we both glare at him.

'Holly,' Mitch chips into the discussion with a firmness I've not heard from him before. 'I like Holly. I like Holly a lot.'

'That's a lovely name,' I interject. '*Really* lovely.' I dig Rick in the ribs.

'Oh, yes,' he pipes up. 'Beautiful. Modern, without being ...'

*Stupid* is the word that's left dangling.

'Festive without being frivolous,' I add. 'It would be a nice reminder that she was born at Christmas.'

'Yeah?' Chloe holds out her hands for her daughter, and I duly hand her over. 'What do you think, Baby? Would you like to be called Holly?'

Cradled in her mother's arms, the baby blows an enormous spit bubble.

Chloe laughs. 'I think that's a yes.'

There's a collective sigh of relief around the bed.

'They say I can probably come out tomorrow,' Chloe tells us. 'With a bit of luck I'll be home in time for Christmas lunch.'

'That'll be lovely. I'd better set an extra place then.'

'I'll keep Jaden overnight,' Mitch says. 'That way I can see him open his presents in the morning. Just let me know what time you want me to bring him back.'

'Mum,' Chloe says, 'Mitch could come and stay for lunch, couldn't he?'

'Of course he can. There's no need to ask.'

Mitch smiles. 'That'd be great.'

'Come round whenever you're ready. I'm planning to make lunch for about two o'clock.' I look at my watch. 'We'll leave you to it now. Dad will come and get you when you're ready to leave in the morning. Just text us.'

We say goodbye to baby Holly, making an extra fuss of Jaden, then arm in arm Rick and I walk back to the car.

'So,' he says. 'Mitch is back in favour.'

'Looks like it. Let's keep our fingers crossed.' I sigh happily. 'It's nice to have everyone together for Christmas.'

'Have we got a big enough turkey?'

'The turkey's more than big enough,' I promise. 'But I will be sure to peel some extra potatoes.'

# Chapter 61

The minute we get home from the hospital, I call Dad.

'How's Mum? Any better?'

'Fine,' Dad says. 'She's upstairs in bed, sleeping like a baby.' I don't point out to Dad that babies usually scream the place down rather than sleep – something we are soon to be re-acquainted with chez Joyce. 'I think we'll stay here overnight, love. If you don't mind. The place is looking a bit neglected. I can do a bit of tidying around while I'm here.'

'Are you sure?' I'm not liking the sound of this plan at all. I've grown accustomed to my parents being in the next room, where I can keep an eye on them. 'I'll worry about you.'

'Don't. We're fine. Honestly. We'll come back in the morning, in time for Jaden to open his presents. I wouldn't want to miss that for the world.'

It's a good job that Jaden is spending the night with Mitch, otherwise I'm sure we'd be unwrapping his presents at four in the morning.

'I'll get Rick to come and collect you about ten,' I tell him. 'Chloe will be coming home with the baby too.'

'That's grand,' Dad says, and I can positively hear him swelling with pride even down the phone.

'What about tonight? Can I bring you some dinner round?'

'All sorted, love,' Dad assures me. 'I got something out of the freezer earlier. I can just heat it up when your mum wakes.'

'Are you *absolutely* sure?'

'You and Rick enjoy a quiet evening to yourself, for once. You'll be busy enough tomorrow.'

That's certainly true. 'Promise you'll phone if you need me.'

'Promise,' Dad agrees.

I hang up, still worrying at my fingernails. 'Dad says they're going to stay there.'

'They'll be fine,' Rick assures me. 'We're five minutes away.'

Before I can voice my anxieties further, Tom breezes in.

'Hi, Mum,' he says. 'Can't stop. Big night.' He stuffs a mince pie whole into his mouth.

'Someone *has* told you that it's Christmas tomorrow?' Rick asks.

'Chill, Dad.'

'You *will* be here for lunch, won't you?' Now it's my turn to nag him.

'Yeah, yeah.' He kisses me. 'Just don't make me wear the paper hat, though. Totally naff.' This is a tradition that I like to insist on. 'What time?'

'Twelve,' I say. Given that Tom excels himself at lateness, that gives him a good window to make it here just as the turkey hits the table. 'You're not sleeping here tonight?'

'No. Better offer.' He grins at me as he takes another mince pie, wisely exiting the kitchen before Rick's head comes off. Then he bounds up the stairs, taking two at a time. Within five minutes he bounds down again in a different shirt. He shouts, 'Laters!' and is gone again, banging the door behind him.

'He gives me a headache,' Rick says, rubbing his temples.

'Stop!' I hold up a hand. 'Listen to that.' There's not a sound in the house. Absolutely nothing.

'*Silence*,' Rick says, perplexed. 'When did we last have that?'

'I don't know. I think it was possibly the late eighties.'

'I normally have to lock myself in my shed to find such all-encompassing peace.'

'You know what this means?' I wiggle my eyebrows at him while he stares at me blankly. 'We have the house to ourselves tonight. Just the two of us.'

'And Buster,' Rick adds.

I concede. 'And Buster.' Obligingly, the dog thumps his tail against the floor, assuming that if his name is mentioned, then it must be time for food or walkies.

'Wow.' My husband breathes the word with awe.

'Wow indeed,' I say, excited now. 'This is a fantastic opportunity. I can make us a nice dinner – *just the two of us* – and then we can have a few hours of peace and quiet. I think we deserve it after all that's happened in the last few days.'

'I'm not going to argue with that,' Rick says.

I don't say it out loud, but it could be the last time for months – *years* – that we're on our own, and I think we should take advantage of it. I should make an effort. Show

Rick that we can still have passion and spontaneity in our lives, once we get rid of the family for the night. This could help to bring us back together as a couple. Remind us of how we once were. Now that I'm on a roll, I think Rick and I will have a very romantic candlelit dinner, perhaps open a bottle of champagne. And I haven't forgotten that I still have some very sexy lingerie in my drawer upstairs that I bought for our abandoned trip to Bruges. If I've got any energy left later on, Rick could well be in for an early Christmas treat.

# Chapter 62

I have run round like a thing possessed for the last few hours, and now I finally believe that I am ready for anything that Christmas can throw at me. No: I shouldn't say that. It would just be tempting fate. All I want is a lovely, quiet Christmas at home with my family with no arguments, and no Rick threatening to put his foot through the telly if we have to watch any more repeats. I would just like everyone to be nice to each other and to end the day without blood on the carpet.

Tonight, we're having a quick pasta dish for supper and a salad – saving up all my calories for the onslaught of food tomorrow. Plus on our only free night for the foreseeable future, I don't want to spend the entire evening cooking. My Delia lattice-topped mince pies have gone unmade, and I can only hope that I've got enough bought ones in the cupboard to see us through to Boxing Day and thus avoid a mince-pie crisis. The fizz is chilling in the fridge. Doesn't 'chilling' sound so much better than 'getting cold'? I, on the other hand, am getting warm with a long soak in the bath that has been squeezed into the proceedings. A thrill of excitement runs through me. I haven't felt like this in ages. It feels like Rick and I are on a 'date night'. Something that I believe is very popular with the likes of the Beckhams, but is not widely embraced in Chadwick Close.

When I'm dry, I slip on the sexy lingerie, which I'm pleased to see still fits despite the amount of Christmas cake and mince pies I've eaten over the last few weeks. Then I remember that tucked in the back of the drawer – away from prying eyes and little fingers – is a sexy red feather boa and matching hand-cuffs. I laugh to myself and drape the boa round my neck, pouting in the mirror. Could be the last chance I have to get my money's worth out of these babies.

Sex is funny when you've been married for twenty-seven years, and I don't mean funny ha, ha. How do you still find excitement, lust, in a body that is every bit as familiar to you as your own? Any form of regular sex life is now but a distant memory. Rick and I are usually just pleased to have survived another day intact, and any thoughts of joining our bodies together requires more effort than is feasible and is, by necessity, way down the list of Things To Do. Though we normally try to mark high days and holidays. Birthdays never go un-celebrated, though sometimes it might be a week or two after the actual date.

I can't say that Rick and I have ever really had a wild time in the bedroom department. We peaked in the back of Rick's car when we were teenagers. Tom was born just after we married. Chloe pretty soon after that. There's nothing more destined to banish passion than a toddler or two crashing into your bedroom at an inopportune moment. There have been a few crazy occasions, but only a few. We once made love on a beach as dusk was falling. I can't remember where, now. It wasn't anywhere white-sand exotic like the Caribbean or the Maldives. I think it was in Newquay, in the days before it was populated by well-heeled sixth-form students being sick. Rick complained a lot about the sand. He's never been a big fan of sand. I think it was being regularly buried in it by the children whenever we were on holiday that put him off. I always fancied being taken at the edge of the sea with the waves crashing over us like Burt Lancaster and Deborah Kerr, all very *From Here to Eternity*. It never happened. And I don't remember Burt Lancaster complaining about the sand.

I can tell when Rick wants sex now, as he has a shower and a shave before he comes to bed. When we were younger we would tumble into bed, heedless of what our breath smelled like or whether I would end up with stubble rash. I wouldn't care whether my make-up was scrubbed off or if the light was on. But it can't stay like that, can it? Passion must surely diminish with the passing years. The best we can do is hope to tickle our fancy with a festive feather boa and that we still make it to bed by twelve so that we're not too tired to function tomorrow. After half a lifetime together, I guess we should be glad we have the urge at all, no matter how infrequent.

Slipping on a dress and heels, my seduction outfit is complete. In the kitchen, I pull out all the candles I can find, including the IKEA bag of a hundred tea lights that every home harbours, and fill the room with them. I'm still lighting them all when Rick returns from walking the dog.

'Bloody hell,' he says. 'Are we having a romantic dinner, or are you planning on burning down the house?'

'Don't be a killjoy. I'm getting us in the mood.'

'Right!' Rick rubs his hands together. 'Have I time for a shower and a shave?'

'Ten minutes. I'll put the pasta on now.'

He slips his arms around my waist and hugs me. 'This is a nice idea. We don't do it often enough.'

We don't do it *ever*, I want to reply, but decide to keep my mouth shut.

# Chapter 63

The pinger on the oven goes and I shout up the stairs, 'Dinner's ready!'

Rick appears in the kitchen seconds later. He has even put on smart jeans and a crisp white shirt.

'You look lovely,' I tell him.

'Thought I'd make the effort.'

I can't believe that Rick is having an affair. Apart from the frequent mystery texts, there's nothing in his behaviour to suggest that he's anything but the same husband he has been for the last twenty-seven years. He's just as solid, just as caring, just as grumbly, just as infuriating. Perhaps I'm just being paranoid. If he is thinking of straying, then I hope tonight will show him that he still has a wife who is hot, hot, hot! We just have to find the time to fit the hotness in among everything else.

While I serve the pasta, Rick opens the champagne. We're not natural champagne drinkers, and only ever buy it when it's on offer in Morrisons. Rather than making me want to dance on tables, it usually has me dozing off.

On cue, Rick yawns. 'Sorry, love,' he says. 'It's been a tough few months. I can't wait for this break.'

Normally Rick hates the enforced downtime that Christmas brings in his job, but he's right – this year he needs some time off to relax. Though how much of that will be done with a new baby in the house is another matter. I can see him spending a lot of time in the shed.

I put some soft music on the CD player – not Christmas songs, for once, but a bit of Adele – and we have a lovely dinner together, chatting and laughing, catching up with news that we've missed in the general hurly-burly of life. I tell him that I phoned Chloe again at the hospital, and both mother and baby are doing fine. I can't wait until they come home tomorrow. What a lovely Christmas treat.

Afterwards, when we've thrown everything into the dishwasher, we take a bottle of advocaat through to the living room. Rick normally calls it the devil's advocaat because my mother drinks so much of it. I've filled this room with candles too, and the lights on the Christmas tree are sparkling. Very romantic.

'I still can't believe it's just us,' he says in wonderment. 'It's been great.'

It's been a very busy day, and now I stifle a yawn too. 'Fabulous.'

We cuddle up on the sofa together and I pour us out a generous measure of advocaat.

'I don't really like advocaat,' Rick says.

'It's Christmas,' I point out. I don't really like it either, but you only have to drink it once a year. I think it's the sickly yellow colour that's so off-putting.

'Oh, OK.' Rick shrugs his compliance. So we knock back a couple of glasses of the sticky liqueur. We both wrinkle our noses.

'That's terrible,' Rick says. 'Shall we have some more?'

'Why not?'

He tops up our glasses again and, second time, it doesn't taste quite so bad.

'Hmm,' Rick says. 'I'm getting to like this. I've heard that it has aphrodisiac properties.'

'Advocaat?'

'Mmm.' He leans in to kiss me deeply. 'See. It's working already.'

I giggle and we kiss again. More advocaat. And, pretty soon, we're lying full length on the sofa and are kissing like teenagers again. If this is what advocaat can do for you, then bring it on!

'Shall we leave them all here,' Rick whispers against my neck as his hands rove my body, 'and go and buy a one-bedroom apartment somewhere far away?'

'Mmm,' I murmur back. 'Sounds good to me.'

Undoing Rick's shirt, I kiss his chest, now covered with a fine fuzz of grey hair but still taut due to the physical work he does. I have been intimate with this chest since it belonged to a skinny boy, and I know and love every inch of it.

He unzips my dress and helps me to slip it off, surprised to find the sexy underwear secreted beneath.

'Wow,' he says. 'You still have it, Mrs Joyce. You are one sexy lady.'

'Ha! You ain't seen nothing yet,' I tell him in my best Mae West voice. Reaching back, I produce my red feather boa and fluffy handcuffs from behind the cushion where I'd hidden them earlier.

Rick laughs. 'Oh yeah?'

Seconds later he's taken off all his clothes – even his socks, and Rick does not part with his socks lightly – and we're on the living room carpet, rolling around on the rug.

Oh, this is lovely. We haven't had fun like this for a long, long time.

'Come on, you saucy minx,' Rick says. 'Come to Daddy.' He pulls me to him with my feather boa. Seconds later, the handcuffs click round one of my wrists.

I don't think I've ever been physically restrained before, and I get a buzz of excitement. I did once quite like the idea of being bound and blindfolded by silk scarves while Rick had his wicked way with me, but we somehow never quite got round to it. So this is very risqué for us.

I'm trying not to think of the fact that we could do with a new carpet in here, or how comfortable our bed is in comparison, when Rick clips my wrists to the leg of the coffee table. We both giggle together. 'I feel very silly.'

'Not sexy?' he asks.

'This is not what we do, is it?'

Rick grins at me. 'Oh, I don't know. I think I'm rising to the occasion.'

And so we make love on the floor with me handcuffed to the coffee table and draped in nothing but a feather boa. It's funny rather than steamy, and we laugh a lot, which is nice.

We do our very best to be passionate, and I think it's a night that we'll remember.

Sometime later, I'm happily basking there in my sleepy afterglow, Rick lying along the length of me, when a yawn overtakes me again. Oh, I need my bed now as I've got an early start in the morning. The turkey is massive and will have to go in first thing. I think I'll take the legs off and roast them on another shelf. Then, while I'm pondering my culinary dilemma, I realise that blood is no longer reaching my arms as they're still above my head and attached to the coffee table. 'Rick,' I murmur, 'undo the handcuffs now. I'm getting pins and needles.'

Nothing but a grunt comes from my husband.

'Rick!' More urgently now. 'You're not asleep, are you?'

More grunting.

I nudge him with my knee. 'Rick! Wake up!'

He snuggles against me.

'God almighty,' I mutter, 'I could be here all night!' I know just how soundly Rick sleeps once he nods off.

I try to lift the coffee table from my prone position to slip the handcuffs underneath the leg, but it's far too heavy. Trust it to be the one piece of furniture in the house that we actually spent a decent amount of money on. So I wriggle and wriggle and jiggle and jiggle for what seems like hours – giving Rick the occasional rousing boot. But to no avail – on he sleeps. I try to make my hands as small and narrow as possible, not that easy when you've got workaday hands. Finally, one last big jiggle and I do manage to get one hand free! Hurrah! Rick snores on, oblivious. It's a good job these cuffs aren't *too* tight.

But then, just as I'm twisting and turning to free the other wrist, I hear the sound of a key in the front door, followed by a lot of laughing.

'Oh no. Oh, *no*!' I make a valiant snatch for my feather boa, and not a second later the living-room door bursts open.

I don't know who screams first, whether it's Tom or me, I can't tell.

'Aaargh,' he shouts. '*Aaargh!* What are you *doing*?'

I would have thought that was obvious enough. My son has more than his fair share of experience on which to draw.

But what's worse, it seems as if he's brought a bunch of his mates back to the house for a party. When they hear him shout out, they push behind him in the doorway as, ineffectually, he tries to stop them peering at his mother in the nip and half handcuffed to the coffee table.

With the commotion, now Rick wakes up. A bit bloody late! 'What on earth's going on?'

He sits up and rubs his eyes. What bit of him was covering my nakedness now isn't, and I try in vain to make the feather boa as big as an overcoat.

'I don't need to see this!' Tom cries. 'You're my parents! This is gross.'

'Close the bloody door!' Rick shouts, hands positioned in a futile attempt to be modest. 'You don't need to keep staring!'

'It's like a car crash,' Tom protests. 'I want to look away, but I can't. I didn't even know you still had sex. Let alone like this!'

His friends are all agog now. I can feel that my face has turned the colour of my fancy feather boa.

344

'Just go, Tom!' I say. 'Please go.'

With that, my son shuts the door and a second later the front door slams too.

Rick turns to me and our eyes meet. Myriad emotions cross our faces – horror, embarrassment, shock. I can't believe that our son has seen us in this compromising position. Normally it's the other way round.

'Was it good for you?' Rick asks.

Then we both dissolve into fits of giggles. And I'm sure that we'd fall into each other's arms, but these bloody silly handcuffs prevent me from moving.

# Chapter 64

I am never drinking advocaat again. Or having sex on the living-room carpet.

Rick and I sit in the kitchen drinking tea, the start of a heavy, bright yellow headache threatening. All the candles have been blown out, the feather boa and handcuffs hidden away again. Now we're not feeling fruity any more, just silly. But we're still holding hands across the table, so it wasn't a complete disaster and, in one way or another, it will always be a night that we'll remember. I'm sure Tom won't forget it in a hurry, either.

We're both in our dressing gowns now, ready for bed. I thought about going to midnight mass, perhaps take Mum and Dad, but it's far too late now. We're not regular church-goers, but try to make the effort at Christmas mainly because the church looks pretty and everyone else we know goes. The Church Women's Committee bake very good mince pies, too.

Now that our romantic evening is well and truly over,

my mind is drifting to all the things I have to do in the morning.

Rick nods towards his shed. 'What do you think of my new lights?'

'It looks lovely.' In truth, it looks like someone has transported a mad Santa's grotto to our back garden. 'Very festive.'

'It's a shame that Neil Harrison can't see it.'

I suspect, like the Great Wall of China, you could actually see it from the moon. Then, as I'm staring at it, I see a shadowy movement. 'Rick? Is that someone going inside?' The hairs on the back of my neck stand up. 'I'm sure I just saw the door open.'

My husband is up and out of his chair in seconds. He sprints across the kitchen, flings open the door and races out into the garden, even though he's in his pyjamas and slippers. 'Hey,' he shouts as he's powering across the lawn. 'Hey, you! What are you doing in my shed?'

Abandoning my tea, I'm hot on his heels, as is Buster who, as usual, is barking and wagging his tail in a more cheerful manner than is suitable for a crack guard dog.

The door of the shed bangs open and a dark figure comes out and starts to run across the garden towards the fence. Whoever it is has on a hoodie with the hood pulled over his head. It looks like he's trying to make his getaway.

This time Rick won't be thwarted, and he gives chase even though he's slithering and slipping on the snow. Buster barks happily and bounds playfully after Rick.

The figure starts to climb our fence, but bravely Rick hurls himself at his legs and pulls him down.

My heart is in my mouth. What if the intruder's got a knife or a knuckleduster? What if he's high on drugs? What if there are six of his mates waiting on the other side of the fence?

The man collapses to the ground and Rick sits astride him, panting heavily. Doesn't seem too long ago since we were in a similar position.

'What are you after?' Rick shouts. 'There's nothing in there.' I finally catch up with them and drop down on my knees next to Rick. Then he pulls the man's hood from his face. Rick gasps, wide-eyed. Buster goes and licks his cheeks.

My husband turns to me, open-mouthed, lost for words.

'Merak?' I say. 'What on earth are you doing here?'

# Chapter 65

Back at the kitchen table. More tea. And biscuits. We all need a sugar rush. Including Buster.

Merak hangs his head. 'I am sorry, Rick.'

My husband rubs his hands through his hair, making it all stand on end, trying to get his brain to take this in. 'You're *living* in the shed? *My* shed?'

'Yes.'

'*You're living there?*'

Rick has been repeating the same thing for some time now. 'Why?'

Merak sips his tea and then clears his throat. 'I realise that it is wrong thing to do. But to rent – even small room – is expensive. I send money home every week. My family in Poland are poor. Your shed is very comfortable.'

'But you *live* there?'

I touch my husband's arm. 'I think we've established that now.'

'I can't believe it,' Rick says. 'Do I not pay you enough?'

'Yes. But money here does not go far.'

'Tell me about it,' Rick agrees.

'Oh, Merak,' I offer. 'All this time I thought we were looking after you, and yet you've been living rough under our noses.'

'Living in *my shed* is hardly living rough,' Rick says indignantly.

'It's hardly ideal either,' I point out. 'You can't sleep on a sunlounger when you've got a full day of physical work ahead of you.'

'I manage,' Merak says.

'I don't want you to *manage*,' I tell Merak. 'I want you to be happy and comfortable.'

His face takes on an even more serious expression than usual. 'I do not wish to lose my job.'

'There's no question of that, lad,' Rick says. 'I'm just, just ... *flabbergasted* that we didn't know. How did you get in there?'

Merak's pale face flushes furiously. 'I borrow spare key from drawer.' He glances guiltily at the relevant drawer.

Oh. As easy as that. So much for the security-conscious Joyces. The key was missing all the time and we didn't even notice.

'We thought someone was trying to burgle us,' Rick says.

'I am sorry.'

'No. *I'm* sorry. You shouldn't have to do this. It's not right. Where do you shower? Go to the loo? Eat?'

'The manager of the bar I work in lets me use his shower. I use the public conveniences in the town centre and, mostly – ' he looks sheepishly at me '– I eat here.'

'At least we've got something right, then,' I tell him.

'I lost my room,' Merak says. 'The landlord says that he can rent it for more. But I cannot get back my deposit. He is a bad man and keeps it.'

'Did you not threaten him with the "Russian mafia"?'

'He *is* Russian mafia.' Merak sighs. 'I do not want my legs broken. So I lose money. I cannot take another room as I have no money for deposit. My mother has six children. My father died many years ago. I am oldest son. She needs me to help her. This is why I come to England. To work hard to provide for them. How can I spend money when they need it more?'

'Why didn't you come to me, lad? Why didn't you tell me that you couldn't afford to rent anywhere?'

'You have both done enough for me,' Merak says. 'I did not want to trouble you more. I thought if I could sleep in shed for short time, it would help me to save money.'

Rick tuts sadly.

'You're like family to us now.' I glance at Rick as I say this, and he knows where this conversation is going and nods imperceptibly. 'We want to look after you.'

'Thank you, Juliet.'

'I take it you're not going home for Christmas?'

He shrugs. 'The flight was too much money.'

'You must stay here tonight and join us for Christmas tomorrow.'

His face, his pale solemn face, lights up in a big grin. 'Really?'

'Of course. I won't have it any other way. I've been asking Rick for weeks to find out what you were doing.'

'You are not angry?'

'Only angry that you didn't feel able to come and talk to us about your difficulties.'

'You are both too nice to me.'

'Please say you'll stay for Christmas.'

Merak smiles shyly. 'That would make me very happy.'

'Then it's settled.'

He comes over and hugs me. 'You are very kind lady.'

'You can sleep in Mum's room for tonight.' Or is the spare room free? Oh, I can't remember. We're going to have to start a booking system at this rate. It's easier if I just go and change the sheets. 'Tomorrow, we can sort out something more permanent. Something that *doesn't* involve you sleeping in the shed.'

Merak's eyes light up. 'You mean this?'

He looks so happy that it brings a tear to my eye. 'Absolutely.'

Rick claps him on the back. 'I must say that you've kept that shed very clean and tidy, Merak. A man after my own heart.'

They laugh together, and it's good to see them both happy. Then I make a mental note to myself to remember that we've got an extra mouth to feed and to peel some extra potatoes in the morning.

# Chapter 66

When Merak is settled for the night in Mum's bed, I go and put Buster in the utility room – much to his consternation. The turkey is defrosting in the kitchen and, though I love our dear dog, I don't want him helping himself to a tasty snack in the wee small hours.

It's nearly two o'clock now, and my eyes are rolling with tiredness. I hear that some couples enjoy a lie-in on Christmas morning, a gentle walk perhaps in a snowy landscape, some convivial drinks and canapés with neighbours before a relaxing lunch. Not me. I'll be up and at the coalface shortly after six o'clock, making sure all is ready for the tribe arriving. Looks as if we'll be having a few extra mouths to feed this year. But that's fine. I'm never knowingly under-catered. The turkey's so big that it probably won't go in the oven – *again*.

'We're all locked up,' Rick says as he slips his arms round my waist. 'Ready for bed?'

'I can hardly stand up straight,' I concede.

'It's been quite an entertaining evening, all things considered,' Rick concludes.

'Yes, but I didn't imagine that *we'd* be providing the entertainment.'

'True.'

'One last job,' I tell him.

He looks at me quizzically. I go over to the fridge and produce a carrot.

'Ah!' The penny has dropped. 'Shall I pour the sherry?'

I nod and put a mince pie on a plate.

In the living room, we take in the Christmas tree, still sparkling away, a pile of presents waiting beneath it. On the hearth I place the mince pie and carrot. Rick puts down the sherry.

'Got to look after Santa,' he says.

'We've been doing this since the children were born.' We twine our arms together and hold each other close. 'Do you think they'll do it for their children too?'

'Chloe won't,' we say in unison.

I laugh. 'I hope she'll be OK with this new baby.'

'She will be,' Rick assures me. 'And we'll still be here for her.'

'How do you think we'll face Tom tomorrow?'

'I think he might understand how it feels for us now when we keep interrupting his sex life.'

'It was funny,' I say.

'You know we'll never live it down,' Rick tells me.

'I'm not sure I want to live it down. I rather like the idea that we're the last of the Chadwick Close groovers.'

'I think the fact that you're using the word "groovers" shows that we're not.' Rick pulls me closer. 'I love you, Mrs Joyce.'

'Are you sure?'

'Of course I am. What else could I want? I've a beautiful wife and a wonderful family. Well, mostly.'

'And you're happy?'

'Very.'

I should accept that, whoever these mystery texts have come from, they're not a threat to our relationship. Rick loves me. I know that and I should trust it. 'I love you too.'

'Who knows what kind of madness tomorrow might bring? If we're too busy fighting fires, I just want to wish you a very happy Christmas, Juliet.'

'Happy Christmas, Rick.'

'Oh,' he says with mock surprise. 'Look what I've found!' From behind his back, my husband produces the mistletoe that was, previously, hanging at the front door.

He holds it above my head and, despite the fact that we've already used up our annual quota of romance in one night, we put it to jolly good use.

# Chapter 67

Christmas morning. I'm up with the lark. Except I imagine even the lark is still, quite sensibly, in bed.

Rick too is wide awake. He came down and hacked the legs off the turkey so that we could shoehorn it into the oven. Now it's safely in there doing its thing.

He and Merak brought the dining table in from the garage and set it up at one end of the living room. Now that our numbers have swelled, with the addition of Merak and Mitch, I'll need to open the middle leaf, and if we all squash up close it will just about accommodate us.

'Anything else you need me to do right now?' Rick asks.

'I don't think so.'

'Merak will help you out if you need an extra pair of hands, won't you, lad?'

'But of course,' the unfailingly helpful Merak says.

'I'll go and get Chloe. The sooner we have her home, the better,' Rick says, and off he goes to the hospital. She texted us at first light to say that he could go and pick her up at ten o'clock this morning. I think the wards are probably trying to get rid of everyone they can over Christmas and, thankfully, both mother and baby still seem to be doing just fine. Like Rick, I can't wait for them to be home at Christmas too.

Merak joins me by the sink and we both set to peeling potatoes, carrots and parsnips. I show Merak how to do the sprouts, putting little crosses in the bottom so that they cook properly, and he does them all methodically without complaint.

While he's busy, I set the table. This time of year, I bring out the best china, the crystal glasses, the silver-plated canteen of cutlery that just gathers dust for the rest of the year and has to be given a good old polish before it's fit for purpose. I fold the luxury red napkins into the shape of a fan. Each glass is decorated with a twist of star-studded tinsel. When Buster trots in to see what's going on, he gets a tinsel bow on his collar. He trots out again looking very festive and pleased with himself.

When I'm done, I sneak a present from beneath the Christmas tree. I've bought Tom two shirts, and he can manage perfectly well without one of them. Upstairs, I take off the label, write out another one for Merak and then replace the present under the tree. As Rick had given him a good Christmas bonus, I wasn't planning to buy him anything else, but now that seems mean. I want him to have something to unwrap today and not be left out.

Back in the kitchen, Merak is rapidly disappearing beneath a mountain of peeled vegetables.

'You're doing a great job there, Merak.'

'Thank you, Juliet.'

'Let's crank up the Christmas tunes. That'll put some power in our elbows.' So Merak and I, side by side, work our way through another bag of potatoes, both singing along to Wham and 'Last Christmas'.

Then the doorbell rings, and I wipe my hands down my apron and go to see who it is. Standing there is a tiny, bird-like girl who looks as if she might originally be from Thailand or somewhere. Behind her are two hulking children who are pushing into adolescence. She's wearing a red leather mini-skirt, a low-cut blouse and heels that are so high I don't know how she can stand in them, let alone walk. Her face looks like it has seen some life.

'Hello,' she says in a shrill voice. 'Very nice to meet you.'

'Hello.'

Then she totters past me and into the hall before I can ask who she is.

'You have very nice house. Come, come,' she says to her boys who, somewhat sulkily, follow her inside.

'Er . . .'

'I'm Mali. We have not met.'

'No,' I agree. 'We certainly haven't.'

'Tom has told me very much about you.'

Ah, Tom. 'I'm afraid Tom's not here at the moment.'

'I know,' she says, taking off her coat. 'He texted me. He will be here soon.'

'Oh, good.'

The woman tosses her coat on the stairs. As it looks like she's planning on staying, I pick it up and put it in the cupboard. 'Come, come,' she says to the boys and, with more sulking, they too strip off their coats.

'He has told me to make myself at home,' she informs me.

'Oh.' She's certainly taking Tom at his word. 'And who are these charming chaps?'

The woman looks blankly at me until she realises that I'm talking about her children. 'This is Niran and Kamol. Say hello.'

Neither of them do.

'Pleased to meet you, boys,' I say into the silence. They both glare at me in response, so I show her through to the living room. 'Can I get you a drink? Tea, or something?'

'White wine,' Mali orders. 'Not too dry.'

'Right.'

'I put TV on for boys?'

'Er, yes.'

'Come, come,' she barks at the sullen youths. 'Watch TV.'

In the kitchen, I ring Tom and, by some sort of miracle, he actually picks up. 'Where are you?'

'Bit tricky to explain, Mum.'

'There's a young lady and two children waiting here for you.'

'Yeah, I know. I'll be back as soon as I can.'

'What's she doing here?'

'You told me you wanted me to bring someone home to meet the family.'

I did. But I wasn't thinking on Christmas Day and with two kids in tow. 'Is she your girlfriend?'

'Well,' he says. 'Sort of.' Very cagey. It probably means that he met someone else last night and is currently with her or him, all thoughts of Mali flown from his head. Also she's a good ten years older than Tom, with two teenage children. But does the fact that he's bringing her home for Christmas lunch mean that he's planning for their relationship to be something more permanent? I've only met her for two seconds and, already, I'm hoping not.

'Are they all staying for lunch?'

'Yeah.' He answers as if it was a very stupid question for me to ask.

'You could have warned me.' Or, God forbid, even have been here to meet them.

'Chill,' Tom says. 'There's always enough grub to feed an army. A couple more aren't likely to make a difference.'

My son hangs up before I can protest. But he's probably right. I'd better get Merak to peel some more potatoes just in case.

# Chapter 68

Rick pushed Chloe in a wheelchair to the car park while she carried the precious cargo of her new baby daughter in her arms. He unlocked the car door and helped her to stand up. It had taken him ages to secure the baby seat in the back of the car according to instructions. Even with Jaden, he was out of practice with these things, and he felt more nervous than when he brought home either of his own children.

Perhaps the advancing years just made you more aware of all the things that could go wrong. As a youth he thought that the future would always be bright, the sun would shine and everything would be well. Now life had worn him down to his knees and he was terrified of bringing another little bundle of innocence into it.

Chloe was subdued when he helped her to fix Holly in the Moses basket and then assisted her as she shuffled into the passenger seat. It was clear that she was still tender and feeling weak. Her face was puffy, and it looked like she'd been crying.

Rick slid into the driver's seat. He patted his daughter's knee. 'What a present to be bringing home for Christmas.'

'Thanks, Dad,' she said quietly, and then promptly burst into tears.

Oh, how he wished that Juliet was here. He was so rubbish at this sort of thing. 'Hush, hush.' He wrapped his arms round her. 'Why the tears?'

'It should be Mitch taking me home,' she sniffled. 'Mitch and Jaden.'

'I know,' Rick said. 'I know.' He patted her back.

'I haven't got wind, Dad,' she pointed out.

'Right.' No patting.

'I want us all to be a family again.' Pained wailing. Oh, God, where was Juliet when he needed her? Peeling spuds for England, no doubt. 'Me, Mitch, Jaden and Holly.'

'You can be,' Rick assured her. 'But it takes hard work.'

'It shouldn't be hard work if you love someone,' she countered.

'That's nonsense, Chloe, and you know it. You don't drift through life with everything all hearts and flowers. Most of it is just everyday grind that you've got to get through. Even more so with two young babies to contend with. You and Mitch didn't come together in the most ideal of circumstances,' Rick reminded her.

'Neither did you and Mum, but you've been happy together.'

'We've had our moments, Chloe. Times when it wasn't going so well, when we had to grit our teeth and get on with it.' Now wasn't the time to talk about the days when he'd just felt like packing a bag and walking away from the lot of them, or weighed down by the sheer relentless responsibility of family life. Or, even more recently, the time when Juliet came close to leaving them all and sailing off into the sunset with her old flame. They had weathered the storms and had come through them stronger. 'You can't just leave at the drop of a hat. So far, Mitch has been sitting waiting patiently for you. He might not wait for ever. If you want Mitch back, it's up to *you* to try hard.'

Perhaps there had been too much emphasis on the *you*, but he knew what hard work his daughter could be. She was the one who found domesticity suffocating, not Mitch.

'He's a sound bloke,' Rick continued while he was on a roll and, for once, while his daughter seemed to be listening. 'You'd go a long way to find better.'

'I know,' she conceded reluctantly.

'By the time we get home he'll probably be waiting there for you with Jaden.'

Her face brightened. 'You think so?'

'I'm sure so. Shall we go? Think it's safe to leave the car park?'

'Yeah.' Chloe risked a smile. As he went to pull away, she touched his arm. 'Thanks, Dad. Thanks for the other night and . . . well, you know, everything.'

'You're welcome, love.'

'You're the best dad in the world, you know.'

Flushed with pride, and despite wanting to put his foot down so that he could get home in time to help Juliet, he drove at a sedate thirty miles an hour so as not to jiggle his granddaughter on her first car journey.

# Chapter 69

Merak and I are making good progress on the lunch preparations when I hear the front door go and a voice from outside the kitchen asks, 'Is it safe to come in?'

Tom.

'You have got your clothes on?' he calls.

'Tom! Get in here *now*.'

My son edges round the door, hands over his eyes. Merak looks perplexed, as well he might.

'Merak, could you go and ask Mali if she'd like another drink?' She's already knocked back three glasses and the sun certainly isn't over the yardarm, but that doesn't seem to trouble her.

When he's gone, I turn to Tom. 'I don't want you to mention last night,' I say. 'Nothing. No jokes, no cheeky comments.'

'But you're my parents.' He pulls a disgusted face. 'What are you doing still having sex?'

'This is our house, Tom,' I remind him. 'If Dad and I want

to swing from the chandeliers then we damn well will.' My son shudders at the thought. Rick would probably shudder too, but I don't mention that. 'It might make you think twice about the parade of casual partners that you bring through here. From now on you'll have some respect for our home. I hope you realise what it's been like for me and Dad to keep walking in on you in compromising positions.'

Tom has nothing to say to that.

'Have I made myself clear?'

'Yes, Mum,' he says suitably penitent. Then his face breaks into a grin. 'But it was very funny.'

I whack his bottom with the tea towel. 'It was not.'

He breaks down into a belly laugh, and I can't help but join him.

'Who knew that my mother was such a raver?' he says, shuddering.

'Enough of that,' I chide. 'You have some responsibilities to attend to. There is a very drunk young woman and two surly children in the living room who I believe belong to you.'

'Oh, yeah.' He now looks like he's regretting inviting the lovely Mali for Christmas.

'I suggest you go and entertain her until lunch is ready.'

Tom comes over and wraps his arms round me. 'Sorry, Mum.' He pecks my cheek. 'Happy Christmas, old girl. I love you.'

And, of course, that defuses all my irritation. 'Merry Christmas, love. It's good to have you home.'

I realise that there'll come a day when Tom will have a family of his own, and it may not always be possible to spend our Christmases together. I should be grateful to have him here while we can.

'Can I do anything to help?'

'We might not have enough room round the table with Mali and her sons. Can you and Merak bring in the garden table?'

'Yeah.'

'Give it a wipe down before you bring it indoors.'

'I'll get Merak to do that,' Tom says. Clearly handling a j-cloth is beyond my university-educated boy.

So Tom and Merak manhandle the table inside and I find more cutlery and glasses – though I'm all out of the best ones – and red napkins and tinsel twizzles. Then I turn my mind to stuffing balls.

I have prepared two trays of perfectly spherical sausagemeat, sage and onion stuffing by the time that Mitch arrives with a totally hyperactive Jaden.

'He was out of bed by four,' Mitch tells me, barely suppressing a yawn as he strips off Jaden's coat. 'We have played non-stop with his Roary racing-car garage ever since. Only one of us is showing signs of losing interest. That right, buddy?'

Jaden nods his agreement.

'Brought it with you?'

'In the boot of the car.' Mitch has got this parenting lark down to a T, I think.

I touch Mitch's arm. 'Congratulations on being a daddy again. You're a lovely father.'

He sighs. 'I only wish the circumstances were different, Juliet.'

'Don't give up now,' I urge. 'I think Chloe may finally be changing for the better. I'd love to see you all as a family again.'

'Me too.'

'You know that I'll do all I can to help. You only have to say the word.' Then, before we can talk any more, I hear the car in the drive and say, 'That'll be Mummy back from the hospital, Jaden.'

My grandson claps his hands together. 'Mummy! Mummy!'

On cue, Chloe comes through the door, precious bundle in her arms. On seeing Mitch, she bursts into tears. He rushes to her and holds her and the baby close, making soothing noises.

'Everything OK?' I whisper to Rick.

'I think everything will be just fine,' he says with a smile.

# Chapter 70

'How's your dad and Dr Jekyll?' Rick wants to know.

'Don't call Mum that,' I tut.

'Are they ready for me to pick them up?'

I nod. 'Dad called a little while ago. They're up, dressed and have had breakfast. Mum, by all accounts, is behaving herself beautifully.'

'Wonders will never cease. It won't last.' He looks at his watch. 'I'll go and get them now. Do you know, they're forecasting snow again?'

'How lovely. A white Christmas.'

'You old romantic, you,' he says, and comes to nuzzle my neck.

'Rick! Someone might see.'

'I don't care. I love you, Mrs Joyce.' He nuzzles some more. 'Did you enjoy last night?'

'The part where our son and his friends burst in and found us naked on the floor in the throes of love, or the bit before that?'

Rick laughs. 'I was thinking of the bit before. And, technically, we were asleep.'

I nudge Rick in the ribs. 'Well, one of us was!'

'Tom wasn't to know that. In future, he might just have a bit more respect for his old man's virility.'

'I think revulsion is the main emotion. He can't believe we're still "at it" at our age.' Our son, I'm sure, would rather imagine that we've only ever had sex twice in our lives – once to conceive him and the next time for Chloe. 'I've spoken to him this morning. He turned up shortly after his girlfriend Mali and her two sons.'

'What?'

I shrug. 'You know Tom.'

'Is it worth remembering the name of this one?'

'I sincerely hope not.' I don't normally judge Tom's eclectic taste in partners, but I feel I'm justified with this one.

'Is said girlfriend staying for lunch?'

'Looks that way.'

'Have we got enough food?'

'As long as everyone likes lots of potatoes.'

'I'd better go and introduce myself to this lady.' Rick straightens his collar.

I don't bother to tell my husband that she's no lady. He'll find out soon enough.

'Go and get Mum and Dad first please, love. I'm worried about them. I won't relax until they're back in this house and under my wing again.'

'How the tides turn,' Rick notes. He kisses my cheek. 'All right. I'll be back in ten minutes and then I'll be your kitchen slave.'

'Merak has been doing a sterling job in your absence.'

'You're happy to have him living here?'

'Of course. He's a great kid. Easier than either of our children.'

'Any ideas where we might put him?'

'Not yet,' I admit. 'I'm going to have to rethink our bedroom allocations.' I could probably do with creating a spreadsheet, it's getting so complex.

He kisses me on the cheek. 'See you in a few minutes.'

Then he's out of the door and I make gravy with some cheap red wine, and bread sauce. Merak sorts everyone out with drinks.

'Have you phoned your mother yet?' I ask Merak.

He shakes his head. 'It is very expensive to call Poland.'

'But you must do it on Christmas Day. Go upstairs to our bedroom and call them from there.'

His face lights up. 'I will not talk for long.'

'Take all the time you need. Give them our best regards, too.' Then I relieve him of his apron and usher him out of the kitchen. Rick will, no doubt, faint when we get the phone bill, but so be it. He can't not talk to his mother on Christmas Day, for heaven's sake.

I'm just parboiling the potato mountain when a mobile phone on the table tings to say that there's a new text. It's Rick's phone, and he's getting as bad as my mother for leaving it behind everywhere he goes. I'll bet he doesn't even realise it's not in his pocket. Picking up the phone, I glance at the message and, despite trying not to think the worst, already a feeling of dread has settled in my heart.

Sure enough, the text is from Lisa. It reads: *Thanx for lovely pressies. Have a great day. CU in new year. Lots of love Lisa and Izzy xxx*

I toss down the phone as if it's burned me. So Rick's buying this woman presents, and Izzy, I assume, is her daughter. She has a daughter. I hope to God that Rick hasn't been doing an Arnie Schwarzenegger and has got a love child somewhere that I don't know about. We have been so tight financially that I can't believe he would buy gifts lightly. And she hasn't just sent love, but *lots* of love.

I wonder why Rick hasn't been more careful about taking the phone with him? If this is an affair, then surely he might have guessed that she would text him today, of all days? Why didn't he call her when he was out collecting Chloe, or take the phone so that he could do so while picking up Mum and Dad? In his shoes, that's what I would have done. And I'm well aware that I have, myself, been in this same situation. I know that it takes skill and cunning to conceal a lover, and I have never considered Rick to be a deceitful man. But then I never considered myself a deceitful woman. We all have dark places inside us, below the surface.

Then I hear the car pull into the drive. Rick's back with my parents. In a minute he's going to be opening the front door, laughing, chatting and he won't know that I've discovered his secret. What to do? How can I behave normally when my world could be crashing round my ears?

Sure enough, the key's in the lock. I can hear Mum and Dad. Quickly I slip Rick's phone into the kitchen drawer. I don't want him getting a message from her. Not on Christmas Day.

I know that we'll have to deal with this in the new year, but for now I can't face it. It's Christmas, and I want a perfect day, to pretend that my family is happy and united, that there aren't cracks and flaws threatening to break us apart. I push all negative thoughts aside. This is the season to be jolly.

The pan of potatoes boils over just as Rick comes through the door. 'All right, love?'

'Yes,' I say. 'Just running out of hands.'

'I'll be with you in two ticks. Let me get your mum and dad a drink.'

'Are they OK?'

'Your mother's perfectly well. Her old self.'

'You mean she's being rude, obnoxious and difficult.'

'Absolutely.'

'I heard that,' comes her voice from the hall.

'Whatever else is wrong, her hearing isn't suffering,' I whisper.

Rick nods and lowers his voice too. 'I'll get her started on the snowball cocktails early.'

Rick fusses about making drinks. He seems like my normal husband, exactly as he is on any other day. But he has a secret, and that's not like him at all.

# Chapter 71

The turkey is browning nicely. When the potatoes are safely roasting in the oven, I nip upstairs and change into my scarlet dress. If Rick can have his secrets, then so can I. Taking the jewellery box from my dressing-table drawer, I slip on the beautiful necklace that Robin Westcroft bought for me – ostensibly for providing administrative and shoulder-to-cry on services. The necklace I haven't yet told my husband about. Knowing Rick, he won't even notice it.

I fluff up my hair and quickly put on a bit of slap and my brave face before going to join my family and friends. I ignore the fact that my heart is tight in my chest.

The living room is crammed full, with virtually every seat occupied. Rick has brought in a couple of kitchen chairs. It all looks very festive in here, and it's nice for our home to be filled with family and friends. And strangers. Someone has turned off the television and my favourite Christmas songs ring out – I suspect that may have been Rick, too. It means that Mali's two children are sitting, arms folded, emanating waves of hostility at their source of entertainment being curtailed. I look across at Tom, but he's oblivious to the children, entranced as he seems to be by the acres of Mali's smooth, coffee-coloured thigh on show beneath the red leather. My father, though he is now supposed to be gay, looks pretty interested in it too. My mother, in her own world, sits next to her ex-husband, knocking back snowballs like they're going out of fashion – which, I believe, they are. Behind her back, Rick holds up three fingers. I don't know if he means that she's had three fingers of advocaat in one glass, or three glasses. Either way, I hope she's not sick later.

Rick comes over and slips his arm round my waist. 'Nice necklace,' he notes. 'Have I seen that before?'

Damn! Rick never notices jewellery. I finger it self-consciously. 'It was a present from Robin,' I say.

His eyes widen. 'That's a very generous gift.'

'I know.' Too generous. I think the art of gift-giving at Christmas is to be generous rather than ostentatious. But secretly I'm glad that Robin has been so lavish. 'He's been having a hard time at home,' I tell Rick. 'I've been trying to help just by being there to listen, nothing more. His wife's getting a ruby bracelet worth over two grand in her Christmas stocking.'

His eyes widen a bit more at that amount. 'Oh.' Thankfully, it seems as if he's decided to drop the subject. Perhaps he realises that if you can't compete, it's simply better to keep quiet. 'Can I get you a drink, love?' he asks.

I nod gratefully. 'Red wine please.' He goes to pour me one. 'Small,' I add – even though my heart cries *Large!* I usually try not to drink too much before serving dinner, as I don't want it to end up decorating the walls or on the floor. I've found it's generally best if the cook stays sober.

'You ought to keep your children under control, young woman,' Mum says to me. 'They're very rude.'

'They're not my children, Mum. Tom and Chloe are *my* children,' I start to explain, but that blank look comes into her eyes again, and I decide to give up. 'Shall we open the presents before lunch?'

'Those two fat boys have eaten all the chocolate decorations off the tree,' Mum continues. 'Look at them. They don't need anything else to eat!'

I turn to the boys who lower their heads, but not before I see telltale smears of chocolate round their mouths.

'I'm *so* sorry, Mali,' I begin, but she is too engrossed in her wine and Tom to care about what Niran and Kamol are doing. Perhaps Mum has a point. I just wish she wouldn't make it so loudly.

'Eh?' Mali says, as she drains another glass.

'Never mind.'

Still, even without the enhancement of chocolate coins, the tree looks stunning with its lights twinkling and colourful presents heaped underneath. Mitch and Chloe are snuggled up side by side on the sofa, cuddling their new daughter between them, and my heart soars to see them as a family together again. Christmas can be a difficult time, a catalyst for rifts and arguments. But it can also be one for healing wounds, too. I hope that happens in this case. Jaden, at their feet, is getting fractious, and it's clear that he can't wait to start opening the pile of gifts with his name on.

Rick and I have bought our grandson an electric guitar and keyboard, and I wonder how soon it will be before we live to regret that moment of madness in Argos.

I also wonder if Tom has thought to buy anything for Mali or her boys, or whether I should nip upstairs to find something to wrap for her. But really it's too late and, while I might have been able to find a suitable scarf or some perfume for Mali, I don't know if I have anything suitable for two boys/men/trainee gangstas in my emergency present stash. They probably want Wiis or Xboxes or sawn-off shotguns. I dread Jaden being this age, and I hope he's never too old to play with trains or be totally enthralled by his Roary racing-car garage.

Out of the corner of one eye, I watch my son and his new girlfriend. Does Tom seem committed to this rather tarty woman and her brooding offspring? It's hard to tell. Tom falls in love quickly and heavily, and just as quickly out of it again. I don't know where he gets that trait from. It's certainly not from Rick or me. Perhaps it's from my mother.

'Presents?' My voice sounds shrill, and I realise that despite my vow not to drink too much, my glass is already empty and I've barely tasted it. Oh, well. Should have gone for the large one.

We all gather round the tree and Rick hands out the presents. He used to perform this task in a Santa's outfit for the kids, while they pretended not to know it was him. But now it's gathering dust in the loft, and he won't even entertain wearing it. Not even for Jaden's sake.

By far the largest stash of presents is for Jaden, and I do hope we're not spoiling him. But that's what Christmas is all about, isn't it? It's for the children. It's to make it a magical time for them. Chloe leaves Holly in Mitch's arms and slides off the sofa to sit on the floor with Jaden and help him to rip open his parcels. Not that he seems to be having a great deal of trouble. Shreds of paper fly everywhere.

He pounces on the guitar and keyboard with glee, and starts playing away with more enthusiasm than skill. Already I can read the expression on Rick's face. The batteries will be coming out of that guitar very soon.

We hand presents to Mitch and Chloe, all practical things, and some bits and bobs for the baby. For Dad I've bought the latest Stephen Fry book, as I know he and Samuel were big fans.

'Thanks, love,' he says. 'That's champion. Just the ticket.'

'Happy Christmas, Dad.' Surreptitiously, I squeeze his hand.

I've bought Mum some toiletries and a jigsaw, in the hope that it will keep her brain active.

'What do I want a jigsaw for?' Mum says when she opens it.

'I thought we could do it together in the evenings,' I tell her.

'I'd rather watch *Escape to the Country*. I fancy that chubby one with the red cheeks.'

'It'll help to keep your mind active.' Though, from her last comment, some parts of her mind could do with being *less* active.

'There's nothing wrong with my mind, Miss Bossy Boots.' She tosses her present to the floor with disdain.

I can see that I'll end up doing the jigsaw by myself.

Merak is thrilled with his shirt, and he's bought us some of my favourite Hotel Chocolat goodies at great expense. 'You shouldn't have, Merak.'

He's shy now. 'But I wanted to say thank you for all your kindness.'

'You're very welcome.'

From Rick, I get a voucher for Marks & Spencer and a hot-water bottle. 'Thanks, love.' I give him a kiss. Some women get two-thousand-pound ruby bracelets but, in all truth, I'm more than happy with this.

'I'll get you a new coat too,' he says. 'In the sales.'

'Thank you.' There's even a gift for Buster, and he sits wagging his tail as I unwrap a new squeaky toy for him. 'Oh. I've left the price on.'

'I'm not sure the dog will mind that oversight,' Rick says.

Buster jumps on his toy and then leaps back when it squeaks. A bit like Jaden's guitar, we'll all be glad when the squeak goes out of it.

Then Mali opens her present from Tom. He's bought her a garlic crusher.

'What this?' she shrieks.

'A garlic crusher,' Tom points out, just in case there's any doubt. Sometimes, he truly is his father's son. 'I thought it would come in useful.'

'You buy woman like me *garlic crusher*,' she spits. 'I want perfume, fancy knickers, big bling-bling!'

'Oh.' He looks at me for help, but I can only shrug. It's too late to raid my emergency stash now. But I don't think that would contain suitable knickers or big bling-bling.

The offending garlic crusher is tossed on the floor, in a similar manner to my mother's jigsaw, where Niran and Kamol use it to try to maim each other.

'Cheap, *unemployed* man,' Mali grumbles under her breath.

Hurriedly, the rest of the presents are distributed and are, generally, more gratefully received. Then I remember that there are some missing. Where are the trendy jumper and child's outfit that Rick had secreted under our bed? There has been no sign of them. I thought they were for Chloe and Jaden, but it seems I was mistaken. Are these the presents that have gone to this Lisa and her daughter, Izzy, I wonder? I can think of no other explanation. Bile rises to my mouth and I swallow it down. I look at my husband smiling, laughing, helping his grandson to play with his guitar, showing him how to strum, and I am struggling to deal with his duplicity. How can I ask him about it on Christmas Day? This is a conversation we need to have. But, for now, it will have to wait.

'Right,' I smooth down my dress. 'Top up everyone's glass if you will, Rick.' Rick, who is buying another woman presents that have probably involved more thought than a voucher and a hot-water bottle.

And though, inside, my heart is silently breaking, I paste a big smile on my face and say, 'I'll get the lunch ready.'

# Chapter 72

In the kitchen, I bite back the tears that threaten to come and, instead, bang about with the pots to make me feel better. I won't cry on Christmas Day. Whatever happens, I won't cry. This day has to be perfect. I grip the work surface and steady myself.

Rick comes in behind me to fix the drinks. 'Everything all right, love?' he asks.

'Fine.' My voice sounds tighter than I'd hoped.

'Sure?' He curls his arms round my waist. 'I know your presents aren't much, but we can go and choose something together – that new coat I promised you, for one thing. You know what I'm like.'

*Do I?* is just about to spring to my lips when, from the kitchen drawer, Rick's phone tings. Another text.

Rick looks round, wondering where the noise is coming from.

It's up to me to pull it out of the drawer and put it on the table. When it tings again, Rick glances at it casually. I look at him expectantly.

'Nothing important,' he says with an uncomfortable shrug.

Then, when I've vowed that I won't do this today, I look my husband squarely in the eye and say, 'I know.'

'What?'

'I know about Lisa and Izzy.'

He starts, taking a step back. His mouth drops open and he stares guiltily at the phone. I see a gulp travel down his throat before he says, 'It's not what you think, Juliet.'

'How do you know what I think?'

'You think it's some woman that I've been having an affair with,' Rick offers. 'But it's not. Nothing could be further from the truth.'

That, of course, is exactly what I think. 'So tell me.'

'She's just a girl. A young kid. A single mum who's struggling by herself. I laid some flooring for her a couple of weeks ago, and we've sort of stayed friends.'

'Friends?'

'Nothing more,' Rick swears. 'She's got no one, love. Her house is a tip. There's no heating or hot water, and she's trying to bring up a little girl there with no help. It breaks my heart to see her struggle.' My husband's eyes fill with tears and he's not a man who shows his emotions easily. 'I've given her a few quid, bought her some groceries. That's all. I think of all that we've got, all that our kids have got . . .' His voice trails away.

'And Christmas presents?'

'A jumper for her, and a little outfit for the kiddie. That's all.' Rick takes a shuddering breath. 'She's just a young girl who hasn't got anyone in the world to care for her. Old fool that I am, I thought I could make a bit of a difference.'

I'm hugging myself tightly while I listen. I really do want to believe Rick. Has he lied to me before in all our years together? If he has, then I can't think of an occasion now. 'And that's really all it is?'

He nods. 'You *do* know me, Juliet. I might be an idiot sometimes. But I've *always* been a faithful idiot.' Rick hangs his head. 'But I have come to care about her and her little girl.' He fiddles with his phone. 'She and Izzy are on their own today. Completely alone. Just the two of them in that miserable house with no Christmas cheer, nothing. They've not even got a tree up.' A tear squeezes out of Rick's eye, and I go to hold him.

'Why didn't you tell me? Why keep it secret?'

'You've had so much on your plate already. What with Samuel's funeral to sort out and all this stuff with your mum, and then Chloe, how could I tell you about someone else's problems?'

'I have been absolutely out of my mind with worry,' I confess. 'I've seen the texts. I've wondered where you were when you've been out in the van. My brain has been stuck on overdrive for weeks.'

He looks at me bleakly. 'Why didn't you mention it?'

'I could say the same to you.'

Rick sinks into the chair in front of him. He puts his head in his hands at the table. 'Has it come to this, that we can never even find time to talk to each other about our worries? Are we so busy with everyone else's that we ignore our own?'

'Yes,' I say to him. 'That's exactly what it is.'

'Come here,' he says, and holds out an arm.

I abandon the lunch preparation and go over to him. He pulls me down onto his lap. 'I love you,' he says. 'More with every passing year. You're a wonderful wife and a fantastic mother. No man could ask for more. Believe me when I say that I'd never do anything to hurt you.'

Tears prickle my eyes. 'I do.'

'I was just trying to help out someone in trouble. I should have told you. Of course I should. But, in my own stupid way, I was trying to protect you. I may have been misguided, but I didn't want to put any more pressure on you.'

'We should have taken five minutes to clear the air,' I acknowledge. 'It wouldn't have built up in my mind out of all proportion like it has.'

'We need to find time for each other, Juliet,' he says. 'In all this madness –' he gestures to where our rabble of guests are waiting for their lunch '– let's not lose sight of ourselves.'

'You're right.'

'We need to make time for us.' He holds me tightly, and I melt into the comfort of his arms. 'We should have a romantic night, like we did last night when everyone was out, on a regular basis.'

'I'm not sure I'm up for being tied to the coffee table again.'

We both laugh at the memory.

'We could go to a hotel,' Rick offers. 'Just overnight. They could cope without us.'

'Yes. We should do that.' Then I find myself crying. 'It would be nice.'

'Hush, hush,' he says, rocking me like a child. 'No crying on Christmas Day.'

383

'No.' I sniff back the tears.

'I'm sorry,' Rick says. 'Forgive me?'

'Of course I do.'

'You can put me on potato-peeling duty as punishment.'

'I think Merak has done you out of a job.'

'Then I'll make it up to you some other way, Juliet. You'll see.'

'And this girl, Lisa? You say that she's all by herself today?'

'Yes. I think that's why she keeps texting me. She's lonely. It's just her and her little girl – a waif of a thing – by themselves with no heating.' Rick's voice cracks again. 'Imagine spending Christmas Day like that!'

'I can't,' I admit. Not now. Not now, when my home is filled with warmth and laughter and plenty. But it's easy for me to think back to when I was a child and it was just me and Mum and Dad sitting quietly round a meagre turkey and dreaming of what it would be like to have a big, happy family Christmas filled with fun. That's the image that rips at my heartstrings. 'Phone her,' I tell Rick before I think better of it. 'Phone and tell her that, if she wants to come and spend Christmas with us, you'll go and pick her up.'

Rick's face brightens. 'Really?'

'Get her to bring some overnight things, too. She might as well stay.'

'Are you sure?'

'Of course. I just wish you'd told me earlier.'

'So do I,' Rick says. 'I should have known what you'd do, too.'

'Go on, then,' I chivvy. 'Call her.'

384

'The dinner won't spoil, will it?'

'I'll keep it all warm until she gets here.'

While Rick phones the girl and asks her to spend Christmas Day with us, I think – for what must be the umpteenth time – that I had better peel some more potatoes.

# Chapter 73

While Rick is going to collect Lisa and Izzy, I tell our guests that lunch is going to be delayed slightly and top up their glasses again. I try to miss out my mother, but she's having none of it. I drain the dregs from the advocaat bottle, mix it with some brandy, lemonade and lime juice and she knocks back yet another glass. Dad rolls his eyes at me, and I wonder whether I should tell her that we've run out, or open another bottle. But she's dangerous whether she's drunk or sober, so I find another bottle in the cupboard. I put out more bowls of Kettle Chips, mixed nuts, the Eat Me dates and some cheese straws that Dad has baked. Everyone tucks in. I hope they don't eat too much, though, as I've got enough potatoes in the oven to sink a battleship.

On the sofa, Tom and Mali are sulking, arms folded in defensive poses, while the boys have a bare-knuckle fight on the floor unchecked.

'Those fat boys are fighting,' my mother notes over the rim of her glass.

'They'll be fine,' I say, trying not to look. As long as they don't kill each other before lunch.

It wouldn't be the first time I've spent five hours in A&E on Christmas Day. One year, Tom broke his arm when he came down in the dark just before dawn to see if Santa had eaten his mince pie and went headlong down the stairs. Dinner was delayed that year, too. Then there was the time that Rick sliced through his finger with the K-tel cordless electric carving knife that has remained unused in the drawer ever since. The Christmas that Chloe got her first bike ended in tragedy and a trip to the hospital when she went straight over the handlebars and knocked out her two front teeth. In fact, there have been too many disastrous Christmas dinners to recount. This year, I hope, will be different.

Jaden is entertaining them all with his electric guitar at full volume. Chloe and Mitch are trying to look encouraging, and I notice that Chloe has her hand tucked into Mitch's. Only dear, sweet Holly is sleeping blissfully through the din. I don't think Jaden will be on *Britain's Got Talent* any time soon, and I'm glad to retreat to the kitchen.

I put some more potatoes to roast in the oven and Merak, bless him, follows me into the kitchen and peels more veg to add to the pans that are starting to bubble on the hob. He's probably glad to escape the noise too. I can only hope we've got enough to feed everyone. I don't like anyone to leave the Joyce household hungry.

When everything is under control, I think about texting Robin Westcroft. It's only now that I've got a moment to do so. I don't know why, but my thoughts have turned to him several times this morning, and I'm hoping that everything is OK with him and his wife.

I tap out a text. *Hope you and Rosemary are having a lovely day. Merry Christmas from Juliet, Rick and family xx*

A few seconds after I send it, my phone rings and it's Robin at the other end.

'Hi,' he says. 'Merry Christmas.' But I can tell from his voice that it's not very merry at all.

'Is everything all right?'

'No,' he says without preamble. 'She's left me, Juliet. This morning.' A sob chokes his throat. 'Who leaves home on Christmas Day?'

'Oh, Robin.'

'She's got someone else, and she's gone to him. Just like that.'

I don't know what to say.

'What am I going to do?' Robin asks. 'What am I going to do now?'

'Don't be alone,' I urge. 'Not today. Come over here.'

'I'd be terrible company, Juliet,' he says. 'But thanks for the offer.'

'Have you been drinking?'

'Not yet.'

Does he sound a bit slurry? He might. 'If you have, then Rick can come for you.'

'No, no. I promise you I haven't touched a drop. But I warn you, I *do* plan to get seriously and heartily drunk.'

'That's fine by me. If you're still sober, then get in the car and come straight over,' I insist. 'I don't want you to do any-

thing silly. I won't have you drinking alone on Christmas Day.'
The Westcrofts live in an enormous house in a village outside Stony Stratford, and I can picture him rattling around in
there by himself. Don't they say that the majority of relationships break down at Christmas? But it must, surely, be a rare
one that actually ends on Christmas Day itself. 'We can just
sit you in a corner and ply you with red wine, if that's what
you want. Please don't stay at home and brood. Lunch is nearly
ready, so you'll have to get here as soon as you can.'

'I'm still in my dressing gown.'

'It'll take you five minutes to have a shower and get dressed.
You can be here in no time at all. We'll wait for you.'

'I don't like to intrude.'

'I won't take no for an answer, Robin.'

'Then I'd better jump in the shower,' he says, and now I can
hear a glimmer of a smile in his voice.

'See you just as soon as you can get here.'

I hang up.

'More carrots and parsnips?' Merak asks.

'Yes,' I agree. 'I think we better had.'

# Chapter 74

Rick arrives back with Lisa and Izzy. Both are scrubbed shiny and are wearing what are clearly their best clothes. I can see why Rick was concerned about them, though, as both mother and daughter look as if they could do with a damn good meal in them. I'm hoping we'll rectify that very soon before everything is a dried-up mess.

'Hello,' Lisa says shyly. 'This is very kind of you.' She pushes Izzy forward. 'Say hello to the lady.'

'Juliet,' I tell her. 'Hello, Izzy.'

The child sucks her thumb and clings to Lisa's leg.

'Make yourself at home,' I tell her. 'You're family now.'

'I've heard a lot about you,' she says.

My husband and I exchange a glance. Rick knows that my expression says that until a short while ago, I had heard nothing very much about *them*. I smile at Lisa. 'And I'm very much looking forward to getting to know you and Izzy.'

Rick puts down Lisa's overnight bag. We're going to need to have a serious bedroom reshuffle before the day is out.

'We've got another visitor on his way too,' I tell Rick.

'Oh?'

'Robin Westcroft's on his own today. *Wife's left*,' I mouth, so that Lisa can't see. 'I thought he might like to join us.'

'The more the merrier,' Rick says. 'We'd better put the kitchen table in the living room, as well – if it'll fit – and move the sofa to one end.'

'That sounds like a fine idea. I'm going to need to serve this dinner soon.' The turkey is beginning to look like a barbecued budgie.

'I'll get Merak to do it with me in a minute,' Rick says.

'He's in the living room doing another drinks round at the moment.' I turn to Lisa. 'Let's take you both through to meet everyone. I apologise in advance for my mother. She's not herself.'

In the living room, Jaden is still on the guitar. My mother is accompanying him by singing 'I Am Sixteen, Going On Seventeen' from *The Sound of Music* in front of the Christmas tree, though my grandson is actually playing a completely different and somewhat unidentifiable tune. Some of the tinsel is draped round her shoulders and she has two crimson baubles dangling from her ears. Liesl she isn't.

'I tried to stop her,' Dad says, head in hands. 'God knows I tried.'

'Come on, Mum. Sit down now. We're about to have dinner. And we've got some guests.'

'Give it a rest, Gran,' Chloe shouts. 'You'll scare the baby.'

Thankfully, Mum stops singing. Suddenly, it catches me unawares that it would normally be Samuel standing here, belting out a tune or two. My throat closes and tears rush to my eyes. I bite them down. This is neither the time nor the place, but the absence of Samuel cuts like a knife.

Rick, blissfully unaware of my turmoil, takes the opportunity to ease the guitar from Jaden and hide it behind the tree. 'You can play that later,' he says with a wink. I know that he's secretly hoping Jaden will forget that he ever had a guitar and that we probably should have gone for the Grand Play Villa option from Toys R Us instead. Or, in fact, any other silent toy.

'Everyone, this is Lisa and Izzy.'

'You're a pretty little thing,' Mum says, and I'm so relieved because, frankly, these days it could have been so much worse. I feel like I'm on tenterhooks every time she speaks.

'Hi,' Chloe and Mitch say. 'Merry Christmas.'

'And this is Merak.'

Lisa turns to look at our newly adopted son and everything in the room goes still – even I can feel it. Their eyes lock, and the connection between them is instant and electric. Merak looks as if he might fall to the floor with joy.

Eventually, Lisa breaks the spell. 'Hi,' she says shyly.

'I am very pleased to meet you,' Merak responds when he finds his voice.

I'll swear there are fireworks exploding all round them, and the aftershock of my mother's singing is replaced by the faint strains of Karen Carpenter crooning 'Close To You' in the ether. Hmm. There's a turn-up for the books. I think I'd better sit them together at dinner.

The sound of a car turning into our drive signals the arrival of Robin Westcroft. I heave a sigh of blessed relief. Finally, our long-awaited Christmas lunch can commence. Then, a second later, there's an excruciatingly loud bang followed by the sound of metal crumpling and glass tinkling.

'Oh, Lord,' Rick says.

He and I rush full pelt out of the house. Robin, it seems, hasn't quite remembered where the brake is in time to stop hitting my car which has, in turn, been shunted into Rick's van which has, as a result, catapulted straight forward into the garage door.

As we approach, Robin opens his car door and slumps out sideways into the drive. 'Sorry,' he says with a hysterical giggle. 'Awfully sorry.'

When Robin Westcroft said he hadn't been drinking, I now fear that he was, indeed, lying.

# Chapter 75

Robin staggers into the house, hoisted on one side by Rick and on the other by Merak. He is veering between laughter and sobbing.

'Coffee,' I say to Rick. 'That's what he needs. Strong black coffee. And quick. I'll put the kettle on.'

'My bloody van,' Rick rages. 'Have you seen the state of it?'

'It's Christmas Day,' I remind him. 'Let's not worry about it now. We can sort it out soon enough.' But that fails to dispel Rick's black looks.

They prop Robin up in one of the kitchen chairs and I make him coffee. Rick and Merak go out to untangle the cars.

'Drink this,' I say, and hand him a cup of coffee so strong you could stand the spoon up in it.

It's fair to say that my boss is looking somewhat sheepish now.

'Are you feeling all right?'

'I'm so sorry, Juliet,' he says, head hung low. 'You're kind enough to invite me round, and then I do this.' He waves in the general direction of our crumpled cars.

'Don't worry about that, not today. We'll fix them as soon as the garage opens after the holiday.'

'I'll pay for them, of course. I'll pay for everything.'

That'll keep Rick happy, at least.

'Rosemary's gone off with a younger man,' he continues. 'A fitness instructor half her age. She said I'd become boring.'

'You're not boring,' I reassure him.

'I certainly don't have bulging biceps. Not like *Darren*.'

'Maybe not, but you're a lovely man.'

'When I'm not drunk and wrecking cars?'

'You should have let Rick come to collect you. It would only have taken him five minutes.'

'I didn't want to put him out, if you can believe it. I mess up everything.' Robin sighs, head in hands. 'Rosemary didn't appear until the small hours again. I had no idea where she was. A familiar pattern. We had a hell of a row, and she told me. This morning, she packed a bag and just went.'

'The ruby bracelet?'

'Still in its box,' Robin says sadly. 'She didn't even stay long enough to open it.' He tries a brave smile. 'I wonder if they'll give me a refund?'

'Are you feeling a bit better now?' What I mean is, can he sit up straight long enough to eat? My turkey is probably drying out nicely now to the texture of shoe leather, and at this rate I'll have to make a lot more gravy to disguise it.

Robin nods.

'Can you face some lunch?'

'I'm starving,' he admits. 'Drinking on an empty stomach wasn't perhaps the best idea I've ever had.'

'I speak from experience when I say that the alcohol/no food combo is always a dangerous one.'

'I realise that now.' Robin lets out another stifled sob. 'What am I going to do, Juliet?'

'This could be a new start for you, Robin,' I suggest softly. 'You and Rosemary haven't been right for some time.' To my knowledge, this has been building up for a couple of years. 'In a few months, when you're feeling better, you might be able to view it in a positive light. You never know, but out there the perfect woman might just be waiting for you.'

'When am *I* going to meet someone else? All I ever do is work.'

'Love moves in funny ways,' I say. 'All you need is some time. Maybe some other things in your life need to change.' I pat his knee and stand up. 'Now, if you're OK for the moment, I'd better get that lunch ready, or my guests might start eating the decorations off the tree.'

'I'm sorry to throw your plans out,' Robin says. 'I'm such a fool.'

'Stop apologising,' I insist. 'Kick back and enjoy the rest of the day.' As I plan to do.

I'm going to forget my crashed car, my son's stroppy girl-friend, my mad mother and everything else. This is the one day of the year that I love the best, and nothing is going to stop me from having a lovely time.

# Chapter 76

Merak, of course, is the first one to come and help in the kitchen. Together we carry through the turkey and all the trimmings. Then we make another trip back for the dishes of vegetables and the mountain of potatoes.

It's a good job that the lounge is the most spacious room in the house but, even so, it looks like a cramped and slightly bohemian branch of Harvester. The sofas are pushed back against the wall. All the tables we have to hand have been pressed into service and are grouped together at one end of the room. I can only hope that no one eats with their elbows sticking out, or we'll be in deep trouble.

'Ready, love?' Rick says.

The table is groaning with food. Steam is rising from the dishes of carrots, parsnips, sprouts and potatoes. The turkey looks plump and golden. There's cranberry sauce, bread sauce and gravy waiting. Christmas crackers are nestling next to everyone's dinner plate. 'I think so.'

'Right, lunch is ready,' Rick says. 'Come on, everyone. Let's sit down before it goes cold.'

With much shuffling in the tight space, everyone manoeuvres to a chair at the dining tables.

'We should take a photograph.'

'Camera's in the kitchen drawer,' Rick says. 'I'll do the fizz.'

So, while I dash to get the camera, he pops the champagne cork and pours everyone out a little bit – even Robin. When I get back, everyone has settled themselves but, as I go to take the photograph, I realise there's an empty chair. Mitch and Chloe are here, next to each other. Jaden's alongside them and Holly is in her Moses basket in the corner. Then there's Tom, Mali, the two recalcitrant children and Robin. Merak, Lisa and Izzy have got their seats. Mum's here, and me and Rick. So who's missing? I check the number of heads at the table.

'Where's Dad?'

Rick looks round. 'He was here a minute ago.'

'Perhaps he's popped out to wash his hands.' But as the minutes go by and everyone waits patiently, there's still no sign of him. 'I'll be two seconds,' I say.

Out in the hall, I shout, 'Dad! Dad!' I call upstairs. 'Dad!' Then, as I head to the kitchen, out of the dining-room window I catch a glimpse of him in the garden. What on earth is he doing there, just as dinner is about to be served?

I go outside, shivering in the cold, and I'm glad to see that Dad has, at least, slipped on his coat. He's sitting on one of the garden chairs on the patio, gazing straight ahead.

'Dad?'

When he hears me, he pulls his hanky out of his pocket and

surreptitiously dabs at his eyes. I go and sit next to him and take his hand. There are icy tears coursing down his face.

'Oh, Dad.' In all the hustle and bustle of this morning, I'd forgotten how much Dad must be suffering without Samuel.

'I miss him,' Dad says. 'Nothing more than that, love.' He pats the hand that covers his. 'Don't you worry about me.'

'Of course you miss him. We all do. I should have been more considerate. I've been rushing around like a mad thing, and I've dumped you with looking after Mum when you probably wanted some time to yourself.'

'It's my duty to look after your mum,' he says. 'She was my wife for more years than I care to remember. For the most part, her terrible singing took my mind off it. Then, a minute ago, when we were all getting ready to sit down and all of the family were there and your new friends, I realised that the person I wanted to see most would never have Christmas with us again.' Dad stifles a sob. 'And Samuel did like a good get-together.'

'I know he did.'

'You go back inside,' Dad says. 'I'll be in soon.'

'We won't start without you. I'm not having someone else missing from the table.'

'You've worked very hard to make it all nice, love,' Dad says. 'Thanks for everything.'

'Come on.' I put my hand under Dad's elbow. 'Samuel wouldn't want your lunch getting cold.'

'No.' Dad stands up, and it feels like his bones are weary. 'He was a good man.'

'The best.'

Then it starts to snow. Fine flakes that dust our faces.

'A white Christmas,' Dad says.

'Perhaps Samuel sent it for us.'

'It would be just like him.' Dad tries a smile. 'Do you think he's in a good place?'

'I'm sure he is.'

'I'd like to think that I'll see him again,' Dad says.

'I'm sure you will.' I link my arm through his and kiss his cheek. 'But not just yet, I hope.'

'No,' he agrees. 'Not just yet.'

We walk back to the house, taking it easy as the patio is getting slippery. The snowflakes land on our faces and very nearly disguise the fact that Dad is still crying.

# Chapter 77

'Where have you been, Frank?' Mum wants to know. 'The wedding's about to start.'

Dad takes his seat. 'It's not a wedding, Rita, love.'

'Are you sure? I thought Juliet was marrying that awful boy, Rick.'

At the end of the table, my husband makes stabbing movements with the carving knife and a *Psycho*-style noise in the direction of my mother.

Me: 'Rick!'

'It's Christmas,' Dad continues. 'You like Christmas.'

'Really?' Mum looks down at the cracker in her hand. 'What are all these people doing here, then?'

'They're our family,' he says, patiently. 'And our friends.'

Mum looks suspiciously round the table and harrumphs. 'I don't bloody know any of them.' My mum points at me. 'Who's she?'

'Turkey?' Rick says loudly as he begins to carve. I hope he's remembered to sharpen the knife. It's one of the very few jobs he's charged with.

'I should have remembered to sharpen the knife,' Rick says with a tut at himself.

I smile. Though I'm not sure if he wants it sharp for the carving of the turkey or the filleting of the mother-in-law.

'I'll take a photo.' Before anyone can argue, I whip the camera out. 'Say cheese, everyone!' I back up to the end of the room so that I can get our whole gathering in.

Everyone raises their glasses in a toast. 'Merry Christmas!'

The shutter clicks. Another Joyce Christmas recorded for posterity.

Finally, I sit down.

'Pass your plates along,' Rick says and he starts to dish out the slices of turkey.

Me again: 'Shall we pull the crackers?'

Taking one, I turn to Chloe and pull it with her. She's put Holly down in her Moses basket and, at the moment, the new baby is sleeping right through her first Christmas with the Joyces. Long may it last. Chloe and Mitch seem to be getting on famously, and I can only hope that it carries on beyond the festive season and that they can be a proper family once more.

The cracker bangs and Holly flinches in her cot. Chloe gets the body of the cracker and I'm left holding a piece of ripped crêpe paper and a roll of cardboard.

'A plastic fingertip,' Chloe laughs as her novelty gift drops out. 'That'll be useful.' She slips the fake, red-manicured nail over one of her own and waves it in the air.

'They were cheap in ASDA,' is my only excuse.

'I'm not putting that hat on, either,' she says.

Having no shame, I unfurl the bright green paper crown which has fallen onto the table and put it on. It's slightly too tight for me.

Chloe reads out her joke. 'What's Santa's favourite pizza?' She waits for me to guess but I'm useless at jokes.

I don't know.

'One that's deep-pan, crisp and even.'

We chuckle together at that, and then pull another cracker. This time I win, and my novelty is a pink plastic ring.

'Great bling,' she says. 'You really have pushed the boat out with these.'

'You can have it.' I slide it onto her engagement finger over the fake manicured nail. 'Hmm. Suits you.'

'As if,' she laughs. 'You can have the fake nail, I'll keep the ring.'

'Want to hear my joke?'

'If I must.'

'How do snowmen get around?' I raise an eyebrow. 'They ride an icicle.'

We fall about laughing again, more than the joke requires. Then she turns to pull one with Mitch.

Across the table from me, Izzy, Lisa and Merak are all pulling a cracker together. Merak helps Izzy to fold her little hands round the brightly coloured paper while still gazing in awe at Lisa. That's nice. When the cracker splits, they don't even care that the novelty inside is a totally useless magnifying glass about a centimetre wide. I hand Chloe's abandoned plastic finger to Izzy, who is much more thrilled with it than

403

my daughter was. The little girl smiles shyly at me from beneath her lashes.

'Thank you,' she whispers in her shy, lispy voice. 'I like Christmas.'

My heart twists. 'That's nice, sweetheart.'

I won't trouble Lisa or Merak to read out their joke, as that would mean tearing their eyes away from each other for a few seconds and I'm imagining that would prove quite difficult.

Tom and Mali are sitting at opposite ends of the table, which is not a good sign. I don't think they're turning out to be love's young dream after all. Mali, instead, is ensconced next to Robin, and is fluttering her eyelashes at him. My boss, I have to say, looks quite enthralled. It may simply be the amount of cleavage on display that's turned his head. He certainly seems to have forgotten, for the moment, that he has very recently been abandoned by his wife.

'You estate agent?' she cries out in glee. 'Very good job. *Proper* job.' She looks slyly at Tom. 'You make lot of money?'

'Oh, yes,' Robins answers affably.

Her eyes light up. 'You pull cracker with me. I very lucky lady.' So they pull a cracker together, and Mali giggles as a plastic packet containing two dice fall out onto the table. 'I told you! Maybe I throw double six,' she says. 'Get very lucky!'

Tom scowls across the table at her and she gives him a death stare in return.

'Let me put hat on.' She unravels the red paper crown and places it at a jaunty angle on Robin's head, a man who is clearly lapping up the unexpected attention. He strikes a pose and Mali claps her hands. 'Oh! Very handsome!'

Niran and Kamol, bored with pre-lunch rituals, are already eating roast potatoes straight from the bowl.

'Pull crackers!' Mali clips them both round the back of the head and, reluctantly, the boys pull crackers and put on their hats.

'My joke! Who hides in bakery at Christmas?' Mali shouts out. 'A mince spy!'

Only Robin laughs uproariously. 'Very good, Mali. Ha, ha. Yes, excellent.'

Mali looks puzzled. 'I no get this! Why funny?'

'Can we read out the rest of the jokes later, love?' Rick says, his patience clearly wearing thin. 'The food's getting cold.'

'Of course.' No one wants a cold Christmas dinner. I quickly hand round the dishes of vegetables and everyone digs in. Dad helps Mum so tenderly that it makes the tears that never seem so far away prickle my eyes once more.

'Thanks, Arnold,' she says, breaking the moment. Arnold, the toy-boy pensioner that she abandoned to his fate in the desert. Why has he popped into her mind now?

'Mum—' I go to correct her, but Dad shakes his head imperceptibly.

'Let me cut up your turkey, Rita, love,' he says, and does just that, God love him.

When everyone's served, I sit for a moment and take stock. I'm not a religious person, but I offer up a small and silent prayer for my family, our friends old and new and our loved ones who aren't with us this year, but who are sadly missed.

Then, before I feel too maudlin, I go and turn up the Christmas songs. I help Jaden to some turkey and veg, then pile my own plate high. This is one day on which I don't count the calories. Delia has done us proud. As always. The roast potatoes are perfect and plentiful. The turkey, despite its extended stay in the oven, looks bronzed and succulent and is, thankfully, plenty big enough to serve our rush of unexpected guests. Through the living-room window, I can see the snow falling – more heavily now – and my very ordinary garden is transformed into a winter wonderland. Just perfect.

'Come on, Rita,' Rick says, 'have you got enough turkey?'

'Yes, thanks, love,' Mum answers, and Dad helps her to hold the gravy boat.

'This looks delish,' Chloe says. 'Thanks. You're a top mum. No one does Christmas dinner better than you.'

'Thank you very much, Juliet.' Merak tears his attention away from Lisa. 'You are a very kind family for having me here. I am honoured.'

'I agree,' Lisa adds. 'Izzy and I can't thank you both enough.'

I look round at the smiling faces at my table and lift my glass. 'A toast,' I say. 'Merry Christmas to one and all!'

'Merry Christmas to one and all!' is echoed back to me.

This is *my* family, for better, for worse. They may not be perfect. Sometimes they may not be all that nice. But they're mine. And this is what it's all about. This is the point of life. Being surrounded by the ones you love at Christmas.

# Chapter 78

If I'm not mistaken, I'd say that the rather silly grin that's appeared on Robin Westcroft's face would indicate that he's feeling up Mali underneath the table. And, judging by the silly grin on her face too, I'd say that she really doesn't mind all that much. Oh, Lord. Tom, at the other end of the table, is drinking too much and, by no stretch of the imagination, could the dark expression on his face be classed as a 'silly grin'.

'Everyone finished?' I ask. General agreement and thanks come back from our family and friends.

Rick and I clear the table. There's very little food left, and I'm glad that I bought a big ham too as that will have to be brought into service for sandwiches tonight.

In the kitchen, Rick says, 'Round one done. You're doing a great job.'

'Think everyone's enjoying it?' I nibble my nails anxiously.

'Some more than others,' Rick answers sagely.

'You've seen Robin and Mali?'

'I think the only person who hasn't noticed is your mother.'

'Thank God for that. She'd no doubt announce it at the top of her voice if she had.'

Delia couldn't help me with the Christmas pudding as I ran out of time, but Morrisons did, and I have two of their top-of-the-range Christmas puddings on offer for dessert. Bumper-sized ones, which is just as well. One year I will make my own. I will remember in September or October that I need to get cracking. But for now, I take the supermarket own-brand puddings out of their packaging and put them on the table. At least with these there's no boiling for hours – they just need a quick ping in the microwave.

'Robin seems to be recovering from his wife leaving very quickly,' Rick notes.

'I didn't want him to have a miserable day by himself, but he's starting to take it to the other extreme.'

'We need to split them up,' Rick says. 'Move everyone round when we have the Christmas pud.'

'Good idea. Though I don't want to separate Merak and Lisa. They seem to be getting on famously.'

'Even I noticed that. I'm pleased for them. They're both good kids. Lisa needs a break.'

I touch his arm. 'I can see why you wanted to help her.'

'You don't mind?'

'Of course not. To be honest, I haven't had much chance to talk to her yet, but she seems lovely.'

'She's trying to do her best for her little girl with no support at all. It's not easy for her.'

'I don't mind taking another one under our wing.'

He winds his arms round me. 'That's why I love you.'

And, in the kitchen, while our guests are waiting for their pudding, we kiss each other long and hard. 'We'll have that romantic night yet, Mrs Joyce,' he promises.

'I'll hold you to it.' I straighten my dress and my hair. 'Now I'd better feed our guests.'

When I turn back to the table, I shout out, 'Rick!' While we were having our moment of what classes as passion in the Joyce relationship, Buster has quietly crept out of the utility room and has climbed onto one of the kitchen chairs. He's currently giving one of the Christmas puddings a good old lick, clearly before deciding which bit he should sink his teeth into first.

'Buster!' Rick shouts. 'Down, boy!'

Buster, knowing when he's been rumbled, climbs down and slinks off to his bed, tail between his legs.

'We can't tell him off on Christmas Day,' I say, feeling guilty. I have some turkey set aside for him, but I can hardly give it to him now or he won't realise what he's done wrong.

'He should know better than to pinch food off the table. We didn't bring him up to be like that.'

We didn't bring up *any* of our family to be badly behaved, but they quite frequently are.

'What shall I do? I can't serve them now. Supposing he licked the other one too, while we were canoodling?'

'Give them a good wash,' Rick advises. 'No one will be any the wiser.'

'Can you wash a Christmas pudding?'

'Run it under a hot tap, put plenty of brandy on it and then we'll set fire to it. That will kill any germs.'

'If it doesn't, it might well kill our guests.'

'We'll miss some of them more than others,' he assures me. 'It's worth the risk.'

So, against my better judgement and vowing to blame my husband if anyone goes down with food poisoning, I rinse off the Christmas puddings under the hot tap and then tip them one by one into the colander and blot off the excess water.

'Do you think they'll notice?'

'A blind man on a galloping horse wouldn't notice that,' Rick says.

Which doesn't reassure me. 'Do you want to taste it first?'

'No,' he says. 'I think we'll leave that honour to your mother.'

# Chapter 79

Rick and I trail back into the dining room. 'Pudding,' I announce, over-brightly. 'Anyone for pudding?'

There's a general murmur of consent around the table. Despite all the food we've packed in, at Christmas there's always room for more.

'Robin,' I say, 'could you possibly give me a hand bringing it in from the kitchen?'

'Absolutely,' Robin says. He retrieves his hands from beneath the table and goodness knows where. He seems to be fulfilling his promise to get roaring drunk today, as he staggers away from the table and lurches after me.

In the kitchen, I pull dessert bowls out of the cupboards. As there are sixteen of us sitting down, not all of them match. However, that's the least of my problems.

'Are you enjoying yourself, Robin?' I ask, forcing a casual air.

'Wonderful,' he enthuses. 'Excellent meal.'

'Mali is a lovely girl, isn't she?' I'm actually not sure that she's a lovely girl at all, if I'm honest. She seems like a gold-digging opportunist who can't control her children, if you ask me. But you know what I mean.

'Oh, yes,' he says. 'Top drawer.'

*Bottom* drawer would be my assessment but, as a mother, you can't help but be protective of your children no matter how misguided their choice of partner might be.

'She's also Tom's girlfriend,' I remind him gently.

'Ah, yes,' he says, slightly shamefaced.

She may not be for much longer, I suspect. But for the moment, at least, that's her classification. For Mali, I fear the garlic-crusher present sealed the fate on their future. For Tom, I think it was her trying to get off with my boss, who clearly is a better prospect than my boy.

'I understand that it's the season of goodwill to all men. I do, however, think that Mali might be taking it a bit too far.'

'Message received and understood,' Robin says. 'Just enjoying the attention, really – and she *is* very nice.'

I'm not sure Tom would agree with him right now, but I feel I've made my point.

'Would you carry the bowls through for me please, Robin?' I was going to get him to light the brandy, as it's a man-type job, but I think he's too far gone to be trusted with a naked flame. If he accidentally breathes on it, he might spontaneously combust.

I ping both of the hosed-down puddings and then put them on a silver platter that I keep in the back of the cupboard for the other 364 days of the year. To garnish, I stick a sprig of holly picked from my single precious bush in the garden on the top of each one and carry them into the dining room.

'Ta-da!' I say with false bravado as I put the puddings on the table.

Mitch stands up. 'Can I say something please, Juliet?' I notice that his hands are shaking.

'Of course you can, love.' I tap with my ladle on the table and everyone falls silent. Without further ado, in front of Chloe, Mitch goes down on one knee. From his pocket, he produces a ring box and flips open the lid. Wow. That ring doesn't look like it came out of a cracker.

Mitch clears his throat. 'Chloe,' he says, voice wavering. 'Would you do me the very great honour of becoming my wife?'

'Oh,' Chloe says. She swivels to look at me, eyes wide, questioning. I smile encouragingly at her and urge her silently, *Go on, girl. You can do this. Please say yes!* Then she turns back to Mitch. 'Yes. I'd love to.'

He slips off the plastic ring she's wearing and replaces it with the sparkling diamond. It fits perfectly. She flings her arms round his neck and they hug each other tightly.

Round the table, we all clap and then queue up to hug Mitch and Chloe.

'Congratulations,' I say to them. 'I couldn't be more pleased.'

'It'll mean a new hat, Juliet,' Mitch teases.

'I'll consider it money *very* well spent.'

'Welcome to the family.' Rick claps Mitch on the back.

'Nice one, mate,' Tom offers. 'Thanks for taking her off our hands. I might get my room back now.'

Chloe kicks her brother in the shin, as she's been doing since she was about three years old.

'What's going on?' my mother shouts.

'Chloe and Mitch are going to get married,' Dad explains.

'Now? I thought you said this wasn't a wedding.'

'Not now, Rita. But soon.'

'Oh,' she says, perplexed. 'That's nice.'

'It is,' I agree, dabbing a tear away. 'It's lovely.'

# Chapter 80

Pudding seems a bit of an anticlimax now. But when I fill my ladle with brandy, set it alight and pour it over my puddings, my guests gasp with delight. Little do they know that I'm disinfecting it as much as anything. God, I hope it doesn't taste of dog slobber. That would be a terrible end to an otherwise lovely dinner. Also, having taken all this time to decide to get married, I don't want to kill off the bride and groom before they make it to the altar.

I start to dish out the pudding and, as I do, notice that Niran and Kamol are missing from the table. They must have sneaked out when everyone was congratulating Chloe and Mitch. 'Where are the boys?'

'I dunno,' Mali says, already focused on Robin again. Who, quite quickly, seems to have forgotten our little kitchen pep talk.

'Let's move places,' Rick says loudly. 'Chat to someone else.' There's much reluctant shuffling of chairs. 'Merak and Lisa, you can stay where you are. Mali, you go and sit next to Tom. Chloe, come and sit next to your old dad.'

'It's Christmas lunch, Dad,' Chloe complains. 'Not bloody musical chairs.'

'Bring my lovely grandson with you too.'

Chloe huffs, as she always must, but does as she's told.

'I'll sit next to Mum,' I offer. 'Dad, you come and talk to Mitch.'

'Right-oh,' my ever-compliant father agrees, and toddles to the other end of the table. Every time I look at Dad I feel a rush of love, and I can't bear to think of him crying alone in the garden. Now his cheeks are rosy from the fizz and he looks like he's enjoyed his lunch. All I want is to make his life easy for him from now on.

Rick has made a good stab at defusing the Mali–Robin situation, but I notice when she sits down next to Tom that they glare at each other.

When everyone has some Christmas pudding, I excuse myself from the table and go in search of our errant teenagers. Frankly, I'm also glad to be away from the table at the moment when they actually taste it.

I search the house, but can't find them. So I slip on my coat and wellies and go outside. Buster, Christmas-pudding fiend, takes the chance to stretch his legs and check out his favourite trees. I call the boys, but get no answer. It's nice to take five minutes in the fresh air away from the warm fug of the house. Since my mother arrived, it always has to be the correct temperature for growing marijuana or she complains about the cold. Then I notice a trail of footsteps heading towards Rick's shed and follow them.

Sure enough, inside I find Niran and Kamol. And, sure

enough, they're up to no good. The boys are sprawled out on the sunloungers playing with Nintendo DS's. Between them is the bottle of advocaat, and they're both smoking cigarettes in a practised manner. Neither of them seem overly concerned that they've been rumbled.

'I think you need to come back to the house now,' I say firmly. 'Your mother will be wondering where you are.'

The shrugs that they give me indicate she probably won't be. Nevertheless, I make them stub out their cigarettes in the snow, confiscate my mother's advocaat and march them back inside. Do they walk in a slightly unsteady manner? I'm not sure. But I am sure that there's a lot less in that bottle than there was. And, indeed, when we arrive back in the living room, their mother hasn't noticed their absence at all. On the plus side no one, it seems, has died from eating the Christmas pudding.

The boys sit sullenly at the table and I consider telling Mali of their misdemeanours and then decide that I'd more than likely be wasting my breath. Even though she's sitting next to Tom now, all her focus is back on Robin and I don't think anything I say will shift it. She's flirting down the full length of the table, and I can't understand why Tom wanted to bring this odious woman and her offspring to our family gathering – even if I did nag him about settling down. Perhaps he did it in a misguided attempt to appease me. Then I glance over at my son and my heart squeezes. Tom looks as if he's regretting being so fast and loose with his Christmas-lunch invitations and has hardly spoken a word all afternoon.

You can't choose your children's partners, but I damn well

wish I could. But Chloe has done well with Mitch, and I just hope she starts to appreciate that more. Next year I will be vetting our guest list. All girlfriends and boyfriends will have to have been here at least once before, and anyone we've discovered naked in our bed is banned.

# Chapter 81

After lunch is over, Rick and I wash up. Weeks and weeks of shopping, stress and preparation, and that's it. All done. I always think that with the end of lunch, that's Christmas pretty much over. Now it's all about eating leftovers and tidying up. And paying for it.

Merak, of course, wanted to help us in the kitchen, but after he'd carried a few dishes out from the living room we dismissed him from duties for the day. I'd rather he spent some time getting to know Lisa and Izzy, as I'd quite like to think that a romance may be blossoming from our Christmas gathering. That would be a nice way to start the new year. Actually I think there may be *two* romances blossoming, but I choose not to think about the other one.

Tom and Rick move the drafted-in tables back into the garden and the kitchen, so the living room now looks less like a restaurant and we can all spread out a bit when they've returned the sofas to their usual positions.

'Enjoy it, love?' Rick asks.

'It's been great to have everyone here.' But exhausting. I can't wait to put my feet up for an hour now.

'It's good news about Chloe and Mitch,' he says.

'I'm delighted for them. I really hope they make a go of it, for the sake of the children. Perhaps Chloe is finally growing up.'

'Not before time,' Rick says.

'It just takes some people longer than others. We'll have to help them out with the wedding.'

'I'm hoping they'll have a low-key affair.'

'Chloe? Low-key?' Perhaps that is wishing for too much. I don't remind Rick that her favourite programme on television is *My Big Fat Gypsy Wedding*, and that she doesn't gasp in horror as she's watching it, as I do. We ought to start saving up – and fast.

'We'd better get on,' I say. 'They'll all be wondering where we've got to. Have you taken the tea and coffee order?'

'I'll do it now,' Rick says and disappears, taking the shopping notepad with him like a waitress, while I fill the kettle.

Buster risks coming out of his bed and wags his tail cautiously as he approaches me. 'You're in the clear,' I tell him. 'They all ate the Christmas pudding.' In fact, everyone commented on how tasty it was this year. If only they knew. 'No one died.'

At that, his tail wags more enthusiastically. Putting my Christmas hat on him, I ruffle his ears then hand-feed him a few of the last remaining bits of the turkey. I think, all in all, it's been a good Christmas Day for Buster too.

Chloe pops her head round the door. 'Mitch and I are going

to disappear for half an hour to bath and feed Holly. Can you keep an eye on Jaden please, Mum? Grandad's got him for now, but he looks like he's about to nod off.'

I'm not surprised. He must be worn out.

'Let me have a proper look at this ring first.' My daughter holds out her hand proudly. I angle the diamond towards the light and it sparkles fiercely.

'Who'd have thought?' she says. 'Had Mitch said anything to you?'

'Not a thing.' It was as much of a surprise for me as it was for Chloe. 'You are pleased?'

'Yeah. I'm over the moon.' Her face is glowing. 'He's a really great bloke, Mum. And, more than that, he's a fantastic father.'

'I'm pleased for you both, and the ring is gorgeous. Any man who can buy jewellery like that is worth hanging on to.'

'I'm so lucky, aren't I?'

I hug my child. 'Yes. Don't ever forget that.'

'I'll try not to,' Chloe says. 'I'd better go before Holly starts to scream the place down.'

'Do you want me to bring some tea up to you?'

'Nah. We'll have it when we come down.'

'Is Mitch going to stay tonight?'

'Yeah,' Chloe says. 'Is that OK?'

'If you can all bundle in together. It looks like we might have a full house. Merak's staying here, and I hope Lisa and Izzy will, too.'

'They'd make a nice couple.'

'I think so.'

'We'll get out of your hair.'

'There's no rush. We love having you all here.'

She shrugs. 'I think we'd like a quiet day on Boxing Day. I'll probably go back to our place with Mitch tomorrow.'

I smile at her. 'If you're going to get married, it would be a good idea to move back in with Mitch at some point.'

Chloe perches on the kitchen table. 'I'm frightened, Mum,' she admits as she fiddles with her new ring. 'I really want to marry Mitch. Honestly I do. But it scares me, too. When it's just me, there seems to be so much responsibility. I've got to make decisions about everything. All the time. Running your own house is hard.'

'The more you do it, the more you'll find you're able to manage,' I assure her.

She doesn't look convinced. 'I've liked being here with you to help me. Life is so much easier. I can hardly cope with Jaden on my own. How am I going to handle two?'

'You'll do just fine. Dad and I will still be here for you. That won't change.'

'You're a great mum. You've always been so fab, and I've taken it all for granted. Now I'm going to appreciate you more and try to be more like you. I only hope that I can do as well for my kids.'

'Give them a proper home, Chloe. A proper family. You won't go far wrong then.'

'I don't know if I'm really cut out to be a wife and mother.'

'It's too late to be dwelling on that now,' I point out.

'All my mates are still single and out clubbing. I can't help thinking that, at my age, that's what I should be doing too.'

'You've got two little ones who depend on you.'

'Yeah, and *that* milkshake isn't going to bring the boys to my yard,' she jokes.

Perhaps that's part of her reticence to embrace motherhood. Chloe has always enjoyed a lot of male attention. Maybe she sees this as diminishing her sexuality. I don't like to tell her that it only gets worse. By the time Holly is a toddler, she'll be so tired that she won't care if she ever has sex again. Then, when her engine is set to start revving again, the menopause hits. Life as a woman is not always easy. I think she's only just discovering that.

Instead of heaping doom and gloom on her, I say, 'You've got a wonderful man, Chloe. One who loves you and cares for you. One who's waited patiently. It's a big responsibility to bring up a family. It's no good wishing that you could turn back the clock now. That's not going to happen.' I put my arm round her shoulders. 'There might come a day when your friends wish they had what you've got. Lots of women find themselves in their thirties wanting to settle down and start a family and yet not being able to find the right man. Instead of focusing on the downside, you could start looking at what you've got and think how fortunate you are. You've got two beautiful, healthy children, a man who obviously adores you and a lovely home waiting for you.'

'I know that.' She hangs her head. 'And I've got great parents who'd do anything for me.'

'Don't be frightened by it; you're just moving on to a different stage in your life. It's called growing up, Chloe. We all have to do it sometime.'

My daughter grins at me. 'Are you absolutely sure about that?'

'This is your time to shine. Embrace your future. Enjoy building your family.'

'I'll try,' she says, and tears sparkle in her eyes as shiny as her new diamond. 'But we can still come back here every Sunday for roast dinner?'

I laugh. 'Of course you can. I need to know that you'll all have at least one decent meal a week.'

'You're the best mum in the world,' she says. 'I want my kids to say the same about me one day.'

'I'm sure they will.'

'Love you loads.' My daughter – my beautiful, lazy, stubborn, headstrong, selfish, infuriating, wonderful daughter – cuffs the tears away.

'I love you too.' Then Chloe jumps down from the table, as she's been doing since she was twelve or thirteen, a child herself, slips her arms round my neck and gives me a hug. Then she goes to look after her baby.

# Chapter 82

I'm feeling quite teary when Rick comes back with the drink orders. Not that he notices.

'I hate to tell you this,' he says, 'but I can't see Mali or Robin anywhere.'

'You're joking.' But I know that he's not.

'What do you want to do?'

'Let's get everyone settled and then I'll go and look for them. Where's Tom?'

'Pouring beer down his neck in the living room.'

I sigh.

Rick reels off what everyone wants and I make the drinks, then pile up a plate with mince pies. I'm hoping that they're all too full to want more than one, as I've just about enough to go round. I'd better bake some more tomorrow.

When I've dished them all out, I put on a lovely Christmassy film, *Nativity!*, to keep the tribe entertained. Within seconds, Mum and Dad have fallen asleep in front of it, which is fine by me as Mum is a lot less trouble asleep than when she's awake.

Jaden and Izzy are playing happily together on the floor with his racing-car garage, while Lisa and Merak are sitting chastely side by side on the other sofa, chatting away. Mitch and Chloe have taken the chance to disappear so that they can feed and bathe baby Holly, who has been a model of good behaviour all day.

I sit down next to Tom and take his beer can from him. 'I don't think that will help.'

'It might do,' he counters.

'Drink is never the answer to anything.' I take his hand. 'Just because your young lady isn't behaving very well, it doesn't mean that you should do the same.'

He raises his eyebrows. '*Young lady?*'

I dig him in the ribs. 'You know what I mean.'

Tom risks a smile. 'The day hasn't quite panned out as I'd expected.'

'I got the impression that you might already have lost interest in her by the time you got here.'

'Taking on someone else's kids is never easy, is it?'

'No.' The two teenage boys who are the subject of our conversation are currently fast asleep on the rug in front of the fire. Or they could be passed out drunk. Whichever way, I could actually quite like them if they were always like this. I nod towards them. 'These two do seem to be quite a handful. I'm not sure you're ready for that.'

'You're probably right.' Tom sighs. 'Besides . . . ' He turns to me with a shrug. 'I did meet someone else last night.' My son grins at me. 'He's a great bloke.'

'Oh, Tom.'

426

'He's a lot nicer than Mali. I don't know what I was thinking of there.'

Ah. Here we go again. Perhaps it's as well that Tom stays footloose and fancy-free until he can actually decide which team he wants to bat for.

'You won't let us find you with him in our bed, will you?'

'God, no! I realise now what a traumatic experience it is. Next time I want sex, I'm going to a hotel.'

'You should let Mali go,' I advise. 'If there is something between her and Robin, then why try to stop it if you're not interested?'

'You don't think I should fight my love rival to the death for her?'

'Does she really mean that much to you?'

He shakes his head.

'Then just move on.'

My son leans over and kisses me on the cheek. 'Has anyone ever told you that you're far too nice, Mother?'

'I'm just trying to be philosophical.' I pat his hand. 'I don't want to spoil Christmas Day, either.'

'Do you think it was the garlic crusher that did it?'

'I think the present-buying model that your father uses isn't one you should necessarily emulate.'

He laughs at that. 'All those years of wheelbarrows and frying pans hasn't put you off him?'

Looking over at Rick, I see that he's chatting to Merak and Lisa, and is oblivious to our talking about him. 'It was a close-run thing sometimes.'

'I want what you've got,' Tom says. 'Just not yet. Not for about another ten years. Or maybe twenty.'

I don't point out that it's taken us the best part of twenty-seven years to build up what we've got. I guess Tom will just have to find his own way in life.

Patting his knee, I say, 'I should go and find Mali. These boys look like they're ready to go home.' I could be charitable and say that perhaps they've either worn themselves out with all their fighting or the excitement of the day, and forget about the advocaat binge.

'You're the best, Mum,' Tom says. 'I know that I'm a crap son and I don't say it very often, but I do love you.'

'That's made my Christmas Day,' I tell him. 'It's better than any present.'

'Ah,' Tom says. 'Sorry about the present. Or lack of it. I owe you one.'

'I can live without another garlic crusher,' I tease. Then I set off to track down the missing Mali and my boss.

# Chapter 83

With much trepidation, I make a tour of the house, gingerly opening the bedroom doors. I knock and look in on Chloe, and she and Mitch are cuddled up together on the bed while she feeds Holly.

'Everything OK?'

'Fine,' she says, a look of sleepy contentment on her face that's equalled by the same expression from her child. 'We'll be down soon.'

They're a picture of happiness, and I wish that they could capture this moment for ever. I close the door on them again with a warm smile in my heart.

Having checked all the bedrooms, I come to the conclusion that Mali and Robin must be outside. And there's only one destination I can think of. Oh, dear. In the kitchen, my coat and wellies are pressed into service again. It's dark outside now, and I notice that someone has switched on the Christmas lights that adorn Rick's shed. The pink HO-HO-HO flashes out into the garden.

I walk down the path, not sure that I want to be doing this, but they've been gone for far too long now. 'Robin,' I shout out, tentatively. 'Mali! Are you out here?'

I'm regretting coming out now. Perhaps I should just leave them alone until they've done what they're doing and had their fun.

As I get closer to Rick's shed, I can hear much frantic rustling. That has to be them.

'It's probably time you came back to the house,' I venture. They are, after all, both supposed to be guests in my home, not bonking in Rick's beloved shed. He'd be furious if he found out. No one messes with the shed. 'Mali, your boys look like they need to be taken home. I'll leave you to it. I hope we'll see you in a few minutes.' Then I turn to make my way back to the house.

As I do, the shed door bursts open and Robin staggers out. 'Sorry, Juliet,' he says. 'So sorry.'

His shirt is buttoned up all wrong and he's only wearing one shoe. Inside the shed, I catch a glimpse of Mali rearranging her clothing.

'It's fine,' I say, averting my eyes. 'No harm done. But it's time you came back now.'

'I must apologise to Tom,' he continues. 'We were simply overcome by passion.'

Ordinarily, I'd view that as a good thing, but on Christmas Day it's all a bit much for me to cope with. 'There are mince pies and coffee,' I tell them, as if that's any consolation for my breaking up their private party.

Then the back door bangs and Rick comes striding down

the garden with Buster in his wake. 'What's going on here?' he wants to know.

'It's fine, Rick,' I say, and hold up my hands in a placatory manner.

'Who's been in my shed?' I knew that he would be more concerned about the usage of his shed rather than the usage of Tom's girlfriend.

But Robin doesn't realise which misdemeanour Rick is most concerned with and starts to back away. 'I can explain,' he says. 'I'm so very, *very* sorry.'

Rick advances, Buster barking excitedly. My husband's face is black. No one, but *no one* switches on his HO-HO-HO but Rick.

Robin moves away more quickly. He hits the cobbles at the edge of the pond and, owing to the fatal mixture of alcohol and ice, he topples. I lunge forward and try to catch hold of Robin's shirt. Buster, eager to join in, bounds in front of me and jumps up at Robin's legs. The dog is more successful than I am and hits Robin squarely in the thighs.

'Buster, no!' I shout. But it's too late. The motion propels Robin backwards and onto the ice that covers the pond. The ice creaks alarmingly and I gasp. And the sad thing is, I think it might just have held his weight if Buster hadn't then jumped right in on top of him.

The ice cracks and Robin sinks through it into the freezing water. 'Aaaggh!' he shouts, flailing about.

Buster, assuming that this is a marvellous game, keeps jumping on him.

'Buster,' I call out. 'Come out, boy. Come out now!'

'Oh, Lord,' Rick says. He stands at the edge of the pond, rubbing his hands through his hair until it's all on end, trying to work out how to grab the dog or Robin without himself getting wet.

'Do something, Rick,' I urge.

'Like what?'

Mali is out of the shed now and dressed again. 'Help, help!' she cries, rushing up and down in the snow in her high heels. 'Help! Help!'

That brings everyone else dashing out of the house and into the garden. Even Mum and Dad totter down the path. When Tom sees what's going on he starts to laugh, and pretty soon is doubled up.

Mali starts to smack him. 'You no laugh,' she says. 'You no laugh. No funny!'

'What's that man doing in the pond in this weather?' Mum asks. 'Is he mad?' For once, it's a good question.

Merak, Lisa and Mitch appear. They've dressed Jaden and Izzy in their coats and boots and the children run about the garden in the snow. Mali's boys follow. Merak starts a snowball fight and pretty soon he, Lisa and Mitch and all of the kids are joining in, rolling around on the ground, shrieking and laughing. I can see that Chloe is watching from the living-room window, safe in the warmth of the house, a smile on her face, Holly cradled in her arms.

Fat snowflakes start to fall and Mum holds out her hands. 'This is lovely,' she says, and she twirls round and round.

'Be careful, love,' Dad says. 'Mind you don't slip.'

432

'Dance with me, Frank,' she instructs.

'Now?'

'Can't you hear the music?'

'Oh, yes,' Dad says. 'It's lovely.' So my dad takes her in his arms and they waltz about in the falling snow. Mum, still wearing her red paper Christmas hat, throws her head back and laughs. She hums to a tune that no one else can hear and sounds happier than she's done in years.

'Help!' Mali shouts. She stamps her foot. 'Help!' She's clearly annoyed that the attention is drifting away from herself and Robin, who is still in the water, gasping and waving his arms. The dog is still enjoying himself too.

'Oh, God,' Rick mutters. 'I live in a madhouse.'

'We do need to do something,' I suggest to my husband. 'If we don't get Robin out in a minute, he's going to get hypothermia.'

'You're right.' Rick takes a deep breath. 'Robin, mate. Stand up.'

Robin, spluttering and floundering, stops. 'What?'

'Stand up,' Rick repeats. 'It's not even two feet deep.'

'Oh.'

Robin stands up, dripping water and weed. Buster, sensing that the game is over, paddles out and shakes himself off. All over Mali.

'Nasty dog!' she yells. 'You nasty dog!'

Buster takes this as an invitation to lick her.

Robin wades out of the pond, looking sheepish. He's starting to shiver.

'I'll run you a hot bath,' I say. 'Get you warmed up.'

'Thank you, Juliet,' he replies, sounding a lot more sober now. 'That would be very kind of you.'

So I lead a very soggy and shamefaced Robin back inside, Mali stomping after us in her short skirt and her low top and her high heels.

# Chapter 84

The side gate swung open and Neil Harrison's head poked round it. 'Merry Christmas, Rick,' he shouted out. 'Mind if I come in?'

'No, no,' Rick said, waving him into the garden. 'Merry Christmas to you.'

'Heard a bit of a commotion,' Neil told him. 'All OK?'

'Someone went into the pond,' Rick explained. 'Bit too much Christmas cheer.'

'Ah. So easily done. I'm glad to get away for a breather.' He flicked a thumb back towards his own home. 'All my lot are rowing. It's the same every year. The entire family descend on us. They all hate each other. We're lucky if no one gets killed. But it's Christmas.' He shrugged. 'What can you do?'

They took in the kids building a snowman, Lisa and Merak mooning over each other, his mother-in-law dancing with her ex-husband, and Rick said, 'Families, eh?'

'Yeah,' Neil agreed. 'Families.' Then his neighbour stood with his hands on his hips, surveying the garden. 'The lights look great here, Rick. Fine show.'

'Can't compete with yours,' Rick said, hoping the bitterness didn't show in his voice.

'It's not a competition, mate,' Neil said. 'Those lights are my only solace. Cathy is a complete Christmas nut, and it drives me mad.'

'Same here, mate.'

'The only pleasure I get is putting those decorations up.'

'Really?' Rick brightened. 'That's exactly how I feel.'

'I saw you and Frank bringing stuff in and wanted to come over and have a look, lend a bit of a hand. But you can't just barge in, can you? I didn't know if you'd resent the intrusion.'

'No, no,' Rick said. 'Come over any time. You're more than welcome.'

Neil moved down the garden, taking in Rick's new lights and making appreciative noises. 'Fine work. Fine work,' he muttered to himself.

Along with his neighbour, Rick admired the lights that he and Frank had bought – the pretty Christmas tree, the Santa and reindeer silhouettes gracing the shed; Samuel's pink HO-HO-HO and the rope lights bordering the pond. He'd been so busy, he hadn't had time for a proper look himself. Now that he did, he felt rather proud. It did look good. Even though Rick said so himself, he and his dear old father-in-law had done a great job together.

'The shed looks excellent. Star on top is a touch of genius. I particularly like the arrangement of the pulsing light rope round the door.' Neil nodded in approval. 'Very classy.'

'Want to crack a beer, Neil? I've got a fridge in there.'

'A fridge? Now I *am* jealous. I've always wanted a shed of my own.'

'Really?' Rick felt a warm glow in his chest.

'*Very* jealous,' Neil reiterated.

'Let me show you round it,' Rick said.

So the two of them left the rest of the family in the garden and retreated to the sanctuary of the shed. When they were comfortably settled on the sunloungers and Neil had expressed his effusive admiration, Rick opened them both cans of beer.

'Merry Christmas,' they toasted together.

'I like the flashing HO-HO-HO. Magnificent.'

'B&Q's finest.'

'Get a lot of mine from the States,' Neil told him. Rick had thought as much. 'I worked over there until last year, and they really go to town. You should have seen what I used to do to the house out there. Drove Cathy mad. I'll have to show you some photos. There's even more stuff in the garage – boxes full – that I can't use.'

'Really?'

Neil sipped his beer. 'You know, we should get together next year. Do something mega. You could use some of my spare lights on your house.'

Rick felt his heart soar. 'I like the sound of that.'

'Maybe we could do it for charity. Put a couple of little boxes outside for donations. People like that kind of thing.'

'Sounds fantastic. As soon as Christmas is over, we should have regular planning meetings in my shed. It could be our headquarters.'

Neil clinked his tin against Rick's. 'It could indeed.' His

neighbour sighed. 'This is the life. I'm glad to get away for half an hour's peace.'

'My sentiments exactly,' Rick agreed. He felt that he'd found a new friend. Who knew that, behind those flashy Christmas decorations, his neighbour was such an affable chap?

# Chapter 85

I run Robin a bath while he perches, still fully clothed, on the loo seat. His teeth are chattering. I put in plenty of foam – lavender-scented. That skanky green pond water is going to take some scrubbing off. Then I bring him a towel, hot from the airing cupboard, a pair of Rick's jeans, a shirt, some socks and a new packet of pants that I was going to give my husband for Christmas but forgot about. Fortunately for Robin.

'There you are.' I hand them all over.

'Thank you, Juliet.'

'Just come downstairs when you're ready.'

'I don't know how I can face you all again,' he admits.

'We have very short memories in this house,' I tell him. 'Though you might offer an apology to Tom. It's not exactly broken his heart, but you have pinched his girlfriend from under his nose. He's probably feeling embarrassed.'

'No more than me. Please don't tell anyone in the office about this,' he begs.

'Of course not.'

'You're a good woman, Juliet, and I don't like to think that I've abused your hospitality.'

I have to laugh. 'You did liven up Christmas Day somewhat.'

He hangs his head and I go to kiss his cheek.

'We'll put it down to stress,' I say. 'You've had a lot to deal with.'

'You're very understanding.'

'You need to get in the bath now. I don't want you to catch your death of cold, so I'll leave you to it.'

Back downstairs, Mali and the boys are standing in the hall. She's called a cab and is waiting for it.

I brace myself to be polite. Very soon she will be out of our lives and, hopefully, that's the last we'll see of her. 'It's been very . . . interesting . . . meeting you, Mali.'

'Likewise.' She views me through narrowed eyes.

I can't say I'm disappointed that I'm not going to become Mali's mother-in-law any time soon.

'Robin? He OK?'

'He's fine.'

Headlights flick into the hallway and the noise of a car pulling up says that her taxi is here.

'Boys,' she says. 'Come, come.' Mali thrusts a business card at me. All it has on it is her name, mobile number and the image of a red stiletto shoe. I don't think I want to know what kind of business Mali engages in. Perhaps I should have viewed those six-inch heels with more suspicion. 'Give this Robin. Tell him call me.'

She totters to the door and lets herself out. The overgrown boys lope after her.

'Merry Christmas, Mali,' I say. But, as she gets into the taxi, there's no reply.

I look out of the kitchen window. In the garden, everyone is building a snowman together. Even Mum and Dad are joining in. So I wrap up warm, find a carrot in the fridge and take out a hat and a scarf and some gloves to dress our latest addition. He's a bonny snowman. The family have done a good job.

Outside, I take Tom to one side and say quietly, 'Mali and the boys have gone.'

'Oh, great,' he says. Not quite the reaction I expected. 'Would you mind if I call Chris and see if he wants to come over later?'

'Chris?'

'The guy I met last night.'

Seems like his broken heart is soon mended. Oh, well. I shrug. 'Why not?'

'Cheers, Mum.' He wanders off, pulling out his mobile as he goes. Looks like we may yet have another visitor before the day is out.

Lisa is brushing snow from her daughter's hair. 'Have you had a nice day?' I ask. 'Dramas aside?'

'It's been lovely,' Lisa says. 'It would have been so boring to be by ourselves.'

'Yes. That's one thing I can say about this house. It's never boring.'

'I promised myself that one day, I'd give Izzy the best Christmas I could,' she says. 'But you've done that for me, Juliet.'

'It's been my pleasure to have you both here. She's a lovely little girl. You should be very proud of her.'

She grins, suddenly bashful.

I smile at her. 'You seem to be getting on very well with Merak.'

'He's really nice,' she says shyly.

'We love him to bits,' I tell her. 'He's like family.'

'Then he's a very lucky man.'

I slip my arm round her shoulder. 'Why don't you stay here for a bit longer?' I suggest. 'If you can put up with us. I don't want you going home to a cold house. Stay here for the rest of the holiday.'

'That would be great,' she says. 'If you're sure.'

'It might be a tight squeeze, but we'll manage. Jaden will be company for Izzy. I'll get Rick to run you home tomorrow to pick up some more things.'

'Would you like that, Izzy?' she asks. The little girl nods excitedly.

'Then that's agreed,' I say.

'Merry Christmas, Juliet. Thank you so much.'

'Merry Christmas to you too.'

The snowman is just about finished, and Rick lifts Jaden onto his shoulders so that he can put the knitted hat onto his head. Rick fixes his carrot nose and Tom winds the stripy scarf round his neck. He's given two sturdy twigs as arms, and Dad slots the gloves onto each one. We use stones for his eyes and his mouth and three for the buttons on his tum.

'He's smiley,' Jaden says. 'Happy.'

Mum stands and looks at him in awe. She claps her hands together. 'We should call him Samuel,' she says brightly.

Everyone freezes and there's a moment of silence, then Dad says, 'That's a lovely idea, Rita. Samuel the snowman.'

The snow continues to fall and Christmas Day is nearly over now. And I think we've come through it relatively unscathed. In fact, I'd go as far as to say that I can't wait until next year.

# Chapter 86

We've all thawed out from playing in the snow. Now every radiator in the house has drying coats and socks on it. We've eaten ham sandwiches, Christmas cake and a fairly good dent has been made in the bowl of tangerines. Most of the nuts and the dates have gone, and I've even forced down a bit of stollen.

'No one likes stollen, Juliet,' Rick says, pulling a face as he tastes it. 'I don't even know what it is. Next year, don't bother to get any.'

'It's not Christmas without it,' I point out. It's like saying don't get a turkey or Brussels sprouts. It's what you have at Christmas. But I have another year to think about that. My thoughts, instead, turn to more pressing matters. 'Now, where are we all going to sleep tonight?'

Tom's new friend, Chris, has arrived and seems like a much better choice of partner than Mali, I have to say. Chris is tall, blond and rather handsome. His clothing is suitable for the occasion and, more importantly, he doesn't have two borderline aggressive children in tow. He's slipped seamlessly into the day, despite being a late starter.

'Who's that?' Mum wants to know. 'Do I know him?'

'That's Chris,' I tell her. 'Tom's friend.'

'Where's that woman gone who was with him? The one who had the fat children and wanted to show everyone what she'd had for breakfast?'

'She's gone home.' Thankfully.

'Oh.'

It's no wonder she's confused sometimes. I have trouble keeping up myself.

My mother knocks back yet another advocaat. She holds out her skirt and starts to sing 'If I Ruled The World' to the Christmas tree. And why not? Dad is snoozing in the corner. He must be absolutely exhausted by now. The way things are going, he might end up spending the night on that sofa. An ancient repeat of *The Morecambe and Wise Christmas Show* is on the television playing to no one in particular. Angela Rippon's high kicks are, I'm afraid, completely wasted on the Joyce household. Robin has finally reappeared. I did wonder whether he'd ever come down out of our bathroom, or if he was going to spend the rest of his life up there. He's looking scrubbed and polished and slightly strange in Rick's clothes. He's also looking rather more subdued than previously.

He comes over to Tom. 'I would just like to apologise,' Robin says. 'I behaved appallingly.'

'No worries.' Tom sneaks a sideways glance at Chris. 'I've moved on.'

I have no idea if Robin realises quite how well. But then he might just understand, as Robin didn't seem to spend too long mourning the hasty departure of his wife.

As we move away from Tom, I slip him Mali's business card. 'She asked me to give this to you.'

'Oh, my word,' Robin says, and hurriedly secretes it in his pocket. 'Thank you, Juliet.'

I have no idea if he'll call her, but I think he'll need some luck if he does. And his large bank account may come in handy.

'Can I just say that you have been the perfect host. Even if I haven't been the perfect guest.'

'It's been lovely having you here, Robin.' And it has. Sort of. At least, all's well that ends well.

Jaden and Izzy are now firm friends, and are ready for bed in their pyjamas. All I have to do is allocate everyone beds.

'Chloe, can you squeeze Mitch and the two children into your room?'

She shrugs. It'll be tight, but there's not much else she can do, really.

'Mum can stay where she is.'

'What?' Mum wants to know.

'Nothing.' I don't want to put Dad in with her because, although he's doing a grand job of looking after her, they're not a couple any more – even though Mum seems to have forgotten this. 'Dad, you can go in our room.'

'Righty-oh, love.'

'Lisa and Izzy, you can have the spare bedroom. It's not big, but there's a single bed in there and we can find a blow-up mattress. It's not ideal, but I hope it'll be all right for a few nights.'

'Juliet,' Lisa says. 'Anywhere is better than where we've been living. I'd sleep on the floor here and be happy.'

'I'm afraid the honour of the floor is going to Tom and Chris. That's if you're staying over?'

When they both nod that they are, I say, 'Rick, you need to go and get the air mattresses out of the loft.'

My husband looks thrilled by the prospect. 'Any idea where they might be?'

'No, but they're up there somewhere. You'll find them.' I'm only hoping that I've got enough bedding to go round.

'Robin, would you mind taking the sofa?'

'I can go home, Juliet,' he says. 'I feel that I've perhaps over-stayed my welcome.'

'What nonsense.'

'I can easily call a taxi.'

'On Christmas night? No. I won't hear of it,' I tell him. 'You're not going home to an empty house.'

'Sofa it is, then,' he agrees.

'Merak, do you mind going on the futon in the dining room?'

'That is fine, Juliet,' he says. 'I am very grateful.'

'Good. That's it.' Excellent. 'All sorted.' Phew. That wasn't nearly as painful as I thought. I had visions of someone having to share Buster's bed.

'You've forgotten just one thing,' Rick says.

I give him a puzzled glance.

'Exactly where are *we* going to sleep?'

# Chapter 87

The clock ticks towards midnight, and that's it. Christmas Day is over for yet another year. My twenty-seventh as a wife and mother. And, perhaps, one of the most memorable.

'Comfortable?' Rick asks.

'Very.' I turn to him, his face illuminated by the flashing of the pink HO-HO-HO. 'This is a very well-appointed shed.'

We have the fan heater on in here, so it's cosily warm. I also have the hot-water bottle that Rick bought me out here, a most useful present after all. Rick has brought out a bottle of champagne and we've enjoyed a couple of glasses together in a rare moment of peace and quiet.

He snuggles up towards me on the sunlounger laid out right next to mine. 'You realise that this is probably the closest we're going to get to a romantic break away for some considerable time?'

'Yes,' I say. 'We're going to be busy with Chloe and the baby. But she is lovely, isn't she?'

'Beautiful.'

'She'll always be special to us,' I say. 'We helped bring her into the world.'

'And we'll help her throughout her life.'

'We will.'

'You were great today,' Rick says. He strokes my face in the darkness. 'Thanks for taking care of Lisa and Izzy too.'

'They were no trouble at all. I've asked them to stay over the holidays,' I tell him. 'I thought you could run them home quickly tomorrow to pick up some more of their belongings.'

'I can't stand the idea of them going back to that freezing-cold house.'

'We'll help her to sort something out. Don't worry.' Then, 'Chloe says that she's going back to Mitch's flat tomorrow. We'll have a spare room for a while.'

'Chloe won't go home tomorrow,' Rick says. 'Not when there's a pile of food here. They'll stay for a few more days yet.'

'You're probably right.'

'I want them to stay,' Rick says. 'There's nothing like having all the family around at Christmas. And a few extras.' He sighs contentedly. 'I was thinking, when they do go, Merak could have the spare room.'

'If you don't mind not having a dining room, we could con-vert that into a bedroom permanently, too. That should just about house everyone.'

'I thought when Chloe and Tom were older we'd be rattling around in this place. I didn't reckon on starting again with a whole new family.'

'Then there's Mum and Dad too,' I remind him. 'Mum needs permanent care now, but I couldn't see her go into a

449

home. It may come to that, eventually. But I couldn't do it just yet.'

'No.'

'I don't want Dad to go home and be by himself, either. I think he's missing Samuel more than he shows.' I think again of him crying alone in the garden, and my heart weeps with him. 'I'd like him here with us.'

Rick thinks on it for a moment, then says, 'We could sell your mum and dad's house. Use the money to build an extension over the garage and make a little annexe for them. Do you think they'd be up for that?'

'That sounds like a good idea. I'm sure they would.'

'We could probably squeeze in two bedrooms and a bathroom up there.'

'I'd like that. I'll talk to Dad tomorrow, see if he's agreeable.'

'Your dad's always agreeable, Juliet. My bet is that he won't mind at all.'

'Thanks, Rick.' I love the idea of having both of my parents here under my watchful eye.

'It's been a good Christmas,' Rick muses.

'One of the best.' We've had a death, a birth, an engagement, a possible new romance, a potential new business liaison, have narrowly avoided food poisoning and witnessed a pond-dunking. And both my car and Rick's van are crumpled wrecks. As is the garage door. In my joy, I nearly forgot about that. Well, you can't say it hasn't been interesting.

'Shall we settle down?' Rick says. 'We're going to be feeding the five thousand again tomorrow.'

'I never mind that. Good job I bought in extra.' There's a pile of sausages and bacon in the fridge, and two dozen fresh eggs. The toaster will be working overtime.

I turn to my husband and kiss him.

'What's that for?'

'For a lovely Christmas.' Then I wriggle in as close as I can. 'I've never made love on a sunlounger,' I tell him.

'Me neither.'

'I'm not all that tired.'

Rick laughs. 'Me neither.'

My husband shimmies over and I climb onto his sunlounger with him. It's a good job that we spent a bit extra and went for the super-duper luxury ones rather than the Argos budget ones we'd first looked at. We slide our bodies together and cuddle up. After all this time, they instinctively know how to mould perfectly. Our dips and curves fit each other's like a jigsaw.

'Merry Christmas, Juliet. Here's to many more together.'

I look back at the house through the shed window: our home. It's all in darkness, and looks still and settled for the night. Calm. A blanket of stars twinkles above it. Fine snowflakes flutter onto the garden. I think of our family and friends nestling down inside, and feel a peace in my heart.

If I could reach our champagne without upsetting the sunlounger, then I'd be tempted to propose a toast. A toast to love. A toast to family. A toast to being kind to each other. But, as that seems highly unlikely, I kiss Rick and, instead, just say, 'Merry Christmas, love.'

# Carole's Tips for Surviving a Family Christmas

## In the Run Up

### Be Organised

For some this will mean starting their Christmas shopping in the January sales, for others July is their starting point. For a considerable amount of the population it will mean thinking on Christmas Eve, 'Omigod, it's Christmas tomorrow,' and running out to see what they've got left in TKMaxx. Just make sure that whatever your style, that you're within your comfort zone. I like to be organised and make lots of lists, but I also like the shops to be in their festive garb before I actually start buying.

### Get Your Invitations in Early

My mother will announce what she's doing for Christmas in about June, so I always know where I stand. With everyone else, we have to bid for Christmas and you'd better get your invitations in quickly before there are too many options. Popular family members well might get an offer to go somewhere better than your house and you'll be left with the ones that no one else wanted.

## Buy Everything

Every year, I buy copious magazines that are replete with the type of Christmas that magazine editors think we should be having. I drool over their pages, thinking that I'm going to dash off handmade place cards for everyone, cut out snowflakes from glittery paper and fashion my own festive crackers. Every year I vow that I'm going to try out some of the fabulous recipes, make my own Christmas cake/pudding/mince pies. And every year I get to December, think, 'sod it,' and go to Marks and Spencer and just buy everything. It saves a lot of time and stress.

## Cut the Present List

I have one brave friend who buys for everyone. No matter how tenuous the acquaintance, they get a Christmas present. She is the start-in-the-January-sales kind of woman. For her family alone, that runs to fifty individual presents. Just writing that makes me feel dizzy. She also buys wonderful presents and I don't know how she does it. I am a great one for the present cull. It doesn't mean that I think any the less of my friends; I just hate shopping with a passion. I hate being bought things that I don't need – unless it's chocolate-based, of course – and assume everyone else feels the same. See below.

## Cut Presents Entirely

No one needs Christmas presents these days. We've got everything. Once upon a time, if you wanted new slippers, you waited until Christmas for them and hoped that after dropping enough hints someone would kindly gift them to you. Sometimes, if you got your timing wrong, that could mean eleven months in skanky slippers and terrible disappointment on Christmas Day. Now, when our slippers or anything else fails, we just go out and buy replacements. Most of the time, we don't even wait for our old slippers to wear out. Need perfume? You might only run out of your favourite scent in November, but you just go and get another one. Now everyone swaps vouchers. You get a voucher for Next from Auntie Margaret, you give her one from Debenhams. They lie in both of your purses unspent until they've run out of date. It's a tricky subject to broach, but I'm sure if you suggest that you don't exchange presents at Christmas, most of your family and friends will be mightily relieved. If not, they'll stop speaking to you and you'll have one less present to buy anyway.

## Buy All Your Presents on the Internet

For the presents that you *do* have to buy, use the internet. Yes, I know this is flying in the face of all the 'Save Our High Street' propaganda at the moment. But if the high street wants us to shop there, then they should make it a more pleasant experience. It's bad enough at any time of the year, but at Christmas it can be a nightmare – trawling round looking for a parking space, being pushed and shoved around the shops by better shoppers than yourself, spending hours finding the right present, then having to queue for just as many hours to pay for it while being served by a surly teenage assistant who's rapidly losing the will to live.

Internet – click, click, click. That's all I'm saying.

P.S. John Lewis, you are the exception to this rule.

**Buy The Perfect Gift**
For yourself. As no one else will.

**Have a Family Outing Instead**
Instead of exchanging presents why not get all your family and friends together and go to a panto, have a nice meal or enjoy a day out somewhere? It saves a lot of squabbling and return-ing things without receipts in the sheer hell that is the January sales. Obviously, the teenagers will loathe this idea as it will involve them coming out of their rooms to socialise, but that is their role at Christmas.

**Budget**
If you are a consummate present-buyer and won't be swayed, then budget carefully. Set a limit per present and stick to it. The last thing you want to be doing is paying for this Christmas until the next one. It's not the amount you spend, it's the thought that goes into it. I was once given a pair of American Tan tights by my ex-mother-in-law for Christmas. She had left the 30p price label on them. I feel she didn't fully embrace  this concept.  If you're a baker, then a box of

Christmas cupcakes is the way to go. If you're a keen crafter, then you already have Christmas all sewn up – pun intended. For teenagers, think cold hard cash. Prevent smaller children from watching any Christmas television at all. They'll no doubt see an advert for the one thing that's the must-have toy and will, therefore, not be available in any of the shops and you will have failed as a mother.

## Get in the Mood

Embrace your inner Christmas elf. Make sure your tree is up in November at the very latest. From the beginning of December onwards, read lots of Christmassy books – including, of course, a range by my good self. Watch lots of Christmas films. Eat lots of Christmas chocolate. Have your Christmas playlist on all the time. You won't get fed up of the songs, they'll just be ingrained into your psyche by the time the big day arrives. The first television showing of *The Muppet Christmas Carol* is when Christmas starts in our house. You can't help but feel just that little bit more festive when Kermit pops up as Bob Cratchit.

# On the Day

## Start Drinking Early

On Christmas Day it has become a pleasant ritual to spend the morning at our next-door neighbour's house. Which means kicking off at ten o'clock with bucks fizz. We normally stay there for a couple of hours and leave feeling a) very giggly or

b) very mellow. Either is an excellent way to start Christmas day. If you have small children this is entirely out of the question as you'll have been up since four o'clock and will be ragged by nine. This is your Christmas until they're old enough to realise that Santa doesn't exist and turn surly.

## Don't Start Drinking Early

The downside of starting to drink alcohol too early – particularly when it's something like bucks fizz where it's so easy to think, 'pah, it's only spiked up orange juice,' – is that you will then be required to produce Christmas lunch while inebriated. In recent years this dreadful mistake has led to me dropping the Christmas dinner twice on the kitchen floor as I was about to serve it. Though turkey sandwiches are an excellent and quick substitute – provided you pick all the fluff off the turkey first. If you have family coming along expecting lunch, try not to be lying comatose on the floor when they arrive. It's probably a good idea to have a designated drinker for the day. Even better if that person is not the cook.

## Handling Tricky Relatives

If you invite your mother-in-law for Christmas Day, then you are truly a saint. You will never do it as well as she does. In her eyes, your family Christmas traditions will always be found wanting. She will remind you of this frequently throughout the day. If you're lucky she won't get you confused with your husband's previous wife after a few glasses of cheap fizz. Never ever, in any circumstances, invite both sets of parents on the same day. Few marriages will survive this.

A couple of well-aimed sherrys for elderly relatives never go amiss. But don't tip them over the edge with brandy butter on the mince pies as well. On the other hand, keep teenagers well away from anything alcoholic. They want to be anywhere else other than at home on Christmas day, but if they are too young to drive, then they are stuck with you. They may retaliate by downing anything in sight and throwing up underneath the Christmas tree.

**The Dastardly Christmas Dinner**
Don't sweat. Christmas dinner is just a Sunday roast with a few extras. Seriously. Wang in a few chipolatas. Job done. Every supermarket now does pre-prepared veg. Use it. No one needs to peel carrots on Christmas morning. If you've got a huge number of family members coming around, get them to bring something with them. If dinner's late, does it really matter? If it's slightly chargrilled round the edges, will anyone notice? The kids normally only eat the chipolatas anyway. If you have a vegetarian relative, remember that turkey omelette is not a viable option.

Don't try to be a martyr and make it perfect all by yourself. Other people can set the table, do the washing up, peel spuds, open microwaveable packets, bring stuff that they have cooked/bought. Also make sure you know which corner shop is open on Christmas Day for the one essential thing you forget.

Don't buy Christmas crackers. They are a waste of money and serve no purpose other than to make every one look stupid in their paper hats and the dinner that you've spent an age preparing goes cold while you're faffing about with them and reading out bad jokes.

Take time with your seating plan. An excellent tip is to put relatives who are likely to kill each other at opposite ends of the table.

It is the one day of the year that the word 'diet' must never be uttered!

When it's all over, put your feet up and get someone else to wash up.

**Post-Dinner Entertainment**
Now that *The Queen's Speech* and *The Morecambe and Wise Christmas Show* are no longer the staples of festive entertainment, you might have to be more creative. Get out the SingStar, the Wii, the Xbox. Some families even still play board games! Though these can lead to serious arguments resulting in previously close and loving families never speaking to each other again. Avoid the minefield of Trivial Pursuit and Monopoly. They rarely end well. Charades – don't even go there. The children will, of course, want to play with their new toys. Just remember that they will all be broken/have run out of batteries by tea time. Never underestimate the recuperative powers of the turkey coma afternoon nap. Everyone will be happier if you just let the teenagers go back to their PlayStations for the rest of the day.

## Whatever You Do Be Relaxed

January is the busiest time of the year for starting divorce proceedings. This is because every married couple has argued their way through Christmas. This, the season of goodwill to all men, is the most popular time of the year for monumental rows. And, even if you survive without a real humdinger, there'll probably be lots of opportunities for skirmishes along the way. Step back. Take a deep breath. It's one day. Go with the flow. Pour yourself another drink. Enjoy it. It's another year before you've got to do it all again.

## Find Some Me Time

Like that's going to happen. If you're a mother, no one is even going to say thank you for putting yourself through all this.

## If All Else Fails ...

Turn off the lights, hide behind the sofa and pretend you're not at home. Next year book to go to the Caribbean for the whole festive holiday.

# Boxing Day

You've survived Christmas Day for another year – hopefully with your sanity intact. Boxing Day is excellent recovery time. Just make sure you've arranged to go to some other poor, unsuspecting relative's house.

If you're one of those rare families who sails through Christmas on a cloud of goodwill without uttering a cross word to each other, then you are truly blessed. And even if you're not, they're your family. Put all the squabbles aside, be kind to each other, enjoy each other's company and have a very merry Christmas!

If you enjoyed *With Love at Christmas*,
you only have to wait until April 2013
for Carole's next bestseller,

## A Cottage By the Sea

Join best friends Grace, Ella and Flick
as they prepare for an eventful week away.

EXCLUSIVE!
Read on to enjoy the first three chapters!

# Chapter One

'*Destination*,' the dulcet tones of the sat nav announces. '*Destination*.'

Harry stamps on the brakes and stops dead in the middle of the road. There is nothing as far as the eye can see. 'Where, you bloody stupid woman?' he asks it, holding his hands aloft in supplication. 'Where?'

'*Destination*.' She is insistent. '*Destination*.'

The sat nav has the disdainful, upper-class tone of my old English teacher. She always hated me too. Normally, we call the sat nav Auntie Flossie. Today, neither of us is really speaking to her.

'Can you see anything, Grace?' he asks.

I gaze out of the car window. It's beautiful here. The road stretches ahead of us, unbroken and there's not another car in any direction. The verdant green fields lie unspoiled beneath the unbroken acres of sky. There isn't a single man-made building in sight to mar the view. It's untamed, remote. And I guess that's the crux of our problem.

'Not really,' I admit. But it's fantastic and I hear myself sigh happily.

'Well, she says we're here.' It's clear that Harry is rapidly losing the will to live.

'Can you just look at the map please?'

I scrabble at the road atlas on my knee. It's a tattered wreck and what remains of the front cover tells me that we bought it from a supermarket in 1992. Helpfully, it has a little red circle where all of their branches are – but none of the major roads built since that year, of course. Somewhat worryingly, there are no helpful red 'supermarket' circles anywhere near here. According to this map, we are in total supermarket wilderness.

In fact, there's not very much near here at all. Currently, the only thing I can see are the miles and miles of rolling fields, hedgerows thick with flowers and sheep. Plenty of sheep.

'Fucking place,' Harry complains.

He is not a happy man. He is gripping the wheel again and his knuckles are white. His handsome face, however, is scarlet becoming borderline puce. My husband, I know, would rather be in Tuscany or Thailand or even Timbuktu. Anywhere, in fact, rather than on our way to a cottage in Wales for a week.

'We can't be far away,' I offer, keeping my tone placating.

The polar opposite to Harry, I'm just thrilled to be here. My dearest friend, Ella Hawley, has invited us to stay with her and her long-term partner, Art. Ella's spending the rest of the summer in Wales and I just can't wait to see her. She's only recently inherited this cottage, but I've heard so much about it over the years that wild horses, never mind a grumpy husband, wouldn't have kept me away. Ella's also invited our friend Flick too, but whether or not Flick will turn up is an entirely different matter. You can never quite pin Flick down. I hope she makes it as I haven't seen her in ages and it will be so lovely to catch up.

Outside the chilled atmosphere in the Bentley – only some of it due to the effect of the uber-efficient air-conditioning – the sky is a blue more usually seen in the Mediterranean and beneath it, on the very edge of the horizon, a silver ribbon of sea shimmers invitingly. We can't be far away because Ella's cottage is by the sea and, if we drive too much further, we'll be actually be in it.

'*Destination*,' the sat nav repeats.

She now sounds slightly weary with life. As am I.

'Get a grip, woman. We're not at the destination,' I tell her firmly. 'Even I've worked that out.'

'Grace,' Harry says, teeth gritted, 'do you mind? We can't stay here in the middle of the road all day.'

To be honest, Harry and I haven't really been speaking since we stopped at Magor Services just before the Severn Crossing. The service station was a glimpse of hell on earth with queues a mile long for everything and the place stuffed with families screaming at each other. Harry couldn't get anything to eat but a plastic ham sandwich on white bread and he's very much a smoked salmon on wholemeal man. His temper, already frayed by the amount of holiday traffic on the road, shredded to breaking point.

It hasn't helped that we've been on the road since silly o'clock and that there was a ferocious tailback to get over the bridge and into South Wales. On top of that, it cost us nearly six quid to cross. Cue much muttering under Harry's breath that people should be paying to get out of Wales, not into it.

'We could have been halfway to the sodding Seychelles by now,' he mutters darkly.

In theory, I suppose we could be. But there's so much else to consider with flying somewhere. It starts with all the vaccinations – nearly the cost of the holiday in itself. Invariably we require malaria tablets too, which make me feel dreadful. The whole experience is just so stressful. All the glamour of flying has long gone. I always feel as if I need another holiday when I've flown for thirteen or more hours just to get back from somewhere. Your memories of the island paradise fade very quickly when faced with a four-hour-long queue to get back through passport control at Gatwick or Heathrow and a week of hideous jet lag.

'I hate long-haul flights nowadays, Harry. You know that. For once, isn't it nice to throw the cases in the back of the car and just drive?'

I get a grunt in response.

Despite my husband's reticence, I'm so looking forward to this holiday and am so desperate for it. Work has been nothing but stress this year – the financial climate forcing everyone to tighten their belts and our business is no exception. I'm an accountant - the staff partner in a small, but successful firm based in north London. We have only ten staff but, believe me, they're a full-time job to manage and I've just had a small mutiny on my hands as we told them that there will be no company Christmas trip this year. Normally, we take the staff and their other halves on a long weekend jaunt during the approach to the festive season. In the past we've been to Paris, Rome, Bruges. All very lovely. All on expenses. But this year we're going to have to do without. Every single one of our clients is watching their pennies and I think it only looks right that we should do so too.

I feel the same about our own holidays abroad. More often than not, Harry and I go away at least twice every year. But how can that be right when so many people are struggling simply to pay their mortgages? I'm more than happy to have a summer just staying at home, although I don't think Harry much likes the sound of it. So, when Ella asked us to come down and spend some time with her at the cottage, it seemed like the perfect solution. To me, anyway.

Harry wasn't keen, of course. Even as we set off he was bemoaning the fact that it would be more 'basic' than he prefers. My other half likes to lie on a sunlounger for two weeks and be waited on hand and foot. He doesn't care if there's culture or scenery. He just wants heat, a swimming pool and alcohol on tap. He likes a turndown service, a chocolate and perhaps an exotic bloom on his pillow every night. Those things don't really interest me. Don't get me wrong, I've enjoyed my fair share of luxury holidays too. But sometimes it can be just a tiny bit *boring*. Does that sound ungrateful? If you're typically British and fair-skinned, there's only so much sunbathing you can do if you don't want the boiled-lobster look. So this year I'm really looking forward to having a holiday in my own country for the first time in many years. I get to catch up with my dearest friends. Harry and I get to spend some quality time together without having to go halfway round the world. It'll be fun. I'm sure. Just the tonic we need.

'Shall we aim to get there before nightfall, Grace?' Harry says tightly.

So I pull my attention back to the map and try to work out exactly where we are.

# Chapter Two

The fact that I get to hook up with my lovely friends is the icing on the cake for me. I'm not sure that Harry's feeling that either. My husband isn't overly fond of my friends. He says that I change when I'm with them. But I think, half of the time, he doesn't like it when he's not the centre of attention and you know what it's like when old friends get together.

Ella, Flick and I all went to university together in Liverpool over ten years ago and, as such, go way back. We're more like sisters than friends and are inseparable. I feel as if we grew up together. Those formative years shaped us into the women we are today. Ella Hawley, Felicity Edwards and Grace Taylor. I smile to myself. We were quite the girls back then. A force to be reckoned with. Mainly due to Flick, I have to say. She was the one who dragged us kicking and screaming into the thick of student life. I'm sure Ella and I would have stayed at home in our skanky rooms every night studying if it hadn't been for Flick. Ella's the arty, thoughtful one. Flick is the fabulously pretty, fickle one. I, for my sins, am the steady and sensible one. Though we're ten years older now and, supposedly, wiser, our roles haven't changed that much.

We all took different courses at university, but found ourselves in the same halls. We hooked up at one of the events in Freshers' Week – I can't even remember what now – and have been together through thick and thin ever since.

After that first rollercoaster year where we struggled to get out of studying to keep pace with our partying, we escaped halls and moved as a team into a totally hideous flat at the top of a draughty Victorian house in one of Liverpool's less salubrious areas. I only have to think for a minute how awful it was and it makes me shudder. The carpet had that terrible stickiness of a back-street pub and, as we were on the top floor, the windows had never been cleaned. They still hadn't when we left two years later. Learning how to exterminate cockroaches, mice and silverfish together is always going to be a lifelong bonding experience. Though it always seemed to be me, with rubber gloves and dustpan, who had the job of clearing up the resulting corpses.

Not only did we share the same hideous flat, but we also worked in the same hideous bar. Honkers. I don't have to say any more, do I? There's a fantastic, sophisticated nightclub scene in Liverpool. Honkers wasn't part of it. We used to run a sweepstake between the three of us – five pounds at the end of the night to the person who got the most gropes. One point for a bottom grope, two points for a boob grope. Flick had the dubious honour of winning most nights.

We put up with the groping, largely without complaint, simply to earn some extra cash to supplement our drinking –

sorry, our studies. If someone got a feel of your tits they tended to give bigger tips. Oh, happy days. Our shared horror only helped to make our little team stronger than ever. Even though we had no money and lived in a fleapit, they were good times. We had fun together. Mostly. But there were heartaches too and we vowed then that nothing would ever come between us. Not men, not fame, not fortune. It's fair to say that's it's only the men that have troubled us thus far.

Harry doesn't like it when we spend hours reminiscing about a life and a time that he wasn't involved with. I'll admit that when we get started on the 'good old days' we do get a bit carried away with ourselves. Once we get going, we can talk for hours. You can't help but do that with good friends, can you? It's not as if we have huge reunions every five minutes. We all have busy lives and often only manage to get together every couple of months for a catch up. We normally go out for a glass of wine and a pizza, nothing more exciting than that. We haven't had a 'girls' holiday together since we all went to Prague on my hen weekend over seven years ago now. So, as reluctant as he is, I'm sure that Harry can't begrudge me a week with my friends.

'I'm dying of thirst,' Harry says sullenly.

My heart sinks. He needs alcohol is what he means. I think this interminable car journey is the longest I've seen him go without a drink lately. I don't quite know what's going on, but recently there have been far too many late nights at work, too much restorative red wine. When he does eventually come home, I can't prise him away from his iPad or his mobile phone. It seems as if he'd rather spend time doing who knows what on Twitter than be with me.

It pains me to say that I can't remember the last time we had a conversation that wasn't in raised voices. We've been married for seven years, but I can't see us making another seven at this rate. It's not so much the seven year itch, as the seven year slump. The last few months in particular have been just awful and, as a couple, we're as far apart as we've ever been. We get up at different times, go to work, eat dinner separately. Sex is a distant memory as I'm usually in bed and long asleep by the time Harry climbs the stairs. The weekends are no better. Harry's taken to shutting himself in his office and I mooch round the house by myself until I too give up trying to have fun and resort to the distraction of paperwork. It's no way to live. It's barely half a life. We are living to work, not working to live.

If I'm honest, there are times when I've just felt like walking out. It's only the fact that I remember the Harry who I married – just about. The man who was charming, sophisticated and great company. It's just a phase, I keep telling myself. It can't be roses round the door all the time. But sometimes it's hard when I look at the stranger sitting next to me.

We're both desperate for this break and I'm so hoping that we can just spend some time together relaxing, having fun and getting back to how we once were. That's all we need, I'm sure. Time. Time to sort things out. Time to have a laugh. Time to work out where it's all gone wrong.

I glance across at him. He's still a good-looking man. Tall, once quite muscular, but now that he's drinking more there's a hint of a paunch as he's never been one to embrace the idea of rigorous exercise. We used to like walking, but now it's all I can do to get him out of the flat at the weekend to go for a stroll down the road. The distance between our front door and the pub is the only walking he likes to do these days. His blue chambray shirt is straining slightly at the seams. I daren't suggest a diet as that would only be another reason to argue, but I'm gently trying to introduce healthier options into our evening meals. Harry's older than me. At forty-four, he's twelve years my senior. Not a lot these days, I guess, but I wonder if it will become more of an issue as the years pass. Still we have to patch up where we are now before I can worry about the future. I want to run my hand through his hair. It's cropped short, greying slightly at the temples. He hates it when I touch it.

This person was once the life and soul of the party. Harry only had to walk into a room to make it light up and I was in awe of him. He was always so confident, so assured that it spilled over on to me and I blossomed in his love. We were great as a couple. We might never have had a wild passion as such, but we were solid. So I thought. We fell into step nicely together. As a couple the whole was better than the sum of two parts. I sigh to myself. Now look at us. Two people circling each other, never quite in time. This holiday will do us good. It will bring us back together, I'm sure. Because, more than anything, I want my husband to fall in love with me all over again.

Harry's voice breaks into my thoughts. 'Found out where we are yet?'

476

'Yes,' I tell him. Though, if I'm honest, I'm not exactly sure. Anxiously, I twiddle one of my curls as I try to figure out where we are on the lines and squiggles of the map. I wasn't blessed with the map-reading gene, hence our heavy reliance on the sat nav. 'It's just over this hill. I think.'

With a tut, he stomps on the accelerator and we set off again. A few minutes later, over the brow of the hill as I'd predicted, I'm mightily relieved to see a sign for Cwtch Cottage – pronounced Cutch, so Ella tells me.

'This is it,' I assure Harry and we turn into a narrow track.

We slow to walking pace as the lane is bordered by high hedgerows on each side and has a tall line of grass right down the middle of it. It's like a secret passage and we squeeze our way towards the cottage. Already I feel as if I'm entering a different world.

'I hope this doesn't scratch the paintwork,' Harry grumbles.

I feel stupid in this car. A Bentley doesn't fit with the scenery. Frankly, it doesn't fit with me at all. But it's Harry's new toy. His pride and joy. He treated himself to it a month or so ago when he had his annual bonus from work. Though I've no idea why anyone would feel the need to spend so much on a car. It's an insane amount of money to blow. To top it off, he bought a personal number plate too. He loves its gleaming black showiness. I just wish that we had something a little more anonymous. Something in beige that the local vandals wouldn't feel the need to run a key down the side of it. This car is criminal damage waiting to happen. To me a man with a flash car is like him walking round waving his willy in front of him. But as I hardly ever drive now – who needs to in

London? – I don't feel that I can really impose my low-key choice of car on my other half. If this is what Harry wants, then who am I to argue?

A profusion of wild flowers blooms in the hedgerow, glorious shades of pink, yellow and white. I open the window to let their colourful heads trail over my hand. The scent is heady.

'You'll get seeds and all sorts in the car,' Harry says. 'Next summer there'll be dandelions growing in the carpet and we'll wonder why. Shut the window.'

Reluctantly, I do.

Thankfully, a short and bumpy ride later, Ella's cottage comes into view. 'We're here!'

The sight of it takes my breath away. Cwtch Cottage stands in splendid isolation on a rocky promontory at the entrance to a small, secluded bay overlooking the sea. It's a simple structure, long and low, painted white and I don't think I've ever seen anywhere quite so beautiful.

'Oh, look at it, Harry,' I say. 'Wasn't this worth that awful journey? It's stunning.'

Ella had shown me photographs of the cottage, but they just hadn't conveyed how spectacular the setting was. There's an unbroken view right to the horizon where the sea meets the sky.

Harry brings the Bentley to a standstill at the end of the bay and stares out of the window, open-mouthed. 'Christ, there's nothing here.'

'It's wonderful.'

The tight band that seems to be melded to my heart these days eases slightly. I think I can actually hear it sigh with relief.

Tears prickle behind my eyes. You can keep your Seychelles and your Maldives, this is paradise to me. How I wish we were staying here for two weeks or even longer. A week seems barely adequate.

My husband is less moved by the surroundings. The expression on his face is bleak.

'Where's the nearest pub?'

'I don't know. Ella said that it was quite remote.'

'You're not bloody kidding.'

'Oh, Harry.' I kiss his cheek. 'It will be lovely, you'll see.'

'I haven't seen anything for miles.' He punches his digit at his mobile phone. 'No signal either.'

Smiling, I offer up a silent prayer of thanks. A whole seven days without having to compete with Twitter!

I put my hand on his arm. 'I'm really looking forward to this. We can have some time just to be together, to chill out, to put things right.'

'There's nothing wrong with us,' Harry says crisply.

But there is, I think. We both know that there is.

# Chapter Three

We park up outside the cottage next to Ella and Art's cars. I climb out and massage my back. Even in a posh car all the hours of sitting have taken its toll. The breeze lifts my hair from my neck and I can taste the tang of salt in the air. The heat of the sun on my cold skin feels like a loving caress. Ella rushes out to greet us.

'Hey!' she shouts and grabs hold of me in as near to a bear-hug as someone who is five foot nothing can manage. We do a little dance while still holding tightly on to each other. 'God, it's so good to see you. I've missed you.'

'Well, now we've got a whole week to gossip to our hearts' content.'

'How lovely.' Ella looks as excited as a child at Christmas. 'Was it a pig of a journey?'

'It wasn't the best,' I respond wryly.

'The weekends are always a nightmare. Too many cars on the road.'

'We're here now,' I say. 'Let relaxation commence.'

Harry is hanging back, fussing with the cases and the gifts that we've brought.

She flicks her head in Harry's direction. 'Is he in a mood?'

'Frightful,' I tell her and we giggle together like schoolgirls.

'We'll soon get the old bugger sozzled,' she promises. 'That'll make him loosen up a bit.'

Ella's not to know that I'm worried about his drinking. Harry has always liked a drink and turns into a party animal after a bottle or two. But, in the last six months, I feel that it's become a more regular habit and has tipped over the edge into something else.

'Liking' a drink has suddenly become 'needing' a drink, I feel, and I'm concerned about the amount of wine that he gets through in a week now. I've even been tempted to hide our recycling box so that the neighbours don't see the amount of empty bottles in there. Whenever I've tried to raise the issue with him, he's just snapped at me. But I'm frightened that Harry can't do without alcohol to get him through the day. I haven't yet mentioned my unease to either Ella or Flick. Somehow by keeping it to myself, I could pretend that it really wasn't a problem and I don't want to start the holiday on a negative note by voicing my fears, so I keep quiet.

Harry comes and takes Ella in his arms. 'Hello, darling,' he says. 'How's life with you?'

'It's good. Sorry that we're in the middle of nowhere,' Ella gushes. 'I know that you like having a multiplicity of bars and coffee shops close to hand. But just look at the view!'

'Fantastic,' he says in a voice that barely disguises the fact that he's disappointed that we're not admiring a white sandy beach in the Caribbean. He eyes the seagulls suspiciously. 'Brought my own booze. Thought I might need it.'

Harry flicks a thumb towards the boot of the car where there are two cases of wine nestling. Inwardly, I sigh. I couldn't persuade him that we didn't need to bring quite so much booze with us. Harry insisted that he needed it to 'get in the holiday mood'.

'Let's take a closer look at the beach,' I suggest. 'Coming, Harry?'

'I'll stay here,' he says. 'See if I can get a signal.' He waves his mobile at me.

Why? I wonder. *Why?* Can't he leave it alone for five minutes?

Ella leads me by the hand to the edge of the terrace. Away from the shelter of the cottage, a stiff wind whips in from the sea. But the breeze is warm and the cool spray spritzing my faces feels wonderful, zingy. It's late June and summer is only just starting to live up to its promise. The weather for the last week has been sweltering, sultry, and it's so nice to be out of London in the oppressive city heat. I lift my arms and reach out to the sun. I should be in an advert for Ocean Breeze shower gel or something. No doubt my mass of brunette curls, untameable at the best of times, will take on a life of their very own here.

'God, this is brilliant.' I want to throw off my clothes and run barefoot in the sand. 'How do you stay away from this place?'

'It's increasingly hard,' she admits.

'I'm not surprised. I'd never want to leave.'

Ella inherited the cottage when her mum died a few months ago after a stroke. It wasn't entirely unexpected as Mrs Hawley wasn't in the best of health and had been in a nursing home for a few years prior to that, suffering from a hefty catalogue of illnesses. But it's never easy to lose a parent whatever the circumstances. Barely a year earlier Ella had helped to nurse her dad through terminal cancer, so she's gone through a rough time. Flick and I have supported her as much as we could but, as she was an only child, the weight of the burden had fallen on Ella.

'You look fantastic,' I tell my friend. 'You're positively blooming.' She blushes at that. 'The sea air must suit you.'

Ella favours the Goth look. Today she's abandoned her trademark black clothes for faded denim shorts and a fitted white shirt. Her dyed black cropped hair is messier than usual and it suits her. Her normally pale face has a smidgen of tan and the pinched look, from nursing ailing parents for too long, has all but gone. She's put a few pounds on her waif-like frame and – though I'd never dare to tell her this – it sits well on her.

'I do feel like a different person when I'm down here,' she confesses. 'Perhaps I've found my spiritual home.'

'"Spiritual home",' I tease. 'You've been smoking those strange-smelling cigarettes again.'

'No,' Ella says, 'not me!'

'Well, whatever it is, it suits you.' I nod back towards the cars. 'I see that Art's already here.'

'He came down last night,' Ella says. She lowers her voice. 'He's a grumpy bastard too. He and Harry can sit on deckchairs and get pissed together.'

'Is he being supportive?'

She sighs. 'In his own sweet way. You know what men are like. Art doesn't *do* illness or death.'

'He probably doesn't know what to say for the best,' I offer. 'It doesn't mean that he doesn't care, sweetheart.'

'I know. Sometimes I feel I'm bottling things up for Art's sake when what I really want is a good blub. He's just so hopeless at dealing with emotion.'

'Tell me about it. After all these years of marriage, Harry still has no idea what to do if, on the rare occasion, I actually cry.'

'I've been down here for a week already,' she tells me. 'Just making sure that the place is spick and span. With Mum having been in the nursing home for so long, it hasn't been used for a while.'

'How are you coping, generally?' I ask, giving her a squeeze.

'OK,' she says. 'Some days better than others. I miss Mum terribly, but she hadn't been herself for ages, so it was a relief in some ways. She hated living like that. She'll be happier now that she's with Dad.' We both start to well up. 'Don't start me off!' Ella cuffs away the tears. 'We're here to have fun this week, put all this out of my mind for a time.'

'And fun we will have,' I assure her. 'I've so looked forward to seeing you. We can have a good catch-up and relax.'

Cwtch Cottage has been in Ella's family for many years. I think it had originally been handed down to Ella's parents by an old spinster aunt of her dad's. Ella spent all her childhood holidays here and always used to tell us how fond she was of the place. Then when her dad fell ill and couldn't travel, her mum didn't want to come here on her own without him. Ella used to bring her occasionally, but the visits were few and far between. Then, in turn, her mum became too frail to make the journey and the cottage was pretty much abandoned.

'The place needs a bit of TLC,' Ella continues. Much like my good self, I think. 'I've tried to get down at least a couple of times a year, but it hasn't always been easy. Thankfully, there's a lovely lady in St Brides who keeps an eye on it for me, makes sure it's not consumed by the sea or too overrun by spiders. But I'm going to have my work cut out getting it back up to scratch.'

'Well, it looks very lovely to me.'

'Thanks. Inside is a bit bashed and scuffed, but it's very cosy. We'll have a great week. I'm so excited to see you. I hope you like it, Grace. I've wanted you and Flick to come down here for ever.'

'Well, I'm glad we finally made it.'

Ella tucks her arm into mine and steers me back towards the cottage. 'You're looking very tired, lovely lady. Everything OK?'

'Work, life.' We exchange a glance. She knows that Harry and I are having a tough time together, if not the specifics. 'Nothing that a glorious week by the seaside won't cure.'

'We'll have those roses back in your cheeks in no time.' She gives my face a friendly pinch.

I breathe in the fresh, salty air and wonder why I live in a flat in the city. Harry, standing behind the Bentley, is still trying to get a phone signal. He gives up when he sees us coming back and busies himself lifting one of the cases of wine out of the boot with a grunt.

'Can I give you a hand with that, love?'

'I can manage,' he puffs as he falls into step behind us.

'You look as if you've come well prepared, Harry!' Ella teases.

'I know what you lot are like when you get together,' he tosses back.

Ella grins at him.

'Is Flick still coming too?' I ask.

'Oh, you know what Flick's like,' Ella says, rolling her eyes. 'She's supposed to be arriving later. But, as we can't get a phone signal here, I haven't been able to ring her and double-check. It's only a ten-minute drive to the nearest phone box, but I haven't had a chance to get there either. I told her she wouldn't be able to get in touch with me, but she's probably forgotten. I bet she's texting me like mad and wondering why I'm not replying.'

'I hope she hasn't forgotten altogether that she's coming.' Our friend isn't known for her reliability.

Ella laughs. 'I wouldn't put it past her, but I've made the bed up anyway.'

'I thought she couldn't make it.' Behind us, Harry sounds tetchy. He's not Flick's biggest fan. He finds her too loud, too attention-seeking. He thinks she's a bad influence on Ella and me. And he's probably right.

I shrug. 'She changed her mind at the last minute.' She could, however, just as easily change it back.

Harry tuts and stamps ahead of us. Ella and I exchange a

glance and a giggle. 'He loves her really,' I say.

Flick doesn't like to commit to anything and, even if she's said that she'll come along to some get-together or another, is always liable to change her plans at last minute. I think it comes with not having a partner to answer to. Ella thinks she's just naturally born selfish, but she says it nicely.

'Is she bringing anyone?'

'I think she must be resting between lovers,' Ella chuckles. 'She said she'd come by herself.'

'Either that or he's married, as usual, and can't get away from the missus.'

'Ah, yes. That's more likely.'

Ella has never really approved of Flick's preference for men who are already permanently attached to other women. Neither have I, come to that, but we've learned to live with it. Unfortunately, the concept of the sisterhood is an alien thing for Flick. Under sufferance, we've met a few of her married lovers over the years. They've always seem unsuitable and shifty. But they've never hung around for too long. It would be lovely if Flick, for once, could meet someone nice, solvent and unattached.

'I've hardly heard from her in the last few months,' I confide. 'I've been texting and phoning, but she seldom replies. She's not avoiding me, is she?'

'Oh, you know what she's like,' Ella says with a shrug. 'She's probably up to no good somewhere.'

'Yes.'

If Flick's in a tricky relationship, she sometimes goes 'dark'. Despite being in her thirties now, she's still exactly the same as when we were at university: flighty, fickle and very frustrating. But we both love her, nevertheless. Ella's right, I'm probably reading too much into it. I can't think of anything that I've done that would have caused Flick offence. She's not one to take anything too much to heart, anyway.

'We'll all have a lovely week,' Ella assures me.

'Of course, we will.' I get a thrill of excitement. I'm going to put all my troubles behind me and just have fun. 'It'll be just like old times.'